J. T. WARREN

HUDSON HOUSE

IT ALWAYS KEEPS ITS SECRETS.

"A Welcome new entry into the world of supernatural fiction."

—Scott Nicholson, *The Red Church*, *Liquid Fear*

HUDSON HOUSE
By Chris DiLeo

Published by Chris DiLeo
Copyright 2018 Chris DiLeo
Cover Design by Kealan Patrick Burke
Originally published under the pseudonym, J.T. Warren
Copyright 2010 J.T. Warren
Original Cover Design by Neil Jackson, page 3

For my wife—love 'ums

And special thanks to LeeAnn Doherty, Karla Herrera, Neil Jackson, Kealan Patrick Burke, Scott Nicholson, Michael Marshall Smith, and Michael Koryta.

"Down there, the house keeps its secrets."

PART ONE
1984

CHAPTER 1

The boys stood together at the end of the gravel driveway with their jackets flapping in the October breeze and the sun setting behind them. Tommy Pomeroy snorted and spat a clump of yellow phlegm onto a patch of crab grass. Eric Hunter and Ed Forlure turned from the looming house, glanced at the spit. They didn't say anything—the spit summed it all up.

Eric stepped forward, *actually* onto the driveway. Tommy snorted behind him and spat again. Eric knew what that meant: *Hurry up*.

Brushstrokes of sunlight painted the front of the house in orange and red; a crimson blade streaked across the second floor windows like a bleeding gash. Those windows were the house's dead eyes and the porch its rancid mouth, the four pillars its rotting teeth. To go up the front steps onto the porch was to walk onto its tongue and smell its moldy wood breath, to enter the front door . . .

"Don't be a pussy," Tommy said.

Eric's mother said Tommy was a *smooth-talker*, a *real charmer*, but sometimes Tommy's voice, and his words, made Eric cringe; it was like when his brother

Steve called him "a little shit" and then grinned at him. Eric nodded.

"Then go," Tommy said.

His feet did not want to. If the house were a monster then the two third-floor windows that protruded from the roof were extra eyes that grew from the house's forehead like tumors. Sometimes things moved in those windows. Sometimes things swayed back and forth.

A girl had hanged herself up there. She used a few of her father's neckties twirled together, wrapped one end around a roof support beam and the other around her neck. Her father didn't even know it happened until late that night when the knot broke and her body dropped to the floor. People said she did it because the house made her do it.

Eric took another step toward the house and Tommy applauded. "This is really exciting, Eric," he said. "Great show, buddy."

Eric bit his lip and continued walking. He heard his mother's warning: *Stay away from Hudson House, Eric. Don't go near it. It isn't safe.*

A sheet of wood covered the first-floor window as did sheets for the second-floor windows and, presumably, the ones on the side and in back—but not the windows on the third floor, the ones that stretched out of the roof like frog's eyes. The gravel driveway petered out into the overgrown lawn. From the driveway, a slate walkway led out into the yard and then turned at a right angle toward the porch steps. The other houses in the neighborhood were not like this; most houses had garages behind them or attached, and if there was a walkway to the porch, it started at the sidewalk.

Eric paused at the edge of the slate path. Evergreen trees lined both sides of the property continuing behind the house, completely blocking the neighbors. A maple tree towered in the front yard like a giant sentry. Its gnarly arms swayed and orange leaves wafted down.

A serial killer had lived here. Hox Grent. Years ago, he terrorized the neighborhood, stealing kids, dragging them back here and slaughtering them. Most of the bodies were never found, only occasional pieces.

Eric stepped onto the slate walkway. Blades of grass stuck out of jagged cracks like the fingers of people buried alive who had managed to break the surface before choking to death on dirt. Somewhere a dog barked; it sounded like a warning.

"Wait."

Eric had been holding his breath and now released it. Ed ran up the driveway and stopped next to him. He held out a flashlight. "Here."

"I don't want to do this," Eric said.

For a moment it seemed that Ed might respond, perhaps offer some encouraging words or even tell him not to go through with it. Instead, Ed nudged him with the flashlight until Eric took it and then Ed ran back to the sidewalk. Eric hadn't brought his own flashlight because part of him hadn't accepted he'd be in this position; the other part of him knew that a flashlight wouldn't protect him anyhow. Despite that, the weight of the two D-batteries inside the plastic casing reassured him. He turned it on.

"Any *day*," Tommy said.

The front steps sagged in the middle like they were made out of cardboard and the color ranged from white on the edges of the steps to dry, peeling tan in the middle where thousands of footfalls had fallen before him. And of those people, how many had stepped here for the last time? How many times had Hox Grent's feet scuffed these steps?

Strong wind beat around the house and made it groan in a million places like the joints in an old man's body. Perhaps the house was waking up. Maybe the girl was upstairs, too, swinging. Maybe she'd come down and say hello.

Eric's skin prickled with freezing gooseflesh. He stopped at the foot of the steps. The house had probably been white or tan but it now radiated in splashes of red, yellow, and orange. The colors swirled across the wood like drops of paint in a bowl of water. Heavy gashes in the screen door made it sag like a limp body about to fall over dead. Someone had spray painted an upside-down star on the storm door behind the screen. Why were the windows boarded and not the door?

It won't be open. There's no way it'll be open. And then we can all go home. He'd sleep with his Ghostbusters nightlight on—he would not tell that to Tommy.

"If you don't get in the house before dark, it doesn't count," Tommy yelled.

He was making this up as they went along. In any trio of friends, there's always a leader and theirs was Tommy. He was probably hoping for a really good laugh, one that would make him fall down with cramps in his sides and tears bursting from his eyes. For that to happen, someone usually had to get hurt. Eric would have to play his part for Tommy's amusement and then they could get back to playing with action figures.

"This isn't so bad," Eric whispered.

The first step squeaked beneath his foot. Shadows from the fractured spindles in the porch railing stretched up the house like mangled fangs.

The moan of the next step screamed for Eric to run back to the sidewalk and beg Tommy not to do this to him. Tommy would only send him back to the house and up the steps again.

Eric took the next two steps rapidly and stood on the porch with the backs of his sneakers hanging off. If he fell backwards, he'd descend into endless darkness. He would fall forever or maybe into hell.

He shivered, rubbed the sleeves of his jacket. He immediately felt stupid. It wasn't the middle of January. He *was* being a baby about this. He just had to enter the house, grab something, and leave. Yes, it was stupid, pointless even, but that didn't mean he shouldn't have the guts to do it.

He stepped toward the door. A fist-sized hole lay between him and the door like someone had dropped a heavy rock through the wood. Or something had tried to break free from beneath. Inside the hole, light glinted off the cat-shaped eye of a troll.

He stumbled back a few steps to the edge of the porch again—*fall off into the darkness*—and stopped. There hadn't been a troll or anything else demonic. He had caught the reflection of a beer can left by a teenager; that was all.

The flashlight beam focused on the curved metal handle of the screen door and Eric went to it. He was mindful to spread his legs wide over the hole without looking at it. Then he was at the door and all out of space.

The screen door handle froze his fingers. The door opened with a squeal. Eric's heart thudded into his throat and his hands numbed; undigested hotdog from lunch roiled in his stomach. He wanted to vomit and cry and run away and never look at this house again but he knew he couldn't do that—running away would label him a coward forever and, even worse, he'd have to admit it was true.

The screen door bounced off his shoulder when he reached for the knob of the storm door. The spray-painted star (*a "pentagram," it was called*) grew larger, stretching across the door in all directions to become a mammoth star, the upside-down legs now gnarled horns. A face emerged inside the star. Eyes blinked open. Eric closed his own. *Just my imagination.* He opened his eyes—the image was a spray-painted star once more.

He grabbed the doorknob and turned—*be locked, please be locked*—and the bolt slipped easily back into the door. He instructed his arm to push forward but it refused. He had gone this far and yet his body wouldn't allow him to go the next few steps needed to prove his bravery.

"Sun's almost gone," Tommy yelled.

The quicker he did this, the quicker he could be back in his room, away from this house. He willed his arm forward again and this time the muscles cooperated to nudge the door open a sliver with a sucking *ooofff* sound—the sound of a sealed coffin breaking wide. Stale air teased his nostrils; it reminded Eric of the way the boxes of Christmas supplies smelled every year when his father brought them down from the attic.

When the door opened all the way with a faint rusted squeak, red sunlight broke through the opening and turned the floating motes of dust into levitating drops of blood.

Eric gripped the flashlight with both hands and scanned for something to grab; anything would do, anything to appease Tommy. To his right, just past a boarded window, a staircase ascended half a dozen steps to a landing and more stairs continued upward at a right angle. He would never go upstairs. No matter what Tommy might call him or how he might threaten him, Eric wasn't going to search the second floor—that was one floor closer to the dead girl.

Just find something and grab it.

Straight ahead, a narrow hallway ended at a shut door that led, presumably, into a room, maybe the kitchen. To his left lay a large empty room which Eric

15

could only partially see because of the jutting wall. The stale smell floated all around him like invisible mold.

Somewhere something creaked like a really large finger cracking its knuckle. Nowhere did Eric see anything he could grab as proof of his visit to Hudson House.

CHAPTER 2

The floor moaned beneath Eric's next step and he paused. He glanced at the stairs and then up, to the ceiling. Was she swinging up there now or lying on the floor? The hair on the back of his neck stood up as a cold chill coursed over his body.

Eric turned his back on the stairs and entered the large room. He immediately knew something was behind him; it had jumped toward him the moment he moved. Right now it stood in the crimson sunlight, hulking over him with blood-soaked arms from wrists that never stopped bleeding, a makeshift noose of ties slung around its neck.

Eric swung the flashlight behind him. The thing had moved back into the shadows where his light could not reach.

A pair of boarded windows divided the far wall of the room. Flakes of paint had peeled off of the wall in large strips like claw marks. Eric imagined the girl in a panic ripping at the wall, tearing at it until her fingertips bled, desperate to scrape her way out of the house that had become her eternal residence. Those same mutilated fingers could seize his neck and break his spine the way the noose of ties had broken hers.

Another boarded window—the front window—was to Eric's left and a large opening into another boxy room was to the right. Three more windows sectioned the walls in that room in a mirror image of this one. Eric had expected old, moldy furniture with decades of spider webs sagging across them. He had at least imagined there would be beer cans and fast food wrappers from teenagers strewn across the place, but he found three completely empty rooms. The musty smell faded and intensified in waves.

The floor moaned with each step and Eric paused after every cry. He kept the flashlight steady while squeezing his other hand into a painfully tight fist that started to numb.

He stopped in the middle of the room and carefully scanned the floor as far into the next room as he could. Bare floors in bare rooms in a bare house. Should he keep searching? He faced the next room. The sunlight was fading rapidly from the front door like a retreating dream.

He could leave the house now, run out slamming the door before the thing leaped onto his back and dragged him even deeper inside. He'd tell Tommy that he searched and scoured but couldn't find anything to grab but that didn't matter since he and Ed had seen him enter the house. Tommy would smile that stupid, proud grin and call Eric a fag.

He passed through the archway between the rooms to the back of the house. The sunlight did not reach this far—maybe it had vanished for the night. To escape, he would have to run back through the last room, turn into the foyer, go out the front door and down the porch steps. And do it with a plastic flashlight.

The floor in this room groaned more loudly and the wood felt softer, weaker. His feet told his brain that the floor had thinned out here like ice and that he needed to tread lightly or he might fall through into the basement. The monster waited down there. The thing of hair and teeth.

That's where Hox took his victims. He tortured them in the basement and then fed them to some hideous beast. Some kids said there was no beast, just some starved dogs, but it amounted to the same: whomever Hox took was never seen again.

With the next step, the floor dipped. He stopped, waited for the wood to splinter and break. Every second he remained in place increased the odds that the floor wouldn't hold but the fear of taking another step, onto an even thinner patch, kept him still.

A closed door stood to his right. He turned toward it, started to take a step, paused. The floor whined. He would walk to the door, push it and see what happened. If something *did* happen, he'd bolt out of the house as quickly as he could. If the opening of the door showed him merely another barren room, Eric would examine it. Then he'd find his way out. He would *not* look upstairs

—homo coward forever or not, he was not going to climb those steps.

He reached toward the door and did not like how his hand shook and blurred in the light. The wood was moist. He pushed on it and his fingers sank into the door like they would into dough or soggy cardboard. His fingers sank deeper. *It's got me.* The door would suck him in, absorb him, and keep him forever.

The door pushed into the next room and his fingers slipped on the surface with a wet squeak. Streaks of blood stretched back from his fingers across the door. The tips had been torn open, the nails ripped out. Blood poured over his hand and splattered on the floor between his feet.

He started to scream but silenced it after only a brief yelp; his fingers had returned to normal. His mind playing tricks on him. Or something *else* playing tricks.

Eric swallowed; his throat felt incredibly dry like he had swallowed a handful of dirt. A slight push swung the door a few inches forward before it swung back just past the door frame and then settled in place. If he kicked the door hard, it would swing wide into the other room and then swing back just as wide into this room. At least that promised easy escape.

He pushed the door open slowly until the hinge stopped yawning and the door could go no further.

Two boarded windows hung above a sink set in the middle of the kitchen counter. In front of the sink stood a woman with long, brown hair, her back to Eric.

CHAPTER 3

Eric's stomach knotted.

The woman's white dress clung to her narrow frame and fluttered around her knees from an invisible wind. It radiated like a white light bulb. She was standing straight, rigid, like something had startled her. Her hands were in front of her, perhaps in the sink; her elbows jutted out from her sides like knotty branches.

Eric froze. The sound of his swallowing echoed throughout the kitchen like a monstrous belch. The woman did not flinch.

If he tried to back out of the kitchen the door would squeak as it had on its opening and that would alert the woman to his presence. Then, as his father said, all bets were off. He couldn't stand in place forever, though. Eventually one of them would move. Once he started, he'd have to run. Could he outrun her? Ghosts could fly —Eric could only pump his legs and hope he didn't trip.

Maybe she wasn't a ghost, just a woman who had gotten lost. Teenagers invaded this place on a daily basis; maybe she was a mother searching for her son. Why was her dress glowing?

Metal scraped against metal, long and slow, high and piercing. Eric's brother had once threatened to make Eric a eunuch, whatever that was, and dragged the blade of a carving knife along a sharpening rod, producing the same sound now vibrating around the room.

He wanted to cry. What was he supposed to do? He squeezed the flashlight, his only weapon. If not a ghost, the woman was some crazed lunatic hoping to continue the slaughter of kids in the memory of Hox Grent.

The scraping metal sound slashed at his ears again and again, louder and louder. Soon the blade would rise over the woman's head and then she would turn, and with a huge grin of spiky fangs she'd bring the giant knife down on him, slicing through his entire body. She'd peel his flesh from his bones and eat it in bloody slurps.

The sound continued relentlessly, a screeching table saw rapidly severing plywood.

The woman turned. Her face appeared behind a curtain of brown hair that hung straight past her chin. She could have been pretty (did he know her?) if not for the blood splotches splashed across her dress. Her arms hung at her sides, palms open. Thick rivers of blood coursed down her arms from deep canyons of mutilated flesh.

Her dead, black eyes rolled backward. She dipped her head back. Her mouth dropped open, and then her hair liquefied and splashed onto the floor in thick, crimson fluid. From her hollow mouth ushered an equally hollow cry.

Eric's own scream burned his throat. He tried to shut his eyes and couldn't. His vision blurred with tears that couldn't hide the thing before him.

The woman stepped toward him. No, *floated* toward him the length of a step. Her feet grazed the ground but did not move. Her arms reached for him. Blood poured from her forearms and splattered on the kitchen floor in blobs that exploded on the tile.

Please, dear God I'll be good so good dear God please.

The woman lunged at him.

Eric's legs collapsed, his knees snapped forward, and he hit the tiled floor first with his knees and then with his face.

The hollow cry morphed into a much more familiar laugh that rose and fell in cackles. It was how his brother laughed after twisting Eric's arm hard enough to make him beg for mercy. Not his brother; this time it was Tommy.

"Get off," Eric cried.

He couldn't budge Tommy. His friend's laughter peaked even higher and he rocked back and forth, riding Eric like a horse.

"*Yeeehaa!*"

Was the woman still in the room? Did her blood now stain his face?

"She'll get us!" Eric yelled.

"Oh, no!" Tommy erupted into a violent fit of laughter. "The dead girl's going to get us."

Eric's flashlight had rolled into the far corner, light facing them. The room was empty. The woman had vanished, but that didn't mean she was gone.

"I'm serious," Eric said more calmly.

Tommy was still laughing when he stood. Eric jumped to his feet so quickly he nearly lost his balance. He hesitated about retrieving the flashlight. He didn't want to pass through where the woman had been. He might *feel* something.

"I saw her," Eric said.

Tommy shined a flashlight directly into his eyes and Eric squinted back. "She didn't die in the kitchen, stupid. She's hanging two floors above us." He gestured but Eric didn't dignify his statement. Tommy knew urban legends; Eric knew truth.

"She was in this kitchen, at the sink."

"Washing dishes?"

Tommy's smirk almost trapped Eric's words in his mouth. "I think she was . . . sharpening a knife."

"Getting ready to cut the Thanksgiving turkey?"

"No."

"And you're the turkey." This fit of laughter stirred a repressed ball of rage in Eric's gut. He swatted the flashlight out of his face, but not out of Tommy's hand.

"Shut up."

"*Ooo*," Tommy said. "Someone doesn't like being called a turkey."

"I know what I saw."

Something about how Eric said those five words weakened Tommy's laugh and his smile waned. They

24

stood in silence for several seconds. Ed stood behind Tommy, eyes wide. Would Ed interfere if Eric and Tommy started fighting, *really* fighting? He'd probably watch and greet the victor as his leader.

"You find anything to take?" Tommy asked. "Or were you too scared of the woman making dinner?"

Eric wanted to tell him to shove that flashlight up his ass and walk all the way home with light shining out of his butt like a giant lightning bug.

"No. The house is empty."

"What's that?"

Tommy's light found a small piece of metal a few feet away on the kitchen floor that glinted like a jewel. It lay almost directly in the middle of the room where the woman had walked only moments ago.

"Go get it," Tommy said.

Eric shook his head.

"Homo."

Tommy pushed past Eric and retrieved the thing on the floor. Eric expected Tommy to start screaming when he picked it up, expected it burn his hand or turn him crazy.

Tommy examined the thing in his open palm with the flashlight beam shining off it. After only a few seconds of inspection, Tommy tossed the thing in the air where it hovered for what felt a little too long, and then caught it in his hand again.

"Your girlfriend left you something," he said.

He tossed the thing underhanded to Eric, who caught it without really seeing it fly through the air. It nestled in his hand like a small, cold insect.

Without his flashlight, Eric recognized the shape and weight of what Tommy had found: a ring. He balled his hand into a fist and fingered the contours of it. Cold spread out from the ring to numb his palm and fingertips. He opened his hand and touched the ring with the thumb and middle finger of his other hand. His fingertips chilled like he had touched a frozen soda can. The cold stung but not bad enough for him to let go. He twirled the ring in a circle between two fingers. The band was thin, almost frail, and something sharp sat on top of the ring, a diamond. Eric had probably seen hundreds of rings on men's and women's fingers in his life but he couldn't picture any of them. He knew his father and mother wore wedding rings, but those were just gold bands. This felt like a real ring, one a woman might adore. One worth something.

Who could have left it?

A gift. From the ghost.

"Hand me my flashlight," Eric said.

"Get it yourself. There's got to be something better in here than some gay ring."

The flashlight was a mile away across a land chartered by paranormal powers. If he walked across that land, would he come back the same? *Little late for that.* He started across the kitchen.

"Perhaps your girl is back here," Tommy said. He was running his flashlight over a closed door at the far end of the wall. Maybe it led outside. He reached for the doorknob.

"Don't," Eric said, without realizing he was thinking it.

Tommy laughed. "Afraid your girl will like me more?"

The flashlight waited a few feet away. The ring was numbing his hand.

"We should leave," Eric said.

"Fag," Tommy said. He grabbed the doorknob. His body tensed. A shiver wiggled through him and he cried out. Eric flinched backward several feet from Tommy and the flashlight.

"Help!" Tommy yelled.

Eric could not move. Electricity, *supernatural* electricity, was passing through his friend's body, frying his brain and melting his skin, but Eric couldn't do anything.

"Help me!" Tommy shook violently, hand stuck to the knob. He was a caught fish on the poisoned hook of the house.

The urge to run came from the depths of his mind that knew, somehow, that if he touched Tommy he would be stuck to him and thus stuck to the house, too. The place would get them both. The only answer was to run, get help, and let an adult come here to risk his life. Kids weren't supposed to die. That was one of the duties parents were assigned when they agreed to be parents. Parenthood meant eventual death.

Ed moved from the darkness of the dining room to Tommy's side like he had been ejected from a catapult. He grabbed Tommy's arm and pulled back. Tommy's hand slipped off the knob and the two boys stumbled backward several steps and collapsed onto the floor. Tommy landed on Ed, who cried out. Eric still didn't move when Tommy's laughter returned and he began verbally ripping into Ed for thinking the house had really been electrocuting him.

Ed backed out of the kitchen into the doorway again, almost hidden in the shadows.

"You guys are stupid," Tommy said. "There's nothing to be scared of."

"But you said . . ." Eric let the rest of his thought dry up. He was only falling deeper into Tommy's trap.

"Babies." He shook his head. He walked back toward the door, dodged to the right, snatched up Eric's flashlight, and tossed it behind him with a rapid, "Heads up."

Eric dodged the flashlight, which smashed against the wall. He jumped at the sound. Tommy sighed. That sigh was worse than the obnoxious laughter, like a disappointed parent instead of a mocking brother. He had made fun of them for being cowards in hope of making them tough and he had discovered that his friends really were wimps.

"I just want to look back here," Tommy said. "Don't go anywhere."

The door was open in a rush and Tommy vanished into another dark corner of this very dark house. The floor creaked with his footsteps until he was gone and then the house went silent.

Behind him, the flashlight had died. Without it, Eric and Ed were stranded in the dark.

"Tommy?" Eric's voice sounded weak and pathetic.

Tommy, of course, did not respond. He was tricking them again. Jokes for kids like Tommy were like drugs for addicts: the more they did them, the more they wanted to do them. And, much like the addicts that they had learned about in school, jokers left a wake of injured people in their path. Hurting people might have been part of the thrill for Tommy. Usually, he hurt others, outsiders and weirdos, but if ever in need, he'd go after Eric and Ed.

Eric started for the door, but Ed's words stopped him.

"We should go."

The calm tone and solid conviction of his words startled Eric. "We can't."

"Soon we won't be able to."

"What do you mean?" Eric asked, but he knew what Ed meant. If they didn't get out of Hudson House right now, they might be doomed to wander its dark passageways. Ed sensed the house's hunger as Eric had, but Ed either lacked the bravery to face the house or possessed the courage to know when it was time to flee.

"We can't leave Tommy," Eric said. He continued toward the door.

"He's already gone," Ed said.

"What?"

29

The kitchen door swung back and forth gently on its squeaky hinges. Eric didn't blame Ed. A moment later, the front door banged in its frame. Had Ed shut them inside the house or had the door shutting been an accident? Maybe the house did that itself.

"Tommy," Eric said. "Ed just left, and I'm going, too. Come out."

Eric couldn't abandon Tommy. Tommy was a prick sometimes but they were still friends. You didn't abandon your friends, not unless you were a coward.

He crossed the kitchen and paused outside the open door. The light from Tommy's flashlight was so faint that it appeared Tommy had taken a candle in there with him. A dry, lifeless stench oozed out of the dark. It was the smell of his grandma's extra bathroom, the one she always kept closed and never cleaned.

Set just off to the right across from the open door a sheet of plywood blocked another window. No escape.

Eric stepped past the door. Tommy stood several feet to the right in a narrow room, flashlight poised on the far wall. The beam was so dim and the splash of light on the wall so faint that the flashlight batteries must be rapidly dying.

"Tommy?"

"I found something," Tommy said in a complete monotone.

"Found what?"

"Something special."

Eric wanted to grab him and drag him out of the house, but the sound of his voice, the lack of any life in that voice, kept Eric in place.

Empty shelves surrounded them, sticking out from the walls like spikes. The darkness wrapped around Eric. He couldn't fill his lungs with air. The room started shrinking.

"This house is really special," Tommy said in that same flat voice. It was an awful voice, a dead one.

"We have to leave," Eric said. "*Now*."

"We can't. Not yet. Maybe never."

"Stop joking around, Tommy. This is serious."

"I know."

Was Tommy breathing heavily or was that Eric?

"We can leave. Ed did."

"No," Tommy said. "He didn't."

"Tommy—" He stepped toward him and stopped. He didn't want to move any closer. Whatever was wrong with Tommy was unnatural and dangerous. Maybe contagious.

"Try to leave," Tommy said. "You'll see what I mean."

"I can't leave you here."

"Sure you can. I'd leave you." Faint emotion floated in those last three words.

Eric paused. Tommy really would leave Eric if their roles were reversed. Part of Tommy probably hoped that something was going to happen to Eric in Hudson House and when, after waiting a few minutes outside with Ed, he hadn't heard any screams, he decided to enter the house and scare Eric with an old-fashioned surprise tackle. But Eric had already been screaming at the bleeding woman. Perhaps Tommy hadn't heard that. Perhaps the house hadn't wanted him to.

Now the house was doing something else. Something to Tommy. He wasn't faking: that brief trickle of emotion in his voice hadn't been mischief but fear. Genuine fear.

Eric turned his back on Tommy. His breathing improved.

"Run for your life," Tommy said. "Not that it'll do any good."

The flashlight beam faded, faded, died. Tommy started moaning, low groans at first and then loud cries.

"Don't you see it, Eric? Can't you feel it? It's beautiful," he yelled. "So *beautiful!*"

Eric ran.

He smacked the kitchen door and sent it swinging behind him, and then he skidded across the dining room floor, shot into the living room, tripped into the foyer, and crashed against the front door, falling to the floor. He leapt up and pawed at the door until he found the knob, and then he was yanking back on the knob, turning and yanking, pulling back with all his might and finding that he couldn't get it open, that the house wasn't going to let him out and that Tommy was right, that there was no escape. He kept turning and pulling back and crying for the damn thing to open and feeling the tears pour down his face and feeling so helpless, so stupidly helpless.

When the door opened, Eric spilled out onto the porch and tripped all the way down the steps and tumbled onto the walkway. Ed was gone. Behind Eric, Tommy's moaning cry echoed within the house.

Eric ran and didn't slow down until he was on the front lawn of his own house.

He grabbed the railing on the porch that led to the back door and into the kitchen—where his mother would be waiting for him to get home so she would know if she had to whip up some dinner because Dad wasn't going to be home until late, like usual, and Eric's brother had already gone out with friends, promising, as usual, not to drink or do anything "stupid."

He ran up the steps and sprang inside the house.

"Mom, you have to—," he started to say but the rest of his sentence, *call the police and send them to Hudson House because Tommy's in trouble and maybe Ed, too,* never came out.

His mother lay on the floor in the middle of the kitchen, arms outstretched, legs splayed, blood gushing from a wound in her head.

CHAPTER 4

His mother had bought him the black suit with the padded shoulders because his grandmother was almost eighty and probably wouldn't last much longer. Grandma had kept on living, however, and Eric's mother hadn't.

Grandma entered the small room in the funeral home where Eric's mother lay in an open casket a few feet off the ground, surrounded by flowers. Grandma spotted someone she recognized, someone she hadn't seen for a long time; this kept her diverted from her dead daughter at the front of the room. What did it feel like to be so old, so close to death, and have to bury your daughter?

His grandmother chatted with the woman, embraced her, cried with her, and laughed. Laughing seemed out of place, almost belittling, but at any given moment someone was laughing. Eric wanted to tell the laughing people to shut up. How could anyone laugh when they knew this woman's son had discovered her dead in the kitchen a few evenings past, her face buried in blood?

Eric's father had said it was an aneurism, something in her brain stopped working, and he had accepted that on the surface at least, but he knew something worse had happened. Brains didn't simply stop functioning. After returning from the hospital, his father had dropped to his knees beside the lake of congealing blood on the kitchen floor and wept loud, fierce tears. He told Eric to stay away, go back to his room, not come out until later, much later, and his father had mopped the kitchen for hours—the mop squeaking—and when he finally left his room, Eric found his father sprawled on the kitchen floor in almost the same position his mother had been. Eric left him alone. His father's cries echoed through the house all night.

The next day, Eric found a clump of scalp and hair wedged into one of the handles of the cabinets beneath the kitchen counter. Long, thin wisps of brown hair curled out of the glob, which felt soft and mushy like Play Dough. Something *had* gone wrong in his mother's brain—something had exploded out of it. This wedge of scalp and hair proved it. He did not show it to his father.

He fingered the piece of scalp in the front pocket of his suit jacket, which was too tight across his shoulders and itched the back of his neck. The fragment of his mother's head had hardened over the past day and now resembled a piece of dried mud. He had intended to put it back, like the final piece in a puzzle, but when his father brought him up to the edge of the coffin and he peered in at his mother, Eric didn't see any missing segments of her head, any gaps in her hair. The people who prepared her body must have covered it up. He'd slip it into her coffin later. It wouldn't be right to bury her when she wasn't whole.

For now, he sat in an uncomfortable chair, caressing the piece of his mother's head, and staring at her still body. He didn't take his eyes from her and she was only blocked when people approached the coffin or stopped in front of him to say they felt so sorry, so bad for him, that she was such a wonderful woman, that she'd be missed for a long time.

These people perused the flowers crowding around the coffin. They pointed at particular bunches and remarked how so-and-so had sent quite a nice arrangement. These flowers of vibrant white, green, yellow and orange were supposed to be a tribute—one of them had a ribbon wrapped around it that read: A Life Celebrated. These were not a tribute; they were a living insult to a woman who could no longer live. The flowers were meant to brighten up the room with its thick, faded red curtains that killed any shred of light trying to come through the windows. The flowers were meant to sweeten the stale stench of a place where corpses laid out for hours, maybe days. The flowers were meant to distract people from the dead woman in the box.

Eric didn't know when exactly it started, but at some point his mother's chest began to gently rise and fall.

He almost stood, started screaming that she wasn't dead, they could stop this stupid nonsense with the tears and laughter and flowers and organ music and he could go back home with things the way they used to be. No one else noticed. If Eric started shouting about his mother breathing, everyone would bow their heads and murmur how difficult this must be for such a young boy. They wouldn't believe him because it wasn't true.

Only an illusion. A trick.

For two hours he watched his dead mother breathing. Then Tommy arrived, sat next to him. Tommy's mother had died many years ago—Tommy said he didn't remember it, or her for that matter.

Tommy didn't say anything at first and Eric toyed with apologizing for abandoning him in Hudson House, but that didn't seem so important anymore. Bigger things had happened.

Tommy spoke first. "Halloween is next week."

"Yeah."

"You think you'll go out?"

"Maybe." He couldn't picture himself running through the neighborhood banging on people's doors for candy.

"We should go back to the house."

"I'm sorry I left you."

"I'm not."

"It was weird in that room. Scary."

"You should have stayed."

"You told me to run."

"We need to go back."

Eric turned from his mother. He had no words to respond but his face flushed with emotion. Tommy told him to relax, hear him out.

"Do you believe stuff just happens?"

"What do you mean?"

"Like by chance?"

"Who cares?"

"You don't fail a spelling test by chance. You fail because you didn't study." Tommy's eyebrows curled toward the middle of his face. "And if you do study, then doing good on a test isn't by chance, right?"

"I'm not going back."

"Your mother didn't die by chance."

Tears threatened.

"What I'm saying," Tommy went on, "is that things don't just happen. Something *causes* them. Your mother died because something caused it." He paused, swallowed. "*We* caused it."

"No."

"We went into that house and then your mother died. She died when we were inside or even when you first entered. We entered the house, so the house killed her."

"Why *my* mother? Why not Ed's? Or your father?"

"You entered first."

Anger boiled in his stomach. "You made me."

"I didn't make you. You entered on your own."

"It was your idea. It's your fault. You killed her. *You killed my m—*"

Strong hands covered his mouth and grabbed him around his chest. They carried him through the people, who glanced and then turned away, and out into the cool where cars slowed as they passed the funeral home.

"What the hell is wrong with you, Bro?" Eric's brother let him drop.

His brother's pale face and dark eyes loomed.

"Nothing."

"Sure as shit didn't seem like nothing." Someone laughed—one of his brother's friends stood a few feet away smoking a cigarette and talking to a woman in a short, black skirt.

"I'm going back in."

His brother grabbed Eric's suit jacket. Eric beat his free hand against his brother's while squeezing the piece of his mother's scalp in his pocket like a talisman. His brother shoved Eric against a pole holding up the corner of a long awning. Eric's back stung with the vibrations.

"Stop acting like a baby."

"Steve," one of his brother's friends said. "Why don't you take it easy on the little kid?"

Steve laughed, released him. Eric knew better than to run. No matter what his brother's friends said, Steve would do what he wanted, especially when it came to his little brother.

"Calm down, bro," Steve said. He pulled a packet of cigarettes from a pocket in his leather jacket, worn over a Metallica T-shirt. He lit the cigarette and puffed the smoke over Eric's head. Eric tried not to cough.

After a few more drags, Steve asked, "What got into you back there?"

Silence would invite an arm-twist, even a kidney jab. "Tommy said stuff."

"Yeah? Like what?"

"About mom."

"It's messed up, that's for sure." His eyes narrowed, poised on Eric. "You found her just laying there?"

Eric nodded.

"Dead already?"

Nodded again.

"And then you called 9-1-1? That's really messed up. I'm sorry you had to find that, bro. It should've been me. I was . . . busy."

Steve rarely offered a gentler side, so Eric kept his defenses up. At any moment, even at mom's funeral, Steve could morph into his abusive true self. Especially in front of his friends.

"Tommy being a prick about it?"

"No, he's fine."

"You were about to tear his head off."

Even if Steve's caring side proved an illusion (like mom's breathing), it might be worth it to ask about the house. Steve had probably been in it a million times. He and his friends were the ideal candidates for drinking in an abandoned house.

"You ever been in that house on Mangle Lane?"

Steve sucked on his cigarette for several seconds, nodded and exhaled the smoke, which masked his face. "What about it?"

"Nothing," Eric said. "Tommy wants to go there."

"Look at it?"

"No."

"Go inside?"

"Yeah."

"Hey," Steve called to his friends. "My brother and his buddy think they can survive Hudson House."

His friends laughed, too loud, too obnoxiously. "Bet they run off the porch before they touch the front door," Steve's friend said, to the giggling amusement of the girl in the black skirt.

I've already been inside the house, Eric wanted to say. *I didn't run away. I'm not a fag. I walked through the house and I even found the dead girl. That's right, I saw her ghost.*

"Yeah, bro," Steve said. "You don't want to go near that house."

"Why?"

Steve nodded slowly again, appraising him. "It's a messed-up place. I been in there a few times. So has Scooter"—he gestured to his friend next to the skirt girl—"and it ain't exactly safe. We've partied in there. Trashed the place. Beer cans, food, other crap . . ."

Did *other crap* mean drugs? He had once sneaked into Steve's bedroom and discovered a small contraption that resembled a pipe only it was made of metal and smelled rotten. Tommy said it was for smoking weed.

"We used to party in the basement. Avoid the cops. Then we found out the truth. The cops won't even go there and the neighbors never complain. You know why? Cause no one wants to go in there. And if you have the balls to go in, good luck."

"But you did." Had he found the thing living in the basement, the thing of fur and fangs? Had he discovered a piece of one of Hox's victims?

Steve admired his cigarette for a moment. "I'd go back, too. But I wouldn't go alone, and I wouldn't go with someone who didn't *know* the house. You have to be smart when you go in there, and you're not smart enough yet."

"Smart how?"

"One night a bunch of us were in the house. Partying. Tim Lebston and his girlfriend went upstairs to . . . to be alone. Maybe fifteen minutes later, one of them screamed. We kicked off the music and stood there. We didn't want to move, fall for some stupid joke. Tim came running downstairs, his face dead white. He said something had happened to his girl. They were . . . together and then she just checked out.

"We went upstairs. He had taken her to the third floor—the attic." Steve paused. "You know what happened in that attic, don't you?"

Eric nodded. The girl swinging back and forth in the window, blood dripping from mutilated arms.

"We get up there and his girl is laid out flat like he punched her or something. She was unconscious, passed out. Her eyelids were shaking like her eyes were moving wildly and her lips were trembling. When I touched her arm, I jumped back because she was frozen cold, like she had been left out in a blizzard. Then this white foam started dribbling from her lips and she started seizuring."

Steve inhaled a deep drag from his cigarette; it had disintegrated to a small stub. "I reached out to touch her again and a cold rush passed through me. My skin

43

prickled with the cold and my teeth chattered. For a second, I thought I was going to pass out, too—got all lightheaded. It passed, but I refused to touch her again. The other guys said I was freaking out, getting spooked too easily, but I know what I felt. It was a ghost, or something worse."

Eric swallowed. "Worse?"

Steve half-smiled. "You believe in ghosts, bro?"

Eric nodded.

"Well, ghosts ain't bad. Ghosts are nothing. What's worse than ghosts? There are many, many things that are much worse. Like demons. You know what those are?"

Eric pictured horned beasts with long talons and lizard tongues. "Yes."

"And there aren't even words for the things worse than demons. It may sound stupid, but there is evil in the world and for some things there is no better term to use than *evil*. Understand?"

Eric nodded again.

"No wonder that serial killer loved that place. There's something seriously wrong there." Steve leaned over toward Eric. "They said Tim's girl OD'd, but I know something got her. I felt it. That's what I mean by smart. Don't go into that house until you're smart enough to handle it. That place will eat you alive, Eric."

The concrete sagged beneath him like the floor in Hudson House. It might crack, split wide, and swallow him into an abyss. Steve could be lying, hoping for a quick scare, but Eric had reason to believe him; he had a Hudson House story of his own.

Steve relaxed, finished his cigarette, and dropped it. "We used to party there every month or so. Trash it, like I said. We haven't been in a while, you want to know why?" Steve waited but didn't appear interested in a response. "Every time we'd go back, the place would look exactly as it did *before* we partied there. The trash gone—all of it. The floors clean. We'd piss in there. Scooter took a dump once. Whatever. It would all vanish. No matter how badly we wrecked that place, it always returned to the way it had been."

Color drained from Steve's face. "I don't want to go back in there," he said softly. "Stay out of that house, Eric. Don't even go near Hudson House, not if you know what's good for you."

Steve gestured toward the entry to the funeral home and Eric headed up the walkway. When he entered, his brother laughed followed by his friend and the woman in the skirt. They laughed, but it sounded hollow like Steve's voice when he said, *I don't want to go back in there*.

CHAPTER 5

A fat priest in black with a pasty face asked for God's mercy to ascend Eric's mother's soul to His heavenly quarters. The laughter had stopped. Maybe the people were thinking of their own deaths and the likelihood of their ascensions.

After the prayers and sobs—his father's eyes burning red—the people who had come to see Eric's mother a final time began to leave. Tommy, however, stayed next to Eric.

"We should go back," he said.

"No."

For once, Eric wanted to heed his brother's advice. *Things worse than demons*, his brother had said.

"You didn't let me explain."

"I don't want to hear it. There is no reason." His father was hugging some old woman Eric had never seen before. They were both crying.

"Can I explain? Are you going to scream again?"

Eric bit his tongue.

"I told you that I think the house killed your mother," Tommy said. "It makes perfect sense. We weren't supposed to go in there, we did, and then she died. That's not a . . . what's it called?"

"Coincidence?"

"Yeah, whatever. It's not that. Can't be. Entering the house screwed things up somehow. We invaded its territory so it felt the right to screw with ours. It went after your mother because you entered the house first, but that doesn't mean I'm not next, or Ed."

Where was Ed? Eric hadn't seen him. Had he even escaped the house?

"So what if it did," Eric said. "My mother's dead and we can't change that, can we? We can't make her alive again, right?" The urge to scream rose again. He touched the piece of his mother's scalp in his pocket.

"No," Tommy agreed. "We can't."

"Why go back then? So the house can kill my father this time?"

"We need to go back so that the house won't kill anyone else."

"By talking to it? Making a deal with it?" Would the woman in white listen to their offer or would she slice them as she had her arms?

A heavy hand settled on Eric's shoulder and he thought his brother had come back to drag him outside again. Or worse, his brother might be in his presentable and loving mode, the disguise he wore when strangers were around. Eric always wanted to tell those people that Steve really wasn't a caring big brother; he was a mean bastard who loved hurting Eric any way and any time he could. But the hand belonged to his father's best

47

friend, Uncle Pete, so called even though he had no family relation.

"You holding together?" Uncle Pete asked.

Stupid adult questions. "Yeah, I'm okay, I guess."

"Glad to see you're with your friends. Times like these are why friends exist. Be good to each other, boys."

They nodded and Uncle Pete lumbered past them toward Eric's father. When he reached him, they embraced and Eric's father gushed out fresh tears. Eric tried to picture Tommy and himself sharing a similar moment.

"I saw something," Tommy said.

Had he noticed Eric's mother's chest slowly rising and falling with life?

"When you left me in there, I saw something."

The punch of guilt subsided rapidly. "I saw something, too," Eric said. "I saw the woman."

Tommy's mouth hung for a moment. "I know I didn't believe you, but—"

"What does it matter? I saw her. Bloody arms and everything."

Pause. "Did she say anything?"

He heard her piercing moan. "No," he said. "She vanished when you hit me."

Tommy thought for a moment. "I saw something else."

"Like what?"

"After you ran out—"

"You told me to."

48

"I didn't care that you left," he said. "I'm brave."

"And my mother's dead."

"So's mine. Welcome to the club."

Silence between them. The exiting parade of mourners dragged on. Still, his mother kept breathing.

Tommy's father entered from an adjacent room. He was tall, as Tommy would no doubt be one day, and thin, though broader in the shoulders. He and Tommy could win a father/son look-alike contest; eventually, Tommy's face would broaden and tighten, forming a hard jaw-line common to male movie stars.

He walked slowly like moving in a dream. His red eyes matched Eric's fathers' and the dark crescents beneath both men's eyes competed for Most Tired. They embraced and then Eric's father pushed Tommy's father away; he stumbled backward, almost hit the wall.

"Sorry, man," Tommy said. "I know this is a tough time but—"

"You were messed up in that room," Eric said. "You weren't *right*."

"I saw something amazing. It was so beautiful."

"I could tell you were scared."

Tommy blinked. "Not scared, Eric. Stunned."

"What was it?"

"The wall came alive."

What was he supposed to say to that? *Sounds great, let's check it out?*

"The house is very special," Tommy said. "You didn't see the wall come alive, didn't see *beyond* it."

"You told me to run for my life."

49

Tommy waited. Their fathers had launched into a discussion of whispers and pointing fingers. They both leaned toward each other, Eric's father trying to stare Tommy's father down even though the man was an inch or two taller. Their words were lost among the waiting mourners.

"What do you mean, beyond the wall?"

"Maybe that's why the house went after you, because you ran when you were supposed to stay," Tommy said to himself. "I stayed and that's why nothing happened to my family."

What about Ed?

Tommy shook his head. "Either way, it doesn't matter. We need to go back. You can't enter that house and then never go back. It'll come for you."

In the pantry when Eric had told Tommy that they needed to leave Tommy had said, *We can't. Not yet. Maybe never.*

"What was it?" Eric asked. "What did you see?"

"I saw that we can't escape, not by ignoring the house. We must go back."

"Why?" Eric almost screamed. A few people glanced their way. Another outburst. Poor boy. Hard to survive in this world without your mother. Probably need counseling. Eric's father had stepped within an inch of Tommy's father, who had raised his hands at his sides as if in surrender. Probably need *family* counseling.

Tommy leaned in like they shared a secret and no one else was supposed to know about it. "I can't tell you."

"Why not?"

"I don't know how to describe it."

"I don't want to go back."

"You have no choice. The house wants you back."

Words did not come in response. They stared at each other. Ed's parents strolled over. Ed was not with them.

"Eric, how are you?" Ed's mother asked from beside her husband.

Another stupid adult question.

"I'm getting by, I guess, Mrs. Forlure." It sounded like something an adult might say.

"That's good, honey," she said.

Her husband gripped her shoulder with one strong hand. "We're very sorry for your loss. Your mother was a wonderful woman." Tears threatened at the corners of Mrs. Forlure's eyes.

Tommy had the guts to ask the obvious: "Where's Ed?"

The tears came then, slow at first, only one or two drops, but once the flood gates opened, the deluge soon began. She buried her face against her husband's chest.

Mr. Forlure cleared his throat. "Ed isn't feeling well. I'm sorry he's not here for you, Eric."

"That's okay."

"Can we visit him?" Tommy asked.

Mr. Forlure bit his lip, a slight gesture but one that betrayed emotions. "You better not," he said. "Not yet anyway."

From the front of the room the sounds of a brief scuffle pulled everyone's focus. Eric's father was shoving Tommy's father out of the room. His hands had come down to stop the shove, but Eric's father was proving stronger than he appeared.

"Get out!" Eric's father shouted and a woman somewhere gasped.

Tommy's father's hands came up again and he backed away. Eric's father turned to the remaining mourners and offered quick handshakes. He worked the rest of the line rapidly.

"It's probably best you stay home with your dad for a while," Ed's father said. "This is a time for the family."

With that, they left, hugged Eric's father on the way out. Eric's father then shook the priest's chubby hand aggressively like they had just made a big money deal. Steve was no where to be seen.

"What was that?" Eric asked.

"Ed's parents are weird, just like Ed."

"No, your father."

"I'm not saying we have to go back tonight," Tommy said. "But we have to go back."

"No."

"Before you decide—"

"I've already decided." He squeezed the piece of his mother's scalp.

"Give me one more chance."

"Why was your father fighting with my dad?"

"Look like the other way to me."

Eric wanted to refute and couldn't. Adult business was best left to adults. "I'm not going back."

"Let's talk to Ed."

"His parents just said no."

Tommy shrugged. "If I convince Ed to go back to Hudson House, will you go, too?"

In his pocket, his mother's scalp crumbled between his fingers.

CHAPTER 6

Before the coffin was sealed and taken to the church for the final rites, the immediate family was allowed to view the deceased once more.

Eric stood center in front of Steve and their father, dad's hands cupping their shoulders—a macabre family picture, forever absent the matriarch. The woman who would never stand among them again, never mind smile in a family portrait, laid before them in a wooden box the color of cherry, with fluffy white fabric puffed around her body.

Eric's mother didn't resemble the woman he had called "Mom" for eleven years. Her face appeared different, recognizable but changed. Eric wouldn't pinpoint the reason until many hours later: make-up covered her face, which made it greasy and false. His mother had never worn so much make-up in life. The red splotches in her cheeks resembled swirls of blood. This illusion of life reminded Eric of the blood puddle on the kitchen floor.

As during her "viewing," Eric's mother breathed slowly and steadily—a gentle rise and fall that only he noticed.

His father choked back a few tears. "She was a wonderful woman, an amazing mother to both of you, and a caring wife. I loved her so much. So much."

He squeezed Eric's shoulder; the padding in his suit crumpled. His mother kept breathing. He wanted to be somewhere else.

"I never imagined this," his father said. "We were supposed to grow old together. This wasn't supposed to happen. I love you, Laura." After another stifling of tears, he told his sons to say goodbye.

Steve nudged Eric toward the coffin. The kneeling thing had been taken away. The flowers that had surrounded the casket last night had been removed, shipped off to the church. The arrangement of white roses that draped over the lower portion of the coffin remained. The flowers smelled of vinegar.

Eric stepped to the edge of the coffin. He fingered the piece of his mother's scalp in his pocket. He couldn't take it out and drop it on her. His father would say something. Hell, Steve might even grab it, want to know what it was, maybe throw it out. He could drop the piece of her head into the hole when they buried her.

"I'm sorry," he said. His father started crying. His hand shook on Eric's shoulder. *This wasn't supposed to happen.* "I'm sorry," Eric repeated. He started to turn back but Steve nudged him again. Without seeking confirmation, he knew what he was supposed to do, for his father.

Eric leaned forward, over his mother's slowly breathing body, and kissed her blood-red cheek. Contrary to the image of blood, her flesh cooled his lips, like kissing a frozen slab of meat.

His brother pushed him to the side and kissed their mother's forehead where no red makeup had been applied. Then his father told them to wait outside. Steve and Eric walked out of the room and listened to their father cry over his lost wife. Steve went outside to smoke. Eric waited and listened.

Sometime later, Eric's father came out, shoulders hunched, eyes red again, tie crooked.

This wasn't supposed to happen.

* * *

The church service went on forever. Eric's suit made his armpits sweat and his pants wedged his underwear into his butt crack. He tried unsuccessfully to remove the wedgie by tugging at his pant legs but stopped when Steve gave him a warning stare. Like this was his fault.

Behind him, Tommy nodded.

His mother's casket—completely closed and sealed now—sat in the main aisle that led to the altar. The roses had been moved to the center of the coffin. Was her head toward the altar or her feet?

Eric didn't recognize most of the people crowding the pews in the church. The priest was the same one from the funeral home. The temperature in the church rose steadily during the service. The hymns were endless.

At one point, the choir belted out three songs, which meant everyone had to keep standing. Would he pass out from standing in this heat? Eric did not sing these songs, nor did he follow along in a hymnal. Neither did Steve. Their father tried his best to sing, but the tears stopped up his throat too many times for it to resemble anything better than strangled coughing.

Eric didn't hear the songs, only begged for them to end. Later, well into the service, the choir started, "Thine be the Glory." For whatever reason, this song broke through the cotton in Eric's ears. The hymn was about Jesus' conquering of death, how He rose from the dead, ascended to heaven, and now greeted each new soul that ascended to His kingdom to live forever in His glory. *Endless is the victory, thou over death hast won.*

Eric had heard of life as a poker game—play the cards you're dealt—but if losing at the poker of life meant death, loss was nothing when God was the dealer. God didn't deal you a new set of cards; He escorted you from the table to the private lounge where the party never stopped. His mother had been freed from the game and invited to the party. Tears ran out his eyes. He didn't wipe at them; it felt okay to cry here in this church surrounded by singing strangers. Perhaps, as the song said, *death hath lost its sting.*

By the final refrain, Eric had taken up the two-lined chorus. The words did not sound beautiful or holy falling from his tone-deaf mouth, but the words did calm him. His mother was okay. She had lost, yes, though in reality she had really won the ultimate prize: eternal life. He even managed a slight smile when the song peaked its final note.

When the post-song hush swept through the church, Eric thought he could accept this. His mother was gone. She'd played the game and left him behind. That was okay. He'd join her at the party one day.

The priest stood near the coffin but not too close, Bible in hand, preparing to deliver the Gospel. The priest was supposed to walk past the coffin to the middle of the church and begin reading from the large book in his hands, but he had stopped during the song and stared at the casket.

From within the coffin, Eric's mother screamed; it sounded like she was yelling through a pillow shoved over her face. The cry was desperate, longing, hysterical. The coffin shook on the casters beneath it. His mother was rocking it side to side, beating at the wooden box for exit. Sealed. She had been sleeping after all and had awoken during that song—*arisen*—to find herself trapped in a wooden box with soft, white fabrics suffocating her.

The priest rested a hand on the cherry wood. Next the fat man would cry out that Laura Hunter was alive, that God had created a miracle and given life back to this most deserving woman, and did anyone have a crowbar? And someone would run toward the front with some kind of metal tool and pry open the box and Eric's mother would lurch up from her intended final bed with a horrified, desperate gasp.

The priest nodded at the shaking coffin and proceeded the rest of the way down the aisle and started the Gospel. Everyone turned to eye the priest while he read some holy passage. The coffin continued to rock back and forth, threatening to tip over and crash onto the floor. His mother screamed from within, panicked now, air rapidly vanishing.

Only Eric knew her horror. He poked his father. His father bent down. "Do you see, dad?" He pointed toward the coffin that rocked violently like it might explode. His father nodded, mouthed, *I know*, and hugged Eric against him.

Eric pushed out of his father's grip. The Gospel according to whoever concluded and the priest began the sermon, which was really the eulogy. The coffin stopped shaking. Life renewed had once more been taken. When the service culminated with "Amazing Grace," Eric wanted to scream at everyone for pretending to see when they had each been blind to his mother's desperate plea for help. Even he had been too afraid to help her.

That night, he suffered the first of the nightmares. He ran to the coffin, smacked into it, and knocked it off its rolling stand. It crashed to the floor with a deafening bang that shook the entire church. The coffin lid creaked open. He dove inside to embrace his mother and couldn't stop when the woman in white reached toward him with her mangled, bleeding arms. Her eyes were white again and her mouth open in that hollow scream.

He awoke with a start, covered in sweat. "Things worse than demons," he said through panting breath.

CHAPTER 7

Tommy came by the next day. Eric told his father he felt ill and though his father's eyebrows rose in suspicion, his father relayed the message. Eric watched from his bedroom window as Tommy walked down the driveway to the street. Tommy stopped and glanced up. Eric jumped back, his window blinds snapping into place. Tommy had seen him and knew Eric wasn't sick.

He didn't have time to waste with Tommy's plans for the return to Hudson House. Tommy's belief that they needed to reconcile the wrong done to the house made a certain amount of sense and Eric knew there was no way to talk Tommy out of returning, but he wanted to delay the trip as long as possible. Could he delay it endlessly?

Eric had his own theory to explore.

His father kept a study downstairs, a room that in other people's houses might have been a bedroom or a family room or a storage area, but Eric's father had claimed it as an office with a large desk at the far end (perpetually covered in papers) and shelves stuffed with books on all the walls. "Why is your office so messy?"

Eric had asked him a few years ago. "Yes, dear," his mother said, "Why is that?" Eric's father smiled. "It's not an office, son; it's a study." Eric asked what the difference was and after a moment, Eric's father said, "An office is a place of rigid work. A study is a lounge of intellectual exploration." His mother burst out laughing.

When not at work, Eric's father spent most of his time in the study. Had he not been napping right now, he would be behind his desk, shuffling papers. Eric entered the room carefully, as if a wrong step might set off an alarm. He went right to the set of encyclopedias. His father had pointed them out once with pride. "If you ever need to find something out, look no further." Eric hoped he was right.

He removed the one marked number four: Birmingham to Burlington. The book weighed more than he expected and strained his arms after only a few moments. He set it on the floor and flipped through pages of black and white text and pictures until he found BURIAL. The entry told him to See DEATH CUSTOMS AND RITES. That led him to book eight: Corot to Desdemona.

He finally found the entry on page 568. He read through the reasons for burial rites (dispose of the body, aid the passage of the soul, reorganize the family/society) and skipped over the various Methods of Disposal—primitive man ate the brains of the dead to gain their knowledge while Polynesian people remove the skin of the dead to free the spirit. Two pages of double columns in tiny print later, Eric found Live Burials.

It was once almost commonplace for people to be buried alive. During the earliest days of civilized society and into the twentieth century, the limits of medical knowledge meant many sick people ended up under ground before their time. Some people came alive during funeral services, knocking and beating on the inside of their coffin to be freed. Some people, the article explained, refused to acknowledge the cries from within the coffin—a kind of group paralysis took hold of entire churches full of people. Though a coffin might have rocked back and forth, people didn't always save the suddenly alive. The person in the box was supposed to be dead. The cries for help could have been tricks of the mind or even a trick of the Devil. Though not common, it was documented at least a few times. A few times, however, was all it took to create a pervasive fear of live burial.

To allay those fears, numerous concoctions were devised for the dead, once interred, to signal that he or she had been buried alive. One of these inventions was a bell attached to a string with the other end attached to one of the presumably dead person's fingers: if the person came alive, he or she could pull on the string and ring the bell placed at the base of the tombstone above. The family would visit daily for weeks after burial hoping for the bell to ring. There was at least one documented case in which the bell did ring but during the exhumation the weight of the dirt collapsed the coffin lid, crushing the person inside.

Eric would convince his father to install a bell system at his mother's grave. He would visit it every day and wait for the bell to ring—he'd prove his mother was not dead, that she had been screaming sealed inside her coffin during her funeral. It had not been a trick of his mind, but rather a collective paralysis that kept the other witnesses in denial.

Eric moved the encyclopedias around so the gap for Number Eight wasn't as obvious and then he slipped back upstairs to his room. He read the paragraphs on live burial twice more, the last time taking notes. He even drew a depiction of the bell and string device. He'd make it himself if he had to. His mother was alive—she had to be.

"Son."

Eric yelped. His father had snuck into the room without making a sound.

"Tommy's back again. He said he has to talk to you."

"Dad, listen. We have to help mom."

His father's face scrunched together like he had bitten into a lemon. He led Eric to the bed where the encyclopedia lay open; Eric's drawing lay beside it. Action figures and Match Box cars were strewn around the floor. After the funeral, Eric had tried to play with his toys, but none of them had been able to grab his attention for longer than a minute or two.

"Not much fun playing by yourself, is it?"

"We have to help her," Eric said again.

His father's gaze went from the toys to the encyclopedia to Eric. "Your mother is dead, Eric. You know that, don't you?"

Eric was shaking his head before his father finished. "There's a chance, dad. Listen. At the church, I heard her. I heard mom crying for help. She was alive. She even rocked the coffin back and forth. We have to set up this bell at her grave so we'll know when she wakes up." He showed him the drawing.

His father's grip tightened on Eric's shoulder and the tears returned. He pulled his son close and cried into Eric's hair. He cried for several minutes before speaking. "Your mother's dead. She's not coming back no matter how much we want her to."

"I checked the encyclopedia. Mom may be buried alive. It's happen before. It used to happen all the time. It could have happened again."

His father battled off more tears. "She's not alive, Eric. You have to accept that. Don't spend time trying to bring her back. You can't. I don't want you reading about such stuff." He shut the encyclopedia. "She does live on. She is still alive in our minds and our hearts. Remember that. Go play with Tommy. You're only causing yourself more grief."

"It *is* possible."

"No," his father said loudly. "It's not."

Eric cringed from his father, who had seldom raised his voice. He didn't even scream when Steve crashed the family car into the fire hydrant down the street. Steve had probably been high on something.

"Dad, she didn't die by chance. There's something else that—"

His father pressed a finger to Eric's mouth. "Listen to me now, Eric, and listen very carefully. I'm sorry that I raised my voice to you. This is a very difficult time. We all loved her so much, but she is dead and I'll tell you how I know that."

Eric sensed something heavy coming, words that might crush him.

His father withdrew his hand from Eric's face and counted on his fingers. "One, she was dead. You saw her in the kitchen. I know that was hard for you to come home and see that. But she was dead. She didn't suffer. Her brain stopped working and she died. The doctors at the hospital confirmed that.

"Two, your mother was embalmed. They didn't used to do that years ago. It means that the blood is drained from the body."

Eric pictured vampires surrounding his mother's coffin, fangs slicing into her flesh, blood splattering on their chins and spilling at their inhuman feet.

"Three, she was cremated. That means that we didn't bury her. We had her returned to ashes, like the priest said."

Eric shook his head. His mother might have been alive when her coffin rolled into the fire pit. What had her last thought been before the fire engulfed her brain?

"She's not dead," he said. "Not embalmed. Not cremated. Not dead! *Not dead!*"

His father hugged him close, soothed his cries. "You don't have to get over your grief yet, son. It's okay to cry or be angry. But you have to accept that she is gone. Your mother is dead. We are not, so we must carry on as she would have expected us to."

He hugged his father, who cried into Eric's hair again. All was lost. None of it mattered anymore: the screaming in the casket, the bell contraption for the mistakenly buried, the hope to save his mother.

The order of his family had been permanently changed. The sky could be green now, the oceans purple.

Tommy was right. The house did this.

It had caused, at least in some way, his mother's death. The balance of Eric's family had been shattered because Eric had intruded on Hudson House. It was only keeping things balanced. Eric had done something wrong, offended the house, or the woman, and so his mother's death was on his shoulders. Just like the girl who had OD'd in the house, Eric's mother had paid the price. Why had she suffered instead of Eric? He didn't know but he knew that it was his fault. He would not turn his back on that burden. He had wronged the house somehow and the house had taken its revenge, but the house might not be done. What if the house had only begun its vengeance? How many more would die?

Worse than demons.

When his father finally broke the hug, Eric said, "I'm going to hang out with Tommy."

His father's smile seemed pathetic, weak. *This wasn't supposed to happen*, his father had said. He had been right and now Eric had to make sure nothing worse did.

"I know you saw what happened at the wake," his father said. "Tommy's father and I, we go back a long way. There's a lot of history. We said some things we shouldn't have. I let my emotions take control."

Eric shrugged. He no longer cared what had happened between them. He had to get to Tommy and get back to Hudson House.

"It had nothing to do with you," his father said. "I just wanted you to know that and not to worry, okay?"

He nodded.

His father picked up the encyclopedia. "Your mother's in a better place."

Before Eric left his room to meet up with Tommy, he retrieved the token taken from the house, the proof of his visit. He placed it in his pocket next to the piece of his mother's scalp.

CHAPTER 8

On the way to Ed's house, Eric told Tommy how the visit to Hudson House would go down. They would go together, as a group. They would not separate, not even for a moment. They would each have a flashlight and some kind of weapon, maybe a baseball bat or a hammer. Tommy nodded throughout Eric's litany. When Eric stopped, Tommy laughed. "You're too uptight."

"You don't think we should be?"

"The house may be dangerous, but hammers? You going to drive nails into ghosts?" Tommy patted him on the back. "We should go in prepared, I agree. But we don't need to freak out about it. You'll understand once you see."

"See what?"

Tommy smiled.

It was pointless pressing him to elaborate. If Tommy didn't want to share something, it might as well be locked in a safe. Still. What was he hiding? No matter what Tommy knew, they had to go back to Hudson House. Tommy was right about that, though

Eric suspected his reasons were different from Tommy's.

Tommy's smile faded after a while. They didn't talk. Eric kicked at small rocks in the street along the curb. Tommy tried to balance-beam his way across the curb but kept slipping every few feet and cursing. Their shadows stretched behind them like alien bodies. They crossed over Mangle Lane, where Hudson House stood at the opposite corner of Mangle and Jackson Drive. Eric paused in the middle of the street. The tall trees surrounding Hudson House obscured it from this angle but Eric still felt the house's presence. The gravel driveway jutted out past the tree line and the sight of it, so completely harmless, triggered a deep shiver from his butt to the back of his neck.

The swaying trees called to him, invited him to stop by, come in for a moment out of the cold, let the house warm him up. He stepped toward the house, actually toward it, stopped, and stared at his foot. What was he doing? Going to the House unprepared was stupid and going now just before sunset was so stupid it was asking for death. His foot did not want to retreat and his other wanted to join it. His legs had disconnected form his brain. They had decided to take him where they wanted to go and that place was Hudson House.

"No," Eric said. He felt pathetic, saying no to his own legs. The vocalization may have been a moment of weakness but his legs fell back within the control of his brain. He turned from the house and warmed. Tommy had kept walking.

Eric ran after him. When he reached him, Eric grabbed Tommy and pulled him off the curb. "You didn't feel that?"

"Knocking me off the curb?"

"No, the house. You didn't feel it . . . pulling?"

Tommy smile again. "I feel it everywhere."

Eric yanked him off the curb again. "What do you mean?"

"Don't worry, Eric," he said. "You'll be back inside the house soon."

"Not because I want to."

"You're going back because you have to. The house wants you back." Tommy jumped on the curb and scurried along it for several feet before slipping again.

The house didn't want him. Eric needed the house to back off, stay away from his family, that's all. If Tommy was right then Eric's intention was irrelevant. He convinced himself that he had to go back to the house but in reality the house wanted him back. The place might even hunger for him. Reentering that house with good intent didn't mean anything if the residents had malicious ones. *Things worse than demons.*

He couldn't back out now. He had agreed to go back on the condition that Tommy convinced Ed to do so, too. Eric could do his best to work against Tommy and get Ed to refuse, but doing that risked Tommy's aggression and, even worse, the house's anger. That sounded so ridiculous. The house expected him back— *had those trees been waving to him?*—not going back would incite its evil, bring more death. No matter what

73

he did, though, he might be trapped. If the house wanted another life, Eric hoped it would take Steve.

He didn't feel guilty for thinking that. In fact, wishing harm against Steve felt good, right. Maybe that would be the deal: the house could take Steve and Eric would never even look at Hudson House again. Fair is fair, after all. He grinned but quickly covered it as though he had snot hanging out of his nose. He should be embarrassed, ashamed. What would his mother say? She'd say better Steve than Eric.

Would she?

"Yes," Eric said.

Ed lived in a bi-level house where they called the first floor the basement and the kitchen was upstairs with the bedrooms. The sun had nearly set when Tommy knocked on the white storm door. Ed's mother answered. The fading light accentuated the wrinkles around her eyes so they resembled the long, thin legs of a spider.

"Hello boys," she said.

"Can Ed come out and play, Mrs. Forlure?"

She gazed past them in the direction of Hudson House. Had it called to her? "It's late, isn't it?"

"Tomorrow's Saturday," Tommy said. He had put on his *I'm-a-good-kid-whom every-parent-should-trust* mask.

Still distracted, she said, "I'm very sorry about your mother, Eric. How's your father?"

Eric shrugged. His father's eyes had been dark red when Eric left. "Okay, I guess."

"You tell him to come over with you and your brother anytime for dinner. We are always happy to have you."

Eric didn't say anything. He didn't want his father crying at the Forlure's dinner table.

"So," Tommy said. "Can he?"

She sighed. "He's not feeling well."

"Sick? On Friday?" Tommy had let that comment slip without realizing it.

"I'll be honest with you. Ed hasn't come out of his room since your mother died. I think he's taking it hard."

Shame flushed inside Eric. He should be at home, too, locked in his room weeping.

"Maybe we can brighten him up," Tommy said.

Mrs. Forlure smiled just enough to show appreciation. "He said it was his fault your mother died, Eric. Do you know why he might say that?"

"No," Eric said instantly and wanted to add: *because he didn't kill her, Hudson House did.*

"Sounds like he needs his friends," Tommy said.

She smiled more believably this time. "Perhaps you're right. It's so amazing the three of you are so close." She stepped aside. "You know where his room is."

Eric followed Tommy up the stairs and down the hall to Ed's bedroom. Tommy's performance was nauseating. How could a kid have so many different sides to him? Which one was real? *A smooth-talker,* Eric's mother had said. Did that mean he shouldn't be

75

trusted? And what had Mrs. Forlure meant when she said it was amazing how close the three of them were? It sounded like something adults just said, one of those confusing but pointless phrases they dropped like *One day you'll understand*. It seemed like one of those throwaway phrases, but not completely. Had she meant that close friendships were amazing? Or had she meant that their friendship was amazing because the three of them were so different?

Tommy knocked on Ed's door and entered without waiting for a reply. "Hey, buddy," Tommy said. "Are you on house arrest?"

Ed sat on the edge of his bed, leaning over with his elbows on his thighs, hands between his legs. He wore jeans and a Ghostbusters T-shirt. He did not look up as they entered.

Tommy stepped up to him, asked if he was superglued in place, and waved his hand in front of Ed's. Ed did not respond, which made Tommy laugh and encouraged him to wave his hand faster and closer to Ed's face. It was like watching a cruel experiment on an animal too sedated to respond. Or too horrified. Ed might be dead, frozen in that hunched-over position. Tommy finally grew tired of the game and mashed his open palm against Ed's nose.

Ed glanced at both of them, blinked several times. "What?"

Tommy laughed. "What do you mean, 'what'? You're not leaving your room anymore?"

Ed shrugged.

"You eat in here, too? What about pissing? Don't tell me you have a bottle under your bed."

"What do you want?" Ed's voice drooped with exhaustion. It sounded like he hadn't slept in days. Maybe he hadn't. Eric sympathized.

"You'd think we'd get a little more appreciation than that." Tommy winked at Eric. The nausea returned. "We're trying to help you, buddy. You ought to be happy we aren't letting you rot in here. I mean, it stinks. You're not crapping in here, are you?"

Ed stood. "Don't bother asking."

"You don't even know what—"

"I'm not going back."

"I think the stench in here is clogging your brain."

"You want to go back to Hudson House." Ed's voice strengthened. "I'm not going. There's no way. That place is . . . wrong."

"It's not—"

"We know," Eric said, cutting Tommy off. "It *is* wrong or haunted or something, but that's why we have to go back. We need to straighten things out. We need to make everything right again."

Energy drained from Ed. "We killed your mother, Eric. She died because we went in there. I'm not going back."

The reality of the situation seemed absurd, yet there it was. "We didn't kill her," Eric said. "The house did."

"Because of us." Ed dropped back onto the bed, leaned forward again to stare at the floor.

"We didn't do anything bad," Eric said, though he didn't entirely believe it. They had entered where they were not welcome. They offended the house, which took action against them—against him.

"The house wants us back," Tommy said. "You feel that, right?"

Ed considered him. "I'm not going back."

"The house took my mother, but that doesn't mean it is finished taking. It may go after you next, or Tommy."

Tommy grunted as though the suggestion was laughable. No house would dare hunt Tommy or his family. It knew better, just like the kids at school knew better. Tommy had once punched a kid so hard in the nose that blood spurted from the nostrils and the nose was permanently crooked. The victim had called Tommy a homo.

"Going back into the house will only make it more angry," Ed said.

"It doesn't get angry."

"I don't think so either," Eric said. The house was a living thing but not something with emotions. It was an entity devoid of feelings or human response. "The house is evil," he said and believed it completely.

"It's not evil," Tommy said. "You two are such cowards. You'll think different after you see what I saw."

"No," Ed said.

"I think we need to try," Eric said. "We need to do it to protect our families and ourselves."

"You can't reason with it."

Eric opened his mouth to disagree, stopped. He had imagined doing just that. He'd search for the woman in white and then make a deal with her: stay away from our families and we'll never come back here. What did he expect the woman to do? She wasn't the pinkie-swearing type.

"We're not going back to reason with it," Tommy said. "We're going back because we have to. It wants us back and so we will go. It doesn't want to hurt us. It wants to help us."

That was an interesting surprise.

Ed beat Eric to the obvious question: "How?"

Tommy smiled. "That's why you have to come with us—to see how."

"Go without me."

"No." Tommy said in his bully voice, the one he used to get kids to move out of his way in the hall or allow him to cut in the lunch line. "We go together. No excuses. Don't make us drag you there."

Ed's expression exposed the very real fear that Tommy would tie up Ed and drag him back to Hudson House if he didn't go willingly. Eric wondered, not for the first time, if Steve had been like Tommy when he was younger. If Tommy tried to forcefully move Ed, Eric would not want to help but he'd have to. He couldn't refuse Tommy. Besides, Tommy was right: the three of them needed to go back to the house. It at least offered better odds for survival.

"Since I left that house," Ed said, "I haven't gone out of this one. I try not to leave my room except when I have to. My mother said I have to go back to school on Monday, but I don't want to. I'm safe in this room, away from that house. If I go outside again, it'll get me."

Eric hadn't been in school all week, either. He couldn't go back after the events in Hudson House and his mother's death. The balance of his world had been shattered. It needed to be restored.

Tommy stepped closer to Ed and dropped to one knee. He might have been proposing. "Stop worrying about the house getting you," he said in that bully voice. "It's already got you."

"I didn't run out of the house," Ed said. "Not immediately. I didn't leave for a long time."

"I heard the door bang shut."

"Sounds don't make sense in there," Ed said. "That's something I learned. I turned from the kitchen, but I didn't have a flashlight. I thought I remembered the layout of the house but I didn't. Or the house didn't let me."

Eric didn't want Ed to continue. He wanted to keep Ed's experience away from him like it was a diseased person.

"You hit the wall?"

"Not *a* wall, all of them. It doesn't make any sense, but it happened. The darkness surrounded me, hit me, *froze* me in place."

"You were too scared to move," Tommy said. He moved toward the door.

"I was scared but I couldn't move because the house didn't want me to move. It wouldn't let me. Maybe the walls did move and cornered me or maybe something else happened; either way, I couldn't move, trapped in the dark. It was so dark, I couldn't see my hands."

In the subsequent pause, Tommy grunted and Eric stared at his friend. Ed was a timid kid who preferred to follow others than risk appearing stupid as a leader. He could crack some good jokes, but he only did that when he was relaxed and comfortable, not afraid of being mocked. Around Tommy, Ed kept his mouth shut and his step in lock with Tommy's lead. What he was saying now was contrary to his typical manner. He wasn't afraid to let Tommy laugh at him because what he had experienced had scared him too much to care.

"The walls tried to crush me. They closed all around me. I couldn't breathe. I screamed as loud as I could but my shout was gone the moment I let it out. It was like the darkness was sucking up my yells. Then the walls retreated. I don't know how long I was stuck like that in the darkness. It felt like forever. I couldn't hear anything except my heartbeat, which was exploding in my ears. It got so cold that I was shivering by the time I found the front door and ran home. The whole way home I felt the house behind me, running after me. I ran to my room and I've tried to stay here since. I don't want to go back. What if the house decides not to let me go again? What if the house crushes me in the dark?"

Ed knew enough not to cry in Tommy's presence but his voice quavered on the word 'dark' and he rubbed his eyes. Silence sat among them for a minute.

"We'll each have flashlights," Tommy said.

"And weapons," Eric added.

"Why didn't the house grab me when it had the chance? Why did it let me go?"

Eric couldn't respond, but Tommy had the answer. "Because it knows you'd come back."

Eric wanted to tell Ed that he didn't have to go back. He and Tommy would go by themselves and face whatever was coming. Ed could stay confined in his bedroom for the rest of his life if he wanted to. Eric wanted to say that but didn't, couldn't. Eric didn't want to reenter Hudson House with only Tommy. He needed another friend, someone more cautious, and someone he could trust.

"When do we go back?" Eric asked.

That smile again. "On Halloween, of course. At sunset."

CHAPTER 9

Halloween wasn't until Tuesday, three days away. Eric recommended that Tommy and Ed get flashlights as he would for himself and weapons, too. Tommy said he'd bring an axe.

"You can't bring an axe," Eric said.

"Why not?"

"Because you might hurt one of us."

"Don't you trust me?"

Eric ignored the question. "No axe."

"You were the one who wanted to bring weapons," Tommy said.

"Not an axe. Something appropriate."

"Like?"

Eric shrugged. He knew what he would bring. "A baseball bat or something."

"It doesn't matter," Ed said. "The only way to stay safe is to stay out of that house."

"We'll be looking out for each other."

"And the house will be all around us, like those dark walls."

Eric wanted to get out of Ed's room, get back into his own. Ed had always been a good friend—more responsible than Tommy when it came to borrowing action figures or a baseball glove, but always more reluctant to do things outside of his room, to explore the unknown, to search for adventure. Ed preferred his bedroom to any other location. That attitude had infected the room like a gas that felt very heavy. If Eric didn't leave soon, he'd have to sit down and then he'd end up on the floor and then hours would pass. Eventually, he'd become like Ed, stuck and afraid.

Something was emanating off of Ed, something toxic. *Cowardice*, Tommy would have said. It wasn't that simple. Ed was afraid but this feeling of off*ness* about his friend went deeper than fear. The house wasn't the reason; it was the cause. With invisible fingers, the house had reached into Ed's body and began pulling it apart. That Ed had actually entered Hudson House was amazing.

Ed said no more and Tommy and Eric left. Tommy commented several times on the walk back about what a fag Ed was but Eric didn't take the bait. He felt better walking away from Ed's house; the gas had cleared, making it easier to think. The sun had set while they were in Ed's room; a chilly October evening had settled in.

Eric didn't realize he and Tommy had turned onto Mangle Lane until they stood in front of Hudson House. Eric rubbed his eyes. Was this a dream? How had they gotten here? The house stood out from the night, its outline definite and pronounced but also completely dark. The house should have vanished into the night but it stood out, as if the night couldn't conceal it. That didn't make sense, but at least the third floor windows were empty.

Tommy stared at the house and a smile stretched his cheeks. When Tommy stepped onto the tall, yellow grass of the front lawn and dry leaves crinkled beneath his sneakers, Eric grabbed his arm. "You said Halloween."

"Relax," he said. "We're not going in. We're just checking it out."

"Why?"

"Think of it as a military mission. Before we can attack the house, we've got to know what we're dealing with. We'll check around back, the yard, whatever. We won't go inside, don't worry." He added something under his breath that might have been *fag*.

"It's dark."

Tommy laughed and shook his head. He withdrew a lighter from his pocket and showcased the small flame. The light didn't reach farther than the two of them but it wouldn't do to explain that to Tommy. His eyes glimmered in the flickering flame.

Eric followed Tommy across the yard next to the slate walkway toward the porch. The four pillars leading from the porch to the roof were giant fangs in an enormously dark mouth. Tommy headed toward that mouth for a moment and then diverted away to the left corner of the house. The crunching leaves could have been firecrackers.

"People might see us."

"Like your girlfriend?"

The neighbors never complain, Steve had said. *You know why? Cause no one wants to go in there.*

The maple tree in the front yard was set just left of the center so that even as the tree grew taller and taller every year, it never blocked the third floor window. Like it knew that the woman in the window didn't want to be blocked. Most of the maple's leaves had fallen so the tree stood as a dinosaur skeleton.

The tree line started just before the porch. Evergreen trees stretched up to the third floor of the house and created a solid fence deep into the backyard. A car passed on Jackson Drive. The headlights flashed in between the trees making them appear on fire. No light penetrated along the lower half of the tree line— the bushy bottoms of the evergreens created a solid blockade. It might be enough to trap them, if the house wanted. Tommy walked past the porch along the side of the house. The grass tangled up their legs like tentacles.

Tommy stopped, stepped closer to the house. He held the lighter before him so that it lit up the plywood nailed over the living room windows. The numbers 666 had bled considerably when someone spray-painted them on the wood. The blood had dried a dark red. *PAINT, not blood—paint, not blood.* Tommy turned to Eric with one of his smiles. The flame in his hand turned his teeth a sickish yellow.

A demon face adorned the plywood covering the next window. The face was crude, like something a kid might scribble in the margin of his notebook. Eyes larger than Eric's hands and a gaping mouth with razor teeth big enough to chop off his head in one bite; it should have been comical, especially with the pointy horns on its head. Eric did not laugh.

"Let's go," he said.

Tommy stepped toward the image and brought the lighter close enough for the flame to touch the wood. Maybe the house would catch fire. Good. Let it burn. That would solve everything. The flame flickered a few times and expanded, stretching over the giant mouth toward the eyes. The lighter had become a flamethrower or a medieval torch.

Eric stepped back but Tommy didn't move. "Cool."

"Careful," Eric said. The flame might jump onto Tommy's face. Would Tommy still smile when his eyes melted down his cheeks?

"The house is glad we're back," he said. "This proves it."

"Fine. Let's go and we'll come back on Halloween." The giant flame danced before the demon's face, making it appear to move. It gave the face eyelids that blinked.

Tommy reached toward the demon image with his other hand and Eric bit his tongue. This was like watching the guy at the circus swallow fire: you expected his neck to erupt in flames.

Tommy's fingers touched the corner of the demon's mouth and traced over its long teeth. His fingers stopped, caught, and his hand smacked the board like the demon had sucked it into its mouth. Tommy cried out. The sudden noise startled Eric back a few more steps and sent his heart galloping like a horse out of the gates. The giant flame burst even larger. The fire lit the whole demon face and the eyes blinked and came alive. They focused on Tommy—a predator assessing his prey.

Tommy screamed louder. Eric couldn't move, didn't want to move. If he touched Tommy, the house would get them both. The best option was to run, flee from this evil house and never return. Shame flooded him but not enough to quench fear. Run or help: Eric could only watch Tommy writhe with one hand stuck to the demon's mouth and the other holding an enormous flame.

The lighter erupted. The flame engulfed Tommy's hand, surrounded it in an instant in a dark blue ball. Tommy screamed as if his hollering might extinguish the fire. His voice echoed between the house and the wall of evergreens behind them. Tremors vibrated throughout his body, which turned his screams into rolling shrieks that made Eric think of a slaughterhouse. Then Tommy dropped back from the house like it had pushed him off (or the demon had spit him out) and he dropped to the ground with flames eating his right hand.

Eric stood in place. This was a horrifying dream that would end soon; it had to. *Like when you found your mother dead in a puddle of her blood? Had the nightmare suddenly ended? Had she really not died?*

Someone else appeared from behind the house—*the woman in white*—and approached quickly, yelling something. Several others appeared from around the corner and surrounded Tommy and the flame vanished but the stink of charred meat hung in the air, which made Eric step back even farther until something poked his back and he thought someone else had appeared from the darkness, but, no, just an evergreen branch, not a person, not a ghost.

"What the hell happened?" Eric's brother glared at him from beside Tommy. The moonlight reflected in Steve's enlarged, glazed eyes, like those of an owl.

Steve and four of his friends had run from the darkness behind the house at the sound of Tommy's screams. Had they been following Eric and Tommy, hoping for such a moment? The fury in his brother's face said no. His brother and his friends had been up to something unrelated but Tommy's stupid behavior had ruined everyone's night. Everyone's except the house's.

Narrow beams of light from flashlights cut across Tommy's charred hand, squirming legs, agonized face. The light could have been electrocuting him from the way his body shook and how the people around him fought against his spastic limbs to keep him still; through the commotion of numerous scared and bewildered voices, Tommy's screams flushed outward in a nerve-jangling pitch.

Steve's hand clenched Eric's jacket and shirt in one tight fist. "What were you doing?"

Eric stammered for words. "Burned . . . Tommy's burned . . . the house . . ."

Steve shook him but no more sensible words fell from his mouth. He could not take his eyes from

Tommy's shuddering body and his blackened hand that kept jumping into the light to the cursing gasps of Steve's friends. The house had done that, not Tommy's stupidity—the goddamn house had tried to kill him. Or teach him a lesson. Did the house want them back or want them dead?

Eric didn't want the answer to that question.

"Shut up," Steve yelled at his friends, cutting through their garbled words and pleas of *What are we going to do? Oh, shit. What are we going to do? Shit. Shit. Shit.* The flashlights turned on him. Steve squinted against the light. "Take him home. I don't care what you tell his father," he said. "Actually, leave him on the doorstep, ring the bell, and run. Better to not answer questions. And don't tell anyone about this."

"What if he says something about us?" a guy in a checkered shirt asked.

"Or him." A guy with a cigarette dangling from his mouth pointed his flashlight at Eric.

Steve's fist pulled Eric's jacket tighter. "Eric isn't going to say anything. Are you?" Eric could not respond. "And his friend won't say anything either or he'll end up with two deformed hands."

Tommy shrieked. He probably hadn't heard the threat; he was in what doctors on TV called "shock."

"Go!" Steve's friends tried to get Tommy to stand but he couldn't quiet his quivering legs. Two of the guys picked him up, one at the shoulders, the other at the feet. They started for the front yard and Steve stopped them. "Jesus. Go around back. Try to stay out of the street

90

lamps. If someone sees you carrying him, you're on your own." They nodded and headed around back of the house. "Give Tori one of your flashlights. She's not going with you."

Tori took a flashlight from the guy in the checkered jacket and walked awkwardly through the tall grass. She was the woman wearing the black skirt at the wake. She had chosen an equally revealing skirt tonight that resembled leopard skin and a black leather jacket that ended a few inches above her waist. She kissed Steve on the cheek; he made no recognition. Steve had no respect for women. What was wrong with her? If only Eric were a bit older and bigger, he'd put Steve in his place. One day.

The darkness behind the house swallowed Tommy and the group carrying him. Tommy's cries reverberated off the trees back to them for several minutes until the darkness also swallowed the sounds. Eric was suddenly sure that he would never see Tommy again. The house had gotten him. Ed had been smart to avoid this place, this horrible, evil place.

Steve shook him. "You gonna to tell me what you two were doing here?"

The collar tightened around his neck. "Tommy wanted to look around."

"I told you about this place, remember? I told you to stay away."

"I was following Tommy."

"Why don't you let him go?" Tori said. She caressed the back of Steve's head but he shook it off.

"No," he said. "Not lettin' him go until he tells me why."

"Tommy wanted to."

Steve lifted him up so that only his toes touched the ground and his collar dug into his throat. "You didn't believe me about this place, did you?"

"No—" *I believe you and that's why I had to come back*, he intended to finish but Steve lifted him completely off the ground in one guttural shout.

"You're lighter than I thought. If you don't gain some weight, you'll never survive high school."

Eric knew better than to resist—that led to more abuse, more pain.

"You think I was full of shit about this place?" Steve laughed. It sounded hollow, dead. "Your friend knows better now, but do *you?*"

"He's choking," Tori said.

"Shut up." Steve lowered his face to Eric's, almost nose to nose. "You want to know what this place can do? You want to learn it so you never forget?"

The spray-painted demon still watched from the side of the house, its eyes blinking and clearing, growing larger. The eyes were hungry like Steve's, like the eyes of a killer.

"I think you need a lesson, little bro."

Steve turned toward the back of the house and dragged Eric behind him. Eric tried to keep his feet moving but tripped every few steps at which point Steve's grip would squeeze and he'd start choking again. Heat filled in his throat and tasted like blood.

"Just let him go," Tori said, more desperately.

"Keep the light on the house."

Steve dragged him behind the house where the grass was up to his waist and more graffiti-speckled boarded windows and a door with stairs in front of it. Steve was going to throw him against the house until his head cracked open. He'd be a sacrifice to the house, a blood offering. Maybe Steve would leave him in the backyard, alone, in the dark. Still an offering, yet much more horrible than being killed outright.

"Please don't leave me here," Eric begged. "*Please,* Steve."

"Stop being a jerk," Tori said. "Let him go."

Steve dropped him onto the grass near the house and laughed at Eric's yelp. Steve grabbed the flashlight and focused it near the base of the house.

"That's where you're going," Steve said.

A glowing metal frame outlined a hollow window filled with the thick darkness of the house's basement.

CHAPTER 10

His brother was only joking. He was mean, sometimes cruelly so, but he wouldn't force his little brother down into the basement of this place. That would be beyond cruel.

"You waiting for an invitation, Bro?"

"I can't," Eric said.

"It's no big deal," Steve said in a *you're-screwed-now* voice. "This is how we get in when we can't get in the front."

He *had* to be joking. Steve and his buddies might drop through a basement window but what girl would do that? Were women so stupid? Why would anyone enter this way when the front door was open? Even if people were watching (and someone was always watching, at least that's what they claimed in school), no one ever complained or called the police.

"Sometimes," Steve said in a serpent hiss, "the front door is a real bitch and it won't open. We come around to this window like backdoor men." He laughed and slapped Tori's butt. She did not sound amused.

Steve didn't need an excuse to torment his younger brother—he had earned that right by birth—so there was no reason for the explanation, which meant it was the truth. If the front door of the house sometimes wouldn't open that meant that the house controlled who entered and who didn't. Sometimes the house didn't want Steve inside it, so, of course, he and his friends broke in through an uncovered window. Eric had entered easily, meaning the house had wanted him. Hell, it had practically rolled out the red carpet.

"You said you never wanted to come back here," Eric said so quickly he barely realized he was thinking it.

Steve paused. His face flattened with the fear Eric had seen outside the funeral home. "I was messing with you," he said. He sounded like he was trying to convince himself.

A cinder block sat off to the side. They probably used it to block the window, prevent suspicion if the police ever came looking. He imagined the rock sliding into place over the hole of a window after he had fallen through, sealing a tomb.

"Please," Eric begged. "I can't go down there."

Steve laughed. It reminded Eric of Tommy's laugh. The same amused nastiness rolled out of both of them when they had control. The grass scratched his face and stank of rotten eggs. The darkness weighed on him and his brother weighed even heavier, bearing down, forcing him to fight, run, or surrender. He could not fight his brother; that would lead to endless punishment, possible injury, and definite humiliation. Running was always an option so long as he got an unexpected head start and, in this situation, Tori prevented a chase. Women were usually good supporters of the weak. Eric's mother had been the protector, his father merely the disciplinarian. He desperately wanted his mother now. Stuck between two choices leads to the final option: surrender. Fighting or running eventually comes back to surrender. Eric could not defeat Steve or run from him forever—one day, maybe, not today—and Steve never hesitated to sneak into Eric's room at night to execute punishment.

Steve grabbed the back of Eric's coat and pushed him toward the open window. Eric dug his fingers into the ground, which slowed the momentum until Eric's fingers twisted and one of them snapped awkwardly, painfully. The grass parted for him and the window loomed large.

"Steve, stop," Tori said behind him somewhere. She might have been yanking on Steve's coat or pulling back on his arm but Eric saw only the widening window of perfect blackness. He would drop through that window head first and crash into the black hole of Hudson House's basement. He'd fall forever, a ceaseless hell of eternal descent. If he stopped falling, he'd break his neck on a piece of moldy furniture—or maybe get impaled on some rusted garden tool. The woman would come down to visit. She might be waiting for him now with a mouthful of hungry teeth. The monster of fur and teeth was down there, too, waiting to pounce.

Just stories, made up myths about some weird, old house.

The window was larger than any basement windows Eric had seen. The windows on Hudson House didn't conform to any standard size because they could morph to fit any size. Any visitor who came here would be able to find entrance if the house wanted it. *Not visitors*, he thought, *sacrifices*. Once you've been inside the house, you never really leave. Eventually, the house never lets you see the outside again.

Steve pushed him harder. Eric's hands twisted and flipped across the ground; a rock sliced his left hand and he cried out. More laughter came from his brother and a more definite protest and pleading from Tori, but still the darkness neared and though he wanted to cry, Eric was too horrified for tears. He grabbed the sides of the window in time to prevent a full drop into the darkness. His head crossed through the hole. Cold immediately seized him, chilling his ears, clouding his eyes. A moment later, his teeth began chattering.

This is what death felt like. Once his hands slipped off the sides of the window and he fell completely into the house's lowest level, he would be dropping into his casket. He would have a wake where people would express sympathies and laugh about stupid things because they were afraid that Death might be coming for them next. They would tell his father they were so sorry, and then they'd turn away and comment about how his wife had only just died. Would his chest rise and fall the way his mother's had? Would he awake in his coffin during the Gospel and cry desperately to be freed only to suffocate in a packed church?

That didn't matter. His mother hadn't died in Hudson House, even though it had killed her. Not the house, no, him. *He* killed her. The house would now take him as the sacrifice intended to restore order. His actions had killed his mother and so the house would kill him. Unlike his mother who had died in her own home, Eric would die in Hudson House so he would have no wake or funeral. His chest would not rise and fall; his coffin would not shake with life. Once he died here, he would stay dead because the house would own him. Darkness awaited. Or hell.

A moan floated from that darkness. Eric wasn't sure he had heard it, not at first when it might have been his own frightened cry, but when the moan came again—louder, closer—Eric knew the thing of fur and fangs was, indeed, waiting for him down here, ready to take him in its claws and sink its teeth into his flesh. The third moan pushed hot air over his face that stirred his bangs. The breath stank of shit.

Eric's scream surprised him. He wouldn't have believed he had so much air in his lungs or so much force behind his cry. As long as he screamed, he could not hear the thing's moan, but he felt it warming his face and yet, also, chilling his bones, making him feel like he would freeze to death while burning alive.

The scream gave Steve what he wanted: power. Eric's hands slipped off the window and Steve yanked back on his legs to pull him out of the darkness. Eric sat back, stared at the window. The moan faded into a distant echo. Eric's skin cooled. The inner chill did not warm, however.

Eric tried to back farther away from the window but Steve held him in place, just outside the hole. "You scream like a little bitch," his brother whispered into his ear.

Tears pushed from his eyes against Eric's wishes. Weakness only made Steve meaner. Why did he have to have such an asshole for a brother? Why did his mother, his protector, have to die?

"Why shouldn't I drop you down there, bro?"

The tears fell faster and Eric could find no reason his older brother should have mercy upon him. He deserved this fate. It was his punishment for entering the house in the first place, for killing his mother. He should die here, tonight. Then Steve could live his life without an annoying younger brother. Their father could drown himself in tears and wonder what the hell had happened.

"Little baby's got no words? Then down the hole you go."

"Jesus, Steve," Tori said, "enough already."

Inspiration hit. Eric couldn't form the words as he pawed at his pockets.

"Looking for a weapon? Bring it on, bro."

Eric found the ring and held it out by two fingers toward Steve's face. It glinted in the beam of the flashlight. Tori's pleadings shut off with a startled yelp. Steve stared at the ring for a several seconds. Then he snatched it away and stared at it in the palm of his hand.

Eric crawled slowly away from the open window. Another moan wafted toward him.

"Where'd you get this?" Steve asked. Tori huddled next to him, eyes wide.

"I found it."

"Where?"

"Around."

"Where are you going?"

Eric stopped crawling.

"It's beautiful," Tori said.

"If I find out you stole this, I will kill you. Got me?"

Eric shook his head emphatically. He had no doubt Steve would kill him. He might not even need a reason. Eric didn't care. He was free of the house and amazed at his brilliant thinking. That little ring was going to save him from the darkness and the moan that still chilled his bones.

"Get the hell out of here," Steve said. "Don't go crying to dad or I'll drag you from your bed and toss you down in that basement without thinking twice."

With that, Eric ran.

He pumped his legs hard through wet concrete. His thigh muscles cramped before he even made it to the front of the house and he feared he might collapse beneath the spray-painted demon—*was it still blinking?* He refused to even glance at the face that had tried to eat Tommy. If he did, the face could change, appear more inviting, attempt to deceive. Eric didn't need evidence to know that. The house would use any and all of its tricks to get him back. *I can never leave.* Cascading tears blurred his vision.

The maple in the front yard was a giant skeleton with flaking skin that floated around it in the breeze. A huge sentry to ward off some people and trap others. Eric scrambled onto the slate walkway and then sprang onto the gravel driveway. Moving too fast—though how could he possibly slow down?—Eric slipped on the loose stones. He thought he could right himself and keep going but his feet tripped and he fell. Rocks sliced into his butt and elbows like knives.

From somewhere deep in the darkness, Steve laughed. Had he seen Eric fall? Was he watching now as blood seeped from his arms? Maybe it hadn't been his laugh; maybe it was the house's. The house was watching him, eyeing him like a spider does a fly when it is stupid enough to land in a web. That's just what he'd done: landed in a giant spider's web. Enormous, hairy legs would protrude out of the house; the arachnid would raise its black belly and open fully its fanged mouth. Venom would pour from that mouth in a waterfall.

The pebbles ripping up his arms were thousands of little spiders that did whatever the mother spider commanded. They had torn his flesh and now they would sink in their teeth and drag him back to the house. They would lead him right to the porch, *to the mouth,* and then the house would grin and devour him.

Eric pushed off of the stones (more spiders biting into his palms) and lunged for the sidewalk. Mere feet from him, the sidewalk and road could have been miles off. With every step, Eric expected the ground to fall away and the spiders to swarm over him. Would he suffocate beneath them before the house could eat him alive? Suffocate like his mother had.

He didn't feel any safer on the sidewalk or in the road or even halfway down Mangle Lane. The house followed. The spider legs had emerged, the body had lifted, and now it was hunting him through the neighborhood. Any second now Eric would feel the thing's hairy legs rub against him before the fangs pierced his chest. It was right behind him, reaching for him. He didn't dare glance back. He could only run and cry.

Huffing for breath and wiping the water from his eyes, Eric trudged up the steps of his house and fell to his knees at the front door. He groped at the knob and couldn't gather strength to seize it. His hands slipped off into his lap. Sobs rocked his body in violent tremors that hurt his stomach. Vomit threatened in his throat. The house had pursued him back here and now waited just behind him. It wanted Eric to turn around and recognize that he had been caught. *Run as hard and fast as you want, and still I'll get you.* The house won because huge predators always beat small prey. That's how the world works. Eric was just another victim.

He refused to turn around. Let the house kill him now if it wanted, but he wouldn't stare at it again. Never again. He shouldn't have gone in there originally and he never would again. He would never use Mangle Lane again, never even cross near it. Simple as that. If the house spared him now, he'd leave it alone forever. Somewhere deep in his mind, however, different logic persisted, the same logic that had made him agree to go back on Halloween and had pushed him there tonight. The fear throbbing inside him might be enough to silence that logic. And keep him safe.

When his father opened the door, Eric was clutching his body and crying that he could never leave, could never get away, never, never, *never*. His father embraced him on the porch; the warmth helped, but the tears kept falling. His father said everything would be all right; it was okay to feel sad and scared because he was, too. Eric just had to remember that his mother loved him very much and she lived on in their hearts.

"I killed her," he said.

"No," his father said. "You didn't. No one did. It was her brain. It just happened, that's all. It's no one's fault. Don't blame yourself, please." He squeezed Eric tighter.

"You don't understand, Dad. I did something horrible. I shouldn't have done it and that's why mom is dead. It *is* my fault."

His father held him a moment longer and then eased up. "What are you talking about? What did you do?"

Did his father wonder if Eric might actually be responsible for his wife's death? How would he react? "I went into Hudson House."

"What?"

"I shouldn't have gone in there. I know. But I never thought this would happen. I didn't know it was really haunted. Really evil."

"Eric."

"It wanted revenge. So it killed Mom. Now it wants me, too."

"Why did you go in there?"

Eric said he didn't know, but that wasn't the truth, of course. He didn't want to indict Tommy, though Tommy would probably do that himself. Eric had been goaded into entering Hudson House to prove his manliness. He had done it to avoid giving Tommy even more power over him. Instead, Eric had succumbed to an even fiercer entity.

That was all true, but it wasn't the complete truth and Eric was only beginning to realize that. He believed he could reenter the house and somehow make a deal with it so it wouldn't kill his father or anyone else. But how would that work? Tommy promised some amazing discovery within, but what could it be? Eric didn't want to completely rule out these possibilities, but he couldn't deny something he hadn't recognized before: he *wanted* to enter Hudson House.

Kids at school would not call Eric brave nor would they call him a coward; he was in the in-between category sometimes called cautious, perhaps even smart. He knew enough not to stick paperclips into electrical outlets (Tommy had tried that and singed his fingernail —the entire hand now charred) and he wasn't afraid of getting shots at the doctor's or jumping into the deep end of the school pool (Ed feared both).

Eric had known about Hudson House, as most people in town did almost intuitively as though the knowledge of the place was inherited, before Tommy ever mentioned entering to prove they were not little kids anymore.

Eric's parents had mentioned the house a few times in passing. Teenagers were known to hang out around the yard and vandalize the place but the police never caught anyone. Of course if the neighbors ever did see teenagers hanging out at Hudson House, they never called. It was best not to get the house pissed at you. His mother had warned him against the place a couple times, once going so far as to tell him, "Stay away from the Hudson Place. It's dangerous and I don't want you there." He had agreed because he was a good son. If she said the same to Steve, he would have agreed and then gone anyway. Eric wasn't like that. It was easy to be a good son if he followed the simple equation: whatever Steve would do, do the opposite.

The kids at school turned to Hudson House as fodder for all kinds of stories that varied from outlandish (pagans had built the house ten thousand years ago) to disturbingly plausible (a secret group of people were continuing Hox Grent's legacy by snatching kids off the street and slaughtering them inside Hudson House every few months). Kids had vanished over the years, and the stories of how they vanished were just as varied, but Eric knew only as much about them as he picked up from his friends.

Hudson House was a place you stayed away from, unless, of course, you had a death wish.

Crying against his father on the front porch of his house, Eric still wanted to go back to Hudson House. The place may have gotten its hooks (*fangs*) into him and he no longer had a choice, but he couldn't say he didn't want to give in to that pull. The more he thought about the house, the more reasonable it seemed to go back. Moments ago he had resolved never to even look at the house again; now, a mere viewing did not seem enough. He had to return.

Maybe that would change. Maybe he'd come to his senses.

"Stay away from that place," his father said. "No matter why you went there, just stay away."

"I will," Eric said. He wanted to believe that but couldn't. He would go back. He had no choice.

That night he suffered another nightmare.

Trapped in darkness so dense he felt it on his skin like wet towels, Eric couldn't move anywhere except where the darkness wanted him to go. His arms and legs wouldn't function and he could only move his head a few inches before the dark stopped him. When he tried to speak, the dark invaded his mouth and stuffed his throat so that he choked and fought for breath. He felt like he had last summer when he inhaled underwater by accident. The water flooding his body set his lungs on fire and he vomited water and choked for almost an hour after Steve pulled him out of the pool.

The dark turned bitterly cold. He shivered so furiously that his teeth chattered loudly. His bed had turned into an ice pit. The dark pressed against him from all directions, trying to crush him into a small cube. His muscles screamed in pain and his bones ached with the strain. He tried to fight his way out of the dream, to scream his way free, but the thick blackness dove deeper into his lungs and burned them while his body froze.

The woman in white arose from the darkness as if she had been hiding behind a black sheet. Her hair hung down past her shoulders and her face shone as if sunning in a warm world somewhere, the light too bright to make out her features. Her white dress clung to her body in heavy wet spots. Her breasts, which Eric had not noticed before, pushed tightly against the wet fabric and her nipples poked the dress so that it appeared they might break through. Water slipped from her neck down between her breasts, which perked even larger. She moaned, not hollow as before, but softly and erotically.

Eric tried to reach for her but remained paralyzed in the darkness. The woman's eyes pierced through him in a deep, dark stare that stirred him, though he couldn't explain how. She approached. He wanted her to touch him, wanted her to caress him, to warm him, to please him. He knew suddenly that she could free him; she could save him. She moved closer until her face nearly touched his. Her stare cracked through his face and plundered his brain. She grabbed the dress above her chest and pulled the wet fabric down beneath her breasts, which jumped out. Her right breast entered his mouth and Eric sucked on it eagerly. The breast was cold as a block of ice. His lips stuck to it; skin from his tongue ripped off on her nipple. Her eyes changed. She found what she needed inside Eric's brain and now her eyes projected pure vehemence. She meant to kill him. He tried to pull off of her breast but it drove deeper into his mouth. It froze his throat. The hollow, supernatural scream echoed out of her mouth. In a moment, the freezing vanished in an eruption of intense heat that burned hotter than any Eric had felt. When his face exploded in flames, he awoke. His sheets were covered with sweat and his penis was so rock hard and hurt so badly that he couldn't stop from humping his pillow until he stained the sheet with his gunk.

It took him a long time to fall back asleep.

CHAPTER 11

Eric avoided everyone as best he could—eating cereal for all his meals, hiding from Steve whenever home—until Sunday night when his father knocked on his door and mentioned that Tommy had been severely burned. He sat on Eric's bed while Eric remained on the floor, matchbox cars surrounding him.

"Do you know anything about it?"

"About Tommy's hand?"

His father smiled just slightly. *What did that mean?* "Yes."

"What did Tommy say?"

His father's hands rubbed together. "He said he was playing with a lighter and it exploded."

"Yeah."

"Yeah what?"

"That sounds like something Tommy would do."

"You didn't see it happen?"

Had Tommy mentioned Eric was there? "No," Eric said.

"You know how dangerous it is to play with fire." *Was that a question?* "You wouldn't do that, would you?"

Eric shook his head.

"Tommy's quite burned, but his father said he'll be in school tomorrow."

Would Ed be in school as well? Could everything return to normal? No, of course not. His mother was still dead.

His father stood, walked to the door, turned back. "How did you know he had burned his hand?"

"What? You told me."

"No, Eric," his father said. "I didn't."

Eric's face flushed. He cast his eyes down at his father's loafers. He could never look either of his parents in the face when caught in a lie. He felt like a disobedient dog with its tail between its legs.

"When you want to talk, I'm here for you. Anytime. But it should be soon."

After a moment, his father left the room. When the door shut, Eric released a lungful of hot air. Eric had never felt as comfortable talking to his father as he did his mother, but that would have to change now. His father had sounded concerned at first. His words before he left—*should be soon*—stung with accusation and knowledge. His father knew he had been with Tommy when he got burned and he probably also knew it led back somehow to Hudson House. What if Eric didn't tell his father? How long was *soon*?

* * *

He decided that soon was not immediate and that a full confession could wait until after he spoke to Tommy

112

and they put an end to their relationship with Hudson House.

Thick, white bandages covered Tommy's burned hand and he cradled it with his other hand like a baby as they walked the perimeter of the cafeteria. Rain splattered on the large windows overlooking the football field. It felt like they were in prison, but school usually felt that way.

Eric knew before the words came out of Tommy's mouth that nothing had changed. The original plan was still in place.

"We'll go back on Wednesday," Tommy said. "Just as we planned."

"But your hand."

"It's fine. I have medicine but, honestly, it doesn't hurt much. It's really burned. You want to see it? It looks like I cooked it."

Not you, the house, Eric thought. "Not right now," he said.

"Somebody might hurl anyway." A table of girls shied from them as they neared and then erupted in giggles once they passed.

"What about Ed?" Eric asked and immediately felt bad. Ed was the only sensible one of the three of them and knew enough to stay away from the house but Eric couldn't let him escape another visit. They all had to go. The house wanted it that way.

"He'll agree," Tommy said.

They stopped at a lunch table where Ed was finishing his soggy fries. He was writing something on a piece of loose-leaf. No one sat next to him. Tommy took the bench across from him and Eric sat on Ed's right; they were bullies getting into position. Some things couldn't be helped.

"This is bigger than us," Tommy said.

Ed did not look up and his pen kept moving. "I know."

"We're still going back. Halloween."

Ed nodded.

"No more excuses?"

Ed glanced at Tommy's bandaged hand, which lay on the table like a piece of evidence, and then returned back to his paper like that's all that needed to be said.

"I know you don't want to go back," Eric said. "Neither do I"—*a lie to make Steve proud*—"but we have to."

"It's what the house wants," Ed said.

"Yes," Tommy agreed.

"I don't think it's safe not to go back," Eric said. "The house wants us and not doing what it wants is going to get us hurt."

"Either way," Ed said, "we're already hurt."

They sat in silence for several minutes among the scattered shouts and laughs of their peers. Life went on as usual for every other kid in the school. Those kids knew of Hudson House and knew to stay away. Tommy, Ed, and he had dared to break that boundary and set themselves apart from everyone else. The other kids didn't know about the visits to the house or the upcoming Halloween return, but they sensed that the three of them had changed. They would never again be accepted as they once were. The house had marked them. Eric's mother had been killed, Tommy's hand burned, and Ed confined in a box of fear.

When the bell rang, Ed got up quickly and left. He walked in between groups of students. No one said anything to him.

"What's the plan?" Eric asked.

"We go in with flashlights and weapons and that ring we found. Finding it was like communicating with the house. We'll take it back and then you'll see what the house has to show you."

The ring.

"Getting nervous?" Tommy asked.

"No," Eric said. "I think I'm going to be sick."

* * *

Back in his bedroom that night, Eric replayed his exchange of the ring for freedom from Steve and the horrible darkness in the basement of Hudson House. Giving the ring away had seemed like inspiration, but it now weighed on him as a cowardly act. The house had given him the ring—or the woman in white had—as some kind of communiqué and he had given it away because he had been scared. The house would want it back or at least see that he had it as a sign of good faith that they weren't trying to outsmart the house. Going back without the ring meant risking greater harm. It didn't belong to him; he had no right to give it away. The house had burned Tommy's hand—what would it do to Eric?

Steve had not been home for dinner and neither Eric nor his father had mentioned it. Steve's plate had been taken off the table and put back in the cabinet. An hour after dinner, Steve had still not returned home and Eric stopped wasting time. His father was in his study, had been since dinner ended. The house sat still, silent and seemingly empty.

In the hallway outside Steve's room, Eric heard only the sporadic creaks and snaps of the house as it settled in for the night. Eric opened the door to his brother's room, which was smaller than his. The room was completely dark and for a moment Eric was back in his dream, trapped in thick blackness. Thinking the woman in white might appear any second, Eric smacked his hand against the wall repeatedly until he found the light switch and flipped it on.

He didn't remember what color the walls were and could no longer tell because posters covered every inch of the walls and ceiling. Most of the posters were in shades of black or bright red and featured long-haired guys with guitars or barely clothed women in provocative poses. A woman in a skin-tight bathing suit sucked on her finger in one of the posters. Her breasts were pushing through the suit and above her head the poster read, *Slippery When Wet*. Eric felt himself get hard.

Many of the posters showed human skulls and splashes of blood with the names of heavy metal bands like Metallica, Anthrax, and Megadeath screaming off of them. Eric hated that music. Steve blasted it in his room so loudly that the walls shook. Whenever he heard that music, Eric would hide. Sometimes Steve would look for him; sometimes he wouldn't. The music scared him, made him feel like the world was spinning out of control. The posters conjured the same feelings.

Unlike the blinds in Eric's room, the ones in Steve's were black, which blocked out all the light. The lamp he had turned on with the light switch was faint, casting the room in a dream-like world. Steve's clothes speckled the floor and unmade bed in rumpled piles like sores. Beneath his bed, magazines poured out like food from a stuffed mouth. One of the covers showed a woman baring her breasts. Eric wanted to grab it and take it back to his room but he knew Steve would find out.

Eric turned to the first of two dressers in the room. Crumpled tissues between bottles of cologne atop a sheet of thick dust masked the top of the dresser. A mix of socks, coins, belts, and various other things Eric couldn't identify filled the top drawer. He found another metal pipe like the one he had discovered years ago. He smelled it and cringed. It stank of something rotting but the faintest sweetness hovered beneath the stink. Eric knew his brother did drugs, and he knew drugs were bad, but he didn't know exactly what drugs were.

Eric searched through the stuff, stopping every few seconds to examine something. He found several plain rings but not *the* ring. Eric would keep looking but he could guess what had happened to the ring: Steve had given it to Tori. Steve would have done that gladly and without thinking twice about how he had scared the ring

117

out of his little brother and then passed it off as a gift to his girlfriend.

Buried beneath the socks, he found several gray boxes of condoms. Sex had to be more forbidden than drugs because Steve had taken the time to conceal the condoms under his shirts while the metal pipe had been practically showcased. One of the boxes was open. Eric removed a circular, yellow object inside a foil wrapper. What was he supposed to do with it? How did you put one on?

"What are you doing?" His father's voice turned Eric around to face the looming silhouette in the doorway. Eric could not answer, nor could he drop the condom. "Why are you in Steve's room?"

Eric ran through the possible excuses that would not arise too much curiosity from his father but settled on the old standby: "I don't know."

His father made no move to enter the room. "You don't know why you're in your brother's room?"

"No."

"What's in your hand?"

"I don't know." At least this time he wasn't completely lying.

"Put it back and come out here."

Eric dropped the condom into the drawer, closed it, and approached his father. His father started lecturing before Eric made it back to the hallway.

"This is your brother's room and you are to respect his privacy. Do you understand?"

Eric cast his eyes down again. When he made it to the doorway, his father grabbed him, yanked him into the hallway, and shut his brother's door. "You want me to tell him you were in there?"

"No."

"Then you tell me why. *Why* were you in there?"

"He has something of mine."

"What?"

"Something I found."

"Found where?"

"Nowhere."

His father's hands tightened on Eric's shoulders, his red-tinged eyes burned with rage and then the grip relaxed, the eyes softened and his father sighed. He knelt in front of Eric. "Look at me," he said softly. Eric did. "I'm sorry I got angry. We're all under a lot of stress. I understand if you're curious about your brother's life and more adult things, but you can't go through other people's stuff. If you want to go in his room, ask him. And if you have any questions about anything—*anything*—you can ask me."

Eric nodded. Was this the beginning of what Tommy called The Sex Talk?

"You need to talk to me," he said. "I can't pretend to know what you're feeling about Mom; you need to tell me. Things are confusing, but we need to stay honest. Right?"

"Yes."

"Good. Now, can you tell me why you were in Steve's room?"

The revelation of everything that had happened at Hudson House, the full description of events and consequences and the ever-worsening situation, was at the tip of his tongue but he could not spit it out. Something stopped him. *Not something*, he thought, *the house*. It didn't want others to know, not yet, not before it had Eric and his friends. Had them forever.

But it already has us.

"Is this still about Hudson House?"

Eric could neither confirm nor deny.

"Stay away from there, Eric. I'm serious about that."

Eric stepped forward, leaned his face against his father's shoulder and cried. He thought of his mother on the kitchen floor in her own blood and the tears flooded out easily. Perhaps partially dishonest, Eric could think of no other way to end the interrogation. His father hugged him and cried as well. The tears might never stop. The pain of their loss would forever fester beneath the surface and even a slight scratch could release the poison of their grief. They would have to live with it or surrender.

Eric wasn't going to surrender. The house would not control his life. He could not save his mother—*burned alive ashes to ashes*—but he could face the house and prove he wasn't a scared, little boy. He might still have to fight the house off for the rest of his life, but he might also be victorious. The best way to deal with bullies was to stand up to them. Eric was going to put that logic to the ultimate test.

CHAPTER 12

Eric had always loved Halloween. The weeks leading up to the holiday were filled with costume-hunting and prank-creating. Tommy, Ed, and he would rush home from the bus stop on Halloween, jump into whatever costume they had chosen (last year, Eric had gone as an axe murderer complete with plastic axe and blood-stained ensemble), and start trick-or-treating before the little kids dressed as pumpkins and fairies got all the candy. Tommy, who had gone as Michael Myers for the third straight year last year, would lead the group and instigate ambushes on other kids in which they'd jump out from behind bushes to scare the kids and, in some lucky instances, make off with extra candy.

Last year was the first time Tommy had said that trick-or-treating was for little kids and they should pursue more exciting activities. He wanted to keep scaring other kids, of course, and if those kids dropped their bags and spilled their candy, well, then that was good, but what Tommy really wanted to do was join the roaming teenage gangs that traversed the neighborhood every Halloween night, fighting other teenagers in epic battles of shaving cream and eggs.

This type of behavior started the night before Halloween but the three of them were always grounded for "safety's sake." They were also forbidden to go near any of these packs of teenagers and had to be home by eight. By the morning of November 1st, shaving cream and egg shells plastered the streets of the development and any cars unlucky enough to get caught in the crossfire. Eric's father had said that teenagers vandalized property on purpose, but Eric didn't think so. What was the point of destroying property? Things didn't scream or cry out when an egg splat on them.

Tommy had smuggled some eggs and a can of shaving cream out of his house. After telling Eric and Ed that trick-or-treating was for little kids, Tommy revealed his weapons. They hung out past their 8 p.m. curfew, and when the gangs took over the streets, Tommy tried unsuccessfully to convince Eric and Ed to take an egg each and stage a surprise attack. Tommy had called them "pussies" but hadn't pressed about it for long. Instead of fighting with and against teenagers, Tommy cracked an egg on Ed's head. Ed then smashed one against Tommy's chest, and Tommy covered Eric's face in shaving cream. And from there it only got messier. When Eric got home, his mother grabbed him, started to scold him, and then tossed him into a waiting bath. He had played with the bubbles like a little kid.

As usual, the three of them had been grounded last night on what the teenagers called "Devil's Night." It was no use arguing that they were almost all 13 which, technically, made them teenagers. None of their parents bought the logic. Eric's father had almost started crying again. Eric didn't press the issue. He had only hoped for a few moments of fun with his friends before they went to Hudson House tomorrow. Returning to that house felt incredibly final, like none of them would ever return. Ever the optimist, or simply the coward unwilling to accept his fate, Eric spent the evening gathering supplies. He laid them out on his floor: Maglite ("borrowed" from his father's tool box in the garage), wooden baseball bat (his father had attested that wooden bats were the only ones worth using), a small silver cross on a chain (a gift from his grandmother that hadn't meant much until now), and a pocket knife (Steve had given it to him as a birthday present last year but Eric had been too horrified to carry it or show it to his parents). He didn't want to fight the house, but he wasn't going to lie down and die, either.

He did not sleep well the night before Halloween. Every hour he awoke in a fresh mist of sweat and the darkness in his room startled him every time—*did I fall into the basement? Am I trapped? Is she coming for me?* When he finally got up for school, he did not recall any of his dreams (nightmares, surely). His eyes were sore with exhaustion but his body trembled with anxiety. When he got on the bus, the countdown to Hudson House began: sundown was fewer than ten hours away.

The school day surged and slowed; it propelled at the rapid pace of his nervous heart and also fatigued to

125

an agonized crawl. He couldn't pay attention to any of the lessons and Mr. Houston had to tell him twice to take notes in math class. During lunch, the three of them sat together, ate quietly amid the chaos of costumed kids screaming and running around the cafeteria, already high on the candy teachers had been giving out all day.

"Sundown?" Eric asked.

"Sundown," Tommy said.

Ed did not acknowledge them but they knew he had heard: he was squeezing his fork so tightly his knuckles turned white.

Last period was always the most difficult to focus in, but Eric had no trouble today. Mrs. Bolton did not take the route Eric's English teachers the previous two years had taken by reading "The Legend of Sleepy Hollow," which may or may not have been like the cartoons Eric had seen of the same title but he would never know because the story put him to sleep within five minutes. Last year, a kid dropped a bag of candy on his head that the teacher had passed around. His peers laughed while Eric picked up the treats and then fell back asleep. Mrs. Bolton said she was going to lecture for the period. The kids groaned and Eric's palms wetted: sundown was only a few hours away. His attention came back quickly, however, when Mrs. Bolton said:

"Halloween may have started over two thousand years ago when Celts burned people alive in wicker cages shaped like giants. Druid priests set fire to these cages to burn the people, typically male, allegedly

126

criminals, as a sacrifice that would redeem the sins of the recently deceased, granting them access to the afterlife."

The room was silent save for the sound of a few crinkling candy wrappers.

"The people who gathered to watch these sacrifices clothed themselves in the heads and skins of animals. This may have been the start of Halloween costumes. To celebrate and honor the freed souls, people lit bonfires on hilltops. They believed that these fires chased away evil spirits. The Celts, ironically when compared to today, believed that evil spirits feared fire."

Fire. Tommy's hand. The evil spirit spray-painted on the window. She wasn't speaking of Halloween; she was referring to Hudson House. In her lecture, Eric might find the secret to beating the house, or at least surviving another visit. Luckily, Tommy did not have Mrs. Bolton, because if he heard this story, he might kill his cat and wear the skin as some kind of sacrificial costume.

Mrs. Bolton wrote a strange word on the board and then gestured to it. "Samhain is the Celtic name of the Lord of the Dead. Halloween was originally called Samhain because the celebration, the burning of those criminals in cages, marked the last day of the Celtic year, which started on November first. On that last day of the year—October 31st, *today*—Samhain allowed the souls of those who had died within the last year to walk the earth to visit with the living."

Charlie Bryer raised his hand. "Like ghosts?"

"Yes," Mrs. Bolton said.

"Like haunting people?" Charlie asked.

"Maybe. But the Celts really believed that the souls walking the earth had returned because they wanted to visit their families. The souls were not tormenting the living; they were communing with them. Does anyone know what that means, *communing?*"

Jeremy Goldman raised his hand. "Talking or conversing with others." The kid was a walking dictionary. He wore khakis and button-up shirts and did himself no favors in class by answering questions. Someone mumbled that he was a "teacher's pet."

"Many of you think Halloween is all about candy and scary stuff, but its roots are steeped in Celtic faith and tradition, which was, at times, very bloody. They were not an evil people. I'm not suggesting that. They were people who believed in sacrifice for a good cause, the love of their deceased family members."

Mrs. Bolton kept lecturing, but Eric only caught bits about the origin of trick-or-treating and the jack-lantern. He had retreated far within his mind.

The connection to fire may have seemed coincidental on the surface, but Eric knew better. The house was toying with him. Celts had believed that evil spirits feared fire but the house, a genuine evil spirit, had used fire against Tommy, and might use fire again, perhaps against all of them. Forces greater than Eric could fathom were at work, manipulating his life to prove that he did not have control. He had lost that ability when he entered Hudson House. To think otherwise could be deadly.

If Mrs. Bolton was right—if the Celts were right about the dead returning—then his mother might have the chance to return tonight, and if she did, Eric could explain how her death was his fault, how he killed her though he had only meant to be brave. Confessing to his mother wouldn't bring her back, but it would at least give him a venue for his emotions. His father wouldn't believe him even if Eric got the nerve to explain the full situation. Only his mother would understand. Would she forgive him?

He didn't want to dwell on that. Forgiveness didn't matter so much as confession; he knew that, too. How could his mother possibly forgive him for killing her? No matter how much love she had for him, his mother could never be expected to relieve him of the guilt. Strangely, part of him did not want to be freed from the chains of his culpability. Responsibility for her death lay with him and there it should stay for his entire life. Even at his age, Eric knew his entrance into Hudson House and his mother's subsequent death would shape his life —if, that was, he lived long enough to have a life.

If she came back, how would she look? Would she be her old self or would blood be spilling out of her head, soaking her face, flooding her mouth? Would she be able to talk or would all her words rumble in an anguished death moan? Would she return with love in her heart as the Celts believed or would anger boil in her veins and vengeance sharpen her teeth into fangs?

Would she come for love or hate? Or would she return as nothing more than a puff of translucent smoke that vanished without recognition. Of all the scenarios, that was the worst. If she returned, Eric wanted to see her—regardless of her appearance or intent.

Eric couldn't wait to jump off the bus and run to his house. When he did, he blended with the other kids filled with frantic excitement for the holiday's adventures. Those kids ran into their separate houses and immediately donned their costumes and begged their parents to let them start the candy quest. Eric, however, ran to his room, tossed off his bag, and hunted for his father; he found him in his study, staring at a picture of Eric's mother. Puffiness swelled beneath his eyes.

He glanced at Eric and then back at the picture. "I asked Mrs. Forlure to follow you guys around the neighborhood but she said none of you planned on trick-or-treating. If that's still the case, I assume you want to talk to me about something else. Are you here because you want to talk to me, finally, or have you changed your mind about going out today?"

His father's sorrowful tone gave Eric pause. "I want to talk—about school."

After a moment, his father placed the picture face up on the desk in front of him and stared at Eric, waiting.

"Mrs. Bolton taught us about the beginning of Halloween."

His father sighed.

"It was a Celtic holiday for the Lord of the Dead and on this holiday the souls of the people who had just died could visit with their families. That day is today."

His father's eyes flitted down to the picture and back again.

"Mom can come back tonight to visit. We can see her again."

That ushered fresh tears from his father's eyes. He let them roll down his cheeks and off his chin. The pattering of drops on the desk drew his attention once more to the picture. He wiped tears from the photograph. "I miss her so much," he said through a sob. "So much."

Tears threatened in Eric's eyes but he refused to let them out. "Do you think she'll visit us?"

"I hope so," his father barely said. "I hope I can hug her again."

"The Celts believed the living could commune with the dead. Do you think we can do that with mom?" He was careful to pronounce *commune* just as he had heard it.

His father finally wiped his eyes. When he lifted his gaze to Eric, his face had changed. He was trying to conceal his sorrow beneath his *I'm-your-father-so-listen-to-me* mask. "I know you want your mother back. I want her back, too. But you need to understand that she's gone. She isn't coming back. She can't talk to us, not anymore. You can't hold on to fantasies because one day they will hurt you."

Parents could be so stupid sometimes that it was a wonder they lived as long as they did. He had ignored everything Eric said about the Celts.

"I loved your mother very much. I thought we would always be together. We'd watch you and Steve grow up, get married, have kids of your own. I *believed* those things. I wanted them desperately. But those fantasies hurt me, Eric. I was deluding myself. Your mother is dead and those dreams did nothing but make this harder for me. Everyone dies. It's a sad fact. Death comes to everyone and we need to accept that. Dead is final. It means the end; it means never again. Don't delude yourself, son. Be honest with reality or it will crush you."

His father had opened a window into the adult world for Eric. That world sometimes seemed illogical. That world languished in misery and depression. That world did not believe in anything but gloom. Eric wanted to shut that window, draw the blind, and turn his back on it forever, but he knew somehow that once you peered through the window, you could never turn away. Even if you could turn away, the world would be different somehow now that you knew what waited for you.

"Your mother loved you," his father said. "And we loved her and that's all that matters."

Eric waited for more but his father said nothing. After almost a minute of silence, Eric backed out of the room, leaving his father to cry over the photograph of his wife. Before he reached his room, Eric wondered if his father's picture-worshiping was an example of those self-deluding fantasies. He could never mention that to his father but he thought it just the same. That was something else he was learning: growing up meant thinking more and saying less.

He hoped he'd live through the night to tell his father everything. He needed to confess, to his father if not his mother. He owed it to them.

Sundown was two hours away.

CHAPTER 13

When the sun's descent painted the sky in deep reds and oranges, Eric gathered his supplies (cross around his neck beneath his shirt, knife in his jacket pocket, Maglite in one hand, baseball bat in the other), and assured himself that he wasn't being stupid; he was doing exactly what had to be done. "If you're here, mom," he said to his room, "I'm sorry. Please watch out for me. I'm only doing what I have to. I know you understand." He stopped short of saying, *I love you*; it didn't feel right to say it aloud to an empty room, almost like a violation. Besides, his mother knew he loved her. Mothers always knew things like that.

Tommy was already waiting at the corner of Jackson Drive and Mangle Lane in the same Michael Myers mask and jumpsuit he had worn the last three years. He did not have the comically large carving knife that went with the costume, but he was holding a pillowcase: the preferred method of treat collection for the serious trick-or-treater. Things inside the case pushed it out at odd, sharp angles.

"Hey," Eric said.

"Hay is for horses," Tommy said from behind the mask. "What's your costume, nighttime baseball player?"

Eric didn't laugh and felt suddenly very stupid. He had been so prepared, so confident, and one remark from Tommy had dashed that certainty. Good old reliable Tommy.

"For protection." Eric swung the bat in a small arc.

Tommy snorted. Eric wasn't going to show him the pocket knife. Once he saw what was in Tommy's pillowcase, however, his pocket knife no longer held the threatening power it once had.

"Check it out," Tommy said and opened his pillowcase.

Eric peered in, saw nothing but shadows, turned on his Maglite and shined it inside the bag. The light reflected off of an impossibly long metal blade that must be meant for cutting people's heads off. Eric gasped and Tommy laughed.

"It's my father's," he said. "He'll never notice I took it out of the kitchen."

"What is it for?"

"It's a carving knife, stupid. You know, cooking?"

"Why did you bring it?"

"Protection. What good is a bat going to do, anyway?"

Other items surrounded the knife. Thick rope bundled in an "8" snuggled next to a hammer that partially covered a mirror, on which rested an envelope and the giant knife—eight inches long, at least. "He

136

won't suspect any of it," Tommy said about his father. "My dad was counting the eggs and hiding his shaving cream."

Tommy's amusement did nothing to calm Eric. "What are we supposed to do with that stuff?"

"You'll see," Tommy said. "And I have this, too." He pulled a plastic flashlight out of a pocket in his overalls. It seemed his outfit had many pockets. At least Eric had him beat with the flashlight. That plastic one might break if he dropped it while Eric's would endure extensive abuse.

"You think he'll show?" Eric asked.

"He better."

A group of kids in torn and bloodied bed sheets shrieked past them down Mangle Lane like a chorus of ghosts. They moved so quickly they could have been flying. Somewhere else a kid screamed and a cackle of laughs followed. The sun had almost disappeared and flashlight beams shook across the roads and houses as dark figures marched up strangers' front porches to demand something sweet.

A burst of wind plastered Eric's jacket to his body like a wet-suit. With it came a chill that seeped through his clothes, onto his skin, and into his body. The cold dug deep, burrowed into caverns of ice, buried hooks that would not shake loose. Halloween was always best when the weather tilted below fifty degrees but this weather stung with an extra bitterness that made Eric shift his weight nervously from one foot to the other.

This Halloween didn't feel like the others; this one was nastier.

"You got to pee or something?" Tommy asked.

Eric was about to respond when the final member of the trio appeared out of the darkness amid a group of giggling trick-or-treaters. Ed blended with the darkness as he walked like it might swallow him if he turned in the wrong direction. Only his face shone brightly. Eric and Tommy's flashlights revealed Ed's secret: black jeans with a thick black sweater. He wasn't carrying anything. He stopped before them, hands in his pockets. He might have been wandering aimlessly.

"The sun is almost gone," Tommy said. "Thought you were going to fag out."

Ed shrugged and lowered his eyes. Eric remembered when the three of them used to play touch football all summer long and often in the winter, too. They had laughed so much back then. Ed hadn't laughed in a long time, it seemed. That bothered Eric not because he thought Ed should laugh; it bothered him because he knew there was nothing to laugh about. All the fun in the world had drained away, leaving the three of them alone with each other. And the house, of course.

"You bring anything?" Tommy asked.

Ed shrugged again. "Why?"

Tommy started to say something and then shook his head. "Whatever."

Eric squeezed the bat in his hands. It felt like it might snap in half or crumble into a million pieces. Ed was right. What was the point in bringing protection?

138

The house had burned Tommy's hand without warning. It could destroy them easily. Fighting was pointless. The bat sagged in his grip and he almost dropped it—almost.

"Let's go," Eric said, amazed the words had left his mouth. Tommy and Ed appraised him for a moment, perhaps surprised as well, and then Tommy nodded and led the march down Mangle Lane.

Eric and Ed walked next to each other behind Tommy. They didn't say anything. Eric wanted to open the lines of communication with his friend, to get him to confide in him, to maybe hear him laugh again, no matter how far fetched that seemed. He tried to start the conversation a few times and aborted each time. Their footsteps echoed off the pavement. Kids in costumes dashed around them and vanished into the dark like momentary dreams. What was very clear, however, was that none of those kids was headed for Hudson House.

The trio stopped in the road before the dark and silent house. Eric expected (hoped) a parent or even a group of kids would stop and ask them what they were doing so that the plan—*what plan?*—would have to be postponed. No stray beams from flashlights touched the house. The world spun wildly behind them in typical Halloween fun and mayhem but that did not include them. They were completely alone on a street thriving with running and laughing kids and parents. They could not re-enter that world. They had surrendered that right when they first dared to test this house.

"Well," Tommy said. "Go on, Eric."

"What?"

"Lead us."

"Why me?"

"You went first before so it only makes sense for you to go first again. We shouldn't change anything from last time, not if we hope to really find out what makes this house tick."

"I don't want to know what makes this house tick."

"Sure you do. You just don't realize it yet. *Go.*"

Eric stepped onto the gravel driveway expecting the rocks to snag at his shoes with those hungry, spidery mouths. The rocks shifted under him but did not part to reveal a hellish cavern.

The wind rushed through him again and deepened the inner cold that had taken root. The branches of the naked tree in the yard rattled like bones cracking against each other. Dried leaves kicked up around his legs in tiny tornadoes. Eric tried not to think about what he was doing (*I'm going back into hell*) and instead focused his Maglite on the ground a few steps ahead of him. Baby steps of bravery.

Each step, however, was a step closer to his grave. At only twelve years old, Eric already had an idea what people experienced when Death arrived in his black cloak, scythe at his side. Would he recognize the moment when the scythe finally swung toward him or would Death attack from behind?

"We have to leave," Eric said. "I forgot the ring."

"No going back," Tommy said.

"You said we needed to bring the ring back."

Tommy laughed. "We don't need the ring. Figured you'd 'forget' it. There's a better way."

Eric was afraid Tommy was going to say that. If the ring wasn't important, why had he first mentioned it?

The porch steps moaned beneath his feet. The wood sagged, threatened to break. Tommy poked him with his flashlight. What was the rush? If Eric tried to run, Tommy would tackle him and drag him up the steps.

Eric stopped at the top of the steps, flashlight focused on the hole in the porch. The light dissipated after a few feet into the hole. It could descend forever. He lifted his leg to step to the door and paused. The beer can that had glowed in the hole like a troll's eye was gone. Steve had said the house cleaned up its messes. Steve and his friends partied in the house, left their mess behind and discovered it completely cleaned when they came to party again. The house wanted to keep up appearances. *Or keep the cage clean and ready.*

Where did all the beer cans and garbage go?

Into the dark. Eric stepped over the hole, grabbed the cold handle of the screen door, opened it with a deafening screech from the hinges, and seized the doorknob to the storm door. The spray-painted pentagram loomed over him.

"The sun is gone," Tommy said. "Open the damn door."

Sometimes the front door is a real bitch and it won't open, Steve had said. Eric knew it would open easily. The house was expecting them.

Eric turned the knob and pushed. The door opened. He thought again of a coffin lid snapping wide. The stale air hit like a wave. Another smell fluttered beneath the musty air that Eric couldn't place, something sweet.

Tommy squeezed between Eric and the doorframe. "Smells like candied apples," he said. He pushed all the way into the house before stopping in the foyer. "You smell that?"

Tommy was right—the smell was clear now and growing stronger with every second they stood in the house. The smell of such a delicious treat should have relaxed Eric, conjured up images of July nights at the Orange County Fairgrounds, but instead the smell nearly made him gag. The smell was *off* like the way synthesized music is always faintly wrong.

The trap is set.

Tommy shined the flashlight on his own face. Pockets of light circled his nose and eyes, casting the rest of his face in shadow. The campfire ghost story trick was corny at best but Eric shivered despite himself. It wasn't right adding more creepiness to this excursion. "Well, let's go," Tommy said in his deepest tone. "It's time for a tour."

Eric told him to cut it out and shined his flashlight on Tommy's face, flushing the shadows away. Tommy laughed, clutched his pillowcase closer to him (*what was he planning?*), and beckoned for them to follow him with his bandaged hand. He was a marked animal returning to the beast that had scarred him.

Tommy headed for a door straight ahead, to the left of the staircase. Eric started to object when Ed tugged on his jacket from behind. "Let's leave him," Ed whispered. "We can run. Maybe the house will get us and maybe it won't, but we don't have to be stupid."

That wasn't friendship; that was each man for himself. They used to call themselves the three *amigos* —one for all and all for one. Now the three *amigos* had disintegrated, crumbled to pieces inside an abandoned house.

For a moment, Eric almost agreed. Running sounded good, sensible, safe. He couldn't do that, though—no matter the consequences. "We all have to do this," Eric told him. "It's the only way."

"I can't." Ed's voice wavered on the cusp of hysteria.

"You have to."

Tommy's flashlight washed over them. "You fags coming?"

Eric handed Ed the baseball bat. Ed took it eagerly. The loss of its grip left Eric forlorn. He had wanted to help his friend but he felt he had made another stupid choice. He slipped his empty hand into his pocket and clutched his knife. As long as they worked together, they would be okay.

"Shouldn't we go the way we went last time?" Eric asked.

Tommy snorted and pulled open the door. He entered the darkness beyond. Eric waited a moment for a scream or a scuffle or a splatter of blood. "Coat room," Tommy called. "Complete with scary coat hooks."

"Very funny," Eric said.

The coat-room door swung gently shut.

"We can leave now," Ed said.

Before Eric could respond, Tommy's shrill scream pierced the air and reverberated from the coat room like the door might explode off its hinges from the pressure.

All for one, Eric thought and ran to Tommy's aid.

Tommy's scream echoed outward from behind the door like the eye of a hurricane spiraling out its winds. Eric pulled his hand out of his pocket, almost dropping his knife, and grabbed the door handle. He swung it wide, expecting the woman in white with her bleeding arms to howl into his face. Instead, Tommy stood directly in front of him, flashlight turned upward on his face again. Eric tried to skid to an immediate stop but couldn't.

He collided with Tommy, finally silencing the scream, and they stumbled deeper into the coat room, smacked the wall and then fell through it. The darkness swallowed them and Eric tried to brace himself for an endless drop. Their fall ended abruptly on the tiled floor of the kitchen. Tommy's pillowcase of goodies clattered next to them. Maybe the mirror had broken. How much bad luck could they endure?

Tommy's laughter ignited a fire in Eric's belly. Why was Tommy such an asshole? "That wasn't funny," Eric shouted.

Tommy laughed louder and said repeatedly that yes it was funny, really funny, and that he had to get their attention before they were frozen in place forever at the doorstep.

"This is serious," Eric said. He stood, scanned the double sink beneath the boarded windows as a cold wave deepened his inner chill. They had fallen into the kitchen as if that's what the house had wanted. *Part of the trap.*

"Yeah," Tommy said. "Seriously funny." He checked the contents of his pillowcase. After a moment, he said, "We're good. Let's get on with it." He headed across the kitchen to the pantry door.

"Where's Ed?" Eric asked.

"Crying on the porch, I imagine."

The door between the kitchen and coat room swung gently back into place in slowing arcs. "Ed?" Eric called.

"Forget him." Tommy stood at the pantry door.

"We need him."

"Don't worry. He's not going anywhere. None of us are. Ever again."

The front door crashed shut. The house had them now.

CHAPTER 14

The door slam still echoing in his ears, Eric almost laughed at his notion of reasoning with the house. It had been a childish belief that if he stood up to his aggressor, he'd persevere. The house would respect his bravery and agree not to bother him any more. A chuckle did spill out and Eric immediately covered his mouth. Only crazy people laughed in situations like this. If he let himself laugh, he'd end up screaming.

The candy apple smell intensified like the vat of caramel candies was directly under his nose. Perhaps it was. The woman in white might be in the basement beneath them stirring the cauldron of goop so that the aroma drifted into the ceiling and teased the boys' taste buds. What would happen if they found that pot and ate the syrupy candy? It might set their guts on fire, and the woman in white would roar with her own laughter while their skin melted like wax.

Tommy pulled open the pantry door and stepped into the world beyond. He kept the door propped open with one hand. "We didn't come here to stand in place."

Eric resisted the urge to call for Ed again. Most likely, Ed hadn't moved from the doorway and the slamming door had blocked him out. Hopefully, the door hadn't crushed him. But these were childish thoughts again full of innocent hope. The house wanted all three of them—Ed had entered the house and *then* the door slammed.

Eric walked to the pantry door, took a breath, and entered.

The same empty shelves protruded from the walls and the same boarded-up door prevented escape. *This house is very special*, Tommy had said. That depended on the definition of "special." The house was not special unless the word meant the corruption of normal, something askew from reality, something tilted toward wrongness. Eric would decry the place as evil when safely outside of it, but not inside, deep inside where the house could get at him anyway it wanted.

Tommy's flashlight cast a circular glow on the far wall as he had done the last time. This time, however, the yellow beam did not dim as it hit the old wood. Dark splotches patterning the wall turned Eric's stomach; they were like liver spots on an old person. Eric's eyes gave him no clue about the *offness* of this place, but his other senses inundated him with warnings. The floor rocked gently from one side to the other as if the house were set on a gentle tide. With each sway, Eric's stomach tightened. The movement increased, the drops to either side deepening.

Eric had gone camping with Ed's family two summers ago and one of the days had been spent canoeing the giant lakes of western New York. Eric and Ed had shared a canoe while Ed's parents shared another. The day had been beautiful and clear, but the deep water had troubled Eric. He hadn't minded the streams they traversed but when they rowed across a wide expanse of water, Eric's heart beat a little faster and he couldn't resist staring into the black depths from which giant seaweed arms reached toward him. What would happen if he dropped into the water? Even with a life jacket on, the seaweed might tangle around his legs and yank him under. That night lying in his tent, Eric had felt the ground swaying side to side for hours. When he shut his eyes, he was back on the boat, only this time he fell in the water and slithery arms wrapped around his ankles. He stayed awake for hours, his mind simulating the canoe's rocking. It had gotten so bad that he almost vomited.

"Do you feel that?" Eric asked.

"It gets better," Tommy said. Did he mean the rocking would stop or they'd get used to it?

The smell of candied apples soured into a stench of decay. The odor coated his nostrils and sluiced into his throat with the weight and vileness of toxic waste. He gagged against the taste and hoped he wouldn't vomit.

The air thickened like during a humid day, only this air was sandpaper; it scraped at Eric's hands and face. He expected scratches to appear on his skin and blood to flow from those wounds.

His heavy breathing almost hid the faint churning sound coming from the wall. It reminded Eric of the sound his mother's mixer made when she was preparing a cake. The sound hummed and throbbed and grew louder. Something on the other side of the wall was gearing up for an entrance. *No*, he thought, *not on the other side—inside.*

The light from Tommy's flashlight vanished. Tommy hadn't shut it off—light still shone from the bulb—but where the light had splashed onto the wall before was now a dark slate. *It ate the light. The wall ate the light.* Eric tried to tell Tommy that this was a seriously bad idea and they needed to leave but when he opened his mouth, bile jumped into his throat and he buried his mouth in the crook of his elbow. The bile came no farther but neither did it retreat. The pantry door shut behind him. His legs wobbled on the unsteady floor. The humming sound whirled louder.

He could not trust his eyes in this darkness where shadows could morph into beasts, but he couldn't deny how the wall changed. One moment it was a solid structure of wood and the next it was . . . *liquefied.* It didn't crash onto the floor in a wave of fluid, but it rippled like the surface of water. The ripples multiplied and swam together in the middle of what had been the wall. The bumps gathered into a circle and then stretched outward toward Tommy.

"Isn't it amazing?" he asked.

The tip of this arm coming out of the wall split open like a clam shell and a potent red light radiated

150

from within it. Then the sides of the arm peeled rapidly back and collapsed into the wall, creating a hole. It widened to the size of a basketball and the darkest red light Eric had ever seen burned outward from it. *Not an arm at all,* he realized, *but a mouth.*

The color deepened to crimson and the hole widened to spread across the wall. Like blood soaking a shirt. Soon the entire wall was a gaping, red mouth. The stench of rotting candied applies filled the room. The bile in Eric's stomach pushed farther up his throat. He wanted to scream and cry and vomit and run and run and run, but he could only stare at the red wall and pray it would eventually release him.

"It wants to show you something," Tommy said.

The color washed the entire wall to the corners and spread across the shelves on either side of them. As the color crawled over the wall it crinkled like burning paper. The closer it got, the more that burning sound resembled hissing. The mouth was opening wide enough to eat both of them.

It's already eaten us, he thought, *and now it's swallowing.*

"I told you there was something special you had to see," Tommy said. He fumbled with the contents of his pillowcase. Eric couldn't move. "You remember what I told you last time, Eric?"

The pillowcase thumped to the floor. The giant knife clanged against something, perhaps the hammer. "I told you to run for your life, not that it'd do any good.

And you did, too." He laughed. It sounded like a cat's screech. "But that's not all I said. Remember?"

The red had almost reached where Eric stood. The color swirled within itself like a lake covered with thousands of bugs. The bile pushed farther up his throat and he bit his forearm, the pain forcing the vomit back down.

"I told you that Ed hadn't left. And I was right. He never left, Eric, and neither did we. This is our place— *forever*."

Large holes appeared three quarters of the way up the wall. The blank spaces in the red mess widened and elongated until they resembled hollow eyes. A large space opened halfway down the wall and stretched across from one wall to the other. Red light, blood, it had to be blood, seeped into the open space as numerous sharp fangs formed. The spray-painted demon wasn't confined to the outside. Teenagers had not painted it, no, it *lived* within the house; this was the face of the house —the face of evil.

"Isn't it beautiful?" Tommy's voice rang with elation. When Eric didn't respond, Tommy said, "Now, turn and look at what the house wants you to see."

Though the red color still hissed along the walls and the floor fluctuated on uneven waters, Eric could move again. Tommy wanted him to move and so he could. It was like Tommy could channel the power of the house. Or the house could channel Tommy.

He angled the mirror toward the wall with both hands. His flashlight had fallen away somewhere.

Tommy's black hair covered his eyebrows in wet patches. He grinned like he had some horrible trick rigged and ready to spring. *That's just what this is. Only the house is the one rigging the trick.*

"Step closer to the mirror and see," Tommy said.

Eric did. The red face on the wall was distorted in the mirror so that the face was more round and yet more angular. The empty eye sockets filled with swirling pupils. A tongue slithered behind the fangs. From behind those fangs a laugh rumbled like thunder in the distance.

"Do you see what the house has for you?"

Another step closer and the face changed. The red slid off like a mask to reveal a woman's pale face. Eric had expected the woman in white and had even seen her in the mirror for a moment before the illusion vanished, the blood pooled along one side of the face, and Eric couldn't deny what the house had to show him: his dead mother.

"Do you see?" Tommy's excitement had disintegrated into maniacal glee.

Eric was back in his kitchen standing before his mother's motionless body where a puddle of blood spread over tile. Her blood kept flowing after she died. He hadn't recognized that before but he knew it now. Her eyes stayed open after she collapsed and stopped breathing. The life had drained from those eyes and yet her blood continued spilling. Eric screamed something that was supposed to be *NO!* but which came out as an almost hysterical howl and shined his flashlight directly into the mirror. The light reflected back in a sudden burst that scorched his eyes.

The kitchen and his dead mother fell away. So, too, did Hudson House. The shining light softened from a harsh glare to a gentle wash that sparkled like diamonds on a white cloth. The sparkles scattered across the white light flickered. It reminded Eric of Morse Code. He couldn't translate Morse Code but the way the small specks shone in successive flashes felt like a message. He had no idea what it might be saying and yet, somehow, that didn't matter as much as how it made him feel. The fear had vanished. Tommy was right: the house was special, and this was beautiful.

"What do you see?" Tommy called.

The mirror shattered in a cacophonous crash that scattered shards of glass around Eric and Tommy's feet. The magnificent light vanished. Tommy grinned. "What did you see, Eric?"

Eric had no strength in his vocal chords, which didn't matter because he had no words, either. The house had shown him his dead mother, had made him recognize how her blood flowed steadily even after death, and then the house had sent him somewhere pleasant where stars glistened in a white sky. *All part of the trick.* The house knew what it was doing, knew how to play them, manipulate them. But why?

Tommy stepped toward him, hands empty. The hammer and knife still safely in the pillowcase on the floor. "Tell me. Tell me what you saw. I *want* to know."

Eric backed away with each of Tommy's approaching steps, almost unaware that he could move again. He wanted to cower in the corner, bury his face between his knees, and wish everything away.

"That's okay," Tommy said. "I know what the house showed you. I always knew. I only wanted to hear you say it. Did you like it? Did you enjoy how the house knew?"

Eric backed into the wall. The door was to his right. Tommy narrowed the distance between them to a few feet. Eric's flashlight beam hit Tommy under his jaw, and shadows stretched his eyebrows back across his forehead.

"What did it feel like, that moment when you stumbled upon your dead mother? Did you see that she was still bleeding even after she died? Tell me: did you see that?"

Tommy had known what Eric would see because the house had told him. Perhaps he had watched Eric discover his dead mother as it happened, the pantry wall showing the scene like a movie screen.

A foot from Eric's face, Tommy stopped. "You can leave this house, but you can never escape it. You belong here. It's easier if you embrace it. The house has wonderful things to show you, but you must always remember your mother, lying on the kitchen floor, blood pouring out of her head because the moment you forget that, the house will teach you a lesson."

Somehow Eric found words. "What was your lesson, then? What did the house take from you?"

155

Tommy smiled. He raised his bandaged hand into the light. "Nothing," he said. "The house took nothing. Actually, it gave me something and I want to share it with you."

"We have to get out of here."

"We have so much more to discover." He raised the large kitchen knife in his other hand. He had hidden it somewhere, tucked in one of the pockets of his Michael Myers overalls, and now raised it before him with the blade curving toward Eric. "The house owns us, Eric. We can never leave. Ready or not, here we go."

Tommy raised the blade and Eric smacked the pantry door open and ran through the kitchen. His feet almost slipped on the tile and then he collided with the door to the coat room. His hands caught the door, fingers squishing between the door and the flashlight, and he rebounded off the wood, stumbled, and fell on his butt. Pain raced up his tail bone. Tommy was laughing, his cackles reverberating within the pantry.

Eric started to get up. The woman in white stood, back to him, before the sink as she had the last time. Who was she? Did she work with the house or against it? Good spirit or evil poltergeist? Eric didn't want to find out for sure, to wait and discover that Tommy could bury that blade in Eric's chest before the ghost turned around, but he couldn't get up.

His leg muscles cramped in his fallen position. The flashlight shone across the floor but, as before, the woman did not need light to glow in her white dress. When she started to turn, Eric tried to as well and could not. He didn't want to see those ravaged arms again, to hear her blood dribble on the floor.

Her long hair obscured her face, but through the strands, her eyes pulsed a deep blue that reminded Eric of the ocean. Her arms were clean as was her dress. This was not the girl who had hanged herself with her father's ties. This was his mother. He couldn't be sure but he sensed he was right.

Eric tried to speak and could not. Tommy's laughter had died out or fallen away into the deepest confines of the house. The previously potent smell of candied applies had faded as well. This woman, his mother, could manipulate the house.

Or she's another part of the trap.

She slowly raised one slender arm above her head until it stood erect above her and then her fingers curled into a fist and her forefinger uncurled to point directly overhead. Veins throbbed against her skin. Did fresh blood flow through those veins or was it some other power that kept her animated?

She moaned deeply, a moan that rumbled through the air and into Eric's body. That shaking stirred his body loose from the floor. Tommy's laugh erupted out of the pantry and the smell of candy bloomed again. Eric scrambled to his feet and crashed through the swinging door into the dining room as Tommy's laugh echoed in the kitchen.

Eric's sneakers squeaked on the dining room floor and into the living room. Tommy banged through a door behind him. Tears blurred Eric's vision. He jumped for the front door and caught the knob. It would not turn. He yanked back on the knob again and again but the door would not open. The house had let them in and now refused to let them out. Tommy was right: they were here forever.

Frantically grunting, Eric persisted at the door, setting one foot on the wall and using all his strength to twist and pull the knob but it didn't even groan under the strain.

A door crashed open behind him. He didn't have to turn to know that Tommy had run through the coat room. Eric stopped pulling, let his body sag, and then turned to face his friend. The flashlight had fallen somewhere but Eric's eyes adjusted to reveal Tommy on the other side of the foyer.

"The house doesn't want to hurt us," Tommy said. "It only wants what belongs to it."

The stairs were closer to the front door; a wooden railing with thick spindles and a carved banister blocked Tommy from easy access. Eric could run and Tommy wouldn't be able to slice him. Not yet, anyway. But upstairs? He had vowed never to go up there, certainly not the third floor. He wouldn't have to, though, just to the second and then out one of the windows. He could jump onto the roof of the porch and then onto the grass.

"We belong here. You have to trust me. None of us can leave."

Maybe Ed left. Maybe he would call the police and they would come barging into the house to end this madness.

Tommy stepped forward and Eric ran for the stairs. Tommy had suspected the move and sprang toward the foot of the staircase. Eric grabbed the banister and lunged onto the second step before Tommy crashed into the railing with a furious grunt. Chancing a glance through the spindles, Eric saw Tommy still brandished the knife in one hand and the pillowcase in his other. The rope and the hammer.

Six steps led to a landing and the stairs continued at a right angle from the first flight up to the second. Eric missed the first step of the second flight, and crashed his knee on the wood. He cried out; Tommy laughed and scrambled up the stairs toward him. Eric jumped onto the second flight of stairs and scurried up the steps as fast as he could. His knee hit several steps.

When his hands found another landing, Eric jumped to his feet and told himself to run right, toward the front of the house, go into whatever room he found and break through the window. How he would break the glass he didn't know. The flashlight would have worked well for that.

When he stood up on the second floor, the woman in white screamed in his face. The hair over her mouth puffed out toward him with a gush of hot air. She raised her arm again and pointed up.

Not straight up. She meant up to the third floor.

Tommy pawed at his feet; the knife clanged on the stairs. He had fallen on the stairs as well. His laughter peaked with every stab that poked at Eric's sneakers.

The woman's scream deepened. Her hot breath stank of rotting garbage. Slivers of her pale face shined in between her scraggly hair—Eric had seen her face before but he didn't want to see it again. This time, something told him, her face would be different. This wasn't his mother; it was an evil spirit summoned by the house.

Her pointing arm shook and the pale skin ripped open in deep, bleeding canyons of blood that poured off of her to splatter on the floor in deafening splashes. The whiteness of her face darkened to crimson. Impossibly, her scream grew louder.

Tommy regained his balance and accuracy; the giant blade sliced through Eric's jeans to sever the skin above his ankle. He screamed and fell forward toward the woman in white.

Her other arm, this one torn open and gushing as well, swung toward him and Eric tried to move out of the way, to fall sideways, to not lose his balance, anything to keep from actually making contact with the woman, but he fell into her grasp. Her frozen hand caught his arm—the coldness penetrated through his jacket, into his skin, and latched onto his bones.

Then he was running up a third flight of stairs, the woman's arm stretching back several feet. That didn't make any sense, couldn't be possible, and still his arm burned with the freezing grip of her ghost hand. He bolted up the stairs, half driven by fear and half propelled by the woman's grip. She was pushing him forward, pushing him away from Tommy. But toward what?

He couldn't stop his feet until he crested the final step and stood in a dark room that echoed like a cave. Everything else fell away: the woman's scream, Tommy's scramble up the stairs, the smell of candied apples. Eric stood in a dark, silent void. Only his heartbeat pulsed in his ears.

After several seconds, his eyes readjusted to this new dark. Some light filtered into the space from the windows that stretched out of the roof like eyes. He was standing on the third floor, mere feet from where that girl had hanged herself. She was not swinging back and forth at this moment; Ed stood there instead, facing the faint moonlight that stretched into the barren room.

"Ed?" Eric asked.

Before Ed could make any response, Tommy clattered up the stairs. Eric darted out of the way, moving several feet from Ed and the windows into the deep darkness. Heavy breathing had overtaken Tommy's laughter. He stopped at the top step, eyed them both, and calmed.

"So, we're together again," Tommy said. "Perfect."

Eric opened his mouth to say something when Ed spoke in a small, frightened voice. "Can you help me? Can someone help me, please? I can't see. I can't move. It's so dark. Help." As the words left his mouth they vanished, the dark squeezing each syllable into silence.

"Ed," Eric said. "I'm here."

"We're all here," Tommy said. Though Eric couldn't see it, he heard Tommy's grin.

"Help," Ed said in that tiny voice. Had he heard them? Was he really only a few feet away or had the house taken him someplace else? Was this his ghost? Or another trick?

Tommy reached into his pillowcase and removed something. The pillowcase hit the floor with a dull thud. He had not removed the hammer; that left the rope. As he spoke, Tommy walked toward Ed. The nearer he got, the more the faint moonlight outlined him.

"Don't blame yourself, Eric. Blame me, if you want, but this isn't my doing. There's bigger things at work. The house hasn't owned you since only last week. No. It has owned you for your entire life; you just didn't discover it until I made you come here. There's a reason for that, too, of course. I told you about being brave and growing up and that may be true, but it's not the truth. You know what I mean? You can run, if you want. I know you want to. I'm sure your leg hurts. I didn't cut you too badly. You might limp for a few days, but everyone will think you were trick-or-treating all night."

Eric did want to run and get the hell out of here and his wound did burn, though not as badly as he would have expected. He couldn't run. Partly out of fear— *could he really escape Tommy?*; *was the front door still locked?*; *could he actually jump from a window to safety?*—and partly out of obligation: all for one and one for all. When Tommy stopped talking, he was standing next to Ed; in his hands, he held the thick rope.

Eric could grab the hammer. No choice felt right. And the consequence of each felt worse than the previous.

"You will realize," Tommy continued as he stood beside Ed, who did not register his presence, "that there is no escape. Run and run and run all you want. Maybe the house will even let you out, but you can't escape. None of us can. We belong here. There is no way to resist, no point in fighting. It's destiny, Eric. Do you know what that means?"

He held out the rope; light shone through the two holes of its number-eight configuration. Then he placed it in Ed's hands. Ed did not respond, but nor did he drop the rope. After a moment, Tommy started walking back toward the stairs, toward Eric. Light glinted off the edge of the blade in his hand.

"You're not like this," Eric said. "We're all friends, Tommy. We have to be cool."

"Cool?" Tommy paused. "Oh, we'll be cool. And we'll always be friends; don't doubt that for a moment. But you will soon realize what I already know. This is where our friendship leads. *This* is where we belong. There's no reason to be scared."

Eric felt the blood soaking his sock. The pillowcase with the hammer was still a few feet closer to him than to Tommy. He slowly approached it as he spoke. "This is not a home. I don't know if it's haunted or what, but I know it's wrong. This place is not where anyone should go—no one belongs here."

Tommy chuckled. Eric paused and realized that the last step might cost him his life. "The house has changed you, Tommy. You might not realize it, but it has. It burned your hand and you don't even care."

"My hand was burned in a pact. You know, like friends have? And what was *our* pact? What did we swear? All for one, you remember that? What happened to that? You don't like where things went, well, boo for you because a pact is a forever thing. We belong here and it's time to accept it."

"This place killed my mother." The pillowcase lay two feet away; Tommy stood just beyond it.

"This house has so much more to show us. Let it and you will be rewarded."

"With what, a *charred hand*?"

Eric jumped onto the pillowcase, clawing at it for the opening. A second later, Tommy dropped onto him, pushing him away from the pillowcase and onto his back. The knife struck the wood floor next to Eric's head with a heavy thud and a metallic snap. The tip of the blade bounced into the darkness. Tommy kept jabbing and Eric blindly squirmed against his weight. A few missed stabs later, the giant blade clattered against the wood and disappeared from Tommy's grip. After that, the fight turned into a wrestling match of hits and kicks.

They had wrestled before, even fought once over the outcome of a G.I. Joe battle in which each one of them claimed victory, but this fight was different than any other time the two of them had struggled in each other's grip: the gnashing of teeth in fury (or panic), the groping fingers that squeezed and ripped at flesh, the rapid slips and punches, the screams and cries—one of them would not survive this skirmish, at least not in one piece.

Tommy outweighed him, and this gave him the advantage of unchallenged top position. Eric was not fighting for control of the fight but for survival. He would only win this battle if he were smart and if Tommy made an error. The first punch to his face filled Eric's nose with snot that backed up into his throat and set his cheeks on fire. The rush of heat across his face ushered fresh tears. Tommy scored two more punches— another face hit that slipped off Eric's cheek and a gut punch that burned into Eric's groin—before sitting back, knees planted on either side of his friend, and wiping the sweat off his face.

"I don't want to make this any worse for you," Tommy said. "But if you want to keep fighting, I'm game. I don't think Ed over there wants to stay in the dark forever, though, do you?"

Eric slipped his hand into his jacket pocket and found his knife. Before he could pull it out, Tommy dropped forward, pinning Eric's arms in place. *How could his burned hand work so well?*

"You said we were friends, Eric, but we're more than that. So listen closely, okay?"

Eric opened the blade.

"We are friends, always will be, but we're not just friends—we're *brothers*."

"I'm not your brother," Eric said.

Tommy leaned close enough to kiss him. "We *are* brothers. United by blood and united forever in this house. Accept your fate and this will be easier."

Eric gestured his head toward the windows. "What about Ed? Is he our brother, too?"

When Tommy turned his head toward their frozen friend, Eric didn't wait for an answer. He didn't want more of Tommy's lies, more of the crap the house was feeding him. He yanked his hand out of the pocket and buried the blade in Tommy's shoulder. Tommy shrieked like a girl but a moment later the scream vanished into a growl of renewed rage. Eric shielded his face with one arm from the imminent punches and slashed blindly with the knife.

A punch crashed into his skull, shaking his brain into a vibrating electric headache. Eric stabbed repeatedly unable to see where he was aiming. The blade found skin and Eric rammed it hard. Tommy's fist ricocheted off Eric's head and then Tommy was screaming. A moment later, he fell off of Eric and rolled toward Ed. Eric got to his feet, wobbling as he had in the pantry when the floor felt set on a turbulent sea. Tommy rolled back and forth, hands covering his face, legs kicking. His hands did little to muffle his howls. Ed hadn't moved from his frozen position.

"Ed?"

Eric stood undecided for a moment and then ran. He practically slid down the first flight of stairs to the second floor (no woman in white screaming and bleeding), thought of breaking a window and then thought again, and ran down the next flight, tripped on the landing, and tumbled down the final steps into the foyer. Tommy's cries drifted down the stairs behind him. Eric ran to the front door, seized the knob—*please God help me*—and yanked the door wide. Frantic seconds later, Eric was running down Mangle Lane. He didn't even notice he was hobbling until he reached his front steps and once he got inside, he discovered the lower half of his pant leg was soaked with blood.

Brothers, he thought. *United in blood.*

CHAPTER 15

After scrunching his bloodied jeans into an old shoe box, hiding the pocket knife in the bloody folds, and stuffing it under his bed, Eric sat with his back to his bed, arms hugged around his knees, and cried. He wasn't sure why the tears flowed but that didn't stop or slow them. He stifled his sobs so that his father wouldn't hear. He was in his study, though, perhaps crying as well, and Steve's room was quiet. He was probably out terrorizing the neighborhood with eggs and shaving cream.

We're not just friends—we're brothers.

Tommy could have meant it symbolically. Certainly Tommy had been more of a brother than Steve if a brother's role was as a supporter rather than a ridiculer. Tommy could be a ball-breaker, even an asshole, but he had defended Eric numerous times in school. They had spent many days laughing and always laughed so long they forgot what started it. They were best friends, brothers even.

Now that Tommy had attacked him, however—hell, tried to kill him—the friendship no longer existed and what made his behavior any more brotherly than Steve's had vanished in the swipe of a blade. At least Eric could rest in the knowledge that he had battled back against lies, had fought and escaped.

Escaped alone. He had fled from Tommy but had left Ed trapped in whatever black world that house had caught him in—left him trapped there for Tommy to do what he wanted with him. He heard Ed's childish begging for help. He had sounded so lost, so alone, so afraid, and Eric had left him there in the dark. Guilt gripped his stomach, twisted it, and wracked his whole body in aching shivers that shook out fresh tears from his eyes and renewed sobs of pain. What was Tommy going to do to Ed? The bundled rope. The hammer. The knife. Maybe nothing. Maybe something horrible.

The pain in his face eased gradually while he sat in his room, his Ghostbusters nightlight casting just enough light to keep the dark away but not alert his father that he was home. He used to feel stupid using that light, but he no longer felt that way. The light wasn't a child's crutch; it was a needed safety net. He might need it for the rest of his life. He never wanted to be in the dark again.

The pain increased in his leg to the point where he had to stop crying to examine the injury. The knife had not cut as deeply as the pain suggested, but blood still flowed from the wound. He soaked up the blood using half a box of tissues and then wrapped an undershirt around his calf and knotted it as tightly as he could. When he crawled into bed, his leg throbbed but did not hurt as much. He thought of infection, of amputation, of death. The house might get him after all. *No escape*, Tommy had said. The house was their destiny.

Eric feared the dreams that would come with sleep but even that fear could not keep his breathing from slowing, his muscles from relaxing, his mind from resting. And in the darkness of his mind, Eric stood in the kitchen before his dead mother, her blood drip, drip, dripping from a deep gash in her scalp onto the tile floor. Her wide eyes were the false stare of a mannequin. The puddle of blood surrounded her face, spreading toward the walls in a steady creep and rising around her like a filling pool so that blood seeped into the corner of her mouth and pushed up into one of her nostrils. The blood stretched toward his feet and, impossibly, he stepped toward it, above it, *into* it. The squishing splash of blood around his sneaker flooded him with a sickening nausea. Yet he stepped closer, both feet in her blood now, and crouched toward her dead face. He couldn't pull back, though he struggled and fought against the straightjacket of this dream world. "Eric," his mother said, and then her mouth filled with blood and more poured from her nostrils and her pale eyes turned crimson and her hair liquefied.

Eric screamed himself out of the kitchen and into a dazzling world of shining white that sparkled with millions of tiny stars, twinkling in a pattern he still could not discern. He walked in this world, though no solid ground existed beneath his feet. Fear ebbed away. His body warmed, that deep bitter chill finally leaving his bones. Warmed and comforted, Eric let this world lull him and diminish, though it could not erase, the images of his dead mother lying in her blood. Those images could fade and crinkle like ancient photographs but they would never disappear. Some things could not be erased. He could live with that so long as he could stay in this world where darkness did not reach.

When his father gently shook him awake and back into the dimly lit reality of his bedroom, Eric remembered what Mrs. Bolton had said about the dead on Halloween night. Was it true? Had his mother come back? Had the house used her to trap him? Had she saved him somehow?

His father peered sternly down at him and Eric feared a midnight reprimand, one of those punishments that lacked rationality and seemed so far away once the sun rose. Instead, he spoke with a quiet voice. "I just spoke to Mr. Forlure. Ed is dead."

The words hit him with a dull thud like Tommy's pillowcase thumping to the floor from the weight of the hammer. His father waited for a response and Eric waited for his own but nothing came. The time had come to tell his father everything and yet he could not. The words would not form.

"You were with him earlier? You and Tommy?"

Had Tommy hammered Ed's skull until his brains spilled out and then gone home and confessed?

Eric nodded.

"You were trick-or-treating?"

Eric did not respond.

"You went to that house again, didn't you?" His father turned angry. "There's no point being silent. Tommy told his parents everything. The three of you were out trick-or-treating and Ed wanted to go to Hudson House. The door was open and he went in."

Eric's tongue weighed a million pounds.

"You and Tommy tried to go after him, but he ran inside, upstairs. You waited, called to him, but he didn't come out. So you left. Tommy told his father but you didn't. Why not? Why didn't you tell me when you got home?"

Eric stared at the wall.

"Don't you care about your friend?"

Tears came easily as they did ever since his mother's death.

His father let out a long breath.

"Were you afraid? It's okay if you were but you need to know what happened. Tommy's parents called the Forlures and they called the police. They found Ed on the third floor. He hanged himself."

Eric saw him swinging back and forth from a ceiling beam, swaying like a tree in the breeze. How had Tommy done it? With the house's help.

"Apparently Ed had been very quiet lately, Mr. Forlure said. But neither Tommy nor you mentioned it. Did you know he was going to do this? Had he ever said anything about suicide before?"

"Suicide?" The word came out awkwardly and tasted foul.

"I know this isn't easy, son, but you need to tell me if Ed ever said anything about it. I won't be upset. His parents deserve to know. Where did he get that rope?"

The rope. He sprung into a sitting position, grabbed his father's arm, and spoke rapidly. "Dad, Tommy did it. Ed didn't kill himself. It was Tommy. *He* killed Ed. The rope is from his house. He had it with him and a hammer and a knife. Ask his parents. He stole them and he tried to kill me. *Look.*" He flung back his comforter and raised his leg with a grunt to show the knotted shirt that had turned dark red.

His father appraised the shirt for a moment and then pushed Eric's leg back down. "Relax. I know you've been through a lot and I'll get you some help if you need it, but Tommy is not a killer. Suicide is hard to accept, but it happens. You can't blame others or yourself."

"The knife. The *knife*," Eric almost yelled.

His father shushed him as he would a baby. "I know you had a pocket knife with you. Tommy told his parents. He said you wanted to go after Ed, to get him out of the house and Tommy tried to stop you. He said you got cut. I'll take care of it, Eric. There's no point hiding your clothes, either. I saw the blood stain on the carpet. You don't have to feel ashamed. Mistakes happen. We all do stupid things. You knew you weren't supposed to go into that house because of what I said, so you brought the knife. It's my fault. I'm sorry."

"No, dad. Listen. None of that is true. Tommy is lying. He attacked me. He cut me. *He* killed Ed. I left them there, in the house. He had the rope. And a hammer. And . . . and . . ." Sobs choked his words and new tears poured out. His father hugged him close and though Eric wanted to scream in frustration and fear, he felt comforted against his father's body.

"This will be hard to accept. But we know it was suicide, Eric. Ed left a note."

"A note?"

"It was found tucked in his pocket."

The envelope. The harmless envelope in the pillowcase hadn't even raised an eyebrow, not when it was mixed with a hammer and a knife. "Dad, that doesn't mean—"

"We can talk more about this in the morning. Things will make more sense then. I want you to give me that knife, too. I don't know where you got it. Knives are not toys, as I'm sure you can appreciate now. Let me clean your cut."

Eric tried once more to explain Tommy's guilt but his father hushed him again and by then tears fell too quickly to keep trying. He cried while his father cleaned the wound on his leg and bandaged it. When his father brought him back to bed, he said, "Tomorrow we will talk more. We need an honest conversation, one without lies. This is not the time to turn against your friends. You and Tommy are practically brothers."

Brothers. Eric wanted to say something and couldn't. Instead, he found the words to say something else, something more important. "Mom came back. I think she did, anyway. She came back like the Celts believed."

"Get some sleep," his father said. "We'll talk in the morning." He left Eric alone with the tiny nightlight fighting back the dark.

Amazingly, sleep took him back very quickly. No dreams filled his weary mind and his body sank into a coma-like state, his sheets wrapped around him in a warm cocoon. Angry voices squawked somewhere too far for him to hear clearly.

That deep slumber shattered some time later with a furious shaking that rocked his eyes wide and stirred fresh pain in his leg. A strong hand clamped over his mouth, pressed him back into the pillow. Steve leaned over him, his face rolling with rage. His hot breath slapped Eric's face with a stench of beer. "Don't struggle or try to scream, you little shit," he whispered, "or I'll make this so much worse for you."

Eric was still half-stuck in the sleep coma.

"Where did you get that ring?" Steve did not lift his hand for Eric to answer. "You found it somewhere, some shit like that. I can't believe I bought that lie. Well, no more. I know the truth. Dad might not realize it, but I do. You're so fucked for this, Eric. You have no idea."

His hand squeezed Eric's cheeks, which flamed up from Tommy's earlier hits, and forced his head deeper into the pillow.

"How long did you think it would take? Or were you hoping it would go this way?" He ground his teeth. "You think you're so smart, stealing mom's engagement ring. Smart asses like you think they can fool guys like me. You're so wrong and you're going to realize just

176

how wrong." He leaned close enough for his lips to touch Eric's ear. "Only shitheads would steal their dead mom's ring. If I have to take the rap for it, you take the pain."

Steve removed his hand and then his fist smashed into Eric's face. Pain radiated through him like electric bolts. Blood coursed out his nose and down his throat. Steve stood over him, smiled. Eric curled into a fetal position and wiped his face across his pillow. The blood blurred his vision. Before leaving the room, Steve smashed the night light with one kick.

Eric hoped the world of white would return again but darkness reigned over him, pain rocked inside him, and no one came to his rescue.

PART TWO

CHAPTER 16

Three days later, Eric was still blowing out clumps of dried bloody snot. A dark brown bruise had spread beneath his eyes like wings and a blot of blood sat in his right eye. Each time he blew his nose, pain erupted behind his eyes and made him cry. He did this just before going to Ed's wake and Eric's father thought he was just overcome with emotion.

"I know this must be impossibly hard for you," his father said.

Eric stared at him through blurry eyes. Eric was wearing the same suit he wore for Mom's wake and funeral. His father was too. That felt wrong for some reason. Eric should have made his father buy him a new suit. The other one, the one originally purchased at Sears for the eventual death of his grandmother should be wrapped in plastic and stored in his closet. It was the suit he wore for his mother's death rites and as such should be kept sacred.

Though the funeral home must have several rooms for the viewing of bodies, Ed waited in the same room, on the same spot, where Eric's mother had been. Eric did not know if Ed's chest was slowly rising and falling, however, because his coffin was closed, a large arrangement of flowers set upon it. Was it closed because Ed's parents didn't want to see their dead son lying there all day? Or was it closed because Ed hadn't just been hanged, he'd been sliced up, too? Eric's father would never share those details with him; it would be too horrible to tell a child. But Eric knew something far more horrible than some supposed suicide. He knew what had really happened in Hudson House three nights ago and he was determined to let everyone know.

There would be no better moment than right here in this room filled with well-dressed people, several large boards crowded with pictures of Ed, and tons of flowers squeezed in between those boards and the casket. Eric would call Tommy out, blatantly accuse him of killing Ed and, with everyone watching, Tommy would be forced to confess. Hopefully, he'd fall to his knees and cry and beg for mercy. No one, not even his own father, would be able to give it to him. The police would be called and Tommy would be taken away.

It wouldn't bring Ed back to life, but at least it offered justice.

Ed's parents stood at the entry way to the room, one arm draped around the other. They both wore black and their eyes burned red in sagging, pale flesh. Eric's father reached out toward Ed's father and then the men were in an embrace. They clutched at each other fiercely; it was a moment that would make witnesses uncomfortable if it wasn't for the dead thirteen year old a few feet away.

Ed's father was whispering something and Eric's father shook his head several times. What was he saying?

Ed's mother bent toward Eric. Snot bubbled in her nostrils. "I guess he should have stayed in his room, after all," she said. Her voice cracked on the last word.

"I'm sorry, Mrs. Forlure," Eric said. "Ed was a great friend." He spoke with such calm and ease that he surprised himself. This was no time to be emotional; he had to be poised for Tommy's arrival and the great showdown.

"Thank you, Eric." She caressed his cheek with one hand, a saturated tissue jutting from between her fingers. She paused for a moment, eyes searching his face. "It is so wonderful that Ed, you, and Tommy are friends. *Were* friends. It makes you wonder about the meaning of everything. There must be some greater purpose, right? God couldn't be so cruel to use my son as some pawn. Right?"

Eric was shaking his head but thinking, *What the hell do you mean? Pawn?*

Her hand gripped his shoulder; she leaned closer. "Your father hasn't been honest with you. Do you sense that? He's been lying to you. Your mother, too, but she wouldn't have wanted this. You deserve to know."

A strange look had taken hold in her eyes. It sent chills up Eric's back and turned his palms moist. "Know what?"

She glanced up at Eric's father—still embraced in a hug with Ed's father. "You shouldn't trust him." She stared past Eric, over his shoulder. "Either of them."

Either of who? Did she mean his father and Ed's father? Why? What was the big secret? "Mrs. Forlure, I don't know what you mean."

That unsettling look faded from her eyes. A small smile crimped the corners of her mouth. She stood straight. "I'm sorry, Eric. I'm not myself at all, as you can tell. Thank you for coming."

She touched her husband's back and he broke the hug. Eric's father whispered one word to Ed's father and then shuffled Eric into the viewing room. Eric had heard the one word enough to know what it was just from reading lips. His father had said, "No."

They sat in the second row. "They'll want you to speak," his father said. "You and Tommy."

Eric nodded. That would make the confrontation even easier. He wouldn't have to suddenly stand up and blurt out that Tommy was a murderer; he could lay the guilt on thick and watch Tommy break. And if he didn't crack, Eric would use his best bullhorn voice and tell the world that Ed Forlure hadn't committed suicide—he'd been killed.

The excitement of this coming moment faded with each new mourner who hugged Ed's parents and then knelt before Ed's coffin. People had been laughing at his mother's wake, sharing stories to lighten the mood, but no one laughed here. Ed was only thirteen, and that was too young for laughter.

A heavy perfume stench wafted off of a woman behind him. It smelled of roses and liquor. Eric's stomach roiled with nausea. His father was talking with people around them. They shared the same one-liners of grief ("such a shame"; "he was so young"; "complete tragedy"; "how you holding up?"; "such beautiful flowers") and Eric only grew sicker. In a wooden box just a few feet away, his dead friend was waiting for justice, but Eric's nerve eroded rapidly.

When Tommy arrived, the room was almost full. The temperature had gone up ten degrees at least. Eric's dress shirt was sticking to his neck. He started to loosen his tie but his father stopped him. He'd have to tough it out.

Tommy and his father entered after a brief exchange with Ed's parents—no hugs, no ominous words from Mrs. Forlure—and stood together before the closed coffin. Tommy's father kept one lanky arm around his son's shoulders. It could have been a touching picture for anyone who didn't know the truth. They stood there for a minute or more and then walked slowly down the aisle between the seats. A red scar puckered the flesh above and below Tommy's right eye forming a spear. Eric had done that—a bit more pressure and he could have destroyed Tommy's eye. They passed Eric and his father in slow motion, both heads turned, all four eyes relaying something, a message that was not entirely clear, and not entirely wholesome.

Did Tommy's father know what his son had done? Is that what the expression meant?

God couldn't be so cruel to use my son as some pawn. A pawn for what? Who was playing a game? What was the real truth? Eric's head began to throb right behind his eyes where the bloody snot seemed to have gathered. He covered his face and massaged his temples. It did nothing to relieve the pressure. When he looked up, Father Randolph, the Catholic priest from Saint Mary's, was reading from the Bible.

Eric barely heard the religious words and phrases. He spoke in a different way from the priest at his mother's wake and funeral. This man delivered the lines with clipped precision as though he had it memorized and was only using the Bible as a prop. At one point, he turned to the coffin, knelt before it and said a prayer over and over again that began, "Hail Mary, full of grace, the Lord is with thee."

Ed's parents sobbed through the repetition of this prayer and Eric wondered what she meant about the greater purpose. Was God involved in any of this at all? If these was a God, why did He let Hudson House exist? Why would God permit evil to live and flourish in a suburban community? Was it punishment for something?

"Now," Father Randolph was saying, "I know Ed had two very close friends. Would you boys come up here for a moment?"

Eric got up slowly. Each step he took was heavier than the last. This was the moment. He would force Tommy into a corner and watch him crack and confess before all these people. He wiped the sweat off his palms on his thighs and then, standing before Ed's coffin, couldn't decide what to do with his hands; his fingers kept twitching, curling with those from the opposite hand and then uncurling.

Tommy strode down the aisle with strong, sure steps. Though he kept his face solemn and grave, his eyes betrayed his real emotion: pleasure. Tommy was actually happy with how this had turned out. He was pleased to be asked to say a few words about his dead friend, whom he had killed.

Tommy nodded at Eric and stood next to him facing the mourners. Eric wanted to step back, raise an accusing finger and shout, *He did it! He killed Ed!*, but his feet stayed anchored to the floor and his fingers continued fighting with each other. His mouth wouldn't open a crack.

Father Randolph said, "We know this is hard, boys, but speak from the heart and you'll be okay."

Eric couldn't pick up his head; he stared at his fingers and their on-going battle. Tommy was staring at him—Eric felt his eyes burrowing into him. Tommy knew what Eric wanted to do and now he was waiting to see if Eric had the balls to do it. If Eric kept his mouth shut, it would confirm Tommy's belief. If, however, Eric mustered the courage to speak, everything would change.

Eric opened his mouth and Tommy began to speak.

"Ed was our friend. We were The Three Amigos. All for one and one for all. We will miss him very much."

A woman in the back blew her nose. A few other people were reaching for tissues. All eyes turned to Eric.

Tommy had spoken so quickly, so confidently, that Eric couldn't imagine carrying out his accusatory scream. Everyone would think him crazy, poor boy's been through a lot, and his father would escort him out while the priest said another prayer.

Still, this was the moment, the time to let the truth come out and show Tommy who really had the guts to act.

"We're very sad to have lost Ed," Eric said, speaking from a reservoir of words he didn't know existed. "We loved him like family and love doesn't die. Tommy said we were the Three Amigos, but now it's only two. Ed is not alone, though, because my mother is there to watch over him."

Fresh tears and scattered sobs rippled through the crowd. People murmured about how beautiful and touching that was and oh, how terribly, terribly sad. Father Randolph stepped between them, hands on Tommy's and Eric's shoulders. Tommy was covering his mouth, perhaps concealing a smile. "These boys are proof that God is not cruel. The love He has for us is right here in this room. Thank you, boys."

Instead of releasing his grip, Father Randolph pulled them toward each other. Before Eric could comprehend what was happening, Tommy embraced him in a strong hug. "You always were a coward," he whispered into Eric's ear, "just like your father."

A few moments later, Eric was back in his seat next to his father and wondering what had happened. Had Tommy really said that? What did that mean, his father a coward? But did it even matter when Eric was definitely a coward? Too afraid of what Tommy might do, Eric had folded under the pressure and fed the crowd what they wanted to hear. Ed was dead, a heart-wrenching suicide, but life went on. These people didn't want the truth: they only wanted to go through the routine and get back to normalcy.

The stink of the woman's perfume behind him turned Eric's stomach again. She was a selfish bitch who cared more about putting on make-up and perfume than she did about finding out how Ed really died.

No, she wasn't the selfish one—*he* was. He had run from Hudson House. He had abandoned Ed (stuck frozen and scared on that third floor), knowing Tommy was bound to do something. If only he had made his father call the police, or called them himself. If only, he had fought Tommy harder. If only he had never gone into that damn house.

If only.

That night, Eric dreamt he was back on the third floor of Hudson House. Ed stood near the two windows, the bundled rope in his hands. Tommy was near the stairs. He held a knife the length of his arm and his smile stretched from ear to ear, like his face was made of rubber. Tommy ran toward him and Eric tried to run away, to at least duck, but his feet were stuck in place. Tommy's smile grew larger and larger, stretching his whole head, and the knife grew, too, now the length of a baseball bat, and then a lacrosse stick. His steps reverberated throughout the room like explosions, but he moved with the ferocity of a speeding train. Tommy passed Eric, somehow just missing him, and then he was upon Ed, burying the blade into Ed's stomach. Eric awoke just as blood spurted from Ed's mouth.

He did not fall back asleep for quite some time.

CHAPTER 17

Someone had punched Tommy in the right eye hard enough for it to swell up to the size of a golf ball. The purple and black bruise stretched down his cheek and over part of his nose. Where the pocket knife had sliced into Tommy's face, above and below his right eye, had turned dark red amid the bruising. Eric had been about to tell him to get off his front porch and never come back here ever again but the black eye stopped him.

"What happened?"

Tommy glanced around. Head bowed, back arched, he stood before Eric like an injured warrior come to seek forgiveness. Was Tommy even capable of feeling guilty? Maybe not about most things like bullying and practical jokes, but murder was different. Tommy had broken. Maybe he had suffered his own nightmare. Maybe he had punched out his own eye from guilt.

"Can we talk?"

Eric's father had gone to work that day for the first time since before Eric's mother's death. He had taken a bunch of cardboard boxes from the attic and told Eric to stay out of trouble. Steve was in his bedroom. The room had been quiet only a few minutes before, but now the deep pulses of heavy metal music thumped through his door. Eric and Tommy walked past on light feet. Even with the music blaring, it was always possible Steve could hear them pass and fling open his door, looking for some morning torture. Of course, he wouldn't torture Tommy—never did: bullies went for weaker prey.

You've always been a coward.

With Eric's bedroom door shut and the heavy metal music dulled to a less threatening beat, Eric turned on Tommy. "What do you want?" He stepped close to Tommy's face, to that swollen eye. "If you want to get me on your side you can just leave. I know what you did. And you'll get what you deserve. Somehow."

Tommy shook his head. "I didn't do anything."

Eric pulled up his pants leg where a bandage concealed his knife wound. "What about this?"

"Or this?" Tommy tapped the scar running through his eye.

Eric didn't back down. "You wanted to trap me there. You killed Ed."

"No. The house did."

"The house made you do it, that's it?"

"This is not a simple situation. Things are more *complex* than you realize."

Eric wanted to tell him to shove it. His mother had been right about Tommy being a smooth-talker, and now Tommy was pulling out all the verbal stops. If Eric let him, Tommy would talk his way out of guilt and into pure innocence. But Eric couldn't tell him to shut up or go away. Hudson House had taken his mother and Tommy might know something about it. Tommy might know a lot.

Eric sat on his bed and slumped forward, forearms on thighs. "Fine," he said. "Explain it."

Tommy took a breath. "You remember in elementary school when I used to go to the guidance counselors?"

Tommy would be pulled out of class, sometimes art, sometimes gym, typically recess. All he ever said about it was that the guidance counselors wanted to make sure he was alright, one of the only kids without a mother.

"My mother died when I was born. My father worked late. All the time. He stopped getting me a babysitter when I was six or seven. He'd just leave me alone in our house. Every night. You have any idea what that's like? I barely slept. Teachers asked questions. That's why guidance kept making me see them. They thought I was being abused or something."

Tommy walked over to the window, pulled the blinds up. Sunlight plastered his face and motes of dust floated around his head. "Nights alone when you're seven, eight, nine years old are nights where horrors stalk you through dark rooms and you cry yourself to sleep. I never saw my father when the sun went down. He threatened me so I'd never leave. 'Stay here or the monsters will get you.' I believed him. But not forever.

"I was eleven the first time I followed him. He'd get in his car, drive away, but he never went far. I followed him on my bike only a few blocks before I discovered the truth."

Eric sensed the revelation before Tommy said the words.

"My father went to Hudson House. Every night. I followed him five days in a row. He'd park on Jackson Drive and walk over. I would wait outside near the trees. I fell asleep outside there one night. When I woke up, the sun was beginning to rise and my father was just leaving the house. Right out the front door, like we did. I raced back to my house so fast that I thought my heart was going to explode.

"When my dad came in to check on me, he said something about the sweat on my forehead. I told him it was a nightmare. He smiled at me, like a molester or something and said, 'Better get used to that. The nightmares have only begun.'" Tommy turned toward Eric, the sun blanching one side of his face and casting the other half in shadow. "He was more right than I could have known."

Was this smooth-talk or actual truth? Eric didn't know how to respond.

"I don't expect sympathy, but I want you to understand, that's all. I followed my father every night. I gained the courage to go closer and closer, even up to the house, tried to peer through the windows. I couldn't see inside. I don't know where he went. Maybe upstairs, maybe the basement.

"I could never go inside. I was too afraid."

Tommy Pomeroy had never admitted he felt fear or even knew what fear was before. This was a grand moment, one to change the very fabric of the world. If Tommy was vulnerable, then he *could* be broken, made to confess.

"So you made me go in?"

"It was the safest way, make you or Ed go first."

"Now my mom's dead."

Tommy walked to Eric's dresser, grabbed the Skeletor action figure lying there. He played with it while he spoke. "While you were inside, I checked Jackson Drive. My Dad's car was parked in his usual spot. He was in the house and now you were, too. I wasn't scared to go in anymore. You gave me the courage to do what I hadn't been able to do for three years. I owe you big for that."

"It was some stupid game so you could see your dad?"

"Not a game."

"You were too chicken to talk to your dad and so you made me do what you couldn't?" Eric imagined leaping up and punching Tommy in his other eye. Then he'd have two black eyes and a charred hand.

"My Dad doesn't matter anymore. I followed him because I wanted to know what he was doing, but that's not why I kept following. I kept returning to Hudson House because it wanted me. It called to me, beckoned me. I went there every night because it had something to show me and it did not disappoint."

"What about Ed?"

"I found something wonderful in Hudson House. You felt it, too. I know things got out of hand."

"You tried to kill me."

"No."

"Yes, you did. You chased me and . . . and . . ." Tears gathered in his eyes. He hid his face in his hands.

Tommy stepped closer. "I would never hurt you. The house got control of me and that's why we ended up on the third floor. It wanted all of us up there to see what it could do. It wanted to show us how it could kill us at any moment. How it killed Ed."

"You did it." Eric's conviction had weakened. His voice cracked.

"Hudson House did. It made me cut you. It made me watch while Ed wrapped that rope around his throat and hanged himself. It let you go, but it made me watch. You have any idea how hard that was? I couldn't move, I could only watch. Ed was like a robot or something until the end."

Eric wiped at his eyes but his vision was blurred. "What happened?"

"Ed turned to me and said, 'Do what it wants.' Then he did it."

Eric clenched his jaw to force back the torrent of tears that had gathered behind his eyes. Hudson House was an evil place and they never should have gone in there. The place had taken his mother; it had killed Ed; it had stolen Tommy's father. How much more damage could it ravage?

Tommy sat next to him on the bed. "I'm sorry about your mom and your leg, but it wasn't my fault. It was the house. You believe me?"

Eric nodded that he did but could not say the words. Belief was not a tangible thing; it was a slippery eel that you could grasp for a moment and then lose forever in a muddy abyss.

"We should tell the police."

"They won't care, even if they believe me."

"Why?"

"People stay away from Hudson House."

"What about all the teenagers?"

Tommy smirked. "How many of those kids you think have actually been inside Hudson House?"

Tommy had a point there. Claiming you'd been inside, if you could do so convincingly, gave you bragging rights bigger than hitting a home run in a varsity baseball game or kissing the hottest girl in school. But Steve had been inside, hadn't he?

"I told my Dad last night just before he was about to leave. I told him that I knew where he went, that I had been following him for years. I told him I knew what was inside. That's why he gave me this." Tommy pointed to his swollen eye. "He said if I ever went in there again, he'd kill me."

"Why does he go there?" Eric asked.

Skeletor bounced back and forth on Tommy's thigh. His goat-head staff fell from his plastic hand. "Because," Tommy almost whispered, "he wants the power all for himself."

A cold chill seized the bottom of Eric's spine. "It's not a safe place."

"Not safe for most people."

"Not safe for anyone."

Things worse than demons.

"It's safe for us."

That smile flirted at the edges of Tommy's lips.

"No."

"We've made it through twice. There's a reason. The house has plans for us."

"Ed made it alive once and then it got him. What's to stop it from getting us the next time?" Was he really talking about going back?

"The house showed us something amazing. It didn't share it with Ed. We have been chosen. *We* are special. We need to go back."

"No."

Tommy placed Skeltor on Eric's leg. The action figure stared up at him with its skeleton face. "Think about it. We're going to have to go back to school soon. The house can help us."

"How?"

"It can give us everything we want."

"My mother? Can it give her back?"

Tommy stood. "Hudson House is a miracle. It has blessed us. It may have taken your Mom and Ed, but that's because it has something much better to give us in exchange."

"How can you say that?"

Tommy nodded his head slowly. "Just think about it." He walked to the door.

"What did you mean when you said my Dad was a coward?"

Tommy smiled. "Like father, like son, that's all."

He walked out of the room and shut the door with the faintest whistling whisper. Eric knocked Skeletor to the floor.

CHAPTER 18

Eric's dad came home late, just before sunset. Had Tommy's father left yet for his nightly trip to Hudson House? Eric's dad carried in two cardboard boxes stuffed with assorted office supplies and folders. He brought them to his study.

"Tommy came by today," Eric said.

His father placed down the boxes. "Did anything happen?"

"Like what?"

"Never mind."

His father squatted and started to unpack the boxes, laying out the materials on the floor, between stacks of newspapers and magazines. Garbage collection had been two days ago but these papers hadn't even been tied up. Mom used to pester him to keep his study clean. Maybe Eric should start doing it now.

"Is there anything else?" his father asked.

"Why did you bring home all this stuff?" He had removed two staplers, a cup full of pens and pencils, several pads of lined paper.

"They gave me an extended leave of absence. I just need some time to get things organized. It's been chaotic since . . . Anyway, then I'm going to start working from home a few days a week. It'll be harder, but I'd rather be home. Someone has to watch out for you."

"I'm okay."

His father sat back on bent legs. "A lot has happened."

"I know."

"No one expects you to recover right away."

"I know."

His father sighed. "You're going to stay away from Hudson House, right?"

"Yes."

He reached out—Eric stepped forward—and placed a hand on Eric's shoulder. "That's good then. It's going to be okay, I promise."

They hugged. His father's body felt so warm and comfortable. Eric could have kept the hug forever. He hadn't hugged his father this often since he was a little kid. That made him feel bad. He should never have denied his father the love he deserved. Eric would never return to Hudson House again and things would get better. Dad had promised.

"I think Tommy needs help," Eric said after a while.

"What do you mean?"

"I think his dad hurts him."

Eric's father thought for a moment. "Maybe you should stay away from Tommy."

"Why?"

"He's . . . unpredictable."

"You believe he cut me?"

Eric's father patted his shoulder again and returned to unpacking the boxes. "Stay away from Hudson House, Eric, and stay away from Tommy, too."

"Are you hiding something from me?" The question came out so unexpectedly that Eric stepped back as though his father might explode.

"Why would you say something like that?"

"Forget it," Eric said and walked out.

* * *

Steve was in the kitchen slurping up Cheerios from a large bowl. "Hey, twerp," he said through a mouthful of cereal. "Bet you *want* to go back to school, huh?"

Eric ignored him, grabbed a can of Coke from the fridge. He started out of the kitchen.

"Hey, fag, I'm talking to you."

Eric turned toward him, tears welling in his eyes. "Fuck you."

The bowl of Cheerios crashed to the floor and Steve had Eric pinned to the wall with one forearm across his throat before Eric could even scream. His throat felt like it was being crushed. He gasped for air, a fish out of water.

"I know your friend is dead, but you better watch it. Got me, fag boy?"

Eric couldn't respond. His arms and legs flailed helplessly. Steve laughed, slapped Eric's face. His nose erupted with a fresh burst of pain. Steve released his hold on Eric and stepped back. "That bruise gets any bigger, I'm going to call you shit face." He headed out of the kitchen. "Clean up that mess, shit face."

A few minutes later, heavy metal music echoed down the hallway. Eric turned toward the spilled cereal and milk. The spreading white liquid could have been his mother's blood pooling around her dead face. Maybe Steve had done that on purpose. Torture came in all different forms.

He was about to leave the kitchen, let Dad discover the mess and lay blame on whomever he wanted, when Eric saw the newspapers on the kitchen table. These newspapers had yet to make it to the study where they would wither and turn yellow, waiting for the day when they'd either be read or trashed.

The papers went back several days. Eric grabbed the one for November 1st. He didn't have to flip far to find what he was looking for. On page two, a headline read: *Local Boy Hangs Self: Child Discovered in Abandoned House.*

The article read:

Local boy Edward Forlure (12) was discovered dead in an abandoned house at the corner of Jackson Drive and Mangle Lane last night, the victim of self-inflicted hanging. The house, known commonly as Hudson House, has been vacant for many years and is an often hang out for teenagers, though police have repeatedly boarded windows and extra bolted doors.

Authorities were alerted when one of the boy's friends called the police. Apparently, the boys had snuck into Hudson House and gotten separated. They had been apart for nearly ten minutes when Ed was discovered dead on the third floor. Police Chief John Carter commented that "the boy was distraught, severely depressed, and looking for an opportunity. He got that chance in Hudson House and it's a tragedy that this town will have to suffer through."

The parents of Edward Forlure declined to comment.

The article listed the day and times for Ed's wake and funeral. Eric hadn't gone to the funeral. His father hadn't even mentioned it. He probably knew Eric had been through enough death ritual for a long time. Had Tommy gone?

Your father hasn't been honest with you, Mrs. Forlure said. *You shouldn't trust him.*

Eric cut out the article. He took it back to his room and found the marble composition book Mrs. Bolton had made them buy to use as a personal journal. Eric had done only one entry. He tore it out and taped the article onto the new first page. He read it again and realized that he wasn't done with Hudson House, not by a long shot. There were too many secrets to uncover. He owed it to Ed and his mother to find out everything he could about the abandoned house at the corner of Mangle Lane and Jackson Drive.

Four years later, over half of the composition book was full of photocopied articles about Hudson House and all the horrors that had happened there.

CHAPTER 19

Eric began his own nightly Hudson House excursions soon after cutting out that first article. He would leave his house when the sun started its gradual descent. That would give him enough time to go to Hudson House and make it back home before total darkness, but also allowed the house to stand before him the way it had before he entered it, streaks of red and orange slicing up its front.

He began these trips because he wanted, needed, to prove he wasn't scared. This house had taken his mother and his friend, but he had to show it that it didn't frighten him. That was a lie, of course. Walking down Mangle Lane, unable to see anything of the house, only that large maple tree, Eric's heart would hammer away in his chest and he'd suffer dizzy spells.

He battled through those moments and always made it to the sidewalk in front of the house. He stood there sometimes as brief as a minute or two and once as long as thirty minutes. He hadn't realized it had been that long until he noticed the sky had gone black and the temperature had plummeted.

The house had a way of making time disappear. Eric would stand before it and watch the large maple branches sway gently, creaking like the sounds of ghosts laughing, and the sunset colors mingle over the windows and porch and forget that the sun would be gone soon and the house would be at its most dangerous.

He started wearing a digital watch a relative had given him for a past birthday, so he could set the alarm, which would break him out of whatever daydream (*trance*) the house had caught him in.

At first, he went every night. He stood outside the house and stared at those third floor windows that jutted from the house like tumorous eyes. He waited for Ed to appear in one of those windows, waited to see him swaying back and forth. But the vision never came.

The thought of what happened to Ed, how those last few minutes of his life must have been so horrifying and lonely the way the house trapped him in darkness, kept Eric in place before the big tree with its gnarled arms. He wanted to run but obligation and responsibility held him in place.

Once, he stepped onto the driveway and started toward the walkway. He made it half way there before he cursed himself and ran out into the street. The house had lured him in. Tommy was right. It wanted him to return. But why?

Tommy had said the house could help him, give him whatever he wanted. Did Tommy still visit Hudson House? Did he now make his evening treks at his father's side? Eric wanted to hide in the neighbor's bushes and wait for Tommy or his father (or both) to arrive, but he could never find the courage to stay there long enough. He always ran home and felt like the house was right on top of him, chasing after him, its front door wide open like the mouth of some predator.

You always were a coward, just like your father.

Eric followed his father's advice and stayed away from Tommy, who never came back to try again to persuade Eric to return to Hudson House. Eric paid better attention in school. He did all his homework. He easily gained entrance into honors English and social studies, but he had to work really hard to get on the honors track in math and science. He did what he had to, studying late into the night, staying after school for extra help. Tommy would never want to get into such classes, so Eric managed to build an invisible barrier between them.

His visits to Hudson House became less frequent. By the end of freshman year in high school, Eric only went to Hudson House once a week. Sometimes he'd go as infrequently as every ten days. He never saw anything in the windows or heard any screams and never stepped on the driveway, but he kept visiting because it was the right thing to do.

The kids in the honors program were pretty nice to Eric, though most of them knew each other since second or third grade when they were pooled together after scoring well on intelligence tests. They spoke of Odyssey of the Mind and field trips to the Museum of

Natural History and the Space-Air Museum. They went on vacations to beaches or foreign countries and they constantly tried to show just how smart they were.

They didn't bother him about Hudson House or how his best friend had died there. Most of the honors kids were more sensitive than the kids in the regular or low-level tracks. Those kids, with whom Eric had to mix in gym and art classes, never hesitated to ask him about what happened in Hudson House when he was 13. Eric should have played it cool and explained it all it detail to them, forcing the kids to stand in awe of Eric's courage, but he couldn't do that. Discussing Hudson House made him sick and nervous. Like the house could hear him talking about it.

"You drawing a picture of your friend killing himself?" James Mecking asked in art class. Eric ignored him. "Everybody knows you were gay for him."

"Shut up!" Eric yelled. The class was stunned into silence. Even the teacher stood with her mouth open.

James leaned toward Eric's face. "When he was hanging there, you offer to suck him off?"

Then Eric was throwing his fists at James and the class was shouting "Fight! Fight!" James earned a day of out of school suspension; Eric got a week of trips to his guidance counselor.

Once, in his locker, Eric found a crude drawing of a stick figure hanging in a noose with an enormous erect penis stretching from its groin past the edge of the page. Someone had scribbled on it, *Hox is back! No more fag sex!*

Eric crumpled the paper and tossed it in a garbage can. He swore several kids were laughing when he did it. Assholes. They didn't know anything about Hudson House or Hox Grent. Eric knew more than he should.

Eric held his own in Honors English and Social Studies, but he still lagged behind the curve in math and science. A few kids helped him when he struggled, though most would have probably enjoyed watching him fail and getting sent back to the regular classes. Katie Lance was one of those who helped him. She was tall and thin and blonde and absolutely beautiful.

Stuck on a math problem in which he had to find for x, Eric would get frustrated, gnawing on his pencil's eraser. A few kids snickered at him, solving the problem with ease. Katie turned around in her chair and smiled. "You need some help?"

Whenever she spoke to him, he couldn't form full sentences. His palms turned wet and his head swam. "Sure."

She leaned over his desk and showed him how to solve the equation step by step. He never learned from her, however, because he was too busy thinking that he was within inches of Katie Lance's face and Katie Lance's lips and Katie Lance's breasts. She smelled of something light and sweet. Eric tried to recall that smell sometimes at night when he was alone in his bed and too afraid to fall asleep.

Paul Brenner, another kid in the honors program who solved math problems before they were even completely written out, told Eric once that he was pathetic for liking Katie. "She's way out of your league," he said. "She may not be the smartest girl in here, but she's too hot for your pimpled ass."

Eric didn't care. He knew he would never have a chance with her. She *was* out of his league. She belonged with other beautiful people, people for whom zits were a temporary setback instead of a permanent affliction. But just because he would never know the pleasure of holding her in his arms and kissing those sweet red lips, didn't mean he couldn't fantasize about it. Or ask for her help even when he didn't need it.

"You know how to do this," she said to him once in tenth grade chemistry class. "I just saw you do it." There was that smile again, the one that scrambled his language and made him feel like he might faint. Her long blonde air hung past her shoulders toward the V of her sweater and the breasts waiting just below.

"I guess . . . forgot," he said, sounding like a foreigner trying to communicate. She giggled and showed him how to balance the equation of aluminum plus oxygen. He should have told her that he did know how to solve the stupid problem but that he had wanted to see her pretty face. That's what girls wanted: smooth-talking confidant guys—not desperate dorks who couldn't do math.

It was the beginning of his junior year when Eric found out Katie was dating Tommy. His smooth-talking ability had won him the right to walk through the halls with the most beautiful girl in school hanging off his arm like some prize won at the faire. She'd look up at

Tommy and smile the way Eric always wanted her to smile at him. She'd kiss him and he'd hug her with his massive arms, lifting her off the ground. She'd laugh so loudly and beautifully that everyone in the hallway would glance. The prettiest girl in school with the captain of the football team.

While Eric dove into honors classes and became part of the Nerd Herd, Tommy spent his time with the jocks in the weight room. In only a few years, he had gained thirty pounds or more of muscle and grown several inches taller. He tried out for junior varsity football in ninth grade, started as an offensive lineman, and then started on the varsity line the next year. He was selected captain unanimously. He wore his football jacket every where he went. And, more times than not, his two new best friends followed him there.

Kevin Tillman and Kyle France were both offensive lineman, though Kevin worked both sides of the ball when necessary. They were taller than Tommy and heavier—Kevin displayed a gut worthy of a forty-year old with a heavy drinking habit. Kevin and Kyle were in the low track classes. They studied long division and wrote paragraphs about how football could be a metaphor while Eric stumbled through pre-calculus and wrote eight-page essays about Victor Hugo's unique use of the narrator in *Les Miserables* or the Christ imagery in F. Scott Fitzgerald's *The Great Gatsby*.

Kevin and Kyle called themselves the KK Krew and would carve KKK into the surface of whatever desk they used. If they were ever caught, they'd smile at the teacher and say it was a football thing, certainly not something about the Ku Klux Klan. Most teachers gave the two of them a wide berth. They weren't expected to do much except say stupid things and push freshmen in the hallway. Most teachers probably thought they'd end up in jail, or dead in a ditch somewhere. Eric would be glad with either outcome.

Tommy never visited Eric's house again and mostly ignored Eric in school, but every so often, he'd throw a glance at Eric or drop some stupid comment. Halloween day of junior year, Tommy was walking down the hall with Katie on his arm (dressed as a punk rocker in a short leather skirt and a top that had been ravaged by a bear) and Kevin and Kyle behind him like bodyguards.

The popular girls waved to Katie. The other jocks slapped Kevin and Kyle on the back. Eric and the other nobodies tried to press themselves into the wall or busy themselves with the contents of his or her locker. Eric had become an expert at looking busy when he really wasn't. He'd shuffle books back and forth, stand for a moment appearing confused, and then reshuffle the books or flip through a spiral notebook.

He was flipping through his AP American History notebook when a heavy hand clamped on his shoulder. He assumed it was Kevin or Kyle, sent over to do some minor harassment on behalf of Tommy but when Eric turned, he faced the leader himself.

Tommy's neck was as wide as his head. His shoulders were rounded beneath his varsity jacket like

Roman warrior armor. "Feel like going back tonight?" Tommy asked.

Kevin and Kyle were mock fighting behind him, pushing each other and laughing while other kids tried to stay out of their way. Katie was talking to one of her friends, another of the beautiful people.

"You can still have it all," Tommy said, "just like I do."

The hand gripping his shoulder was the one the house had marked. It no longer resembled charcoal, but could now pass for a black and flesh-colored piece of granite. Even with his scarred hand, Tommy had ascended the social ranks of high school popularity.

He yanked Katie toward him and before she could say "Hi, Eric," Tommy pulled her close and French kissed her with enough force to pop off her head. They kissed for what might have been a minute. When he pulled out of the embrace, Katie dangled in his arm for a moment gasping for air like she'd been under water.

"See ya, brother," he said. Walking away, Tommy slapped Katie's ass. Her laugh echoed through the hall.

Eric didn't go anywhere near Hudson House that night. Of all nights, he probably should go on Halloween, but he couldn't do it. He didn't want to stand outside that damn house while kids ran all around him in stupid costumes. He could stand there all night and no one would say anything. They might see him but they would not say anything because they didn't want to end up staring at the house, too. Fear kept most people away. For Eric, fear was certainly a part, but it wasn't everything. In fact, it was curiosity that kept him from Hudson House.

The marble composition notebook that had once been for Mrs. Bolton's class was now a collection of articles about Hudson House, about the kids who had vanished, about the serial killer who once terrorized the town.

Amid all his extra studying, Eric had started an informal search for more information about Hudson House. He scanned through his father's encyclopedias and found nothing. He would glean through the daily paper, hoping for any mention, an investigation, anything. Then, in ninth grade, he started spending every study hall period in the school library. He discovered why the place was called Hudson House. He unearthed a string of names that had morphed into town legend. Preston Hughes. Robert Francis. Marge Lewis. Vanessa Wiles. Eric had heard of these people before, their names tossed around as proof of what Hudson House could do. Some were Hox Grent's victims. Some had simply vanished. All were connected to the house on Mangle Lane.

Eric had asked Mrs. Killerton the school librarian if she would photocopy some articles for him. The articles were kept in plastic bags labeled with red stickers proclaiming, HANDLE WITH CARE. She had agreed, though her large eyes—magnified behind enormous glasses—told him she suspected him of something inappropriate. She had that look that could silence students from across the room. She was old and her hands were wrinkled and veiny, but the students feared her.

She scanned through the yellowed and crinkled pages Eric had removed from the newspapers kept in the back room. "Why are you reading about such things, Mr. Hunter?"

"Class assignment. For Mr. Sheboy. Town research project." It sounded convincing enough.

"I see," Mrs. Killerton said. "Well, Mr. Hunter, you will need to see Mr. Sheboy about making copies of these articles."

"But you have a machine back there." He pointed to the room with the glass walls behind the library counter where videos and microfilm were stored.

She set the pages of the newspaper down, ran her hands over them, making tiny crinkling noises. "It isn't healthy what you are doing."

"What?"

"I know, Mr. Hunter, that your friend killed himself in that house."

Eric stumbled for words, found none. The kids knew. The teachers knew. Everybody knew.

"I can't let you continue this quest. It's not healthy."

"It's *research*."

"Keep your voice down, Mr. Hunter, or you will go back to study hall."

"I'm sorry, it's just that I—"

She held up her hand for him to stop. "This is a public school library, and I am a public school librarian. There is no freedom here. I run things. I am responsible for the well-being of the students left in my charge. These articles are not something you should be reading. You may stay here and do your homework, but you will not continue on this path of inquiry."

He hated her, suddenly and completely. "Why?" he asked.

"You would be wise to stay away from that house, Mr. Hunter, and anything relating to it."

"You can't refuse to give me information. I'll tell Principal Black." Adults always thought they knew best. She had probably never even seen the house in person, never mind been inside it.

She paused, glanced around. "Smart people stay away from the dark places. They are afraid to face the darkness—they're afraid of what they might see. You should be, too."

She smiled the way a grandmother might at something ridiculous her grandchild said. "Do whatever you feel you must. I will do the same."

He thought of snatching the pages out from under her hands and running through the halls, but instead he watched her carry them into the glass room. He stood in place until she returned. "Did you want a pass to the office?" she asked.

He turned from her and sat at one of the tables. He did nothing for the rest of the period.

That night, however, he had a revelation. He wrote down as many of the dates of the articles as he could recall. He cursed himself for not thinking of this sooner.

The next day after school, Eric visited the Stone Creek Town Library. The librarians there were old, too, but moved more slowly than Mrs. Killerton and smiled like they were sliding into senility. They got used to seeing him every day after school and were delighted to let him use the photocopier, which they could barely run.

Eric spent his afternoons in the public library reading old newspapers (hard copy and microfilm) and his study hall periods in the school library rereading the articles he had found and copied. Mrs. Killerton kept her distance and Eric quietly went about solving a decades-old mystery.

CHAPTER 20

The nightmares got worse.

He was back on the third floor of Hudson House, again stuck in place. Tommy still brandished the giant knife and Ed held the bundled rope. Tommy charged at him and Eric couldn't move. Instead of stabbing Ed, however, Tommy stopped just before him, turned to face Eric. Then Ed slowly made a noose out of the rope with hands that moved with precision. He didn't even look at what he was creating; his hands worked as if apart from their owner. Ed held up the completed noose and then slipped it over his neck. He tightened the knot and tossed the rest of the rope over a ceiling beam. He stood there with empty eyes and a pale face. Tommy laughed, grabbed the end of the rope and began pulling Ed up. He hoisted him off the ground with ease. Ed didn't flail or cry. He was emotionless. His neck cracked with a hollow snap. "It's what the house wants," Tommy hissed in a serpent voice. Tommy stepped to Ed and drove the knife through his stomach. He sliced it down. Eric awoke before Ed's intestines splashed onto the floor.

That same dream continued almost every night following the encounter with Tommy in the hallway on Halloween in his junior year. If he fell back asleep after awaking, the dream would reset and begin again. Sometimes, Eric got up and made himself coffee. He'd spend the rest of the night studying or reading the articles he had gathered, searching for answers, hoping for a miracle.

The first article, the one he had clipped from the newspaper in the kitchen began the collection. *Local Boy Hangs Self: Child Discovered in Abandoned House.* Next to the article, Eric had pasted a picture from the school yearbook. In his picture, Ed seemed to be staring off at something beyond the photographer. Maybe he was seeing his own death.

"I'm sorry I left you," Eric whispered to his friend.

The next article was something he had found in *American Homes: 1850-1930.* The book was full of pictures and designs for all different types of houses, but it hadn't taken long for Eric to find one that resembled Hudson House.

One of the most popular styles of American home architecture was the American Foursquare. This style, developed and very popular in the early Twentieth Century, offered a simple box design, a four-room floor plan, and two and a half stories of living space. The houses had a boxy feel to them with low ceilings and multiple doors adding to an almost claustrophobic atmosphere. However, each design varied somewhat to help lessen the boxy feel. The Hudson design, for example, offered a prominent front porch and one or two dormers.

Eric had circled Hudson design and then spent hours scouring through old home catalogs until he found *The Aladdin Readi-Cut Homes Catalog* from 1920. The picture of The Hudson showed a beautifully kept house of yellow and tan with a lush garden surrounding the white porch. It looked like a nice place to live. The description said the house was for "lovers of simple and practical architecture" and praised the "Dollar-a-Knot siding" and the "Oregon fir" used for construction.

Eric searched for the blueprints to the actual Hudson House and eventually found them, though not until he had uncovered articles far more disturbing.

From *The Stone Creek Weekly*, November 6, 1949: *Teenager Vanishes: Police Say Boy Ran Away*

Local boy Preston Hughes (17) is missing and believed a runaway, according to police. An accomplished student, varsity football player, and member of the champion Regional Debate Team, Preston Hughes was a well-liked boy who is missed by students and community members. Preston was last seen driving his car through the Stone Edge Development. His vehicle was found parked on Mangle Lane. The police gave no further comment and the parents of Preston Hughes said only that they miss their boy and hope he's okay.

A black and white photograph accompanied the article. In it, Preston was wearing a shirt and tie with a blazer. Eric had circled "Preston Hughes," a name most kids knew, the "was" in the second sentence, and "Mangle Lane." The name Preston Hughes was just another part of the Hudson House legend. He was, people said, Hox Grent's first victim. Eric had circled the "was" because it felt odd that the article would make Preston seem dead when he was, at that point, simply missing.

The next several pages of Eric's composition book covered the on-going search for Preston Hughes. The articles got briefer, but the headlines became more desperate, hopeless: *Search Continues for Missing Teen*; *Family of Local Teen Pleads for Help*; *Still No Leads in Missing Teen Case*; *Missing Teen Case Still Open, Police Stop Searching*; *Mother of Missing Teen Suspects Worst*. None of the articles mentioned Hudson House.

There were no more articles about Preston Hughes, though his name did pop up here and there. Such is the way legends are made.

The next article (*Teen Misisng, Search Full Scale*) was from the *Daily Creek Record*, dated August 5, 1950. It discussed the disappearance of fifteen-year-old Alexander Dradge, who was last seen walking in the Stone Edge Development. The police had commenced a huge search for the teen, canvassing not just the development ("door to door," according to the police), but the entire county and the outer lying regions. The next article—*Search for Teen Ongoing*—suggested that hope for finding the missing boy had grown thin. Much like the articles about Preston, these articles dwindled in size but grew in hopelessness as the dates on them covered weeks and then months.

The next article from the *Daily Creek Record* was a cover story occupying two full pages in September of 1951. *Teen Missing: Police suspect runaway, parents claim kidnapping.*

Sixteen-year-old Robert Francis vanished from the Stone Creek Development yesterday, setting off a police and private-citizen search covering Orange, Rockland, Ulster, and parts of Sullivan Counties. Though police have listed the case as yet another runaway, the parents of Robert Francis are publicly declaring that their son would never runaway and that "he must have been kidnapped." The police have no additional leads at this time.

The articles continued after this one much the way they had after Preston's disappearance. The search continued, grew desperate, and eventually faded away. Eric had heard of Robert Francis, as well. Hox had brutally tortured him in the basement of Hudson House. Then he had fed him to his dog.

Eric found a tiny article from 1952 in *The New York Spectator*. The headline suggested little more than an interesting curiosity: *Teens Vanishing Upstate.*

Three teenage boys have vanished from Stone Creek, a suburban community in Orange County, New York, and the police are curiously reticent. The three boys—Preston Hughes (17), Alexander Dradge (15), Robert Francis (16)—disappeared separately over the past three years. Each one was last seen in the Stone

Edge housing development, an idyllic place of maple trees and sidewalks. The disappearances remain unsolved and the police say only that "all leads are being actively investigated." The favored theory is that all three boys are runaways but the families of each boy claim that their child would not do such a thing. Because the police have listed the cases as runaways, the FBI is not involved. On a final curious note, the real estate market in the Stone Edge development is experiencing a sudden flux of houses for sale. For example, on Mangle Lane in the Stone Edge development, where all three boys were last seen, six houses are currently for sale. Perhaps the sellers have teenagers of their own.

After he added that article, Eric began to keep notes in the journal. He kept track of the names of the missing and the relevant details—or lack there of—for each case. Several pages of articles about missing teens later, Eric wondered why no one else had made the connections. Surely, the police couldn't be so daft as too miss all the connective tissue. The boys hadn't runaway; they had been abducted, but not by a person—a place. Each boy had entered Hudson House and never left. Eric could still go to the police, show them these articles, and explain the link. The police might have been afraid to do anything back then but those officers were gone. The police would have to do something. Wouldn't they?

But Eric couldn't go to the police because they'd laugh at him, just as they would have if he'd try to turn Tommy in after Ed's death. They wanted simple explanations, not excursions into unknown territory. And the simple explanation for Preston Hughes, Alexander Dradge, and Robert Francis? Hox Grent.

Killer Caught: Madman Confesses to Killing Eight.

After receiving a call from Harriet Welters that a man in a "large black car" grabbed a teen off Mangle Lane in the Stone Edge Development, police immediately located the vehicle and, apparently, saved the life of Douglas McDonnell who could have been the latest victim of a killer police are saying is responsible for eight deaths. Hox Grent, 36, is being held on suspicion of kidnapping and murder. The police say he has confessed to killing eight teenagers in a murderous rampage that dates back to 1949 with the disappearance of 17 year old Preston Hughes.

That article was from 1960. The following articles followed the indictment, trial, and imprisonment of Hox Grent who was sentenced to one hundred fifty years, though only one body was ever discovered; he refused to release any information of the others' whereabouts. He expressed no regret and even "seemed to relish relaying the morbid details of each murder during the trial to the horror of the victims' families." An article from *Time* magazine—*The Stalker Among Them*—included lengthy passages of Hox's testimony. Eric circled two sections. The first read:

For much of his testimony, Hox Grent appeared flippant. He offered glib statements ("They died because it was their time to die. I'm just the messenger."), which seemed intended more to rile the crowd than offer an insight into the man's crimes. For example, when Patricia Roberts, mother of one of the victims, stood up in the court and declared Hox Grent a "certifiable crazy who should rot in hell for eternity," Hox smiled and remarked, "Your son was scared until the bitter end. He begged for me to stop. Can you picture that?" Mrs. Roberts ran for the bathroom and did not return to the court.

While these anecdotes are interesting and plentiful for the trial of Hox Grent, the most intriguing moment came late during his questioning when he had tired considerably but the prosecution refused to let up. The attorney, Kyle Williams, demanded Grent offer a reason for his killings. To this demand, Hox Grent said, "You want answers but you won't find any. Even if you stumbled upon something, you'd be too afraid to embrace it. You don't want me to give you the reasons. Not the real reasons. You want something to hang on me. A placard. You want something that proclaims just how bloodthirsty I am. You can't have that answer. It doesn't exist. The people in Stone Creek know the real reason. Ask them. Not that they'll answer you. They're too afraid. Maybe they should be."

The people in Stone Creek did know the real reason but Hox was right—no one wanted to admit that Hudson House was an evil place. Further in the article, Eric had also circled this:

There was no doubt that the jury would convict Hox Grent and give him the longest prison sentence it could. Though Grent's lawyer tried to attribute the killings to the workings of a man out of his mind, and get a sentence in an mental facility, the jury was not convinced. Before the jury retired to deliberate the sentencing, Judge Lyon asked if Grent wished to say anything. Much to his lawyer's chagrin, Grent said: "My defender has claimed I'm crazy. I am not. Do not pretend, you little people, that I am a mere distortion of normality. The world is not as you believe. There are things far darker and far more terrible than you can imagine. Lock me up if you must, but it will not end anything. Lay the eight dead on my head if it calms your hearts, but I only did what was asked. Yes, I embraced it, but I didn't ask for it. When it asks, you must answer yes. I am merely a man, very sane, but there is something beyond me that is not a man at all and It is very mad and very, very hungry."

Grent's words came alive as Eric read them. He saw the serial killer on the stand, the man's wispy hair dangling around his emaciated face, saw him lean forward into the microphone and speak those words clearly: *there is something beyond me that is not a man at all and It is very mad and very, very hungry.*

Hudson House.

The weight of Hudson House threatened to crush him. When Eric walked home from the bus station he would feel the house right behind him, following. He'd have to fight the urge to check over his shoulder. But the compulsion would win. He'd stop, check behind him, and reaffirm that he had never escaped Hudson House and probably never would.

The article, *Killer behind Bars* would seem to put an end to the missing teen epidemic in Stone Creek, but several more pages of articles waited to prove Hox Grent's words—*lock me up if you must, but it will not end anything*—prophetic.

The next disappearance occurred in 1974. The missing teen this time was a female named Marge Lewis. Like the boys who had vanished (destined to be victims of Hox Grent, if the articles were to be believed), Marge had last been seen in the Stone Edge Development. Knowing the history of vanishings and murders, why didn't the residents pack up and move out? Even if they didn't know everything, or tried to dismiss the talk as urban legend, they at least sensed the wrongness of Hudson House; that's why they never went there. They're afraid to face the darkness.

No one had witnessed Marge's disappearance but she had been on her way to her friend's house on Jackson Drive, which could have placed her dangerously near Hudson House, though the article made no mention of that. The police were pursuing all leads and Marge's parents had set a twenty thousand dollar reward for any information leading to her safe return. As the articles continued about Marge, the same desperation permeated the headlines and the pieces shortened by a few hundred words each time. The case was apparently unsolved because after the article *Police Abandon Search for Missing Teen*, the next article was from 1980.

The article was about Hox Grent's latest parole hearing, which much like those of Charles Manson was simply a soap box on which a maniac could momentarily stand before receiving his rejection and shuffling back to his cell. With his parole-rejection a foregone conclusion, the prosecution had also requested that Mr. Grent not be allowed to send and receive mail. The families of the victims had been receiving letters from Mr. Grent since his incarceration. There was also speculation that he had been professing the joys of his kills in letters to untold numbers of morbid admirers. Mr. Grent did not deny this, referring to these letters as "communiqués with my many fans." The judge felt that eternal imprisonment was punishment enough and that the letters could continue. If, however, any of the letters to the victim's families contained threats, the privilege would be revoked.

Eric included that article in his collection not because he had accepted Hox's sole guilt, but because it was proof of the feeling Eric had gotten while in the confines of Hudson House—some places are evil and what happens there can not be explained or attributed to anything or anyone other than the darkest forces of the supernatural world. Hox had discovered it and been warped. The place should be condemned and burned. No one had lived there for at least fifty years, if ever. Didn't that mean something?

Eric thought of burning Hudson House but had never gotten his plans any farther than the idea. No matter how noble and just the reason, Eric didn't want to break the law. He thought of paying Steve to do it, but that was bound to lead to more trouble. He couldn't trust his brother, never could, except to be an asshole. Eric also hesitated burning Hudson House because he was afraid of what might happen if it didn't burn. Suppose he coated the porch in lighter fluid, dropped a match, and it never caught? The house wouldn't take Eric's behavior lightly. There would be retaliation. The place had taken his mother; it might take his father next.

There was one more article, another missing teen case. A female again. Vanessa Wiles. Vanished from Stone Edge like the others. No witnesses and no leads. On the wall in the second-floor Science wing boy's room, someone had scribbled above a urinal, *Vanessa Wiles Sucks Hox Cock in Hell*. Eric had added the details from the article to his on-going lists. He had amassed twenty pages of hand-written notes that he felt amounted to a complete damnation of Hudson House but which the police would claim was a waste of time and perhaps even proof of a troubled mind. That would be the great joke for everyone if Eric ended up in a straightjacket with padded walls around him. *Always knew he was strange*, someone would say. *He never had any friends. I'm glad he didn't shoot up the school*, one of his peers, maybe Paul Brenner, would comment. Even Steve would help lock him away. Safely secured in a world of white coats, would Hudson House still be a threat?

Every time he reread the articles, Eric recalled his excursions in Hudson House and came closer and closer to a revelation (he was sure) and then crashed into a pit of hopelessness. The articles proved nothing except maybe that kidnappers favored his development. Ed's death didn't connect to the disappearances, not for anyone who didn't know the truth. Eric had no idea how to proceed, rethinking the arson idea again and backing away from it every time. His search had grown more frantic as his nightmares became more vivid. He heard Ed's guts slip from his sliced stomach.

Nothing good comes from that place.

On a rain-soaked April afternoon where wind smacked against the large library windows, Eric scoured through heavy dust-covered binders containing all the registered architectural designs for the houses in Stone Edge. When he finally found the one for Hudson House, he wished for the hundredth time that he had never started questioning.

Four pages of blueprints perfectly resembled Hudson House, save for the shield of evergreens. The first page was an exterior view of the front. The next three pages covered the first and second floors and the unfinished third floor. The design transported Eric back into Hudson House. He rested his finger on the crossbeam from which he imagined Ed had hanged himself. Or Tommy hanged him. Beneath the last blueprint it read: *Note: Basement not included as homeowners declined to build. Furnace will be placed beneath first floor stairs.*

No basement. Eric pondered that for some time. There *had* to be a basement. He had seen the broken window in the back of the house, had heard something down there—something alive. It was simply not feasible for a basement to be constructed after a house was built. There had to be a mistake in the filing of the design.

Re-examining the design and asking the librarian to read the address—51 Mangle Lane—Eric was sure the mistake was not with the filing and it couldn't be a mental blooper of the architect. He wouldn't just forget the basement. No, something else was responsible.

If the house had been built without a basement then one had to come from somewhere. The only place was obvious: the house had created it. If so, why? What was down there? What did Hox Grent keep down there for his victims? Or was Hox just another victim?

There were still too many questions. He had never found an article about the girl who hanged herself with her father's ties and then sliced her wrists. He had never unearthed articles about the other kids who disappeared (Hox took credit for eight killings). Where was the proof of those events? Had they been hidden, tucked into dark corners where they could never be found? Why was he the only one gathering all this information? Why didn't anyone else care?

They are afraid to face the darkness, Mrs. Killerton said, *they're afraid of what they might see.*

She said he should be afraid too. He was more scared than she could ever know.

CHAPTER 21

Eric hadn't realized how bad things had gotten for his father and Steve until the summer before his senior year. He had been too consumed with his studies, both with school and with Hudson House. Not that noticing the changes in them would have made any difference. If Eric had learned anything from his delving into Hudson House lore, it was that no matter what you did, you couldn't fight powers bigger than you. Hudson House was just one example of a larger power. Addiction and despair were larger powers, too.

Eric was in his room, rereading Hox's testimony (*there is something beyond me that is not a man at all and It is very mad and very, very hungry*) when Steve knocked open the door and lunged into the room, body bent forward like he was falling. His eyes sat in dark hollows, sunk into a pale face. His hair lay on top of his head in a mess that hadn't been combed, or perhaps even cleaned, for days.

"Bro, you got any money?"

Eric wanted to laugh but he knew that would only enrage Steve. Eric didn't fear him the way he used to. A wonderful thing had happened in the last four years. Eric had gotten bigger and Steve had seemed to shrink. His arms thinned into lanky branches and he always walked hunched over as if his back weren't strong enough for him to stand straight. He had started "getting inked," as he said, and was now almost sleeved with an array of multicolored images that could be random paint splotches. The tattoos gave him a more sinister appearance. He may have weakened, but he could still inflict pain, and sometimes did, thought it was never more than a quick arm twist or a kidney-jab. Eric didn't care how Steve wasted away his days, or his whole life for that matter, but these was one thought that still troubled him. If Steve had gone inside Hudson House before Eric did, why didn't anything happen to their mother then? Why had Eric's entrance been different?

"I don't have any money," Eric said.

Steve scanned the room, moved toward a bookshelf, started fumbling with the things there. "C'mon, bro. I know you holding out on me." He picked up a plastic apple, shook it.

"I'm not giving you any money."

"Don't be a smart ass. I need it."

"Buying books for college?" Eric asked, being a smart ass. Steve had been lucky to graduate high school. Going to college was a delusion.

"Fuck I care about college. Where's your stash?"

Did he mean Eric's porno mags? Was he looking for drugs? Eric had tried pot once at a party hosted by Carla Manning, a fellow honors geek; he hoped it would give him the courage to talk to Katie Lance, but instead it made him drowsy and he slept the party away.

"Where's your money?" Steve opened Eric's closet, pushed around the hanging shirts and pants. "You actually wear this shit?"

"Why do you want money?"

"I need it."

"Why?"

Steve got in his face. Body odor and cigarette stench leaked off of him. "I'll beat it out of you. You want that? Just give me some money."

"How much?"

"You got fifty?"

"So you can get stoned or high or blasted or something?"

Steve forced a laugh. "You don't know a damn thing."

"Then why don't you explain it?"

"You used to cry when I'd twist your arm behind you. Remember? You wanna cry again?"

Eric reached into the middle drawer of his desk. He removed a rolled-up ten dollar bill. His father gave him a twenty-dollar weekly allowance. It wasn't much, but Eric was too busy with school work to get a job. Steve didn't have a job, either. Who knew how he got any money. Maybe he stole it.

Steve snatched it from Eric's hand, unrolled it. "Ten dollars? That's it?"

"That's what Dad gives me."

Steve made a fist. "I find out you lying . . ."

"I'll be right here," Eric said and returned to his articles.

Steve stepped behind him. His stale breath warmed Eric's neck. When he spoke, his voice sounded small and distant. "Why you reading that?"

"What do you care?"

"What'd I tell you about that place?"

Eric grabbed a pencil and squeezed it. He could almost imagine jamming it into Steve's face. "Did you even go in there? Or was that all a lie?"

"You have no idea what you're doing," Steve said. A moment later, Steve was gone, slamming the door behind him.

* * *

Eric's father hadn't been to work since last Halloween. He said they gave him another extended leave of absence, but Eric wasn't a stupid little kid anymore. He knew his father had been fired.

He spent most of his days in his study. He sat behind a desk covered with papers and framed pictures in a room stuffed with stacks of newspapers, magazines, precariously stacked books. The windows hadn't been opened in a long time; the smell of rotting paper and stale air was a stagnant cloud that slowed approach. How could his father spend so much time down here? It was at least unhealthy and at worst physically dangerous.

"Dad?" Eric asked.

He sat in his chair behind that desk, staring at his empty hands.

"Dad?"

His father looked up and twitched. "Oh, Eric. Hi. What's up? You need something?" Red clouds floated in his eyes and several days of stubble was working its way up his face and down his neck.

"I'm going out for a little bit. You need anything?"

"No, no. I'm okay."

"You ought to go outside before the sun sets. It's a beautiful August day."

He smirked, shook his head. "I'm right where I want to be."

"You could open the windows, at least." The once-white curtains had long ago turned yellow and brown from age and dust and were kept shut at all times. The only light came from a small lamp on the desk.

"Watch out for your brother," his father said. "He's on one of his money scavenger hunts."

"Yeah, I know."

"You think he does drugs?" His father was fiddling with his fingers like he couldn't figure out how they functioned.

"I don't know, Dad."

"Be safe and don't stay out too late."

Eric left him in the study staring at his fingers and made his now biweekly visit to Hudson House.

* * *

He didn't want to go, but he did it for Ed. He brought a wind jacket even though it was over eighty-degrees because when he stood in front of Hudson House, he always suffered chills. He walked slowly down Mangle Lane and felt the house pulling him closer. It wanted him to come inside this time, to come back and stay forever. Eric would stand outside for ten minutes and then leave. He'd stare at the third floor windows and wait to see something but nothing would come. Why didn't the house show him something? Why didn't it give him more reason to believe?

Because I already believe completely.

He had at least expected to catch Tommy's father entering Hudson House. He hadn't seen anything, however. Until, that was, tonight.

Before he reached the row of evergreens separating Hudson House from its closest neighbor, Eric heard chatter and stopped. He had to squint to make out the people, of which he counted six teenagers, but he didn't need to squint to recognize Tommy. He could identify him by laugh alone.

They were gathered on the front porch, a few sitting on the steps, as though it was the porch of one of their houses. Two of them were drinking beer and Tommy held a brown paper bag concealing another beverage. A girl, definitely not Katie, hung off his arm, laughing, unsteady on her feet. Tommy groped her ass and she batted him away, almost falling over.

Kyle France tried the front door and then slammed his hand against it repeatedly. The others laughed. "It won't open," he said.

"Have some more to drink," Tommy said.

"You said it would open." The laughter died.

"And it usually does."

"What do you mean? Is there some butler or something?"

Tommy guzzled from the paper bag. The girl on his arm said something to him but he shook her off and faced his friend. "How about I open it with your head?"

Kyle turned to his fellow member of the KK Krew. "Why don't you give it a shot, Kev? You're stronger than a bull."

Kevin shook his head, guzzled a can of beer before crushing it in one hand and tossing it down the stairs.

Almost a minute passed before Kyle said, "I just don't want to get caught."

"You see anyone watching us?" Tommy asked. "I told you, the cops won't come here. Trust me."

"But we're in the open, drinking."

"So go home, queer." Tommy drank again and the others laughed.

The kid kicked the door with an awkward karate smack that almost cost him his balance.

"What did I say, fag?"

At the erupting laughter, the kid said, "Screw you. All of you."

Tommy handed the bottle to the girl next to him and then grabbed his friend in a headlock. This elicited more laughter. "Think you're funny?" Tommy said. "Laugh at this." He torpedoed the top of kid's head into the door.

The kid groaned, stumbled, and Tommy let him fall. The laughter quieted, though not at Tommy's sudden rage—the door was slowly opening. The group gawked for a moment before rising and entering, stepping over their friend.

Tommy grabbed Kyle, raised him up, and stood with him on the porch while the others hooted and shouted inside the house. Eric crossed the line of trees, moving closer, but still staying in the shadows.

"I told you it would open."

"Screw you," Kyle slurred.

"You'll feel better inside. The door opens when it wants to open and apparently your head is tonight's key. So go in and drink, but remember: if you ever cross me again, I will kill you. I'll slice you and leave you trapped in this house and no one will ever find you. Kevin, your other friends, no one'll even care."

The kid bowed his head.

"Now, don't shit the bed because I need you on this."

Kyle nodded and then they were inside the house and behind its solid door.

Eric wanted to sneak up the walkway and onto the porch but to peer in he'd have to prop open the door. The front windows on the first floor were boarded up, had been forever. He could still imagine doing it, but something had changed about the house. The sunlight was fading very quickly, but the house still glowed like it were radiating heat.

He stepped back, knocked into the line of bushes and panicked for a moment, thinking the house had snuck up behind him and was grabbing him with thousands of spiky fingers. He stumbled onto the sidewalk, panting for breath. When he turned back to the house, he almost screamed.

Ed was in the third floor window, swinging from a noose he had made with his own hands. The light hit the window, or the house emanated its own light, and Ed was illuminated on that dark third floor with the protruding windows. Ice seized Eric's joints and a shiver ripped through him. He brought his shaking hands together as if in prayer.

Slowly, Ed raised one arm, opened his hand, and waved. His head rose up and he started laughing. The sound rolled out from the third floor window with a screech. It echoed against the house across the street, ricocheted down the street.

Eric ran. The scream pounded in his ears. Why was Ed laughing? What did that mean? What had the house done to him? *He's in Hell and he's gone mad*. There was no other explanation.

By the time he made it home, his heartbeat had obscured the scream in his ears. The scream returned, however, later in Eric's nightmares. He couldn't block it out, even when he shouted his way out of the dreamworld. Ed kept screaming just beneath the surface and Eric couldn't do anything to stop it.

CHAPTER 22

The first day of school of his senior year, Eric found the card in his locker. The orange envelope with his name scribbled across it in black marker was waiting for him at the bottom of his locker. He first thought it was something he had left behind from last year and then he thought it was a card from a secret admirer. By the time he opened the envelope and slid out the card, those thoughts vanished and he knew who had slipped the card through the slats in his locker.

The card, of the invitation variety as opposed to the greeting kind, was in the shape of a candied apple, complete with cartoon dripping caramel. The front of the card read in black cursive: *Something sour, something sweet, loads of goodies for you to eat.* And the flip-side proclaimed, *You're invited!* over the image of a jack-o-lantern with cornstalks forming the opposite side of the candied apple stick. Beneath that, someone had scrawled, *HH wants you* and then signed it, *Brothers Forever.* Not just any someone, of course: it had been Tommy.

A chill washed through him as all his classmates were erupting with excitement over seeing friends and discussing teachers. Tommy was being a smart-ass, something at which he excelled, but he was also tearing open a wound Eric had hoped was at least somewhat healed. How wrong he was. Rereading the card, Eric was propelled back to that night when he left Ed to die in Tommy's hands. His nightmares crashed inside his mind; his ears filled with the sound of Ed's guts splashing to the floor. That had never happened, only been a dream, just a dream. But Ed had died, made to create his own noose and Tommy had helped to kill him. Meanwhile, Eric had been running home like a scared boy.

Someone brushed past Eric, offering an elbow shove for good measure to the laughing delight of girls in short skirts and boys with necks two feet wide. Tommy glanced back over his shoulder just long enough for Eric to see his emerging smile. Eric hated that more than anything because it epitomized Tommy—that goddamn smile.

Eric wanted to charge after him, waving the card in Tommy's face. He wanted to scream at Tommy for being such a prick and then rip the card to pieces. Everyone would gape in shock, stand back, and wait for Tommy's response. Maybe Tommy would walk away or call Eric a "fag," but it was more likely he'd give Eric a good punch in the stomach and leave him on his knees gasping for air. No one would help Eric. That's how high school worked. Everything was okay so long as

246

you knew your place and didn't try to break the status quo. If Eric challenged Tommy, in the eyes of his classmates, Eric would deserve whatever punishment Tommy dealt.

Instead, Eric tucked the Halloween card in his notebook and went to class. His day started with AP English. He didn't really hear what Mr. Cahill was saying as he handed out the syllabus; Eric was busy re-reading the card. *You're invited! HH wants you. Brothers Forever.* What was the point of giving Eric this card? Tommy didn't need to go to all this work to simply harass Eric. He could do it with passing comments in the hallway or abusive shoves in gym class.

He thought of Tommy using Kyle's head as a battering ram to get into Hudson House and then telling him that he needed him on this. Could this card be the "this" Tommy mentioned? Not the card alone, no; the card was only the beginning of something bigger. Tommy was planning something and part of the plan involved dragging up the horrors of the past and making Eric re-experience them.

Class ended and as Eric shoved the syllabus into his notebook along with a copy of *World's Best Literature* (all 1300 pages of it), he heard Katie Lance say she wasn't sorry it was over, she was only sorry she had been with the jerk for so long.

Katie was getting up from her desk amid a circle of other girls, all dressed in their newest outfits. "He's a slime ball," Debbie Folds said.

247

"And Cathy Punto is a total skank," Lynda Wyman said.

"Yeah," added Ashley Kolar, "if he wants to be with that slut, let him. You're too good for him anyway."

Katie was nodding after each of the comments. She offered a smile at the "slut" remark, but her eyes were heavy and tinted red. She brushed some of her blonde hair behind her ear, grabbed her books, and headed for the door.

"Looks like now's your chance, loser," Paul Brenner whispered in Eric's ear.

"She and Tommy?"

Paul shook his head. "She's fresh meat back on the market."

"Don't be disgusting."

"Oh, sorry," Paul said, "forgot you were in love." He slapped Eric hard on the back and walked away laughing.

The rest of the day, Eric could think only of Katie. The way her eyes sparkled sometimes when she looked at him. The way she smiled with the small dimple on her right cheek. The way her clothes hugged her body but not too tightly like some girls. The way she laughed, sweet and light.

He watched her in AP Economics and AP Biology. In economics, the teacher sat them alphabetically in rows, which put Katie directly behind him. Every time he turned to hand her another sheet the teacher had disseminated, he let his eyes linger over her. She always smiled and once giggled when his stare went on past the point of normalcy. Other girls might be creeped out, but Katie didn't care. She might even like him. He tried to get up the nerve to say something about how sorry he was about her breakup, but he couldn't find the way to say anything.

In gym class, however, Eric's thoughts returned to the card (*Something sour, something sweet, loads of goodies for you to eat*) when Tommy and the KK Krew strolled in. Kyle tried to grab one of the basketball hoops but his meaty body weighed him down too much. Tommy called him a "dick" and shoved him into the padded walls. Kevin laughed, his big belly shaking.

Why had he left that card? What was he planning? Eric kept his distance and they ignored him.

Eric sat near the top of the indoor bleachers during attendance and the laborious explanation from Mr. Phillips about the importance of physical exercise, stretching, and learning the rules of a variety of sports. Tommy and his buddies sat in the front so they could make comments to Mr. Phillips, who kept telling them to settle down, they'd be burning some energy soon enough.

"Tommy's gonna need a new girl for that," Kevin said.

"Shut up."

"Mind if I give her a push?" Kevin made a small pelvic thrust that Mr. Phillips ignored.

"Get her back any time I want," Tommy said.

They were pigs and Tommy was the head hog. He didn't deserve Katie. He couldn't possibly appreciate how beautiful and kind and wonderful she was. If there was any justice in the world, Tommy's dick should fall off. But there was no justice. That was stuff for books and movies. In reality, the bad guys got away with murder and rose to the heights of popularity while the good guys slumped along in the shadows, outsiders forever.

That night, Katie was on the third floor of Hudson House while Ed's hands knotted a noose and Tommy stood by his side with the giant knife. Katie wore a white gown that was almost transparent. Her nipples pushed out the fabric. She glided toward him as if on air. When he touched her, a rush of freezing air ushered up his arm and through his entire body. Katie smiled big, like Tommy, and began to laugh. Ed's crazed laugh rolled from her mouth. Eric wanted to scream, to cry, to do anything to break out of this nightmare. Katie's fingers sprouted enormous talons. She sliced off her gown in ribbons. For a moment, she stood before him in her naked perfection and then rivers of blood gushed out all across her skin. She grabbed Eric's head and thrust his mouth onto one of her frozen, bloody breasts.

Eric woke up and spent a half hour knelt before the toilet, dry-heaving.

* * *

Another Halloween card, identical in every way, waited in his locker the next morning. He ripped open the envelope and then shredded the card to pieces that fluttered to his sneakers. The next day, another card fueled a hot flash of anger. Eric tore up this third card

250

and punched the locker. He spent two periods in the nurse's office with her debating whether of not he had broken any of his fingers. She bandaged it and Eric tried to keep it in his pocket.

"What happened?" Katie asked in AP Economics.

He wanted to tell her that her stupid ex-boyfriend had been leaving him cards meant to piss him off, but her eyes and her smile melted his aggression. "I punched my locker," he said, admiring his hand.

"Why?"

"I was angry."

"Because?"

Eric thought of what to say for a moment and then shook his head. "It's stupid. No big deal. I'm fine."

After he faced forward again, Katie touched his shoulder. She spoke directly into his ear. Her warm breath stirred him. "Tommy hasn't been saying anything, has he?"

"Like what?"

"I know you two used to be friends."

"Years ago. Middle school."

She paused, leaned closer. "He's an asshole. Don't let him bother you."

Katie's kind words and erotic delivery of those words was not enough to keep away the nightmare. Again, she tore open her own flesh with hideous fingernails and again She forced Eric to take her breast in his mouth. He woke up choking on his pillow.

By the end of September, Eric had torn up almost twenty identical (*You're Invited!*) Halloween cards. Each one gave him a burst of anger, but he didn't punch his locker again. He even stopped ripping them to pieces; he simply tossed them in the trash. The best way to beat Tommy was to not let him have the power the other kids let him wield. Besides, Katie was showing active interest in him and that was enough to help him forget the stupid Halloween cards. *HH wants you. Brothers Forever*.

"You need help with this problem?" Katie asked him in economics.

He turned and her smile revealed her teasing. "I didn't get to the heights of advanced placement courses by cheating off pretty girls."

"Oh really?" She said. "You think I'm pretty?"

Eric's hands were wet. His heart thudded like mad. This could be an epic moment, one he would think back on years later when he and Katie had their first child. Eric opened his mouth and Paul Brenner slapped the back of his head. "Sorry," he said, "thought you were caught in a trance."

* * *

A few nights later, Eric was sitting at his desk daydreaming about Katie when his father knocked on the door and walked in. He moved slowly on legs that wobbled slightly. He might, at any moment, collapse. His face had paled even more than the last time Eric had really looked at his father, and dark splotches had taken permanent residence beneath his eyes and across his forehead. He moved to the bed and sat on it with a lifeless drop.

"Dad?" Eric asked. "You okay?"

His father thought about that. "No. I'm not, son."

Eric moved to get up but his father raised a hand to stop him. "I've been thinking about your mom a lot lately." He chuckled without energy. "What else do I do? Sit downstairs and stare at her picture all day, *every* day. I love her so much."

"I know," Eric said. He had watched his father deteriorate for four years and now the poor man had finally hit bottom. This was a spectacle of the power of grief and its ability to ravage body and soul.

"There are things you don't know, things you should have been told. Your mother and I agreed that you shouldn't know any of it, not for many, many years. I can't keep the secrets any longer. I've tried to write it out but there's no way to do it. I need to just tell you. Okay?"

"What is it?"

"In a few weeks, it'll be four years since your mother died."

The splayed body, the pooling blood.

"I wish there was some rhyme or reason to the horrible things that happen in life, but I'm here to tell you, Eric, that life doesn't do fair. Bad things happen and people suffer. People lose everything they have. Your mother was my everything."

"Dad, maybe you need some rest."

He smirked. "You look as tired as I do. I know you don't sleep well, wake up screaming sometimes. What torments you? What is it that comes for you in the night?"

"Dad, I . . ."

"It's that damn house, isn't it?"

Words dried in Eric's mouth.

His father was shaking his head. "Your mother told you to stay away. I told you to stay away. Why did you go? I know who made you. I should have seen it coming a long time before it happened. Tommy's a bad seed, just one of those ill-minded people. He forced you to go there, but why did you go? *Why?*"

Eric fumbled for words. Veins bulged in his father's face like worms.

"Don't bother," he said. "As I said, there is no reason to any of it. Shit just happens. You went because you did. That's all. And now you can't get away from it. Right?"

"What do you know, Dad?"

His father bowed his head and appeared to fall asleep. Eric started to get up when his father spoke in a voice barely above a whisper. "Your mother was a wonderful woman, but she made a mistake. She did something terrible."

"What?"

"Our wedding song was 'Love Me Tender,' you know that Elvis song? We were supposed to be true to each other, but your mother wasn't. I'm not blaming her. It's as much my fault as anyone's, but she's the reason you can't sleep at night. She's the reason you suffer."

"What do you mean?"

"I never thought one thing could cause so much damage. Your mother did, though, she knew what might happen. That's why she warned you."

Eric was sitting on the edge of his chair. "What did she do?"

"Your mother and I were good friends with Tommy's parents. When we moved into this house, they were so kind to us, generous. When Tommy was born, we treated him like our own son. His mother was killed when Tommy was not even three months old. His poor father. He just couldn't cope.

"We helped him all we could. Took him and Tommy in. They were practically family, you see. Your mother helped raise Tommy for a while. Then things got too personal. I got upset because it seemed they were never going to leave and your mother, she defended them. I know she was only trying to help but it hurt so much to have her support this other man."

Eric knew where this was headed and he didn't want to hear it, but he couldn't stop his father. Once the gates holding back the truth were opened, it was impossible to close them again. He knew what his father was going to say, yet he knew he had to hear it.

"We started fighting all the time and . . . I pushed her away. She and Tommy's father . . ."

"Dad, you don't have to continue."

His father shook his head. "I do. You deserve to know. Your mother and Tommy's father had an affair. It nearly destroyed our marriage, but we toughed it out for Steve and, ultimately, for you."

Instead of the truth lifting his father's spirits, each word that fell from his father's mouth made him hunch over farther like they were anchors connected to his heart.

Eric knew he shouldn't get angry, but he couldn't help it. "Why even tell me? What's the point?"

"Parents tell their kids to stay away from Hudson House because it's abandoned. Because some serial killer murdered kids there. Because the ghosts of the victims haunt there. Because it's a dangerous place."

Eric's hands balled into fists. He saw Tommy smiling as Eric was forced to accept that his mother had cheated with Tommy's dad. He thought of Katie. There was something about the Pomeroy men that women couldn't resist. They were smooth-talkers.

"Your mother always told you to stay away from Hudson House because she knew first hand its power. She and Tommy's father went there when they . . . were together. She never told me everything that happened, but she made me promise not to ever tell you any of this, and to always keep you away from that house."

His mother had been in Hudson House? She had had sex with Tommy's father there? Did they do it in the kitchen or in that small pantry with the living wall? Maybe they went upstairs. Maybe they had done it right where Ed later hanged himself.

His father's eyes drooped with tears and exhaustion. "I'm sorry I didn't protect you. I'm sorry I never told you sooner. I'm sorry I let you and Tommy be friends. I thought it would be for the best."

Eric couldn't speak. He wanted to scream and cry and punch a wall and vomit. He wanted his mother to be alive so he could yell in her face, call her a whore, and blame her for everything that had happened, blame her for her own death, for Ed's death, for his father's collapse into depression, for Steve's drug addiction. He wanted to kill her for being such an unfaithful bitch.

His father stood. His legs shook beneath him. "I don't know if I was right to tell you that. I'm so very sorry, Eric."

He turned away from his father. A moment later, Eric swept his arm across the top of his desk and enjoyed the resounding crash of his books as they hit the wall and dropped to the floor. The marble composition book opened to *The Stalker Among Them*.

* * *

Anger clogged Eric's brain too much for him to recognize what his father was doing, why he had told him about his Mom and Tommy's father. It wouldn't be until much later when Eric realized his father had been cleansing his conscience, purging his soul, preparing for the next world.

* * *

For the first night in a long while, Eric suffered no nightmares. In fact, he had no dreams at all. When he woke the next day, he knew exactly what he had to do and, for the first time ever, he felt no hesitation.

He waited until Tommy and his crew were beginning their daily pre-first period march down the center hallway. They strode with arrogance, making comments at some people, receiving high-fives from others. Some girls turned away, others smiled and puckered their lips.

Katie and her friends were standing outside Mr. Cahill's classroom, waiting for the minute bell. Eric couldn't have asked for a better set-up. He took the day's Halloween card in its orange envelope from his locker and waited until Tommy, Kyle, and Kevin were almost upon him. Then Eric walked right up to Katie Lance.

The other girls stopped their conversation mid-sentence. Katie turned to him and smiled. "Hi," Eric said and before Katie could respond, he took her in his arms and kissed her on the lips. He expected her to fight it off but she relaxed, almost went limp.

When he fantasized about actually kissing Katie Lance, Eric imagined it would be a kiss for the ages, one that would grip his whole mind and body, transport him into another existence. He was amazed and shocked at his own bravery, but he could not appreciate the kiss like he hoped he would because he knew Tommy was watching and it would only be a moment or two before he grabbed him and probably beat the hell out of him.

Tommy didn't grab him and neither did his buddies. The moment ended when Mr. Cahill walked out of his classroom and said there was "no fornicating in my hallway."

Tommy, Kevin, and Kyle did get Eric later, however. They grabbed him in the locker room when he was putting on his gym shorts. Mr. Phillips had already gone into the gym along with most of the kids. Anyone left in the locker room knew enough not to intervene.

Kevin grabbed one arm and Kyle the other. They threw Eric against the lockers and held him there. A combination lock dug into Eric's back, making him wince. Kevin and Kyle did not smile or add their own derisive comments. They held Eric in place like robots or zombies. They stared past Eric, off somewhere. Black crescents sunk beneath their eyes and specks of blood dotted the whites around their pupils.

Tommy stepped up to Eric's face, breathed on it with a hot stink that smelled of moldy wood.

"That was some stunt you pulled this morning," Tommy said. "You must think you're quite the hotshot." The wound Eric had inflicted four years ago with a pocket knife, nearly severing Tommy's eye was red and swollen like he had sliced open the scar.

Eric didn't bother to struggle against his captors. They would do whatever Tommy told them, and do it now without any trace of individuality. A skinny kid named Dan was standing frozen in the corner, gym shorts around his knees.

"You want her," Tommy said, "you can have her. That slut. What are brothers for, if not offering up the sloppy seconds of some whore?"

Eric gritted his teeth, forced himself to not make this moment any worse.

Tommy smiled. "You want to say something else?"

Eric managed to control his rage and Tommy told his buddies to let Eric go. They gave him an extra smack against the lockers and then all three of them headed out. Kevin and Kyle walked with Tommy but not quite in-step; they shuffled, lumbering after him like sedated patients in a hospital.

In bed that night, Eric thought about Kevin and Kyle. How they moved, almost lifelessly. How they stared off into nowhere. How their eyes had filled with blood. How it meant they were lost, victims of Hudson House.

PART THREE

CHAPTER 23

Eric found the Halloween card in his locker. It was like the others except for one thing. He found it leaning against his books after seventh period when he swapped his biology notebook for his gym clothes. It came in the same orange envelope with his name scribbled across it in black marker. The card, like all the ones previous, was in the shape of a candied apple, complete with cartoon dripping caramel. The front of the card read in black cursive: *Something sour, something sweet, loads of goodies for you to eat.* And the flip-side proclaimed, *You're invited!* over the image of a jack-o-lantern with cornstalks forming the opposite side of the candied apple stick. On every card, someone (Tommy) had scrawled, *HH wants you* and then signed it, *Brothers Forever.*

Last night was Devil's Night, which made today the anniversary of Ed's death. The nightmares were always worse in October. Last night, it had been particularly bad, so much in fact that he remembered only snippets of screaming, splashes of blood, and the cold chill that raced through him when he woke. Damn Tommy for continuing with these cards, not only ripping open old wounds but gouging them and prodding deeper into them.

This card, this Halloween card *on* Halloween, was the same candied apple card with the same writing on the front (*Something sour, something sweet, loads of goodies for you to eat*) and the same *You're Invited!* on the back image of a cornstalk-surrounded pumpkin. Below that the message was different. Instead of *HH wants you*, the scribbler had written, *This is not a night to be alone. HH is collecting and you're past due. All things come back—will she?* Instead of the *Brothers Forever* signature, the writer put simply, *Bro*.

That's what Steve always called him—*Bro*. Tommy knew that, of course, but what was the point of changing the closing? That probably didn't matter as much as the new content. He read it over three times before glancing around the hallway. Tommy and his cronies were nowhere in sight and a fat teacher with a gray beard was telling everyone to get to class because the bell was going to ring. This was the second card left today. Tommy was hedging his bets that another card on Halloween would send Eric to the breaking point.

Eric grabbed his gym clothes and headed down the hall. He could have thrown the card out like he did with all the others, as he had done with the one that morning, but this one was different. He needed to examine it further. He passed the garbage can without dropping anything in it.

Rereading the card a fourth time, Eric turned a corner and smacked into Katie Lance. His hands collided with her books, which spilled onto the floor, and her hand—so small and delicate—caught his shoulder just before their faces would have collided. The startled laugh was already leaving her mouth when he began apologizing and dropping to the floor to gather her books. She told him it was okay, he didn't have to get her stuff, it was her fault, but he picked them up without hesitation and couldn't stop staring at her pink-painted toenails. Why she was wearing open-toed shoes when it was almost November?

"Thanks, Eric." She took the books, her fingers lightly caressing his.

A warm rush coursed through his body and sweat wet his palms. He nodded, unable to say anything. Since the kiss a month ago, they had hardly said anything to each other. He kept trying to work up his nerve, but he always backed down. He continued to admire her long, blonde hair and her light voice when she answered questions in class or laughed at a joke.

Eric stood in place, waiting for her to move around him, for her to quickly forget this brief encounter. She brushed a lock of hair off of her forehead—it was so wonderful how she didn't spray her hair into some petrified cocoon like every other girl—and smiled. Did she want a formal apology? Maybe he should apologize for that kiss.

He started to give her just that, casting his eyes down from her face to her breasts that made the perfect-size curves beneath her sweater and then quickly down to the ground because he didn't want her to think he was some pervert, some jock who only wanted to get some, and then found his tongue was too thick to make the proper sounds. She probably thought he was a social retard. Even when they worked together on group assignments in class, he had to stay on topic or he'd blunder himself into a nervous stutter.

"Are you ready for the test today?" she asked.

He forced his eyes back to her face and that movie-star smile. "On *Scarlet Letter*? Yeah, I guess so. I mean, the book's pretty dull, I think." The book was dull but he had read it twice to make sure Mr. Cahill couldn't surprise him with one of his patent obscure essay topics.

She giggled—had he said something amusing? "I couldn't finish it."

"Not much happens."

"You have lunch sixth, right?"

"Yeah." She had noticed him in the lunchroom from her table of hot girls and burly boys. Perhaps popular kids kept track of everyone, just to make sure no one was planning a coup.

After a moment, she asked, "Would you tell me what happens?"

This was not an unusual request coming from a popular kid to an ostracized nerd herder. The popular kids were too busy having fun and being teenagers to fit in all that studying. Maybe Katie had been getting through English this way since day one. With the wealth of virgin males in the English class alone, her beauty could get her answers all year long. She had given him more than enough answers in calculus and biology to earn as many private tutoring sessions in English as she could want.

"Of course." Being used was okay, especially when it was by someone like Katie Lance. For a few minutes in lunch today, Eric would be the envy of his nerdy peers. A proud moment for the weird kid.

"Great." She moved past him, close enough for her arm to swish across his, and then she was down the hall, absorbed into a pack of chatty females.

The bell rang and Eric ran the rest of the way to gym. He made it into the locker room before Mr. Phillips locked the door and started berating the boys for moving slower than molasses.

Tommy was mocking a kid for wearing glasses that, according to him, were big enough, and thus heavy enough, to crush the kid's body. Kevin and Kyle smiled in a half-hearted way as though they didn't understand the joke. *Zombies*, Eric thought.

Eric found a locker on the other side. Tommy could send all the damned Halloween cards he wanted, make any written insinuation about their brotherly connection and Hudson House, but Eric didn't want to be sucked yet again into the forefront of high school ridicule. That was the kind of thing that destroyed kids, sometimes forever.

The basketball unit, if that's what it could be called, continued when Mr. Phillips wheeled out the huge containers of basketballs and told everyone to form teams and start playing. Anyone who chose to dribble a basketball alone or try to play a game of horse was quickly shut down when a pack of kids claimed stake to a particular hoop. Eric hated how unorganized gym class was, though, to be honest, he had always hated gym class because even when it was organized and the selection of teams was carefully monitored, Eric was always one of the last chosen, and only then with deep reluctance from the team captain.

When Mr. Phillips slipped back into the locker room, to sip some brandy if Eric's peers were to be believed, Eric sat on one of the benches along the side of the gym. Hopefully, no one would notice his self-exclusion and pinpoint him for derision. No one did, each of them more concerned with forming teams and arguing over alleged fouls once the games started.

Tommy had chosen his football buddies, of course, and were taking on a group of mid-level students, kids who were neither in the popular crowd nor exiles. The middle ground they occupied could be a blessing or a curse based on the capricious mood of the popular ones.

Eric removed the Halloween card from the pocket of his shorts. As with every card since the first, the sight of the drawn candied apple brought back the potent odor from the house. The smelled had pulsated within the house like a living thing, growing deeper and more pungent. He hadn't fully realized it when he was almost thirteen, but he now equated that smell with the witch in the Hansel and Gretal story who lived in a house of candy for the sole purpose of luring unsuspecting kids into her home and then into her oven. What else could be the purpose of the smell if not to make Eric comfortable, unaware that Tommy was about to stab him to death?

But Tommy hadn't been successful, hadn't even scored a major hit. That's where Eric had beaten him, slicing a near blinding hit to his eye with a small pocket knife while Tommy wielded a monster blade. Eric and Tommy had been closer in size then. If the same scuffle happened now, Eric wouldn't stand much of a chance against Tommy's biceps.

Eric still wanted to try. He wouldn't be fighting Tommy for self-respect; he'd be doing it for Ed, for some kind of vengeance, some kind of equilibrium that would prove Tommy couldn't kill someone and ascend to the highest plateaus of popularity without consequence.

Kill someone.

Tommy had done it, had strung Ed up and left him to strangle to death. He had held the end of the rope and watched Ed asphyxiate.

Eric knew his dreams were right. Ed formed the noose from the rope and wrapped it around his neck and tossed the other end over a support beam. Then Tommy hoisted Ed into the air. Eric had left Ed to suffer and to die. Eric had only cared about himself. The Three Amigos had quickly crumbled to every man for himself and Eric had let it happen.

What could he have done back then? Could he have actually stopped Tommy? Could he stop him now?

This is not a night to be alone. HH is collecting and you're past due. All things come back—will she?

Why had the message changed? What did that mean? Why did this night, *this* Halloween carry so much significance? Why was Hudson House collecting now? The house held power. Eric couldn't deny some things—the woman in white, for instance, and the dread that filled him when he had been in that house—but he didn't fool himself into believing that the house had brought about Ed's death. Tommy was responsible for that. Like many bullies, and criminals too, Eric supposed, Tommy placed responsibility for his actions on an outside force. Some people blamed their parents, others God or society—Tommy blamed Hudson House. Only blame was the wrong word. Tommy credited Hudson House, praised it, worshipped it. Tommy sent the Halloween cards because he felt he was doing something the house would want. That made Tommy even more dangerous. The house had gotten Ed; now, it wanted Eric.

All things come back—will she?

Who? Yet that was obvious. Tommy was part of the World's Greatest Assholes, which meant that nothing was taboo for him. Maybe he killed Ed and maybe he didn't, but there was no way he would deny authorship of the cards. When faced with this card Tommy would confess who the *she* was. He would probably do it willingly and with a grin. He thought of his father as a lifeless man apologizing in Eric's bedroom. *I'm so very sorry*. Hot rage swelled inside Eric.

He tore the card in half, loving the feeling of power it gave him and how it fueled his anger, and tore the halves in half again and again until little scraps of the card dropped from his hands beneath the bench.

"Hey!"

He looked up and a basketball nearly took his head off. It bounced off the wall behind him and into the middle of a game somewhere. Tommy stood with his hands still in the air from the throw, his buddies on either side of him laughing. "What the hell are you doing?" Tommy asked.

Eric stood. His legs shook with anger, fear, and anxiety. He had not expected Tommy to initiate a scene. While socially acceptable for him to ridicule Eric, it increased the risk of their connection being discovered. If Tommy started the berating, others would follow and, eventually, someone would wonder why Tommy was picking on a waste of a kid like Eric. It wasn't that he couldn't; it was that kids at the top of the popularity chain didn't waste time with those at the bottom unless they got in the way. Tommy's unprovoked attack could lead to questions. Eventually that could be detrimental to Tommy's popularity.

"Looks like you're littering," Tommy said. Kevin and Kyle stood behind him, dazed but grinning.

"What do you want?"

Tommy stepped forward; Eric fought the urge to back away from him. What was the worst thing Tommy could do here? There'd be witnesses.

"I want to know why you're polluting my school."

"Because someone has been *polluting* my locker."

271

Tommy licked his lips, stepped closer. "I guess you didn't like what they left."

"No. I didn't and I want them to stop. Immediately."

Tommy gestured for his buddies to hang back and then he moved to Eric so quickly that Eric had no time to respond before Tommy's face was nose to nose with his. Tommy spoke quietly, viciously. "I've seen you walking past Hudson House. I know you feel it, too. Stop fighting what must happen. We belong there."

"Like Ed?"

"He's in a better place than we are. The house wanted him and he wasn't as much of a coward as you."

"Then why don't you join him?"

"Not without you—*bro*."

"You're not my brother!" Eric screamed.

Tommy stepped back and the bouncing basketballs behind him slowed to silence as everyone stopped to gawk at the kid who had just flipped out on Tommy Pomeroy.

Courage, or pure anger and hate, pushed him forward back into Tommy's face. He lowered his voice, trying to imitate Tommy's poisonous hiss: "You can say the house took Ed if you want, but I know you killed him. I'm not stupid, Tommy. Something may be *off* about Hudson House, but you're the one who's really messed up. Hear me right now: stop leaving those Halloween cards. I'm not going back there. And stop calling me bro. We are *not* brothers."

Silence hung between them. A solitary laugh echoed through the gym.

Would Tommy simply nod and back down? Was it true what they said about bullies that if you stood up to them they were cowed and left you alone forever? If a simple moment of strength brought on by righteous anger could shake the high school caste system then life was not as hopeless as it seemed for the dejected and deprived—Eric could show them how to rise up, to battle back, to evolve into someone stronger.

Tommy leaned forward, nose to nose again. His breath was rotten. "This is the wrong place for this. I will see you later—at Hudson House. She won't save you again."

Eric had no time to respond that there was no way he was going to Hudson House because Tommy's fist hit Eric's stomach with enough force to cripple him to the floor and make him gasp for air. He was faintly aware of kids laughing at him and complimenting Tommy. The social structure in which they existed dictated that Eric should stay down, subservient, but even if Eric had wanted to start a real fight, he had no strength or air to get up.

"I'll see you around," Tommy said. "Bro."

After Tommy returned to basketball along with everyone else, Eric muttered, "asshole" and sat on the bench. He slowly gathered up the pieces of the Halloween card and stuffed them into his jeans pocket. The punch had vanquished his anger and brought back his timidity and paranoia—he didn't need anyone else finding the card. If it got traced back to him, Eric would end up in the principal's office under suspicion of orchestrating a prank. Life, high school life particularly, was extremely unfair.

As things happened, Eric found himself in Principal Black's office anyway.

CHAPTER 24

Eric slugged his way out of gym class and down to the library. He had study hall ninth period and always spent it in the library. Mrs. Killerton never said anything to him other than hello. She had said her piece back when Eric was in ninth grade. If she knew what Eric was doing, however, she might have a few more words for him.

Smart people stay away from the dark places. They are afraid to face the darkness—they're afraid of what they might see. You should be, too.

Eric splayed out his books and notebooks on a large desk, so it appeared he was studying but what he actually did every day when he came here was to reread the articles he had gathered about Hudson House. He could recite some of them from memory. Especially the pieces about Hox. A few parts ("They died because it was their time to die. I'm just the messenger.") nestled uncomfortably in Eric's brain.

He turned to the same article he always started with, the *Time* magazine piece entitled, *The Stalker Among Them*.

The background for the first page was a picture of Mangle Lane taken from about halfway down the street. Hudson House loomed at the far end, a dark house with a property which never grew so unwieldily as to be an eye sore. The house took care of itself, after all. Set over this picture, next to Hudson House, was a mug shot of Hox Grent. He did not match the image Eric had always carried in his head since he was a little kid and people spoke about the Mad Man of Mangle Lane. Hox imagined a large, roughened man with piercing eyes and a strong jaw line. The real Hox was a balding man with tiny eyes and wrinkles traversing his face like dry riverbeds across a desert. He was smiling in the picture, showcasing crooked teeth that, legend had it, he had filed down to fangs so he could be a cannibal. The caption beneath the picture read, At his trial, Hox Grent professed, "Lock me up if you must, but it will not end anything. Lay the eight dead on my head if it calms your hearts, but I only did what was asked."

He was right. The disappearances and, presumably, the murders didn't stop.

Marge Lewis. Vanessa Wiles. Both taken after Hox had been imprisoned. Both disappeared from the Stone Edge Development like all the other victims. What did that mean? It was pretty obvious, even if the police didn't want to admit it. Stone Creek had another killer living in its midsts, a Hox Grent copycat.

When it asks, you must answer yes. I am merely a man, very sane, but there is something beyond me that is not a man at all and It is very mad and very, very hungry."

The article about Hox's last parole hearing gave a possible explanation. Lawyers for the victims' families sought to rescind Hox's freedom to write and mail letters. He had been sending harassing letters to the families, ones detailing for them how their children were slaughtered. More interesting than that, however, were the hundreds of letters Hox received annually from "fans." Hox was allowed to correspond with people who wanted to know what it was like to kill people, what it felt like. Any of these fans could be the copycat killer. The police must have explored that possibility. Right?

"Excuse me, Mr. Hunter." Mrs. Killerton was standing on the other side of the desk. She wore a floor-length pale blue dress and a heavy white sweater. She kept her hands joined before her as if in prayer. The lenses in her glasses had gotten even thicker over the years.

Eric edged his elbows over the *Time* article. "Yeah?" he asked.

Her lips tightened. "You did not sign in today."

All students using the library had to sign in upon entering. Eric had never forgotten before. "Sorry. I have a lot on my mind."

She raised an eyebrow. "Studying?"

"Yeah. Big test tomorrow on *The Scarlet Letter*."

"Yes," Mrs. Killerton said and leaned slightly over the table. "Poor Hester Prynne. Forced to wear a scarlet 'A' for her sins." Her eyes flitted down to the article, which Eric hadn't fully concealed. "Do you feel you've been forced to wear your own scarlet letter?"

"What?"

She sighed. "I believe I told you, Mr. Hunter, that researching that old house was an unhealthy enterprise."

Eric backed off the composition book, letting her see the article with the mug shot of Hox Grent—balding, beady eyes, crooked teeth. "I found the articles at the town library."

"How industrious of you," she said. "You are far too old to be concerned with the things that happened there."

"I'm not bothering anybody. Why don't you yell at those kids?" Eric pointed toward a table of boys folding paper footballs.

"Don't worry about them," she said. "Worry about yourself and how you spend your time, especially in my library."

"Fine." Eric shut the book.

Mrs. Killerton leaned closer. "That house has been abandoned for years. The man who used to live there went crazy and killed his daughter. He strung her up in the attic with a bunch of his ties and then sliced her up so she bled to death while she suffocated."

Eric couldn't respond. It was like a switch had been flipped inside her.

"I told you once, and now I'll tell you again: It would be wise for you stay away from that place."

After a moment, Mrs. Killerton backed away and headed for the boys making paper footballs. Had she just tried to scare him? Maybe she had her own Hudson House story. She'd probably die with it before she ever told anyone.

Eric opened to the article again.

The attorney, Kyle Williams, demanded Grent offer a reason for his killings. To this demand, Hox Grent said, "You want answers but you won't find any. Even if you stumbled upon something, you'd be too afraid to embrace it. You don't want me to give you the reasons. Not the real reasons. You want something to hang on me. A placard. You want something that proclaims just how bloodthirsty I am. You can't have that answer. It doesn't exist. The people in Stone Creek know the real reason. Ask them. Not that they'll answer you. They're too afraid. Maybe they should be."

Things worse than demons, Steve had said.

Nothing good comes from that place.

"Reading how to be tough?" Kevin stood on the other side of the table where Mrs. Killerton had just stood. He spoke in a dead voice, one with almost no energy.

Eric didn't respond. The best way to handle bullies was to ignore them. They either did something stupid or they got bored and picked on someone else. Hearing Kevin speak again, however, was an interesting turn of events.

"That was pretty stupid thing to do in gym."

"Why is that?" Despite his well-founded theories for handling bullies, Eric couldn't help himself.

"A punk like you shouldn't shit in the king's yard."

"That almost sounds profound," Eric said. "I'd offer to show you what I'm doing, but it helps to be literate."

The kid's fat cheeks reddened. "You can't win," he said.

Several kids were busy at various tables throughout the library but Mrs. Killerton had her eyes on Eric and Kevin from her spot behind the circulation desk. Eric would be safe no matter what this jock tried. If there was one place an ostracized nerd could be safe it was the library.

"I didn't know this was a game," Eric said. He loved the subsequent rush that flooded through him.

The kid's face darkened to a deep crimson. His eyes wandered again as they had in the locker room a month ago. What was wrong with him? Still, Eric enjoyed this small victory. This one was for all the victims of the power-hungry jocks who got their jollies from hurting others. If Eric had a champagne glass he would have raised it high and proclaimed victory.

The kid reached across the table, curled his fingers in Eric's shirt, pulled him onto the table, and punched him in the nose. When Eric fell backwards against the table, he wondered if this hit realigned the damage Steve had done four years ago.

CHAPTER 25

Principal Black dropped his meaty forearms onto his desk that stretched nearly across the room, gripped his hands together, and leaned forward, tilting his head just right to complete the *I'm-only-telling-you-this-for-your-own-good* look teachers and principals favored when doling out punishments. His mouth opened and then closed—Eric was supposed to believe that the lecture and punishment about to fall upon him was from a man who had agonized over it. Such bullshit. It reminded him of Steve, who had evolved from using the physical abuse of primitives to the verbally caustic and condescending methods adults favored.

"I know you are in all the honors courses we offer here. How are classes progressing?"

"Fine."

"The marking period is almost over. You must be stressed. High marks are needed to stay in those classes."

That wasn't really true. Eric knew one of his classmates had failed two quarters of Physics last year and the teacher only threatened to remove him. "Classes are fine."

"You spent a lot of time in the library."

"Honors classes. Like you said." Eric shrugged. Principals often expected honors kids, especially outcast honors kids, to start crying before them and beg for mercy.

"Mrs. Killerton said you aren't studying. She says you've been up to something else. You want to explain?"

Had she ratted him out? "I'm doing research."

"For?"

"Personal education."

Mr. Black pushed out his cheek with his tongue, sighed. "You don't seem to appreciate your situation, Mr. Hunter. I wouldn't be so sure of yourself were I you."

Did his usage of *Mr. Hunter* mean Eric could now call Mr. Black by his first name? "Since when is doing research in a library wrong?"

"When a fight breaks out."

"I didn't—"

One of his plump hands rose and opened, palm out. He sighed again. "We have witnesses of what happened, including what Mrs. Killerton told us. Don't waste our time with shallow defenses. This school has a zero-tolerance policy for violent behavior. An altercation equals *out of school*. I didn't need to bring you in here to discuss that. What concerns me, Mr. Hunter, is that you are foregoing your studies on a dangerous sidetrack in the library."

Out of school? Fine. Eric had never gotten in trouble in school before but he could take it. It might even move him up the popularity ladder. If Eric stayed in his room, his father wouldn't even notice he didn't go to school.

"Dangerous?"

"Mrs. Killerton informed me of your Hudson House . . . investigation."

That bitch. "So?"

"She told me she warned you to not get caught up in macabre things. I wish she had come to me in September. The important thing is to not continue. You agree?"

"Continue what?"

"Many boys over the years have grown interested in Hudson House but each one discovered why it's not a wise endeavor. It won't lead you anywhere but into trouble, as it did today. You are to desist with your amateur investigation. Is that understood?"

"Why should I? I can research whatever I want."

"In the school library, you are to use the resources for class assignments only. Any other use of school property is inappropriate and punishable."

"You can't punish me for reading."

"There's a lot I can do, young man."

"Tell me why."

His eyes drifted from Eric's face to the only window in the room. Outside, a kid was laughing with another while enjoying their lunch. Eric's lunch was next period and Katie would be waiting for her personal study session.

"The place is wrong." Mr. Black's eyes rolled slowly back to Eric. The man's chubby face paled a shade or two. "I don't hesitate to say that to you, Eric. I can't say more than that, but I can tell you that my prohibition on that place is not without just cause. Mrs. Killerton warned you against your further pursuit into that place. You know, more than most, how dangerous a place it can be. So, please, Eric, leave the house alone. For your own safety."

The fear trembling in his eyes stayed Eric's tongue. Mr. Black had his own Hudson House story. For once, Eric felt sympathy for one of the authoritarians in the school. In school, teachers and administrators ruled, but at the corner of Jackson Drive and Mangle Lane, Hudson House reigned.

"What you're saying are reasons *to* investigate."

"You won't find anything you want to know."

"Like what?"

"Never mind. Let me put it simply: if you keep researching that place, your library privileges will be revoked. With all the projects the honors classes demand, no access to the school library will be quite detrimental to your grades. Don't do that to yourself. Or your parents. If you pursue that place outside of school, you will only invite more altercations like you experienced today and what will your parents say about that? Do you think your mother would condone that?"

"My mother is dead." *Asshole*, he wanted to add.

Mr. Black stumbled over his response: "I'm very sorry. I . . ."

Eric did not respond. Let him squirm for a few seconds in the uncomfortable silence.

"I want you to see Mr. Lemming."

"I don't need a psychologist."

"Your behavior is unhealthy and it is affecting your conduct at school and your academic performance. You should have seen him long ago, I think. Mr. Phillips told me about your screaming in the gym today."

Teachers turned on kids in a second. "I'm fine."

"Tomorrow, instead of going to the library during study hall, you are to see Mr. Lemming. He will be expecting you."

"I'm only doing research."

"It's either Mr. Lemming tomorrow or five days out of school starting now."

Eric wanted to tell Mr. Black just how big of an asshole he was, but a glance at the clock on the wall confirmed that lunch was a minute away and Katie would be waiting. Let the principal think he had done some good, been some kind of badass. Good for him. One day Eric would be free of this place and Mr. Black would still be here counting his days to retirement.

CHAPTER 26

She spotted Eric as he entered the cafeteria. From her table of popular girls, Katie rose with a laugh trailing from her lips and brushed her blonde hair behind her ear. Eric drew closer to the table and then started to turn left to zigzag his way through the cafeteria to gather up his courage again, but Katie waved to him and he went to her.

He stood back a few feet from the table of laughing females. Hopefully, they weren't laughing at him, though that seemed the likeliest of reasons.

Katie told one of her friends to be quiet and turned to Eric. "Let's go outside where we can actually hear each other."

Eric nodded. She wanted some quality alone time with him. Sitting outside wouldn't be completely alone —lunchroom monitors were always watching and other kids ate outside, too—but freedom from the endless eyes of the cafeteria was more privacy than he had ever had with Katie.

She grabbed her bag and a small Tupperware container of salad and led the way through the maze of tables to the outside. Eric admired the way her butt moved, how the jeans were almost painted on. Behind them, the girls erupted into fresh laughter.

They sat on the curb in front of the school, the lunchroom windows behind them. So much for privacy.

Katie began eating her salad while Eric took out his copy of *The Scarlet Letter* and the notes he had taken while reading it. She gazed across the student parking lot while he spoke. "So how much did you read?"

"Not much."

That was okay; it gave them more together time. He was staring at her bare feet again for several seconds before he realized it. "Well, there's four main characters: Hester Prynne, her daughter Pearl, Reverend Dimmesdale, and Arthur Chillingworth. So, it's the seventeenth century and the Puritans rule. Hester is accused of adultery and is forced to stand on a scaffold in front of the whole town. She refuses to reveal the man she's sleeping with and is sent to prison, where she has Pearl. When she gets—"

"What are you doing tonight, Eric?"

"What?" Her blue eyes had fallen upon him and in them Eric lost his thoughts.

"Tonight," she repeated. "It's Halloween, you know."

"Yeah, yeah. Of course."

"You have plans?"

"Well, I—"

Loud shouts exploded in the lunchroom. A table of jersey-clad jocks began chanting their favorite football cheer: "*K-I-L-L, Kill, Kill, Kill!*" Tommy cheered loudest. The lunch monitors drew near but did not attempt to silence them. Even they were not above the jocks in the school social strata. Kevin and Kyle pounded their fists on the table with the beat but did not cheer.

"Assholes," Katie said.

Eric smiled. He couldn't help it.

"If you're not doing anything," Katie said, "there's a party tonight and I think it'd be really cool if you came."

Eric had never been to a popular kid's party. He had been to parties at honors kid's homes where they only discussed school and the only exciting thing was flirting while eating pizza and slurping soda. Carla Manning's party had become the most exciting when Alex Fremont pulled out a bag of weed. Even so, they were still geeks, socially inept and hopelessly concerned with academics.

After no response, Katie said, "You don't have to come. I just thought you might have fun."

Letters fumbled into words, which squeezed into nonsensical sentences in his foggy mind. He stopped himself from attempting an answer until his mind was able to clear the fog and create the easiest of responses: "Sure."

Her smile brightened to showcase straight, white teeth. "It's at Angela's house, which is in Stone Edge on Jackson Drive. Number 217. Do you know where that is?"

Hudson House loomed over him, crushing the nervous fluttering in his gut, squishing it into dead fear. Then it passed with a glimpse into those eyes again. "Sure," he said.

"We'll be there after school, but you should come around eight. It'll be just getting started. You know, after the little kids finish trick-or-treating."

"Sure."

She giggled. Katie Lance had invited him to a party. Popular kids would be there; it was potential social suicide for her. He needed to proceed calmly, but the feeling inside him was more than a reaction to her invitation or simply a mere crush—this could become love. And Tommy would have to swallow his pride and endure it. Maybe there was justice in the world.

A minute passed before she said, "So, *The Scarlet Letter*," and Eric stumbled back into review mode.

He covered the highlights of the book, the allegory, and much of the symbolism before the period ended. When she left and said she'd see him tonight, Eric resisted the desire to leap into the air. Things could turn around for him. Life could get better.

Biology brought a pop quiz, which Eric thought he aced, but once he finished he didn't remember anything he had written. After he handed it in, he wondered if he had written *I love Katie Lance* over and over.

He stopped at his locker to drop off some books and found another Halloween card. It was identical to the others (before the one this morning) from the promise of goodies to eat to the *HH wants you*. He grunted.

Someone glanced at him but he didn't care. Tommy was really messing with him now. Because of the incident in gym class, Tommy had dropped off a third card. He stared at the signature—*Brothers Forever*—for several seconds, letting the rage return.

He tore the card to pieces and left them on the floor.

The bus ride home didn't bother him as much as it usually did. He was one of the few seniors who didn't drive (or get a ride) to school, which meant he had to endure the misery of riding with underclassmen. His father had promised a car *after* graduation, for driving back and forth to college. That didn't help him in the meantime. Eric nearly told a squawking freshman to shut the hell up, but his anger from the second Halloween card slowly gave way to the nervous excitement of tonight's party.

Steve was home, a rarity on a weekday afternoon, not to mention a party-holiday. His beat-up Pontiac Trans Am sat crooked on the driveway. Every time Steve returned from wherever it was he went, the car showcased new scratches and dents. *Much like Steve himself*, Eric thought, amused at his insight. Supposedly Steve was working at a mechanic's shop, but Eric doubted he could keep a job longer than an eight-hour shift. If his brother had money, he was getting it from somewhere else.

Eric went to his father's study first. Even with the ceiling fan light and the table lamp on, shadows weighed down the room. Old newspapers sat in stacks all around. Many of the covers had yellowed and crisped. Piles of magazines—*Time, Newsweek*—lay around the room as well. Books had once packed the shelves behind his father's desk and, while some remained and some lay on the floor, several shelves had been cleared and now displayed framed photographs of Eric's mother. The pictures covered all stages of their romance from dating through marriage and parenthood. What books remained on the shelves bore titles like *Surviving with Grief, Coping with Loss*, and *Enduring Sorrow*.

His father claimed he was still working from home, but Eric had never caught him doing anything but wallowing in misery. Eric was not sure how much, or how little, money his father had but it never really crossed his mind. The power kept working and the water running and the milk was usually replaced before it soured.

As usual, his father sat behind the desk, masked in darkness. Scattered papers kept the desk in a constant state of disarray. A paperweight that read, *A Cluttered Desk is a Sign of Genius*, a birthday gift Eric had given him last year, held down a pile of unevenly stacked pages from a yellow, legal pad. More framed pictures lined the edge of the desk. A travel pillow rested off to the side on top of a pile of folders. More nights than not, his father slept down here, surrounded by pictures of a dead woman.

"Dad?"

His father stopped writing something. "Son."

Eric stepped closer. The musty smell of old paper settled around him. "How are you?"

"I'm fine." He forced a smile. Dark blotches patterned his face like a disease. "Why wouldn't I be?"

"Something happened at school today . . ."

"I already spoke with Mr. Black."

With too many angles to take, Eric chose the most predictable. "It wasn't my fault."

"Make sure you don't fall behind in your studies."

"I won't."

"Is there something else?" His father was staring at a picture on his desk.

"I miss her, too."

"It's not the same. She was my one and only. I loved her so much."

"It's not healthy to be down here like this all the time."

"Worry about yourself, son, and I'll worry about me."

It's my fault, he wanted to say. *It really is all my fault*. He couldn't say that, though, because his father would take all the burden of grief no matter what Eric said. His father would refuse to listen to anything that contradicted his self-inflicted punishment. But it wasn't all Eric's fault, either. It was his mother's. If she hadn't been so easily seduced, hadn't given herself to Tommy's father in that house, she'd still be alive and Eric wouldn't have spent his teenage years reading articles about kidnappings and murders.

"I'm going out tonight," Eric said.

"Be safe." His father grabbed the picture holding his focus and pulled it closer across the desk.

Eventually, Eric left. Before the study door closed, a choked sob escaped his father's lips.

No music pounded through the walls of Steve's room, which gave Eric pause. Long ago, Eric had learned to move stealthily past Steve's room. If Steve heard him passing, he would swing open his door and make some insulting comment. Steve once said, "I didn't know shit could walk" on such an occasion. Another time Steve seized him and pulled him inside his room where the real intimidation and pain began. Eric seldom left Steve's room without tears in his eyes and bruises on his body.

Almost seventeen years old, Eric still feared his brother, though not like he once did. Steve didn't torture him anymore. Steve's friends, if he had any, had stopped coming over years ago. Steve's brutality existed solely in his cruel verbal torment. Eric usually retorted with a dismissive curse, but he still feared what his brother might do.

He started tiptoeing down the hall, then mentally told Steve to go screw himself and stomped toward his room.

Steve's door swung open and Steve stood in the doorway, swaying. The sweet, pungent odor of weed drifted off of his brother like the stink off of an onion. He wore only a pair of tight black jeans; his bare chest showcased a collage of tattoos that varied from a skull and crossbones on his stomach to a naked woman wrapped around a pole to a blue rose with thorns that spelled out their mother's name. A piece of clear plastic clung to the bloody imprint of fresh ink on the right side of his chest. The plastic distorted the image, but the newest addition seemed to be an elongated face with hollow eyes and a gaping mouth.

"Hey, crooked face."

Eric wanted to skip the usual berating banter and jump to the climactic derisive expletives, but his brother slouched against the doorway, gripping the molding for balance. Sweat streaked his face and chest. When he spoke, his teeth chattered together in between the words. His brother had not behaved the way a brother should; he had once threatened to burn out Eric's eyes with a lit cigarette until Eric nearly fainted from fear. Now Steve was stuck in the grip of drugs. Hopefully, he was suffering. Hopefully, he spent his days vomiting and shitting himself. Whatever he suffered, he deserved it.

"You don't look good, Steve."

"I'm not, bro. Not good at all."

"So what?" he said and felt ashamed.

His brother sighed. That expressed more than words could: Steve was slowly realizing what a waste he had become and that acceptance and surrender was easier than fighting.

Eric resumed his walk to his room when his brother stopped him with two words. "I'm scared."

Eric appreciated the situation for a moment before responding. How many thousands of times had Steve inflicted torture on Eric and scared him so badly that

Eric stacked books against his door so he had some warning of his brother's midnight assaults?

"Of?" Eric asked.

"You think I'm some junkie."

"That scares you?"

"You think what I say don't mean anything."

"What does it matter what I think? And since when have you cared about what I think or anything else that has to do with me?"

"I love you, bro."

Eric grunted.

"We're brothers and that's serious. That's blood."

Eric thought of Tommy.

"You don't like me. I don't know why."

"You don't remember or are you lying?"

"I want you to know some things and the first one is that there ain't nothing more important in the world than brothers."

"You been reading self-help books?"

"Bro . . ."

Eric shook his head. "Whatever. What do you want from me?"

"I need to tell you why I'm scared, but before I do that, you need to accept me as your brother. You need to acknowledge that the blood in our veins is the same."

"You're on something right now, aren't you?"

Steve grabbed his arm. Past abuses ran through his head. "Don't walk away from me, bro. I need you, and you need to hear what I have to say."

"Why?"

"Sit with me for a minute."

Before Eric could protest, Steve stepped back into the seclusion of his room. The door remained half open and through the gap the heavy stink of weed and body odor floated out like a poisonous cloud. The last time Eric had willingly entered this room, he had been searching for his mother's engagement ring and had discovered condoms instead.

He entered now with the caution of a hazmat responder. He stepped lightly in case the soiled carpet suddenly came alive and he stuffed his hands into his pockets to prevent them from clapping his nostrils shut. Steve wasn't his usual hostile self, but it was better not to press his luck. Steve was a dog that could turn vicious without warning.

Steve sat on his unmade bed, slumped forward, forearms on his thighs. He had left plenty of room for his brother, but Eric stopped two feet inside the room. The endless posters on the walls had not changed; the half-naked women from assorted heavy metal album covers crossed their legs and licked their lips with dirty allure. Eric found himself staring at one of them and felt disgusted. He would think of these pictures later, he knew, and please himself by combining the images with thoughts of Katie Lance. Maybe tonight she'd wear a costume of tight leather.

"I'm not the greatest brother. I know that."

Was this a confession or a drug-induced fumbling of thoughts?

"We're still brothers, and I love you."

"You've said that."

"Just listen to me, okay?" He took a moment, steadied himself. "I know you've been to Hudson House but you need to stay away from there. Stop reading about it. Stop going there. Don't ever go back—or anywhere near it. You understand?"

"You got another story of some girl ODing?"

"That wasn't—never mind. I may have joked with you before about all kinds of things, but when I talk about that place, I don't mess around. I'm serious."

"I already know about the house. I know it's . . . *wrong*."

"Fuck 'wrong'; the place is evil. I didn't always think that, though. I used to party there with my friends. Had a great time. Joked about how it was haunted, how some girl killed herself on the third floor. Yeah, real big joke. Got drunk, drugged, whatever. That story I told you at Mom's wake was true. But even that didn't scare me from that place. The real shit, the horrible stuff, came later."

Eric kept his mouth shut. If Steve really had been inside Hudson House, why did mom die when Eric entered? As Steve continued, the room grew colder.

"Sometimes the front door wouldn't open. We'd pound on it for hours but it was like hitting a wall. This kid Freddy tried to get in through the second-floor windows. He climbed up onto the porch roof and slammed the glass several times without luck. He drank a few beers while up there, too, and no one passing by cared. Maybe they knew. Freddy gave the window another shot, decided it was no good, and then climbed to the third floor window. He had to hold onto the trim with one hand while punching with the other. He really punched the shit out of it. The glass shattered, but not into tiny pieces. It fractured into giant shards. One of them pierced into Freddy's hand, hell, *through* his hand. He freaked out, fell, rolled off the roof. Said he had seen something in the window just before he hit it. A woman in white."

Eric swallowed a dry lump.

"We took him to the hospital and lied, of course. Freddy lost three fingers. He was lucky not to lose the hand. We went back the next day and the window was fixed. Not boarded up like the ones on the lower levels. *Fixed.* The door opened that day for us. We partied pretty good but it wasn't the same. Something had changed and we could feel it. The house felt different, colder and hotter at the same time. I thought I heard the house breathing. I shit you not, bro. It wasn't somebody screwing with me. It was like the house had lungs and was actually breathing.

"We had already been upstairs when my buddy's girlfriend went into a coma, but we had never been downstairs into the basement. We didn't know how to get down there. We once busted a window in the back that led to the basement but none of us had the balls to snake down there and our flashlights didn't do any good. That's the other thing about that place. Sometimes the flashlights work okay and sometimes the darkness swallows the light.

"Not much happened the next few times we went there, though I heard the breathing again. No one believed me, but I know what I heard. Then Brian Thomas found the entry to the basement. There's a hatch in the pantry that opens up to stairs that stretch into an abyss. Once Brian found it, everyone wanted to go down and check it out. I tried to convince them not to but J.J. called me a pussy and said if I didn't join them, I could look forward to that as my new nickname. J.J. was a tough kid, an orphan—bound for failure and he knew it, but his threats were serious. He held grudges longer than anyone, and if he labeled you, that name would stick until he changed it. Everyone went along with it, maybe out of pity.

"I went in last. I even made my girlfriend Tori go first." Steve shook his head. "Walking down those stairs was one of the scariest things of my life. Each step creaked so loudly like it might break. The darkness settled around me, pulled me deeper. The house's breathing was very loud down there. Every step brought me closer to the echoing huff of its lungs.

"It's difficult to really express how horrible it was, bro. I tell you about it and it doesn't sound like much, but when I think about those steps and that darkness, so damn thick. I didn't think I was coming back out of that basement, and I was almost right.

"When my feet finally touched the concrete floor, I could only see Tori in front of me, but no farther. I wanted to call out to Brian and J.J., who were up front, but the lungs sucked at the air so loudly that the floor trembled. Tori walked forward. I followed. Little pebbles of broken concrete shook around my shoes. I see that perfectly—the stones vibrating.

"The temperature rose at least ten degrees, maybe more, while we walked down there. I started to sweat. In the *whooshing* and *flumping* of the house's lungs, I also heard a metallic *ping* and *clang* that got louder and louder until it made me jump every time it rang. It sounded like giant metal teeth, snapping together.

"Then Brian said, 'Check it out,' and the darkness cleared some. His flashlight was suddenly powerful enough to push back the shadows. What had caught his attention was a hulking metal thing that took up the entire far corner of the basement. Huge cylinders sat on the concrete with heavy pipes running between them and up through the ceiling. Heat pulsed off of it. It could have contained an inferno. Touching it would burn your flesh off.

"Brian asked what it was and J.J. said, 'It's the furnace. An old forced-air furnace.' One of his foster families had lived in a house with a furnace like that, though not as big. 'Not even close to that big,' he said.

"We had only found a big furnace, but I wanted to get the hell out of there. The others weren't thinking like I was: why did a house this size have a gigantic furnace? Why were rooms in the house so cold if a furnace was on in the basement? And why was the furnace even on? How was that possible?

"The rest happened so quickly. I wish I had run when I first thought of it. I wish I had never gone down those damn steps. When I finally got out of the basement and away from the house, I felt it on top of me. The house had let me out but it had not let me escape. It followed. It chased me home."

Steve slipped into an inner world ripe with darkness and nightmares. Eric had listened skeptically at first and then interestedly, and finally he was engrossed. His brother had experienced real Hudson House trauma. They had more in common than Eric had realized. That could be something to build on.

"What happened?" he asked.

Steve didn't glance up. He sighed. "The basement didn't smell of anything much, maybe a bit musty, when we walked down the steps, but when we approached that giant thing in the corner, the air filled with the smell of beer. At first it smelled like someone opened a fresh brew and then it stank like someone had poured a keg on the floor.

"It should have been nauseating but it wasn't. It smelled good, really sweet. It made me thirsty. I almost forgot about leaving. Then J.J. said, 'I saw something behind the furnace.' Brian commented about the beer smell—how he wanted to get back to drinking—and dropped his flashlight. It broke. Brian bent to get it. The light from his flashlight caught the edge of something. It could have been a reflection off of the furnace, but I'm not sure. To me, it looked like a claw.

"Tori screamed. Something crashed behind the furnace like it had smacked against the wall and then tried to break through the furnace. I think I heard J.J.

groan. It could have been Brian or even me, but I thought he groaned like he had taken a hit to the gut.

"The furnace kicked off. The silence should have been a comfort, but it wasn't. The sudden quiet was more frightening than the rocking furnace had been. And the darkness closed in. It swallowed up the light, eating the beams of our flashlights. The dark wasn't just moving in, surrounding us; it was attacking.

"I turned for the stairs, hoping I'd find them, and Tori grabbed me. 'Where was J.J.?' I called for him. Brian did, too. As did the others, but he didn't respond. He might have been messing with us, but that seemed unlikely with every passing second. Tori started screaming for him. The others yelled, too. The screams echoed around us. 'Shut up! Shut up!' Brian yelled. But no one did.

"Then someone yelled long and loud. The sound pierced through the chaotic shouts, silenced them. The long scream cut off after a few seconds, but in those seconds, we heard the pain tormenting J.J. We had no doubt that it was him, at least I didn't. That's when I discovered that Hudson House wasn't just a weird place —it's a lethal place.

"We ran out of there, stumbling and tripping on the stairs. We ran out of the house and scattered in separate directions. Tori even ran home. As I said, I felt the house right behind me, almost on top of me while I ran. I didn't even feel safe in this room. J.J.'s scream kept repeating in my head. It was the last anyone ever heard of him. The house swallowed him in that darkness. The worst part was that no one seemed to care, not even his foster parents. They had a new foster kid in two weeks. The talk around school was that J.J. had run away. Even Brian and Tori said he had run away. They didn't want to face the truth. I understand, I guess. I couldn't escape the truth, though, because the house came after me in my dreams."

People are afraid to face the darkness—they're afraid of what they might see.

Eric's fascination gave way to fear, which anger attempted to squelch. "You tried to put me down there."

Steve shook his head. "No, I—"

"Yes." Eric stepped closer. "You wanted to push me down there into that darkness. You knew what could happen. Hell, you probably wanted the house to take me. Is that it? Huh, bro?"

His brother's sorrowful expression held no hate or antagonism. A few moments of that stare weakened Eric's anger enough for the fear to reemerge. Neither brother said anything for two minutes.

"I didn't know, not that time. I didn't go into the basement until after the night Tommy got burned. We thought you two had tried to light each other on fire. The house got him, didn't it?"

Eric did not respond.

"Or maybe you knew more about the house than I did. Maybe you two tried to burn it down, but it wouldn't let you. Either way, you need to believe me: when I threatened to push you down there, I had no idea what it was like. I only went into that basement once, though Brian and some of the others went down looking for J.J. a couple times. They never found anything. Even his busted flashlight had vanished. The house leaves no traces."

"I know," Eric said. "I know about Hudson House. It took Ed."

They shared a nonverbal exchange between fearful eyes.

"Yeah. I know it did. I saw it happen."

CHAPTER 27

Eric stepped toward his brother, hands balled into fists. He wanted to attack him, partly out of anger for not telling anyone and partly out of hate for failing to protect his brother from a place as evil as Hudson House.

"You knew?"

"I warned you about—"

Eric raised a fist. "Fuck you."

"I *didn't* see it happen," Steve said. "I saw what the house wanted me to see . . . in my dreams."

Ed tightening the noose around his neck.

"The night of J.J.'s disappearance was the first nightmare. I don't remember anything except the dark. Deep darkness so thick that it squeezed my throat and drowned me in quicksand. I was so cold. When I woke up, I was shivering in a pool of sweat. I don't know if anything else happened in that dream, but if it did I don't want to know about it. The darkness was enough. Maybe my brain blocked the rest out. That's fine with me.

"But the next night the darkness gave way enough to show J.J.'s screaming face. Tears rolled down his cheeks. I see that perfectly like a picture. The image was frozen but the scream pounded throughout the dream world, hurt my ears. I tried to fight out of the dream but the dark wouldn't let me escape. Long fingers with gnarled knuckles and cracked and yellowed nails smacked over J.J.'s mouth. His scream vanished and the pounding breaths of the furnace filled the void. Then blood dribbled from J.J.'s eyes. I woke up trying to scream. My sheets were wrapped around me like a straight jacket.

"I suffered that one many times. Sometimes I was able to wake up before the hand covered his mouth, but then once I closed my eyes again the dream would resume like I had only pressed 'pause.' After a while, I noticed that while the images and sounds of the dream didn't change, my location did. With every dream, I moved closer to J.J.'s screaming face and the hand that jumps out of the darkness. The hand looks human, but the veins are so large and purple that the person must be diseased or something. The worst part of moving closer isn't the hand, though; it's the blood. Before the dream changed, I could smell his blood, almost taste it. Blood shouldn't be scary but it is when it's right in your face because you see it fill the contours of the flesh like it's a living thing. A blood worm."

Eric's hands had lost the fists, his arms fallen slack. "How did the dream change?"

"That night you gave me the ring—"

"That's when Tommy got burned and you tried to push—"

"I didn't know what I was doing," Steve said. "The dreams were screwing with me, bro, making me crazy. I was barely getting four hours of sleep a night. I couldn't take it. I drank more and more and . . . did other things."

"Drugs?"

"It doesn't matter, but yeah; I did drugs. I don't want to sound pathetic or stupid, but I needed them. They helped me sleep. They couldn't get rid of the dreams—I don't think anything can—but the drugs helped *dull* the dreams. The same things happened but I wasn't as afraid. The house tried to infect my mind and the drugs shielded me. That may sound like bullshit but the truth doesn't always make sense. I needed the drugs and so I took them."

"How did you get the money?"

"I did what I had to. I'm not proud of some of it, but I had my reasons. The drugs helped dull that too—my conscience."

"Lucky for you."

"Forget it, bro. You can hate me all you want for whatever reason you want to, but first you have to hear me out because I want to protect you. I want to be a brother to you for once. Okay?"

Eric waited.

"The night you gave me the ring, I was enraged. High on something and scared shitless because I had been dragged back to that house. Even Tori, who had seen everything I saw in the basement, was fine with going back. I once asked her if she suffered nightmares. She told me she didn't dream. Of course that's not true. Everyone dreams. Some people choose not to remember them. I had no choice with mine; they followed me everywhere.

"I convinced Tori to come back here that night instead of going into Hudson House, though I'm sure the door would have been open. She was really happy about the ring and tried her best to thank me, if you know what I mean, but I couldn't focus. Maybe it was the drugs or maybe it was something else.

"When I fell asleep, the darkness returned, engulfing me as always, but then your friend Ed appeared like the dark had created him. He stepped toward me, held out his hand, palm closed, and smiled. The smile wasn't right. It was crooked like he had been born with a facial deformity. It scared me like the blood on J.J.'s face.

"He opened his hand and the ring you gave me glittered on his palm like a star. The light coming off of it pierced through the darkness, slicing it into flaps, and through those flaps I walked. The dark no longer held me in place. My fear subsided. It was a wonderful feeling to not be afraid.

"I reached for the ring. Ed's smile dropped, his head snapped to the side, and his body flew backwards. Then he was hanging in the dark, swinging by a rope. His hands hung by sides, empty. The ring was nowhere and the darkness flooded in around me until I couldn't breathe. The last thing I saw before I woke up was the blood slipping from the corners of Ed's eyes."

Had blood fallen from Ed's eyes while he hanged on the third floor of Hudson House? Dreams weren't reality but that didn't make them less true. Tommy sliced open Ed's stomach in Eric's nightmares, but that never happened. When dealing with Hudson House, truth and reality didn't go hand in hand.

"Your friend died a few days later. I had that same dream until the night he died—Halloween. That night the darkness opened to Mom's coffin at the wake. I walked to it, afraid how she might be different in this other world. But she looked as she did: dead but not gruesome. I watched her for a while, at least it felt like a while. Then her eyes snapped open and she sat up, grabbed my arm with both hands and squeezed. My arm felt like it had been set on a hot stove. Her mouth dropped open into a horrible snarl with gleaming fangs. Her eyes turned red and her nose fell off, exposing a dark hole. Purple veins sprouted beneath her skin, pushed out her flesh.

"I screamed and screamed. She pulled me toward her, toward her gaping mouth. Blood was filling her coffin, sloshing around like a whirlpool. Just before her fangs would have bitten me, my head snapped down to her hands, and on one of her fingers the ring shined with that same star-twinkling brilliance.

"Dad had asked me about the ring a few days earlier. Said he couldn't find it. I said it was probably on her when she was cremated. He said, 'No, she was wearing her wedding ring only.' He suspected me, of course, and while that's messed up, it wasn't unexpected. I still hadn't put it together with the ring you gave me. The drugs numbed my brain.

"When I woke from that dream of mom, I knew what happened: you stole her engagement ring to bring to Hudson House, maybe to conjure her spirit or something, and she was telling me you did it. She knew I would take the rap for it and she wanted someone to know the truth. From beyond the grave, Mom wanted you punished. So, I went into your room and punished you."

Warm pain flushed Eric's nose. "I didn't steal it."

"The next day, I found out Ed had committed suicide in Hudson House and Dad saw the ring on Tori's finger. He didn't yell or hit me. He saw the ring, saw the smile on Tori's face, and let it go. I expected him to bring it up later after she was gone, but he never did. To this day, I don't know if he blames me or you."

"I didn't steal it. I found it."

"Still sticking with that BS?"

Eric started to respond and changed his mind. "Where is the ring, Steve? Tori still have it?"

"You want to steal it again?"

"I know your brain is clogged or whatever, but you need to hear me: I found that ring, mom's ring, in Hudson House the day she died. In fact, I probably found it at the same time she was dying in the kitchen."

The anger drained from Steve like the tide going out. "It doesn't matter, bro. She's dead and I never had that dream again. I hit you and it made the dream go away."

"No. You hitting me didn't make it go away. The house took the dream away because it was a warning—for you."

"Of?"

"To stay away from that house."

Steve snorted. "I'm trying to warn *you*, bro. I already know that place is fucked."

"I found that ring, and I think it needs to be returned."

"It's gone. Long gone with Tori."

"Where is she?"

"Who knows. Somewhere. Nowhere. It doesn't matter."

Maybe he was right. What good would the ring do, anyway? Eric wasn't going to go back into Hudson House. He would keep up his night vigils, watch out for Ed, and hope the house targeted someone else.

Fear flushed in Steve's eyes. "That dream never came again, but I get others. Every night the darkness returns. It chokes me, crushes me, freezes me, and burns me. The dark shows me blood and death and monsters I can't describe. It shows me places where misery reigns. It gives me glimpses of hell. Have you ever seen babies burn? I have. Their flesh is so soft that it bubbles almost instantly and slides off their bones so easily. And it splatters so loudly. Behind each of these dreams, the huffing furnace keeps its breaths steady. The house isn't haunted. I am."

Eric stepped back from his brother without realizing it.

Steve peeled the clear plastic off the new tattoo. Blood glistened on his skin. An exaggerated mouth with a lizard tongue snapping between rows of razor teeth was set beneath huge, burning eyes engulfed in a cloud of darkness. "I had this done, bro, because it's what I see when I sleep. It's the demon who chases me. Alcohol and drugs don't keep him away. Nothing does. I know he's got me. I'm damned and this is the ink to prove it. Don't let him get you. *Please*, bro—stay away from Hudson House."

After several seconds of silence, Eric said, "I will. I promise."

Steve collapsed backwards on the bed and shut his eyes. Eric said his name a few times but Steve did not respond. Eric started for the door and spotted something strange. In a room like this very little was strange, so perhaps this was more out of place. Eric shrugged it off as another one of his brother's drug habits. He knew a few kids at school who got high huffing. He didn't know if Hudson House had made Steve into an addict or if that was just a convenient excuse. Either way, his brother deserved some time to sleep, and hopefully without dreams. He left his brother's room and gently shut the door.

He didn't think of the can of lighter fluid in Steve's room until much later and by then it was too late.

CHAPTER 28

Eric showered, dressed, and applied fresh cologne. Katie Lance's blonde hair looped through his fantasies of embracing her, feeling her, kissing her. This time the kiss would be magical. He got aroused thinking of it. He had to keep things in perspective. She was popular and he was a geek, an outsider geek at that. She may have invited him to a party but that didn't mean she was ready to drop to her knees and taste him. Imagining her lips wrapped around his penis got him revved up even more.

He focused himself enough to dissipate his erection and smooth out the wrinkles in his button shirt. Was he too dressed up? Wasn't it Halloween? If he had to, he could say he was going as an after-work accountant. That sounded stupid and lame. He changed three more times before deciding on the original clothing. Hopefully, no one would comment about his ensemble.

He paused outside of Steve's room, leaned close enough for his ear to touch the door. The faintest weeping reached him. But that could have been his imagination. Eric had never seen his brother cry, had long ago decided his brother was not a compassionate human and thus not capable of crying. Maybe he would cry in a monstrous fit of laughter but certainly not out of pain or despair. That brother—the one Eric feared so stoutly for most of his childhood—was gone, replaced with a troubled soul who tried to find solace in drugs and alcohol but managed only to bury himself deeper in fear and self-loathing. Eric felt bad, but not bad enough to check on him.

Eric didn't bother stopping by his father's study again, either. The man didn't care. He was too busy living in his own illusion.

He headed toward the party. In his mind, Katie wore lingerie with a white thong that showcased her perfect butt. By the time Eric arrived at Mangle Lane, Katie had exposed her breasts and stood over him asking if he wanted to taste her. That wonderful imaginary moment sank away when Eric realized where he was.

No matter how many times he had walked this road on his excursions, Eric still trembled and turned cold on it. He had gotten better at controlling the feeling over the years but he was unable to prevent its onset. When he neared Hudson House, he reached into his pocket and caressed the small plastic bag he had removed from his dresser before leaving as he always did on these Hudson walks. In four years, the piece of his mother's scalp had deteriorated into crumbs and dust but Eric kept it safe in the plastic bag and never went to Hudson House without it. He would be sure not to let Katie search him. The crumbling scalp of your dead mother was not something a girl wanted to find.

With November only hours away, the trees on Mangle Lane stood bare with their long gnarly branches that reminded Eric of elderly people's limbs. Except those damn evergreens at the end of the block. Those trees never faded, never lost their potent green color or cinnamon smell; they forever shielded Hudson House from its neighbors, for which the neighbors were probably grateful.

Those neighbors, whoever they were, never showed themselves, at least not when Eric was around, and that had become quite often. Since discovering that article about the housing market in this town, Eric had noticed that at least one house (sometimes two or three) usually had a FOR SALE sign posted by its mailbox. Tonight, only one house had a sign—the one directly across the street from Hudson House. Perhaps the people in that house had seen something. Perhaps they had seen a lot.

A ghost of all white ascended the front steps of that house and stood on the porch before the closed door. A moment later, a pirate and a blood-covered butcher (wielding an exaggeratedly large butcher knife) joined the ghost. Eric thought for the briefest of moments that he was losing his mind. Since when did monsters wait on porches?

Eric had been so consumed with his thoughts he had forgotten it was Halloween. Now he noticed several costumed kids running from house to house, parents following along in the street. Farther away, on the next street perhaps, the sounds of teenagers gearing up for the night festivities offset the giggling youngsters. The mix of noises seemed ominous. Halloween was a time when ghouls roamed free and bad things could happen without explanation. Typically those bad things were petty vandalism and stale candy, but that changed for Eric four years ago. Since then Halloween had been far scarier than anything ever placed in a trick-or-treat bag. Eric wished for his younger years, for the time before he learned that evil really does exist.

After almost a minute of waiting (a record for sugar-charged children), the ghost, the pirate, and the butcher ran to the next house over on Jackson Drive. They did not think to try Hudson House; no one did. Even the youngest kids knew about the house. They had heard the various horror stories from peers and perhaps even parents. While most of the kids probably heard a story or two about the place, it wasn't probable that all of them had, and yet not one child tried for the house. The one across from Hudson House was dark and all the kids tried it but they knew better than to cross the street. They sensed its wrongness. Eric had sensed it, too, years ago. He lived now with an intimate understanding of the perils waiting inside the house.

He stood on the sidewalk and watched Hudson House. People silenced themselves while passing as though walking by a burial.

. . . *afraid to face the darkness* . . .

Without assisting wind, the bare maple tree waved at him with its many twisted arms. The house inviting him again. The windows were dark, no moonlight tonight. Eric was sure the house could produce its own lighting if it wanted. If it wished Eric to see something, it would make sure he saw it.

HH is collecting and you're past due.

Eric stood before the house another minute. The tree waved again but nothing lit or stirred within the house. For a moment, Eric almost stepped toward it, onto the gravel driveway. The house was quiet, maybe it was a safe time. *Silent, yes,* he thought, *but far from safe. Far from dead.* The illusion of safety was just another one of its many tricks. Eric wouldn't be free of the house until he graduated from school and got as far from this town as he could. Maybe Texas. Maybe California. Maybe Japan.

Eric left Hudson House behind him. One day he'd be able to leave it behind for good. Hopefully.

The party was already in full swing by the sound of it. The house on Jackson Drive glowed like a giant jack-o-lantern that even flickered from all the moving bodies passing by the windows. A group of teenagers sat on the front steps, laughing. Eric did not recognize anyone. He thought of walking past the house, pretending he was on route somewhere else, but that would be pussy. He might be a wimp but there had to be a point where he grew some balls.

"Hey," he said as coolly as he could.

A kid dressed as a punk rocker with a red Mohawk snorted while two others who had been in a shaving cream fight erupted into laughter. Between laughs, they

319

pulled candy from a large plastic bowl and shoved it in their mouths. More laughter came from inside the house. Were people watching from inside? Had he been invited as a joke, a Halloween prank? Maybe one of the laughs was coming from Katie's mouth. He didn't doubt it, necessarily, but he wanted to disbelieve it.

His face flushed and he was thankful the porch light was not on. Instead of running away with his tail between his legs, Eric kept his balls and stepped toward the stairs. "This the party?"

The three guys exchanged looks. "What does it look like?" the punk rocker said.

"Is Katie here?"

"Katie who?"

"Lance."

Another snort. "Who's asking?"

"I'm Eric. I'm in some of her classes. She invited me."

"Whoa, I see." The punk rocker stood and the other two followed his lead. "Well, we're checking invites before anyone can go in."

"Excuse me?"

"You said she invited you so where's the invitation?"

Eric touched the plastic bag holding his mother's scalp. "She didn't write me one. She just asked me to come."

The punk rocker sought approval from the other two. "Sounds suspicious to me. What do you think, Charlie?"

"Yeah. Suspicious." The shaving cream boys started laughing again.

The punk rocker strode down the steps until he was nose to nose with Eric. "Who are you really? Are you some kind of narc or something?"

"Narc?"

"What are you supposed to be, anyway? This is a Halloween party, not a fag fest."

For once, Eric wanted to be back in front of Hudson House, maybe even inside it. "I'm not a fag."

The punk rocker laughed. "Could have fooled me. It's a really good costume."

"It's not a costume."

"Even better, queer."

"Fuck you."

The punk rocker smiled, glanced at his buddies, and turned back with a sharp viciousness in his eyes. He grabbed Eric's shoulder and pushed him down the walkway several steps. The other two started cheering for a fight.

The front door opened and Katie jumped onto the porch. "Brent, what the hell are you doing?"

The punk rocker stumbled, turned, keeping one hand on Eric. "Just showing gay boy the way out."

Katie pushed the shaving cream boys to the side and came down the steps onto the walkway. She wore a short, puffy skirt with white stockings and her hair in two long braids. "Eric? Is that you?"

"Hi."

She grabbed the punk rocker, yanked him off of Eric. "Go play with your friends, Brent. You're scaring away the trick-or-treaters."

He walked back up the porch but glanced over his shoulder to offer Eric a snide flick of his tongue. Then he was inside the house with his buddies.

"Sorry about that," Katie said. "Brent's a dick."

"That's okay. I'm used to it."

Her face melted into an *oh-that's-so-sad* expression. Would pity earn him a kiss?

"I'm glad you came."

"That's a nice outfit."

She blushed. "It's kind of stupid, but the girls wanted to be fairy tale characters. I'm Little Bo Peep. My sheep cane is somewhere inside. Wait until you see Jenn; she's Alice, but I don't think her outfit is what Carroll imagined."

Eric followed her back toward the house. Butterflies fluttered in his stomach. Hot *and* smart. He wanted to grab her, kiss her, profess his adoration. The skirt was long enough to cover her butt but not long enough to keep it hidden while she ascended the steps. Her white underwear matched her stockings. His hand almost reached for her butt. How wonderful it would be to touch. She glanced over her shoulder and smiled. Had she noticed his reaching hand? What did that smile mean?

"Monster Mash" played in an endless repeat from the kitchen while "Thriller" pounded in heavy bass from the downstairs, and somewhere recorded screams and ghoulish laughter changed to hissing cats and howling wolves.

Not nearly as many people crowded the house as Eric expected. Costumed people were crammed in the kitchen drinking various colored cocktails and eating pretzels and potato chips while the smell of some unhealthy appetizer like pigs in a blanket wafted from the oven. Eric recognized a few faces, though some were slathered with makeup, but no one acknowledged him when Katie gestured to the kitchen and said, "Here's the animal pen. They're feeding now." Eric didn't exactly know the people as much as he knew of them, had seen them around school, could name them. With each step up the social strata, students knew fewer and fewer of their peers. The top kids knew only the other top kids. Being on the bottom, Eric knew just about everyone and none of them knew him.

But what did that matter when Katie Lance was showing him around? He followed her through the living room where a mixed group of males and females were scrunched together on the couch and assembled on the floor before a large television on which Leatherface was busy hanging bodies off of meat hooks. One of the girls, this one dressed as a rag doll with a fake wig of thick, red hair, screamed in surprise when the chainsaw roared to life. The boys around her released a barrage of criticism. She threw popcorn at them and everyone laughed.

From this room, Katie walked down a hallway— past a bathroom in which someone was apparently vomiting—and into a pink-and-red bedroom. A canopy with a silky fringe hovered over the bed and stuffed animals covered the comforter.

A girl in a blue-and-white dress with a black bowtie set between two large breasts and white stockings that ended in smaller black bowties just past her knees had her arms wrapped around a boy whose face was melting in rivulets of blood pouring from his eyes. Blood also gushed from the corners of their joined mouths. The boy's hands slipped their way up the girl's legs.

Katie coughed loudly. The girl broke the embrace and straightened her short skirt, which barely reached mid-thigh.

"Jenn," Katie said, "this is Eric. Eric, Jenn."

"Hi."

Jenn smiled, glanced at Katie, and then said, "Oh, right. Sorry. This is Chris. He's a zombie or something."

"The living dead," the boy said in an exaggerated zombie voice.

"Whatever."

Katie coughed again, stared at Jenn.

"No," Jenn said. "We just got here. Everywhere else is packed."

"This is *my* room."

Jenn shrugged. "Go ahead, but we get the bed."

Katie sighed and pulled Eric out of the room. Before the door smacked shut, Jenn was tackling Chris on the bed, kissing his horrific face. "I told you about her outfit," Katie said. "Like a whore."

Eric didn't know how to respond. Should he agree? Then she laughed and the tension vanished.

Katie glanced into two other bedrooms and shut both doors almost immediately. "Those rooms are no good, either. You'd think someone put something in the punch." She laughed again and grabbed his hand. "Come on. We'll find some place."

She pulled him down the stairs, guided him through a room stinking of alcohol—a guy in a bear costume sucked down beer after beer, crushing each one against the side of his head—and down another flight of stairs to the basement. A few people glanced at them while they passed, and one girl looked appalled, but no one said anything. With Katie's hand on his, Eric's social position no longer mattered. If the princess chose a commoner, the man rose; the princess did not plummet.

A table tennis match raged in the basement between two large guys whom Eric believed were on the football team. That meant Tommy could be around here somewhere. Even if Katie thought little of him, had broken up with him, she'd still invite him because that's how parties worked—if you were popular enough, you could be a total asshole and still make the social rounds.

A group of people were watching the table tennis match, which the players took so seriously they screamed and cursed whenever the ball didn't bounce their way. The rest of the basement, lit in orange and decorated with cartoon cats and vampires, was relatively empty except for a girl dressed as a fairy (another amazingly short skirt) and a boy in a New Jersey Devils jersey. "Night on Bald Mountain" was playing from somewhere.

They sat in folding chairs against the wall beneath the picture of a goofy, howling werewolf. "I'm glad you came," she said again.

"It's some party."

"Yeah, but how many people are going to help me clean up before my parents get home?"

After a pause, Eric said, "I'll help you."

Her hand dropped onto his thigh. "That's sweet, but you don't have to."

The music built toward its crescendo. "I'd like to."

"Eric, I feel really stupid, but I invited you here because I wanted to know something."

He should have known this was too good to be true.

"You're really good in English and I really appreciate you helping me out."

"It's no problem."

"What I mean is when you're helping me it's really great."

"For me, too. The review really helps."

"Eric, I never needed your help."

"What?"

She squeezed his thigh. "I asked you because I wanted to spend time with you. You're so sweet and funny."

"Oh."

"When you kissed me last month, I was so surprised. But I liked it. How come you didn't ask me out or anything?"

What could he say, admit he was scared?

"Tommy threaten you?"

"No, no."

Her eyes said she didn't believe him. "He's such a prick."

The jocks playing table tennis erupted into derogatory shouts and accusations. After a few moments, the rumble faded to an occasional yell.

"This isn't really the privacy I wanted."

"Yeah." Should he touch her?

"You know about Hudson House, right?"

"What?"

"The old place over on Mangle Lane. You've been in it, right?"

Katie's hand suddenly felt very cold on his leg. She had been admitting feelings for him, actual *desires*, and then she mentioned that house. Why? Perhaps the house was manipulating her. Should he tell her that he not only been in the place but knew everything about it, including how it kills?

"Yeah."

"People say it's haunted. Some girl committed suicide there. She hanged herself in the attic. And sometimes you can see her in the window, swinging back and forth on her rope. Why would someone do that, kill themselves in an abandoned building?"

Eric wanted to yell at her for being so ignorant and insensitive and he wanted to hug her close and cry against her chest. "Tommy didn't tell you what happened?"

"What do you mean?" Had he really not told her?

Eric swallowed. "Our friend Ed killed himself in there."

"Oh, God. I'm so sorry. I didn't know."

"On the third floor. Just like the girl."

"That's horrible. Now, I think I remember that. We were in middle school, right?"

"Yeah. Surprised you didn't know I was there. Everyone seems to know."

"Everyone thinks they know everything."

"Yeah."

When she spoke again it was with quiet cautiousness, afraid perhaps that Eric would start crying or something. "The place creeps me out sometimes, especially at night. I know some people who have been inside the house. They said the front door was open. Do you believe that? How could the door be open?"

Her hand neared his crotch.

"They wanted me to go but I wouldn't dare." She rubbed his thigh, licked her lips. "Today *is* Halloween. It's a night made for scary stuff."

"What are you saying?"

"We know the place is empty. We'll have privacy there. And since it's Halloween, a little scare couldn't hurt. It might even make things more exciting." She slid her hand onto his crotch.

He grew aroused and couldn't believe it. She was asking him to go back into the one place he had sworn off but the promise of a sexual encounter had taken precedence. What the hell was he supposed to do? If he

328

said no, he'd lose her, she might even realize how pathetic she had been trying to get with such a geek. Saying yes, on the other hand, would lead him right back into hell four years after he had managed to escape it.

"Maybe it's stupid," she said. "With your friend and all, I understand if you don't want to." Her tongue slid between her lips.

"Katie, I—"

Her fingers teased the tip of his penis.

"You're beautiful," he said, sentencing himself to damnation.

CHAPTER 29

She held his hand while they crossed the street toward Mangle Lane. The tops of the evergreens swayed side to side. Was the wind making them move or was it something else? *The house is excited*, he thought. *And hungry.*

"I don't think we have to go inside the place," Eric said. "I'm sure it'll be quiet behind the house." After he said it, he thought of the spray-painted demon and the basement window.

She shook her head. "Don't be silly. We need *total* privacy."

She tugged him along onto Mangle Lane while his mind danced between images of her giving him oral sex and Ed wrapping the rope around his neck, between her begging for him to put it inside her and Tommy's hand singeing to black.

They stopped at the corner just past the line of evergreens that shielded the residents on Jackson Drive from Hudson House. The trees moved back and forth more quickly and though he felt no wind, Eric grew cold. That cold sunk into his skin and reached for his bones. He had almost forgotten that feeling. It might be fear or it might be the house's way of saying, *Remember me?*

Laughter and shouts from the party echoed behind them. It had been a mistake to go to the party. He should have realized that, but he had let the promise of sex—or at least a sexual encounter—push him to do something he knew would lead only to misery. That misery, he believed, would be when Katie told him what a loser he was and all her friends laughed. That had not happened. Quite the opposite. And yet he was in no better shape. Entering Hudson House was far worse than high school embarrassment.

He resisted stepping on the dying grass that lay like an interwoven afghan of brown. In the summer, the grass grew to knee height. In the fall, the grass died in ugly patches. If the house could clean up after partying teenagers and keep its insides relatively free from the musty smell of abandoned places, why didn't it keep the grass short and presentable? The answer, Eric imagined, was the same for why the house had let its paint fade, its siding crack, its roof sag: the house was clever enough to know what it could and could not get away with it. Abandoned houses had to show some kind of wear. It was only in the winter when it was obvious that something strange was happening. The snow never piled very high on the grass and seemed to vanish before even touching the driveway or the porch steps. Still, people didn't notice. Only Eric.

Katie pulled him harder, promising sexual adventures with the way she pursed her lips. He stepped onto the grass and winced, expecting the ground to cave in. It didn't, of course. Eric was approaching of his own volition and that would make the house even happier. He thought of pleading with her again. He'd beg her to go somewhere else. They could even go back to his house. His father would be drunk on misery in the study and Steve was probably in a drug coma.

The grass crinkled beneath his feet. Each step he took felt final, like he was approaching the electric chair. He was suddenly sure that if he entered tonight, he would never leave Hudson House.

"Katie, this place is really . . ."

"What? Are you scared?" She pulled close to him so her breasts pressed against his arm. "It's okay to be nervous, but I'll protect you."

"We could go to my place."

She frowned. "Don't you want me? Aren't you past due for some fun?"

Past due.

HH is collecting and you're past due. He had evaded the place as long as he could, and now it was time to face whatever horrors awaited him. He hoped his mother would forgive him. That would make it better, at least until the monsters crawled from the shadows.

She stopped him on the walkway in front of the steps. "Spooky, isn't it?"

"Yeah," Eric managed to say. His legs filled with cement but his back and arms turned rubbery. If he fell over, his body would snap in half.

"I hope the door's open."

Something sour, something sweet, loads of goodies for you to eat.

She started to yank him up the stairs; he pulled back. "We can't," Eric said. "It's not safe."

You're Invited!

"It'll be okay. I promise."

"I'm not joking." Her smile waned. "This place is evil."

This is not a night to be alone.

Silence. Then her face broke and the laughter followed. "Stop being an ass and come up here."

"No, Katie. I can't."

Her smile returned and did not falter but morphed with the *oh-how-sad* face, and she stepped down to him, caressed his cheek. "You're really scared? That's cute, Eric. Most guys wouldn't be so honest. But let me tell you a secret"—she leaned toward his face, nose almost touching his—"You don't have to be scared of anything when I'm with you."

Her lips pressed against his. They felt warm and wet and tasted sweet. He pressed back but not too hard. Their first kiss had been too sudden; he had to make this one special. This kiss was his first *real* kiss. And it was with Katie Lance. For a dangerous place like Hudson House, wonderful things were happening here tonight.

She broke the kiss after a few seconds but the feel of her lips lingered. He wanted to grab her, pull her close, and kiss her again, this time longer and with tongue, but he only blinked at her. The moment had come so suddenly and ended so rapidly that he couldn't react in the debonair way he envisioned in his fantasies. He was going to be James Bond and Fred Astair. Instead, he was a bewildered, though pleasantly so, teenage boy at the whim of a girl society deemed too attractive for him.

Laughing, she skipped up the steps and opened the screen door. Eric ascended the steps without realizing it. The kiss played on an endless loop in his mind. The chill had receded some with the kiss but now that he stood on the porch before the front door, the cold swept back into him, and the kiss was safely stored in his memory bank.

"Ready?" she asked with a giggle.

He shrugged. How do you ask a man if he's ready to die?

Her hand touched the doorknob and she recoiled with a loud, "Ow!"

"What happened? Are you okay? Let's get out of here."

She examined her hand for a second, locked eyes with him, and laughed. "Relax, Eric. I was joking with you. Trying to help you relax. It's Halloween, remember?"

This is not a night to be alone.

"I know," he said over his pounding heart. "Four years ago my friend died on Halloween. He died here, Katie, in this house."

She didn't turn to look at him. "It'll be okay. It's just a house."

The pentagram was gone from the storm door. Apparently the house had gotten around to cleaning it off. "He was found on the third floor, hanging from a ceiling beam."

Several seconds passed with no response.

"Katie?"

She spun around, face contorted into an exaggerated howl. "*BOO!*"

Eric stumbled backward to the edge of the porch, almost slipped off. Her face immediately changed to concern and she reached for him, but he didn't need her help. He turned from her and stared down the steps, out across the grass toward the street lamps that cast pale ovals of light that died at the edge of the lawn, but Katie grabbed his arm before he made it down one step.

"His name was Ed Forlure. No one knows why he committed suicide."

Her hand touched his shoulder. She tried to stifle the laughter bubbling beneath the surface. "I'm sorry. I thought you were joking with me. I mean, I know your friend died here, but that was years ago. It's not like it was your fault."

"I don't think he killed himself."

"What?"

"This house killed him. It made someone do it to him."

"Someone killed him?"

"Or some*thing*."

"Who?"

Tommy's name stopped at the tip of his tongue. There was no point spreading an accusation he couldn't prove. She obviously didn't like Tommy anymore, anyway, so he had no reason to make him look even worse. What mattered wasn't Tommy; it was whatever existed in this house, living off people's fear and misery. Eric had no name for it and even after all his research was no closer to understanding it.

"Let's just go, okay?"

She touched his face again. "You poor boy."

"I didn't want to disappoint you."

"I don't think you can do that."

Her lips neared his again. He readied himself. This time he would not let her go until he had proven his worth as a manly kisser, as a guy who knew how to make a woman forget her cares in a single embrace.

The door swung open and bounced loudly off the side of the house. The shock made Katie jump and Eric slipped off the edge of the step. He grabbed the railing before he could fall.

A broad shouldered figure stood in the doorway, its outline standing out against the eternal black of Hudson Houses' insides. Tommy stepped out from the house and seized Katie. She yelled in surprise and then he tossed her into the house where other people reached for her with heavy arms. Tommy then grabbed Eric's arm and dragged him over the threshold into Hudson House. The door slammed shut and the darkness cloaked everyone.

CHAPTER 30

The floor vibrated with living warmth as if giant organs pulsed beneath the skin of the floorboards. The warmth radiated into his palms and sucked his hands into the wood. Eric yanked back on his hands and almost tumbled backwards. He steadied himself, stayed on his knees.

"Sorry to ruin that moment for you, bro, but time is wasting."

"I'm not your brother."

Katie squirmed against the large hands of Kevin Tillman. Kyle France stood next to him holding a pillowcase bulging with items. Both of them stood in place, ready to do whatever Tommy asked. Their eyes had gotten redder, their faces paler. "Let go of me!" she cried. "Tommy, what the fuck?"

Tommy appreciated her for a moment, shining the heavy beam of a large flashlight in her eyes and then laughing. "Women. You think you can rely on them. You think they are telling the truth and then they try to knock out your knees."

"I was doing what you wanted."

"Making out with my brother was not part of the plan."

Eric opened his mouth to say again they weren't brothers but stopped. She knew Tommy had been waiting here for them. The whole thing from the "accidental" bump-into this afternoon to the party-invite had been part of a plan to get Eric to go where he swore he never would again. He should have known her affections were too good to be true. He wanted to be pissed at her, but he also wanted to punch Kevin in the face and be her shining knight.

"We weren't making out," Katie pleaded. "He wouldn't come in the house."

"And kissing would make him do that?"

"Tommy—"

"Shut up. I'll deal with you in a minute." The flashlight switched to Eric's face, momentarily blinding him. "Sorry about the deception, brother, but I had to get you here somehow."

"You're not sorry about anything."

"I'm sorry you haven't accepted your fate. But that's about to change. I embraced my role four years ago, as did Ed."

"You killed him."

"I did not. No matter what you may wish to believe, I never hurt Ed. I wanted only the best for him, but things being as they are dictated that he go somewhere else." Tommy spoke with his usual confidence but it was like he wasn't speaking; the house was speaking through him.

"Bullshit."

"The house wanted him, Eric, and it got him. Now it wants us. You know it, so don't pretend you don't understand. A pact was made four years ago when you entered this house. You promised your soul, as did I."

"You *made* me come in here. You were too scared to go by yourself."

Tommy thought for a moment. As he spoke, he paced back and forth like he was an executive and this encounter no more than a routine business meeting. Katie squirmed against Kevin's grip and started to cry. "You ever hear of the Holy Burden? It's something I heard in church once. Father Randolph said that the Holy Burden was the weight of responsibility set on each person's soul for he or she to do God's will. He said that even without religious instruction, people know what to do and what not to do because we are hotwired to God's expectations. The more in touch with this connection we are, the better we will understand those expectations and responsibilities.

"And when you're in touch with the connection, you're also open to His intervention. I'm sure you know what that means. Sometimes God steps into people's lives to make something happen or prevent something else. Some people call it coincidence; others credit God.

"Father Randolph told us that God was always trying to intervene because He owned us. He gave us free will because He loved us, but He also steps into our lives nearly every second of the day for the same reason. He tries to manipulate and guide, to help us go in His

341

direction. Things happen for whatever reason and God is there to steer you if—that is—you're open to listening.

"God created us, so the logic goes, and bestowed upon us this Holy Burden that we are condemned to live up to or die in failure of. I remember thinking how strange it was to have a creator who claimed to set us free but who really wanted us to do things in a very specific way. God, it seemed to me, created one huge headache for Himself. The burden thing didn't sit well with me. It still doesn't, but I've learned something."

He stopped pacing, stood just inside the living room. Katie was sobbing now and Eric wanted to go to her, wipe away those tears. She had tricked him, but she didn't deserve this. "God is not always what you first believe or what society, even Father Randolph, has taught us to expect. God is everywhere, everyday. You might find Him in the bottom of a cup of Dunkin Donuts coffee or in a public toilet or in an abandoned house. If you can accept that, then the rest will be easy."

"God does not live here," Eric said. "This place is damned."

"I don't know what you mean by damned, Eric, but you are right about one thing: God does not live here. God *is* here. This house is God."

"You know what that sounds like, Tommy? Like you've lost your mind."

For the first time this evening, Tommy's grin painted his face. That smile sent renewed cold through Eric's body. He may have lost his mind, which may have actually happened four years ago, but he was in control and knew it.

Katie cried out, "Tommy please, he's hurting me."

Tommy offered her a glance but did nothing. Kevin and Kyle were in a different world, perhaps not even hearing anything Tommy said.

"I'm not suggesting that people come here to worship," Tommy continued. "That would be silly. This house—this God—is not the one the stupid masses want. They crave the cloud-squatting, beard-wearing listener of woes. He is not here. The God here is far more powerful, far more amazing, far *heavier* with His burdens. But oh his rewards are far more than the other could offer.

"Four years ago, I discovered God in this house, right in the pantry. You don't want to believe it, but you sensed it, too. I know you did. You know what this place is, Eric, and you know it is where you belong. You came here first; do not forget that. This place wanted you first and foremost, but you have resisted the most. Why is that, Eric? Why have you fought your destiny?"

"Get off of me," Katie shouted. "This is stupid, Tommy. You didn't say anything about God or whatever. You said this was a prank. Let go of me." She squirmed and fought but Kyle held her taut in front of the staircase. She began to sob.

"Katie, it'll be okay," Eric said.

Tommy laughed. He took a breath, walked over to her, and cracked her in the face with the flashlight. Her

343

head snapped back and then she went slack. "Don't release her. She isn't finished yet."

Kevin and Kyle nodded slowly and Tommy strolled back toward Eric, who hadn't tried to intervene. He had known what Tommy was going to do, something brutal, it was always safe to predict, but he couldn't get off his knees. Something kept him in place. Tommy hadn't even worried about Eric attacking. He knew Eric couldn't. Katie sagged in Kevin's grip like dead weight, her hair had fallen in front of her. Eric wished he could smooth back her hair, dry her eyes, kiss her.

"This house has placed a burden upon your soul, Eric," Tommy said. "It placed the same burden upon mine and upon Ed's. Ed has paid his due, and now it is time for us to pay ours."

"This place has tricked you," Eric said. "There is nothing holy about this house. Look what it did to your hand."

Tommy took a moment to appreciate the permanent marks on his once-charred hand. "Not as bad as what someone else almost did to me." He gestured to the gash Eric's pocket knife had left four years ago across his eye. "A little more force and you could have blinded me, at least in one eye." He shrugged. "Wouldn't matter, though. I don't need eyes in here." He shut off the flashlight and darkness filled the room like a stifling gas. "I see you perfectly, Eric. You still see darkness, but I see everything."

"What do you want?" Even if he managed to run— if the house allowed him to get out the front door—the race would never stop. Eventually, Tommy would have his say and get what he wanted. Eric slipped his hand into his pocket and caressed the ash of his mother's scalp.

Silence settled in with the darkness.

"I want you to accept your destiny," Tommy said only inches from his face. The sudden closeness jarred Eric backward and he lost his balance. Before Eric could fall, Tommy's strong hand—the marked one, perhaps—seized his arm and kept him in place. He squeezed it hard enough to make Eric wince. His breath was the stink of rotting road kill.

"We made an agreement with God four years ago," Tommy said, much quieter. "When we entered this sacred place, we agreed to accept the burden God had for us. Father Randolph said that once you recognize the burden, you cannot deny it because that brings damnation. Your only hope is to embrace it and let Him guide you."

"I never agreed to any burden."

"You did, Eric. You signed a contract with blood. Your mother's death was the signature and now you must fulfill the terms. Hudson House is collecting and you're past due."

"This placed killed my mother." Saying that simple sentence, something he believed completely for four years, in the place it implicated seemed horribly dangerous. It was entering a church and cursing the priest.

"No," Tommy said. "This place didn't kill your mother. *You* killed her."

"No!" Eric tried to swing his free arm at him but Tommy's fingers dug into the flesh, immobilizing the arm with pain. Eric's other hand scrunched the plastic bag holding what remained of his mother.

"You know how I know you did? Because you're afraid of this place. You know the potential of this house. Once you grasp the depth of its power, you will realize everything.

"This place has haunted you ever since that first visit. It has infected your dreams, troubled your mind, followed you everywhere. I know it has for two reasons: it did the same to me and you have come here hundreds of times, always stopping at the sidewalk, but always staring with curious eyes. I know that because I was always here, just as you will be. Don't be afraid of this place, Eric. If you're willing to acknowledge the burden it has set on you then there is nothing to fear. Refuse it, however, and it will crucify your soul."

Eric didn't believe Hudson House was *the* God—or even a god—but he did believe it was dangerous on a level humans couldn't fathom. Haunted or evil, the place was wrong and it had destroyed Tommy's mind. It had done the same to Ed; only he had given in to the hopeless dark and taken his life while Tommy had surrendered to the promise of power.

No, Ed *hadn't* killed himself. Eric couldn't think that way. Once he started on that path then Tommy's state of mind was right around the corner. If he kept everything straight in his head, kept the darkness at bay, then maybe he could get out of this mess.

"Why did you wait so long?" Eric asked.

After a moment, the flashlight came back on. The beam shot right into Eric's eyes and he screamed. Tommy laughed.

In the darkness, Tommy's face had adopted a sinister accent that Eric couldn't quite identify. His eyes appeared larger but set deeper into his head while his mouth had grown outward so that the edges of his lips ended in the middle of his cheeks. Was that a trick of the light? Eric didn't want to know.

"The house has stepped into my life many times over the past four years," Tommy continued. "As I said, along with the burden comes intervention. After that first experience in the pantry when the house spoke to me, I was suddenly open to all aspects of this world *and* other worlds. The house showed me how to satisfy the burden it placed upon me. It made everything so clear. So many people go through their lives in doubt, bathed in shadows. This house cast back the darkness and illuminated the path. It was godly.

"Once I let the house into my mind, let it guide me, I was no longer afraid the way most people are. I don't fear accidents or death or embarrassment or ridicule. I live completely; I live like a king. The house gave me that freedom. When you see the way, Eric, you will understand. Everything falls away but what is important. You can't lose your way when you accept the burden. The house won't let you stumble from the path.

"The house saved me many, many times. When I suffered moments of doubts, near lapses in faith, Father Randolph would have called them, the house always rescued me. After Ed surrendered to the house's wishes, and you refused to speak to me, I felt abandoned. I know you were experiencing your own nightmares, so I don't blame you, but there I was—alone. I almost died like Ed. I even came here with a bundle of rope like Ed did. But the house stopped me. It intervened."

"You brought that rope, not Ed. You had it with you in your pillowcase." Tommy followed Eric's eyes to the bag in Kyle's hands.

"I'll get to that," Tommy said. "But not yet. The house wouldn't let me in that night when I arrived with my own rope. The front door wouldn't budge. I headed around back to find another way in but I never made it back there. The boarded windows, the one that first marked me, came alive again. It told me to drop the rope and run home. It was not yet time for the ultimate sacrifice. Things had to be done first. Preparations made."

Had the house really spoken to him? What did he mean by preparations?

"Things started to change for me in school. For you too, I imagine. I fell in with the right group of people. I began lifting weights, getting bigger. I joined the football team. I went to parties. I rose through the ranks, you might say. A regular American Dream. Each time I doubted a move or failed to know which way to turn, the house chose for me. This house guided me to them and

348

vice versa. It manipulated events and people to get me where I needed to be. And while I ascended, you turned your back out of fear and plummeted into a pathetic, little world. I tried to convince you.

"You ask why it took me so long to get you back here. The answer is because that is how the house wanted it. I had to get to where I am now before the plan could be crafted and executed. I may have held some doubts but not about the plan or the house's wishes. I doubted whether you could keep living as an exile. I thought you would kill yourself long before this moment could occur.

"You proved me wrong, which only shows just how little we are capable of understanding in a universe where God is perpetually ignored whether He is in your coffee or in an abandoned house. Things were meant to be this way, Eric. Our fates were forever linked when we entered this house."

Eric still couldn't move. His knees were stuck to the floor. *Just the way the house wants*, he thought. *That way I can't fight.*

Tommy walked to the center of the foyer. "I apologize for the Halloween card. I couldn't resist. You didn't seem to be handling it well in gym today." Kyle grunted. Did that mean anything?

Something sour, something sweet, loads of goodies for you to eat.

"Couldn't resist because the house made you write out sixty cards?"

You're invited!

Tommy's face scrunched in confusion. "Sixty?"

HH wants you.

"Why even bother wasting so much paper? You had Katie in on the whole thing. That's all you needed." She hung there, head bowed as if in contrition.

"I only left you one card."

Brothers Forever.

"Afraid of looking like an obsessive freak in front of your hoodlums?"

Tommy's confusion continued for a moment and then the lines on his forehead smoothed out and he laughed. "The only freak in the room is you, bro."

"I'm not your—"

"Shut up. You don't have the information you need to say what you say. Someone has to educate you, and someone will. Not yet, though. First, Hudson House wants you. As I wrote, the house is collecting and you're past due."

Why would Tommy lie about leaving all those identical cards in Eric's locker? He had to have left them because he admitted to today's card (at least one of them), which was like the others except for the slight difference in writing.

Tonight is not a night to be alone.

Eric had to get out of here. He had to run and run and run as he did that night four years ago. Only this time he had to run past his house and keep running. Of course, first he had to get to his feet, which still couldn't move.

Tommy gestured toward the door that led to a closet, which led to another door, which led into the kitchen. "Time to embrace the burden, Eric, and let the house set your path."

"You tried to kill me four years ago. I'm not going any deeper into this house."

Tommy walked slowly toward him. "I was really sore about that night for a long time. Then I realized that what happened was what the house wanted, and then I was okay with it. But you are going deeper into the house, Eric—*much* deeper."

Tommy approached him in three giant steps, seized his arm again—a flare of heat rushed along Eric's skin —and yanked him forward. Eric toppled over. With one hand on Tommy's arm and the other still buried in his pocket, Eric was helpless. Tommy dragged him across the floor toward the doors and for several steps Eric couldn't do anything but watch the door come closer.

The wood floor scraped his knees; even through his pants, it felt like razors tearing his skin. The floor was coming alive, reaching toward him with a million hungry mouths full of fangs.

Eric tugged back on Tommy's arm, which made him stumble and turn. Eric swung his legs forward and over, knocking into Tommy's ankles and tripping the first leg. Tommy fell with a startled gasp, crashed into the floor, released his grip on Eric's arm. Eric tried to turn back to the front door, but Tommy leaped on top of him. He clawed at Eric's face, his fingers tearing at Eric's eyes. "I'm going to kill you this time!"

The fight that started four years ago would finally end. Unfortunately for Eric, Tommy had grown considerably in size, with bulging biceps and concrete pectorals, while Eric had merely become lanky and nerdy with fingernails he neglected to trim on a regular basis.

Eric yanked his other hand out of his pocket and felt the plastic bag catch on his fingers, rip, and slip off into the darkness. Despair so deep he could have wept for days struck him like a mind-numbing punch. He had to find the bag. He couldn't leave a piece of his mother here. He had done too much to her already. But maybe she deserved to be here, stuck in this place where she betrayed her husband and her family.

The light from Tommy's flashlight spilled in many directions but still darkness crowded around them and with each passing second moved closer. Eric shoved Tommy as hard as he could, sending him sliding back several feet, and flopped onto his stomach, shooting his arms out for the plastic bag. *The house got it already. The darkness ate it.*

Tommy leaped onto him. His knee buried into Eric's lower back, making him scream. He squirmed beneath Tommy's weight like a bug on a needle, limbs flailing for escape. "You aren't going anywhere, bro," Tommy said. "You keep fighting and Kevin and Kyle are going to immobilize you. Understand?"

Eric went limp. In the strength department, Tommy had Eric beat a million times over, but Eric still had his brain—and his will to survive.

Tommy stood after a moment, brushed himself off. "I'm glad you understand the situation because it'll make things so much easier."

Eric wanted to wait another moment but the time to strike had arrived and he couldn't delay any longer. He pounced on Tommy. The move startled Tommy enough to twist up his legs and send him back to the ground with a loud crash and a *ooofff* of exhaling air. Eric landed on Tommy and paused for a moment, celebrating his achievement: he had toppled Goliath.

Then Tommy landed a heavy punch across Eric's jaw that jolted him backwards off of Tommy and into the darkness again. His elbows absorbed the brunt of his fall.

Tommy laughed, amused with his accomplishment. "Don't try to fuck around, Eric," he said. "The house has determined how things will go."

"Fuck the house!" Eric shouted and charged him again.

Eric's hands found Tommy's neck. The neck caved in and plowed Tommy back into the floor where he erupted into a fit of agonized, choking coughs. The viciousness of the coughs kept Eric's hands from squeezing Tommy's throat and finishing the job.

Finishing the job? Did that mean killing him? Could he do that? Even if Tommy had killed Ed—which he must have—Eric still couldn't kill to attain vengeance.

The hit to the throat had been strong enough to make Tommy writhe on the floor, groping at his throat and producing the most disturbing hacking sounds. He sounded like he might barf up a lung, perhaps both.

Eric sat up, straddling Tommy, and watched Tommy's face darken from red to purple as he coughed and hacked and gasped for air. He had never seen his friend so vulnerable before, weak and helpless. Kevin and Kyle stood in place. Was Kyle grinning?

"I'm not going any farther into this house," Eric said. "And stay away from me forever." The rush of adrenaline that accompanied those words felt so wonderful. Eric could do anything, be anything. Hudson House had haunted him for so long, tortured him with nightmares, but now he had proven that the malicious creation it had molded from his former friend was no adversary. Evil could never triumph in the face of good will and determination. He had no idea it could have been so easy. "And I'm taking Katie with me."

Katie dropped to the floor and Kevin stepped forward and cracked him in the face with a meaty forearm. Eric collapsed backwards, head bouncing off the floor. Intense white light flashed before him. He hoped for the stars, for that land of brightness and coruscating serenity, but darkness quickly swallowed the white light. His chance at peace and, perhaps, salvation, vanished in a blink.

Kevin stood over him, emotionless. Eric had lost his sense of balance; every time he shifted, his head spun and twirled. He tried to shake it off and only made it worse. The foyer slanted, half of it buried in perpetual darkness that stretched into the depths of infinite hell.

The rest stood in elongated shadows that swarmed up the walls with hungry mouths, stretching to eat him whole.

Tommy sat up. His upper body had grown several feet and his head stretched toward the ceiling. His arms reached toward Eric and were impossibly long with fingers that morphed into crab claws, snapping, snapping toward Eric's face. He tried to scream and couldn't. The sound wouldn't move past his throat.

Just an illusion, he told himself. *The house is trying to trick you.*

But as Tommy's claws neared, Eric found it more and more difficult to accept his brain's logical explanation. "You can't fuck with what the house wants," Tommy said in a voice several octaves deeper than his own. The words vibrated through the air, shivered against the walls, and shook themselves along Eric's skin. "And the house wants you."

His claws seized Eric's neck and ripped into the flesh with sharp spikes. Heat flashed along the wounds. The claws dug deeper into his skin, drawing blood, which coursed down Eric's neck and saturated his shirt. This was it. The house wanted Tommy to kill him and had given him the deadly hands needed to do it. Eric would be found—*if* he was found, that is—in a pile of his own blood. Just like his mother.

Tommy stood over him, impossibly tall with a jaw that dropped down to his waist when he spoke. "Hudson House has been waiting. Tonight is not a night to be alone, Eric."

Then the flashlight was back in his face and its light drove away the distorted world that had infected Eric's eyes and mind. Tommy returned to his bulked-up, though normal, size and the darkness retreated into the corners. But in those corners, Eric noticed, the darkness began eating at the stray beams of the flashlight like termites at wood.

"You grab him," Tommy said to Kevin, who had used his forearm as a nightstick. "And you take Katie," he told Kyle. He leaned into Eric's face. "I know you don't want to go any deeper into the house, but you'll change your mind. Let's start somewhere familiar, shall we?"

Tommy turned his back and pushed through the door next to the stairs. Kevin grabbed Eric by the back of the neck with one hand and placed the other on his shoulder where it sat as a sandbag. Kyle picked Katie up onto her feet who slouched onto him like a weepy girlfriend—still unconscious. He wrapped an arm around her and followed Tommy. Good old reliable KK Krew.

"You don't have to do this," Eric said to Kevin.

"You're definitely wrong about that," Kevin said in a dead monotone. He shoved Eric through the open door and into the dark.

CHAPTER 31

The darkness of the coat closet passed quickly when the second door opened to the kitchen. The jocks carried their own flashlights and now turned them on, Kevin lifted his heavy hand off Eric's shoulder to do so. For a half second, Eric flirted with the idea of turning— if he could snap free of the hand clutching the back of his neck—and smacking Kevin in the face. If the move took him by surprise then Eric could flee.

Tommy walked right through the kitchen and stopped at the pantry door. Kyle rested Katie against the wall by the door. She slumped to the side and he had to keep his arm against her for support. He held the pillowcase. Kevin shoved Eric into the middle of the kitchen and then pulled back on his neck. Tommy hadn't said anything but the guy knew what to do. It wasn't Tommy guiding him, though; it was the house.

Eric thought of that night he watched Tommy use Kyle's head to open Hudson House's front door. They had been planning this for months. Eric cursed himself for not being smarter. He had explored the macabre coincidence of kidnapped teenagers on Mangle Lane when he should have been watching out for the dangers closest to him. Tommy had left all of those Halloween cards. No matter the reason he denied it, Tommy had orchestrated this mad scheme to get Eric back here. And now what?

"Do you remember what I said the first time we entered this room?"

Eric didn't want to answer but the fingers on his neck squeezed one out. "You told me to run for my life."

Tommy paused. "I told you," he corrected, "that this house is really special and that we couldn't leave, maybe never."

"You said you'd leave me."

"The house ordained events the way they fell and we are far too ignorant and meek to question it." If only Tommy's teachers could hear him—*ordained events*.

"You a preacher now?"

Tommy swept his flashlight across the kitchen. The metal sink glinted like a star. "You found her here, didn't you?"

The woman with long, brown hair and a vibrant white dress whirled in his mind. He knew who she was, but he dare not admit it, to himself or anyone. For a moment the image warmed him and then a giant carving knife grew out from her hand and her face contorted into a hideous grin.

"She helped you," Tommy said. "I saw her, too. Tried to trick me, scare me. A bug in the house is all she is. She helped you and I want to know why."

"I don't know."

"Who is she?"

"I don't know." Kevin's fingers squeezed more tightly and Eric winced.

"You don't have to tell me now, but I will find out. You will tell me before we are finished here. You can tell me without pain or . . ." He shrugged. "Whatever you do don't pretend ignorance. I know what the house knows and I do what it wants. And you will, too."

All things come back—will she?

"I don't know who she is or why she helped me." Her arms erupting in gashes of blood that poured out and splattered on the floor.

"You think you can beat this house, but you can't." Tommy gestured and opened the door, stepped into the pantry. Eric resisted but Kevin pushed him easily. They once again followed Kyle and the semi-conscious Katie deeper into the house.

The pantry was much warmer than the kitchen. Eric started to sweat. He didn't remember any heating grates in the room, but the heat seemed to be rising from the floor, warming his feet through his sneakers. *Like standing on a stove burner.*

Instead of the faint musty smell that lingered in the foyer and kitchen, a charred smell of burgers left too long on the grill wafted upward with the heat. At first, the smell was almost pleasant, like the heat, but then it began to burn his nostrils, sour his throat, and make him nauseated. The house was going to cook them.

The pantry door shut behind the jock, trapping them all in the room. "Let's see if you remember better in here," Tommy said. On a silent cue, all the flashlights clicked off and darkness gobbled the space.

The room grew hotter and the stench of burning meat filled the room. The only sound was Eric's rapidly beating heart thudding in his ears. Sweat rolled into his eyes and stung.

When Tommy spoke, his voice sounded much deeper and louder as if magnified through speakers. "You ran away four years ago, but you can't run now, dear brother. The house is very special and it's going to show you just how right now." He snapped his fingers; it sounded like a firecracker. After sounds of shuffling and a grunt, Tommy said, "Perfect."

Could Tommy really see so well in the dark?

Tendrils of crimson color bloomed in the center of the far wall. It could have been a single rose growing in the dark with its petals as its own light. The light pulsed and stretched outward from the wall like an arm reaching out from a vat of motor oil. The tip of the arm split and the sides peeled back into the wall. The red light splashed into the wall, pushing it outward, and then crumpled into concentric waves that rolled across the wall, resembling the surface of a lake disturbed by a thrown rock. The red blob grew fingers that stretched rapidly over (*or inside*) the wall, expanding in all directions. The red color vibrated as it moved, swirling within itself like a spinning can of paint.

The fingers reached onto the side walls, stretched toward them and expanded. As it moved and the color whirled within itself, it also radiated a dark hue that cut

360

through the darkness of the room enough to outline Tommy's body in fire red. Raising his arms, Tommy sounded a cry of triumph that rolled with inhuman tones. Eric's sweating skin pickled with gooseflesh and he feared he might faint.

Katie lay in a heap near the wall where the living red color had appeared.

The color stretched past them along the walls and ceiling toward the back wall. What happened once it surrounded them?

Tommy turned, his face in a profile of red, grabbed Katie by the hair with one huge arm. She squeaked like some dog toy. Along with the illusion of fire, the red walls expanded Tommy's height and muscle girth. *Not an illusion; the house is giving him strength.*

Katie dangled from her hair, unaware of what was happening. Eric's feet grew hot. He had to do something. Had to stop Tommy from whatever was going to happen. But he couldn't move. Either the house didn't want him to interfere or his own fear kept him immobilized. Regardless, Katie was in Tommy's hands now.

Tommy released his grip and Katie's head bounced off the floor. One of her bones snapped. Tommy laughed and stepped back, waited. For a moment, nothing happened. Then the dark red color on the walls stretched onto the floor and reached for her with those fingers.

Eric wanted to scream, to startle her awake, to do something so that he wouldn't live with the memory of his cowardice when that horrible color touched her. But he couldn't. He could only watch.

The color washed over her legs and slithered up her thighs, across her stomach, and over her breasts. Her body twitched. The color paused at her throat for a moment and then surged over her chin and into her mouth. Her jaw dropped open like the color had yanked it downward to make room.

It's eating her, Eric thought. *It's a goddamn python.*

She came out of her unconsciousness with a strangled scream. Her hands thrust toward her throat but her arms stopped halfway there, constricted. The color pulsed brightly around her body. Tremors shook her. She rocked back and forth but no more than an inch or two. The color kept her in place. Fear enlarged her eyes and tears rolled down her cheeks.

She tried to scream; at least that's what Eric believed she was attempting: a garbled, strained choking rasp fought out of her mouth. It sounded agonized, brutalized. The sound came again and again, each time getting fainter but carrying more desperation. Her eyes rolled toward them. Could she see him watching?

Eric wanted to vomit. If he didn't intervene, the image would haunt him forever. Even knowing this, Eric could not step forward. Kevin had dropped his grip, but Eric still couldn't move. The house didn't want him to interfere—it wanted him to bear witness. She may have betrayed him, but Katie didn't deserve to go out as yet another Hudson House victim. In a just world, her beauty would save her.

The color wrapped around her body in deeper and deeper shades. Her arms snapped down, elbows smacking the floor. Her back contorted in a sharp arch but her screams fell to near whispers. That sound grated on Eric's nerves more than a real scream would have. It sounded like someone was snuffing her out beneath a pillow.

The red color passed her mouth, thrust down her nostrils, and seeped into her eyes. Her body shook viciously. Did it blind her? The shaking continued for only a few seconds but it felt longer, much longer. When it stopped, her body dropped against the floor with a heavy thud. Her head bounced off the wood, rolled to the side. Katie's dead, red-covered eyes stared at them blankly.

Above her, rippling on the wall, the demon face with the giant eyes and massive fangs, the same face they had seen here four years ago, smiled. Eric almost screamed. He expected the face to start talking. Its voice would be made of the thousands of wails that had echoed inside this house over the years. It would speak from the power of stored-up fear. It would be evil incarnate.

The demon face said nothing and silence settled back into the room as the color saturated Katie's blonde hair. Eric squinted, hoping he would see her chest rise and fall, even the slightest bit. For Christ's sake, his mother's chest had been moving at her wake. The house couldn't have killed her so quickly. So efficiently.

"Shit," Kevin muttered.

"We're okay, right Tommy?" Kyle asked. His voice cracked mid-sentence. "We're not going end up like her, right? *Right?*" The KK Krew had come out of their trance, just as the house wanted. Now, they would have to face their fears as well.

"Shut up," Tommy said with enough violence to make him do so.

The color seeped over Katie's still head and back onto the floor. She was an awkward shape tucked beneath a crimson carpet. How could he have let this happen? He should have been stronger, more courageous; he should have bashed Tommy's face in and saved Katie. He should have done those things, but instead he had watched her die. He thought of Ed Forlure's mother at the wake saying, *It makes you wonder about the meaning of everything. There must be some greater purpose, right? God couldn't be so cruel to use my son as some pawn. Right?*

Maybe they were all pawns, even Tommy.

The color coated the floor, whirled both within itself and in place for a moment, and then it surged forward toward Tommy.

"Watch out," Kyle said. He backed away until he hit the wall next to Kevin.

Eric stood in place, unable to move or take his eyes from the advancing color as it leapt onto Tommy's boots and slithered up his jeans. Tommy's legs shook slightly,

364

sending tremors up his spine and vibrating his arms at his sides. The color pulsated brighter and brighter while it coated Tommy's legs and rode over his butt and up his back. The color stretched again into gigantic fingers. They reached up his back and over his shoulders like suspenders.

Eric hoped it was burning Tommy's skin. He hoped the color would suffocate him the way it had Katie. He wanted it to strangle Tommy in a slow, agonized death. Eric probably wouldn't have enough time to escape before the color got him, too, but dying was worth watching Tommy die first, knowing that the curse of Hudson House was over.

Though Tommy's body shook, the tremors were not violent. He did not cry out when the color covered his back and coated his hair like a skullcap. Why wasn't it hurting him? How could the color kill Katie but spare Tommy?

The color continued surging up his body but advanced no farther along the floor. "Isn't it wonderful?" Tommy asked. "Isn't it *beautiful?*" Either the color was feeding off of Tommy or Tommy was feeding off of it. The house had already killed Katie, but Eric knew it could do worse things, probably *far* worse.

One of the football players began beating the pantry door. His thuds reverberated off of the shut door: the house was not going to let them out, not until after it got what it wanted. The player cried for help. Tears spiked his pleas.

Tommy picked up the pillowcase. The color teased the edge of the fabric like an animal sniffing a spot on the ground, and then spread over it as well. "Do you remember what I had in my pillowcase?"

Of course Eric remembered: a carving knife, a hammer, a mirror, a flashlight, an envelope, and thick rope, long enough to hang someone.

Tommy reached into the bag where his hand lingered. Was he toying with him or actually deciding what to remove? No matter what Tommy removed from the pillowcase, Eric still couldn't move. The fight would be completely one-sided. Hudson House wanted a massacre.

"You saw what the house can do," Tommy said. "But that wasn't anything. You will see everything it can do, but I want you to see it from my side—not Katie's." That brought out a self-amused chuckle. "Who is she, Eric? You must tell me now before things go any further. Once they do, there's no changing the outcome."

At first, Eric thought the *she* was Katie, but Tommy was pressing about the woman in white again. Eric almost made something up. He didn't, though, because he sensed he shouldn't. The house would detect his lies and either Tommy or that living red color would teach him not to lie.

"I don't know."

Tommy shook his head. From the pillowcase he removed a handheld mirror that might have been the same one if the original hadn't been destroyed. He raised it in front of himself and then angled it enough to see Eric.

The red color had stopped spreading at the edges of his face. It rippled and pulsed there as if anxious or hungry. Tommy's eyes burned with the reflection of red light. When he spoke, his mouth revealed bleeding teeth that might or might not be a trick of the sinister light.

"The house plays tricks," Tommy said. "I know that, and I'm sure you've seen it, too." His voice quivered in a fractured baritone. "Sometimes the tricks are good and sometimes they are nasty, but the house always has its plans. The last time you looked into a mirror in here, you did not see what the house wanted. You saw her. The parasite. She feeds off of the house, Eric. She is a bloodsucker. Why would you protect something so fiendish?"

"I could say the same to you," Eric said.

Tommy smiled. It loomed huge in the mirror. "Catch," he said and tossed the mirror over his shoulder. Eric's arms moved sluggishly and he knew the mirror would miss his fingers and fall and shatter, but his hands made it to the right place at the correct moment and the mirror dropped onto his open palms.

"Look," Tommy said.

"No." Eric didn't want to see a Hudson House trick or the woman in white.

Tommy's hand plunged into the pillowcase again. This time he removed a carving knife with a blade almost as long as his forearm. The red color reflected in the polished metal. "*Look,*" Tommy said. "You probably don't want to see this."

He turned and charged, raising the knife over his head. Eric expected the blade to pierce the top of his head and that would end everything. The last thing he'd see would be Tommy's blood-splattered grin. Instead, Tommy ran past Eric toward Kyle, who was frantically beating on the pantry door that wouldn't open. He spotted Tommy and shrieked, but his horrified cry vanished when Tommy buried the blade in the base of the kid's neck. The scream crumbled into a pathetic gurgle.

Tommy leaned forward, eye to eye with his teammate, whispered something Eric couldn't quite catch (it sounded like "Welcome Home"), and then snapped the knife quick to the side, slicing open half of the kid's neck. Blood sluiced free in a waterfall that splattered on Tommy, the walls, and the floor. Still Eric couldn't move. Kevin started crying. Seeing a guy that big cry only made things more frightening. Why didn't Kevin stop Tommy? Why didn't he at least save himself? Tommy held Kyle up by a fistful of hair. Where the knife had sliced, the flesh hung wide, revealing a hole blacker than the darkness in the house. Tommy jerked the head back and forth, which made the hole open and close like a mouth. Each time the hole opened, the skin stretched and ripped a little more.

Eric turned to the mirror without realizing it and was startled by his own red reflection. He thought the red color had covered him, but the red light was coming from the ceiling and from Tommy, radiating off of his body. The color would get him soon, though. Or if not, Tommy's knife would.

Bringing the mirror closer to his face and staring into his own eyes, Eric saw something glimmer in the corner of the mirror, very far away. Moving closer, Eric watched the speck of light flicker. And multiply. Several spots of glittering white light sparkled across the mirror. Behind him, Kevin begged for his life in tiny whimpers. As more stars appeared, Kevin's cries faded farther and farther away. Eric started to calm.

Powerful white light erupted from the mirror in a blast like a camera flash magnified a million times. The light blinded Eric for several seconds before it dissipated and he could peer into the comforting world confined to the other side of a handheld mirror. When he opened his eyes, he found that the other world had exploded into his (or he had fallen into it).

Eric stood in a world of white where millions of tiny stars flashed and sparkled. He was unaware of any noise, but this place did not feel absent of sound. Eric turned around—finally able to move his feet again—and gawked at the heavenly world. A breeze cooled his skin. This was where he might find God, not in Hudson House.

You're still in Hudson House, a voice told him. *This isn't an escape; it's a trick.*

Eric didn't want to believe that voice but he knew it was right. Hudson House would never allow an exit so easily unless it was part of a bigger plan—or if the escape were merely an illusion. Even knowing that, Eric did not want to leave this world of light and comfort. Here he was at ease; here he was safe. Perhaps this was a distraction, meant to occupy him while Tommy completed his nefarious deeds. Or perhaps this place was not an escape but a trap. The house wanted him here because it knew he would never want out.

The last time this world had arisen, Tommy shattered the mirror, saying the house didn't want Eric escaping into another world. If that was true, then maybe here was a good place to be. It might not fulfill the requirements of an escape, but it could be a refuge. Here the madness ceased. Eric would enjoy it then and prepare for when the light vanished and darkness once again reigned.

After almost a minute, Eric realized from the burning pressure in his chest that he had been holding his breath. He tried to let this world completely relax him but he couldn't. A shred of anxiety trembled beneath the surface, gnawing at his mind. Anticipation was one of the worst emotions when it was born of imminent dread.

A human form stepped out of the white and approached. The white draped off to reveal the woman's face and long, brown hair that had spurred Eric's curiosity and allayed his fear since first discovering her four years ago. He was not afraid. The white remained as a cloak over the rest of her body. When she neared, the cloak looked more like a dress fluttering in the breeze. She reached toward him. Thankfully, the white completely covered her arms.

"Who are you?" he asked, though now he knew for sure.

The woman smiled. Her teeth matched her dress and the background sweeping all around her. In that smile, Eric found the last of his trepidation dissipate and extinguish. He reached for her as well. This woman meant no harm. She had come to protect him. He wouldn't address her the way he should because it felt dangerous, like Tommy might be listening.

"Will you help me get out of here?" he asked.

She shook her head. The action was a flirtatious refusal at first and then her head kept shaking and turned violent. Her head whipped back and forth, hair swooshing around her face and wrapping her head. Both of her arms reached for him. Her fingers protruded from the white, rigid like sticks, and then blood flushed the fingers, saturating the flesh. The blood seeped up her arms and overflowed. It poured off of her like water out of a fountain. Far darker than the red color that had infected the pantry, her blood weighed down her clothes in heavy clumps.

Her head snapped still. Slowly, her hair waved before her face. Her dead eyes peered at him. Tears of blood coursed from those eyes and carved jagged paths down her face. Her mouth dropped open but no howl fell from it. Instead, a clump of blood dropped out and splattered somewhere. *Her tongue. Oh, God, that was her tongue.*

She shuddered forward and Eric backed up. But where could he go? Then she was directly in front of him. Her eyes dropped from their sockets, which were filled with the same darkness living in Hudson House. It squirmed in there—*inside* her. She was trapped here, unable to help anyone, forever doomed because of her transgression.

Her hands seized Eric's arms and his flesh froze. He screamed.

Tommy slapped him across the face. The world of white with the flashing stars and the horrible vision in white vanished. The mirror lay on the floor shattered. The red color had retreated from Tommy's head and was now sliding down his legs, retreating back toward the far wall. Kyle lay in a pile by the door. His head was barely connected. Kevin was on his knees, head against the wall, sobbing. Tommy still held the knife.

He slapped Eric again. His hand was a hot burner. "Who is she?" he screamed.

"I don't know."

"Bullshit. She was here. I saw you. She had you hypnotized or something. Who was she?"

The red color was not retreating all the way to the back wall where the demon face hovered; it was slipping down through the floor as if sucked by something beneath them. As the color dissipated, the darkness moved in.

"Find out who she is—*now!*"

"You broke the mirror," Eric said. "How am I supposed to find out?"

Tommy took a moment, caged his anger. "The mirror is a pathway. She infected it. I need to know who it is so she can be dealt with."

"She's bleeding."

Tommy smiled. "Of course she is. She's in the house of God."

The last of the color disappeared under them but a slight red hue radiated in the shape of a rectangle in the floor. Eric hadn't noticed it before, Steve had said it was there. Maybe it appeared only when the house wanted it to.

"I'm not telling you anything. Why don't you ask this damn house?"

Tommy laughed. "I only wanted to hear you say it. You honestly think I don't know your slut of a mother is here? She thinks she can help you, but she's wrong. She's long dead and gone, Eric. She was a whore and now she's in her Hell."

Tommy knew about the affair. His father probably gloated about it. They probably discussed it here in this very room. Anger turned his hands into fists and he wanted to charge Tommy, but he couldn't do that. Tommy would only knock him down with one arm or slice open his stomach and rip out his intestines. There had to be a way out of here, please God, any way out of here.

"This isn't going to end well," Eric said, eyes fixed on the glowing trapdoor.

"You're wrong about that. Things are going to end very well for everyone. It's time to see what this house is really all about."

Eric heard the smile in Tommy's voice. The red outline of a door in the floor vibrated, inviting them down into the basement.

CHAPTER 32

Tommy found an edge of the trapdoor and lifted it. Red light pulsed from below and a wave of intense heat rolled out. Eric's body ejected a fresh gush of sweat. Something rumbled down there. Something hungry.

Tommy grabbed Katie, dragged her over to the hole, and shoved her down. Her body rumbled down the stairs. He didn't hear her hit bottom. Maybe there was no bottom. The stairs could go on forever. All the way to Hell.

"Grab Kyle," Tommy said.

Kevin sobbed, "No. Please. Don't do this."

Tommy raised the knife. "You won't get off as easy as he did. I'll slice open that big belly. Your intestines will spill out and you'll bleed to death for hours. It could take days."

"Tommy, please—" He pawed at the door like a trapped animal.

Tommy pointed the long blade over Eric's shoulder. Slowly, Kevin shuffled over to Kyle. Sobbing heavily and pleading to God, he grabbed Kyle and dragged him toward the hole in the floor. Tommy pushed Eric to the side with an almost careful gesture. Even well off the bend and brandishing a huge carving blade after almost slicing off a person's head, Tommy still possessed considerate behaviors. *No, he's just protecting you so the house can kill you.* Kevin stopped dragging his buddy. He turned away from Kyle's sagging head, the way it fell too far to one side.

"Push him down the stairs," Tommy said.

"Just let me go," Kevin begged. "I won't say anything, Tommy. I promise. *Please.*"

Tommy thought about it. "Fine. Push him down the stairs and then you can leave."

Eric didn't believe Tommy had suddenly grown considerate *and* empathetic, but Kevin believed him. Desperate people will believe anything if it's what they want to hear. He pushed Kyle to the edge of the hole and then over the edge into the glowing red abyss. The body thumped down the stairs.

"He's not down all the way," Tommy said.

"I can't go down there."

"Sure you can. Let me help." Tommy placed one booted foot over the jock's face and shoved him. Kevin fell backward down the stairs. He screamed as he rolled downward but the shouts dissipated rapidly. He either stopped screaming or actually reached bottom. Tommy had shoved him as easily as he might have shoved a little kid.

"After you, Eric."

Finding more courage than he thought he had, Eric said, "You can bury that knife in my chest because I'm not going down there."

The darkness had completely retaken the pantry. The red light pulsed from below, retreating gradually deeper. "You think I would stab you, my own brother?"

The knife clattered on the pantry floor. The sound was quickly suffocated. The dark ate light and sound.

"Go for the knife," Tommy said. "It landed somewhere. I'm sure you'll find it. Though it may cost you a few fingers. Probably makes more sense to enter the basement."

"Why should I go down there?"

"All the answers are waiting for you."

"Why should I believe you?"

"We're brothers."

"No. We *are* not."

"Everything will make sense. Down there, the house keeps its secrets."

"You have no way of making me."

"I still have this." Tommy lifted and dropped the stuffed pillowcase. Something heavy smacked the floor. The hammer.

Against the fear raging inside him, Eric said, "Go ahead."

"Stop resisting, Eric. This is your destiny. There is a very special place for you here. Embrace the burden and let the fear go."

"Let me out."

"I can't. Only the house can do that and it's not part of the plan." He stepped closer, hot breath pasting Eric's cheek. "Go down the stairs or I will have to make you."

"I don't care what you do. I'm not going down there."

"You can try to ignore the burden this place has set on you, but I know there is one burden you cannot ignore and that is why you will go down there."

"What is that?"

"How you killed your mother."

"What do you know about it?"

"Everything."

"Tell me."

"I know your mother was a whore. I know she tried to save you from this house, tried to keep you from the truth, and she continues to try even after the house has taken her. I know things you have always wanted to know, things you *need* to know."

A moment later, Tommy entered the hole in the floor and stomped down the stairs. His footfalls echoed briefly. The red light was almost completely gone and then Eric would be alone in the dark. Alone as Ed had been when Eric left him behind. Alone as his mother had been when something burst in her brain and she died in the kitchen. When Hudson House got her.

He could try to leave, though he doubted the house would let him. He could wait here in the darkness and remember how he had carried death into other people's lives. His action had ruined his father's life and his inaction had done the same to the Forlures's. That reality weighed far heavier on him than any illusions the house could manufacture. Eventually, Tommy would come back upstairs. That was logical: there were no doors at the basement level, but the people who built the house didn't even construct a basement—so, the house could make an exit for Tommy. Then Eric would be trapped forever. And still the basement would wait. But would the answers? This place had killed his mother and now he could finally learn the truth.

Or fall for a Hudson House trick.

Eric approached the entrance to the basement, paused. The heat pulsed strongly. Somewhere down there something rumbled. It sounded like a giant stomach. *This is for you, mom*, Eric thought, and stepped down toward the red light.

* * *

The temperature raised five degrees or more with each step. Eric hesitated when his head hovered above the door and then ducked beneath it and tried not to slip on the steps. They had not been created with safety or ease of use in mind. *When the house made these steps, it made them for only one purpose: to get people down to the bottom as quickly as possible.*

What waited down there?

He slipped on a step and almost fell. The rumbling sound pounded around him and even with the red light highlighting the steps, the darkness sank heavily over everything. The red light receded so that with each step Eric took, it moved backward the same distance.

Halfway down the steps, Eric knew he should be able to see the rest of the basement, but the darkness shielded his view like a veil. The red light illuminated the bottom of the steps and the wall directly across from it but the darkness cut it off as it swept left. Eric was curious what awaited him in the dark world to the left, but something more imminent concerned him now: Kyle lay sprawled across the last few steps. The skin securing his head to his body had ripped even more, completely exposing the muscles beneath and part of his spine.

Eric stopped. Was he supposed to walk over him? Kevin and Tommy must have, but could Eric be so heartless or afraid for his own life to step over a mutilated body? Kyle might have been an asshole, but he had probably expected a Halloween prank, not death —certainly not his own.

The problem of what to do next was solved for him when Kevin stepped into the glow of the red light and grabbed his friend by the legs. He started to pull him off of the steps.

"You should run," Eric said.

Kevin stopped, glanced up and then behind him. "It's too late for me. For you, too."

"I know this isn't what you expected."

"Expected?" Kevin said. "This is fucking hell."

Thundering over the rumbling sound, Tommy's voice commanded: "Bring the dead to me!" His maniac laughter echoed.

"If you have a weapon," Kevin said, "please kill me."

Eric shook his head and Kevin dragged Kyle into the dark. On the last step, the kid's severed skin caught the edge and ripped up the back of his skull, nearly flaying his scalp. Eric swallowed a ball of vomit in his throat.

He took a tentative step down. And another. And another. He stopped again with one step remaining. The rumbling sound deepened, resembled heavy breathing. The veil of darkness kept his view obscured but he could see farther around it. The red light pulsing on the wall illuminated Tommy's back as he gesticulated directions to Kevin dragging his friend near Katie's corpse. Something huge stood behind them. Something breathing.

"I can wait all night," Tommy called, "but the house cannot. We are waiting for your presence, dear brother."

Eric didn't move. His heart was ready to burst through his chest and splatter on the concrete wall.

"Did you hear me, brother? It's not nice to keep your flesh and blood waiting. Especially when it is time for it to be put to better use." After a pause, he mocked, "Oh, brother? Are you coming? I so want to play with you. *Bruuuuther*."

That final, dragged-out calling pushed Eric down the steps, and he turned out of the darkness and into the light. "I'm not your fuc—" The refutation of sibling connection fell short before the glowing monolith heaving behind Tommy.

It was the furnace, though far, far too large for a building like Hudson House. The giant machine stretched at least ten feet across and touched the ceiling, an eight foot height or more. Numerous metallic tubes reached out from the body and arched toward the ceiling. Some connected directly above while the others twisted across the ceiling toward other destinations. Immense heat radiated off each of these arms. Touching one would burn flesh. The red color squirmed across the body and every arm like a living skin.

Other than the extending tubes, the body was nondescript metal, except for where Katie and the near-decapitated Kyle lay. A large cavern opened at the base of the furnace to a midnight-black hole that might stretch to infinity. *Or to hell.* The sides of the hole moved, flapping back and forth like giant, hungry lips. Eric expected an equally giant tongue to slither out and wrap around Katie. It reminded Eric of a lesson in biology where they watched footage of undersea animals. A deep-sea diving vessel had gotten pictures of a creature right out of a child's nightmare, with a million eyes and clawed tentacles and mouths that opened and closed in circular orifices lined with razors. He hadn't believed such things existed. Where did those creations fit into God's design? Father Randolph might have a theory or two. Eric had his own theory: God didn't create them—the Devil did. And that's what masterminded the thing in the basement of Hudson House. The builders never constructed a basement because they didn't have to; the house built it on its own.

The basement that no man conceived stretched to the left into a dense darkness and went on endlessly beneath the stairs. None of it made sense. The wall of the house ended only a few feet past the entrance to the stairs in the pantry and where Eric now stood would be the backyard of Hudson House. No windows lined the top edge of the room, but there had been a window into the basement that night four years ago. Where was that window now?

The house creates what it wants when it must. And it destroys those things just as easily. And destroys other things, too.

It was no use trying to make sense of this place. The floor might suddenly give way to another set of stairs or the walls might shift to reveal a hallway to nowhere. The house could not change its exterior because people would notice, but it could do whatever it wanted down here. People could be lost in here forever. The house could make them disappear. Eric was closer to the truth now than any of his research could have brought him.

Kevin dropped back from the pile of bodies, heaving, crying. Hands on his knees, head bowed, he could have just finished running laps and was now awaiting the coach's next direction. Driven by fear alone, Kevin would do Tommy's bidding. Escape was a laughable idea, anyway. Standing before the behemoth of a furnace that pulsed and breathed with life, Eric knew the house would not simply let him leave. He would have to make a deal with it as he had planned to four years ago. Unfortunately, he never got any further in planning that scheme than the idea.

"So glad you could join us, brother," Tommy said. He admired the furnace. "This house is more special than you can ever imagine. It is the mystery that intertwines the psyche and it is all the answers that are dared to be believed. The house is everything."

"The house is poison."

Tommy reached into the pillowcase. Eric started to step back and stopped. If Tommy chose to kill him now after everything said upstairs, so be it. An ending was an ending.

He removed the hammer, dropped the pillowcase. He seemed to evaluate the weight of the tool. "This house has so much to offer, if you're open to its gifts." He walked around the pile and approached Eric. "But for those who refuse to accept what is offered, the house has other ways of handling them."

"You won't kill me."

Tommy smiled, paused. "Then there are those for whom the house will never give answers. For them, there is only one option."

He stepped past Eric, raised the hammer, and snapped it down onto Kevin's head before he could release an entire scream. The hammer hit with a heavy thud and cracked through his skull. Tommy stepped back and Kevin slumped forward, the head of the hammer lodged beneath his thick hair. A reddish-grey mixture oozed from the hole. For several seconds, Eric could only stare.

"The human body is more fragile than you think," Tommy remarked, amused.

Nausea stirred in Eric's stomach. He turned from Kevin. Behind Tommy, the other dead bodies lay, waiting.

He couldn't think of the dead. If he even let himself drift off about poor Katie or even the pathetic but most harmless KK Krew, Eric would be reduced to tears. He couldn't surrender. Not yet. "This place has ruined you," he said. "You've always been an asshole, but now you're so far gone there's no hope." It was a complete understatement, but it was all Eric could manage.

"Hope?" Tommy laughed. "That's for losers. And with the house on your side, you can never be a loser. Doesn't that sound good, brother? To not be a loser. To have power. To not live in fear. To always be confident and do whatever you want."

"At what cost?"

Tommy glanced at the bodies. "Take Katie, for example. You wanted her; that's why it was so easy to get you here. And why did Katie do it? Because I had her, Eric. She was easy. Why? Because the house gave me the power to get what I wanted. I got her and you didn't because I'm not a loser. Don't you want that power?"

"You killed three people." Eric's lungs weren't filling with air.

"I didn't kill anyone. That's what you don't understand. You don't see that yet, but you will. The house took them. It merely used me as a conduit. It is my burden for the privileges I enjoy."

"What do you know about my mother's death?" Eric didn't know how he managed to keep talking, gasping between words now, but he feared that if he stopped, he would curl into the corner and completely shut down.

"We'll get to that. First, the house wants what belongs to it."

"Which is?"

Tommy turned to Kevin, looped his hands beneath the guy's arms, and dragged him to the other two. At the pile, Tommy bent over, manipulating the bodies. For that moment, Tommy was entirely vulnerable, back exposed, but Eric couldn't do anything. He didn't know if fear kept him in place or if the house actually protected Tommy, but no matter how hard he wished for his hands to join and raise high like a hammer, nothing happened.

Tommy finally turned around, hammer in his hands. He had moved the pile of bodies closer to the gaping mouth of the furnace. "Watch and know."

The furnace rumbled. The many arms spreading across the basement shook. The huffing, breathing sound deepened and magnified, echoing throughout the basement. The hole at the bottom of the furnace twitched around the edges and grew wider. It spread open across the base until it was as wide as the pile of bodies before it. The air thickened with intense heat that loosened Eric's flesh. A faint smell traveled with the heat but it was too weak to decipher.

Tommy moved next to Eric, an excited grin on his face. *Anxious for the feeding.* Eric felt nauseated again.

The red color pulsed with greater vibrancy. It slithered and swirled across the surface of the furnace, but it stayed away from the gaping hole. The darkness in that hole moved. It moved like an eel beneath the surface of the water, barely detectable but sensed. Something was stirring in the darkness. The house was alive but something else lived in that black hole. Now it was coming out to feed.

The dark stretched out from the hole like a hand but with abnormally long fingers. Each of the fingers squirmed and curled as the whole hand moved forward. Eric thought again of the deep-sea creature with its tentacles and razor teeth. The hand stretched farther out of the mouth. It shimmered. Perhaps it was an illusion, a chimera. If that was the case then maybe everything down here was. Hell, maybe even the entire house. A collective illusion shared by all the people who knew Hudson House and kept it alive through fear.

The fingers touched Katie's still body. Eric flinched for her. The fingers trailed over her arms, chest, and head, squirming like worms. They pushed her shirt up, exposing her stomach, and slipped beneath. When they groped her breast, Eric squirmed. What the hell was it doing?

Then it abandoned Katie and climbed onto Kyle. The fingers did not find anything interesting on his body either until they reached his neck where the soft tissue was exposed and blood still dribbled out. The fingers fondled the torn flesh, lifting it, investigating. They stretched the skin more, burrowed deep into the tissue. Though the sound was slight, Eric heard the fingers pierce the muscle and slither into it. Eric covered his mouth and clenched his jaw.

The nausea ebbed when the smell of candied apples flushed into his nostrils. That's what he had faintly detected before but now it filled the room intensely. There should be vats of candied apples all around them. The smell could only be coming from the furnace— from that hole.

The hand pulled back but the fingers did not slip out of the muscle. The fingers held and the tissue ripped apart into clumps. Some dropped out onto the floor and others stayed stuck to the fingers, which curled into something like a fist. The furnace rumbled again and the hand opened. The pieces of tissue and muscle had vanished. Then the fingers returned to the injured area and removed more internal goop, swallowed it.

The fingers did this several more times and then gripped the base of Kyle's skull, and ripped it free from the body with a bone snap. The fingers surrounded the head, squeezed and pumped it like a basketball. Slowly, the head shrank. The skin hung loose and the scalp bundled. It was eating the skull first. Eventually, the jock's head dangled limply as nothing more than a mask. And the hand devoured that, too. After a moment, it returned to Kyle's body and began removing pieces of his chest starting at the open neck.

Another hand protruded from the dark to assist with the gleaning of the body. Three more hands filled with squirming fingers crawled out of the hole and together the hands diminished the corpse very quickly. Piece by piece, chunk by chunk. Flesh, bone, blood, and clothing vanished in small clusters. As the fingers worked, the candied apple smell intensified so much that Eric tasted candied apples well enough to fool his other senses.

"Quite something, isn't it?" Tommy said as the fingers swallowed pieces of foot and sneaker.

"This is hell," Eric said quietly.

"Not for us. For you and me, this is paradise."

The fingers started eating Kevin, scurrying into his head through the hammer hole. The vomit finally pushed its way out. Eric barely moved, letting the puke splatter on his sneakers. Thankfully, his stomach had been nearly empty.

Eric tried to look away and couldn't.

Tommy exaggerated a deep inhalation. "Festive, don't you think?"

"No," Eric barely said.

"The house has an eternal memory. It can recall anything and everything. It does this, very often I have found, through smell. They say that smell is the strongest sense for recalling experiences. Have you heard that? I guess not. This house knows what it does. I hope you at least realize that, dear brother. There is logic to everything that happens here and to everyone connected with this place. The candy apple smell is for you. Well, actually, it is for us both. It is for memory."

"For what memory? The last time we were here together? For four years ago? For Ed?" Anger concealed his disgust.

"No—for *our* mother."

"What?"

"I promised you answers. But they are not all for me to give. The house must give them to you."

Eric started to interrupt, to ask how exactly the house was going to give answers when, so far as knew, the house could not speak, but the words stopped in his throat. While the hungry fingers kept picking at Kevin, the side of the furnace rippled like the surface of water. A black boot appeared followed by a jean-clad leg. An arm slipped out and then half of a torso was exposed. The person wore a man's dress shirt; Eric could not tell the color but everything glowed red. The person's head came next and then the rest of the body. For a moment, Eric had no idea who it was that had appeared—not stepped from behind the furnace but stepped *out* of it. Then he recognized who it was and knew he was in more trouble than he ever could have imagined.

"Hello, Eric," Tommy's father said.

CHAPTER 33

Eric had not seen the man since the wake for Ed, but he knew it was him. His body was frailer than Tommy's, but the resemblance was strong in the face, especially in the grin that he now flashed. Eric hadn't noticed that similarity four years ago, but now he knew very clearly that Tommy's dementia was a family affair.

Tommy's father stepped forward, glanced at the tentacles finishing the last few pieces of Kevin. The furnace's rumbling had quieted some. "So, the time has finally arrived."

"This is how the house wants it," Tommy said. "Complete truth."

When Tommy's father spoke, his voice wavered with emotion, but his eyes remained fixed and his body stiff. "Your father loved your mother quite a lot, I think. As I loved my wife. She died, my wife, but you know that. She passed away when Tommy was barely two months old, so he has only the memories of her I give him. We had moved to this town when he was born. The American Dream. A family, a home, a beautiful life. When she died, so did that dream. People suffer horrible events and bemoan how things weren't supposed to be like this. Well, I can honestly tell you that it wasn't. I understand the pain people feel when their dreams die. People don't plan for disaster, for devastation, for a car accident. There are no answers—only grief.

"Your parents moved into the neighborhood the year before she died. We all became friends. It was such a wonderful click. We weren't merely friends—the connection was deeper than some families enjoy. We spent so much time together. Wonderful days.

"When a drunk driver killed my wife, your parents were there for me. They truly were my family. Your mother would come over with Steve and make sure I was surviving. She became a surrogate mother to Tommy. When the depression was really severe, your parents took me and Tommy into their home. Your mother raised my boy for a while. Without her, I don't think I would have survived.

"What I'm about to tell you, your father already knows. He would never tell you, though. After your mother died, I felt you should know, but he refused. Your mother and father agreed that it wasn't necessary and he stuck to that. I conceded to them because of all I owed them, but the thought was always there, the words at the edge of my lips. I couldn't tell you until the moment was right, until things came together in the right way. Now they are."

Eric's heart was thumping so heavily. He knew what Tommy's father was about to say, but it couldn't be possible. His mother had cheated, but had the deception gone deeper than sex? The anger started building rapidly. He would not accept it. Even so, he needed to hear the words.

"*I'm* your father," Tommy's father said.

"No," Eric said.

"Your mother was so good to me. We never planned on it happening, Eric. You should know that, but sometimes things do happen and there is no explanation. People connect and that connection gets deeper. Your mother and father fought about me. She insisted I needed their support. He was threatened.

"One night after they fought, your mother came to me with tears in her eyes. I took her in my arms and kissed her. I remember the look in her eyes when she pulled back, a mix of surprise and recognition. She was so beautiful. She knew what I needed and I knew what she did, too."

"No. Stop." Eric wanted to charge him, choke him, kill him.

"You know I'm right. If you search your soul, you know I'm telling the truth. Your mother was not trying to hurt your father, but, of course, that was unavoidable. Your mother refused to have me in her home, however. When she refused, I learned something even more wonderful about your mother. She would give me what I needed, but not at the disgrace of the home she had forged with her husband. For the same reason, she refused to come back to my house. It may seem stupid, but I found it incredibly noble and heartwarming."

"Shut up," Eric hissed. He couldn't do anything else, his body again frozen, ears forced to listen.

"This house has been empty for as long as anyone knows. That's what it wants. Permanent residents would limit its freedom. Without that freedom, it could never open the world to people like us. People who are destined for something greater than what normal life offers. Your mother was one of those people and she discovered the power of this place the first time.

"She had an incredible sweet tooth, your mother. It was amazing she kept such a wonderful figure. It was October that first time. I kissed her and she kissed back and said she had to get out of her house. We went for a walk, but she had to have one of her sweets. She had made candied apples with Steve only the day earlier. She said they tasted even better after congealing in the fridge over night.

"We left the house and walked beneath the stars while she licked and sucked on her candied apple. That did it for me, I think—her eating that apple. I stopped her outside this house, told her that I loved her, and kissed her. We expected the house to be locked. It wasn't, of course, and in this place we had each other."

Eric's stomach swirled with bile. "It's your fault," Eric said. "You seduced her. You made her cheat on my father."

Tommy's father chuckled. It sounded like bones clattering. "I am not ashamed for what happened. I am saddened only that I didn't find her before your father. But that isn't entirely correct. People find each other,

394

Eric, when they need them. Your mother and I came together because we needed each other. That night in the house, we discovered intimate depths that I never knew existed. I want you to know the truth because you are the product of the love we shared.

"You fear this house; I see that in your eyes. This is no place to fear if you are ready to embrace your destiny. Perhaps that fate was sealed so many years ago when you were conceived, or maybe it was ordained far earlier. I know great things because of this house, but I don't know all. It is not for me to know.

"What I do know, however, is how the roof let in the stars while your mother and I lay on the third floor. It vanished or changed, but the stars that speckled the sky came down to us or maybe we rose to them. The darkness gave way to the most magical light you can imagine. A white sky dotted with shining stars. We knew then that this house wasn't an abandoned home, but a magical temple where love could blossom."

The white sky with stars. "I don't believe anything you're saying."

"Yes, you do." He strolled toward them. Tommy remained near Eric, hammer in his hands. "You can't deny truths, especially not in the house that built them. I loved your mother and she loved me. We came to this house many, many times after that October night. When she discovered she was pregnant with you, she confessed to your father. I hoped he would divorce her and then I could have her for my own. But I doubted the

395

depth and capacity of your mother's heart. She refused to let him go."

Eric's hands were fists. His fingers dug into the soft flesh of his palm. Everything Tommy's father said was true and that only enraged Eric further.

"When you were born, as I said, it was decided not to confess this truth. It has haunted me for so long. I am glad to have confessed it. Your mother would bring you over. I think that was against your father's wishes, but she did it anyway because she knew a father should see his son. She was a mother to Tommy, as well. It was so good for a while.

"Things changed. She didn't visit as often. She refused to love me. Refused to come here. Your mother turned her back on this place. That's when she cursed herself. Everything comes back. That's the order of things. Her denial came back to her when you entered this place. The house claimed what it was owed."

Tommy slapped his arm around Eric's shoulder. "See, brother, you *did* kill her."

The rage came out in a torrent so quickly that Eric didn't realize he could move again until he had landed a punch across Tommy's face and tackled him to the concrete. The hammer dropped somewhere. He had control of the fight, purely out of surprise, landing scattered punches across Tommy's face, throat, and chest. A crotch hit from Tommy's knee turned the tide very quickly. They rolled across the floor toward Katie. The fingers of the many hands were sliding over Katie's body, unable to find a place to start ripping. The hammer lay near her.

Tommy stopped them a foot from Katie and smacked Eric across the face three times. Each hit stung worse than the previous. Eric cried out. Tommy laughed and sat up. Eric didn't hesitate. His face burned and blood was falling from his nose down his throat, but he refused to surrender, not in this house of lies. He punched Tommy in the throat. Tommy grabbed his throat immediately, choking. Eric tried to punch the same spot again, but Tommy batted his hand away.

Then Tommy's father was on top of Eric, shoving him back against the floor. Tommy's weight shifted forward as well. Father and son smiled the same. Gasps of air choked in Tommy's throat, but his father didn't notice. He seized Eric's throat and leaned forward. His breath stank of candied apples. "Your mother was such a good fuck. I was so sad she refused me. I could have spent my life fucking her, hearing her cry out in pleasure. She loved when I dominated her, when I showed her I was a man. She liked that, you see, because your father is such a pussy. Little crybaby can't accept fate. But I can and have.

"Your mother would never come here again, but I visited this place every night. And that's when I found the real wonder here. It led me to this basement, to the secrets it holds down here—in there." He nodded his head to the gaping hole. "In there is the most wonderful things you can imagine. But there is a cost that accompanies such glory. A burden was set on my shoulders. The house gives power and glory, but it demands something in return. It showed me what it wanted and I provided it. Do you know what it wanted, Eric?" Spit accompanied each word. "Do you have any idea? It wanted Marge Trent. And I gave her to it."

Marge Trent. 1974. She had disappeared on her way to her boyfriend's house on Jackson Drive. Eric tried to picture the articles about her, but only one headline came to mind: *Police Abandon Search for Missing Teen.*

"The house knew she would be passing by. It knew no one would see. I grabbed her, killed her, and gave her to the house. It devoured her piece by piece and then rewarded me. You know how I killed her? I sliced her throat."

Father and son chuckled like that had been the punch line to a gruesome joke. Tommy's father squeezed Eric's throat more tightly until Eric's face flushed from lack of oxygen and then released his grip. His fingers were long and knotty like branches and his fingernails were yellow and cracked. He and Tommy stood. Eric inhaled several times without success until his lungs expanded and he choked himself into a sitting position. The hammer was only a few feet away.

"Do you remember what's left in my pillowcase?" Tommy asked.

The rope and an envelope. Eric's throat burned too much to speak.

Tommy lifted the pillowcase and removed the envelope. "You think you know what's in here. Can't speak? Throat burns, right? Well, let me speak for you.

You think I killed Ed. You've always believed that, but you're wrong. Just like with your mother—*you* killed him.

"When you ran away, we thought you'd run right to the police. There was no time to do what should have been done. Ed was never supposed to leave this place. That was a disgrace, and you caused it. I never took you for a complete coward, which you proved yourself to be. I really appreciate you not running to the cops, but don't think that I came here with a pre-written suicide note. That was created after Ed hanged.

"He didn't fight it, either. Dad knew he wouldn't. It was my time, you see, to accept my destiny, to embrace my burden. Ed knew there was no escape. You should have listened to him, though I doubt it would have helped. He was right to stay away because he was not chosen for the splendor. He was needed to prove my worth."

"You *did* kill him," Eric managed to choke out.

"Stop thinking so bluntly, brother. Death is not what you imagine it to be. Death is merely another state of existence. And in this house, death is a gateway to something else. For some, it is a path to heaven, a trip to darker lands for others. Murder is not what you imagine it to be. The taking of a life is an empowering thing. You not only know what God feels, you *become* God. When I say I didn't kill Ed, I'm not lying. The house guided me to him and him to me. The house orchestrated what must happen."

"No," Eric tried to yell. "You're insane. Both of you!"

That shared smile again. Tommy opened the envelope and removed a sheet of lined paper that was yellowed with age. "After your slut of a mother refused to be with our father anymore, he found true love in this house. The house led him to a man who had known the Hudson House burden but who had been denied its greatest reward."

Far above them a crash sent tremors down into the basement. The furnace rumbled loudly, perhaps in anger. Still the fingers were not dissecting Katie's body. Was her chest gently rising and falling? Tommy didn't flinch.

"This letter is to my father from that man. It is only one of many but it is the only one that matters because it is where this man bestows the glory of this house onto my father and commands him to share the brilliance as he failed to do." Tommy opened the crinkled letter and read: " 'Accept the house as your destiny and share this responsibility with your sons. In them, the house will know the greatness it deserves. Whatever the house commands, you must do. To turn your back is to guarantee death. I lost my chance, but it may be for a reason. The house knows what it is doing. I was not the chosen one—perhaps you are. And if not you then it is your sons who will know what it is to be gods. The house is very hungry. Open the world for them and let the house have them. Your friend, Hox Grent.' "

"No," Eric whispered. Tommy's father had taken over Grent's gruesome chore of abducting teenagers, killing them, and feeding them to the house. Worse still, Grent said that it was the sons who should continue the house's bidding. Not the son, but the *sons*. "He was a serial killer."

"He was a pioneer," Tommy said. "A chosen one, but not *the* one. That is for us to discover. Stand up brother and accept your destiny. You know the truth now, and it is time to face Hudson House. It is collecting, and you're past due." Tommy dropped the letter and removed the bundle of thick rope from the pillowcase. He curled one end around his hand, dropped the rest, and stretched the rope between his hands.

Hoping he wasn't doing exactly what the house wanted, Eric rolled toward Katie, grabbed the hammer, and stood. The furnace rumbled behind him, the many pipes shaking. And somewhere far away a scream floated. *I'm losing it*, Eric thought. He adjusted his grip on the hammer to hold it with both hands.

Tommy laughed. "Brothers don't fight. They unite." He turned to his father who dropped his arms to his sides. Tommy dropped the roped behind his father, looped it around the other end, and pulled it tight in a crude knot. He wrapped the rope around his father, pinning the man's arms to his body. Tommy's father didn't offer the least resistance. "The will to live, to survive, is strong," Tommy said. "Even though our father has accepted his role, acceptance is not always a guarantee. Things will go much more easily if there's no chance he can fight."

"I am not the one the house needs," Tommy's father said. "I didn't want to believe that for a long time, but I finally realized that I was only a piece of what the house wanted. Your mother was another piece, and the final piece is both of you, my sons."

Eric raised the hammer, no longer sure what to do. "I'm not your son."

Tommy finished wrapping the rope around his father and then added a final knot. The rope covered him from shoulders to knees. Despite his confines, excitement lit his eyes.

A loud crash echoed down from above.

"For several years I knew nothing of this place except what kids say. The girl who killed herself on the third floor. The ghosts that walked the halls after dark. The usual. I didn't learn the truth until the night Ed died four years ago. My father, *our* father, left me alone so many nights when he was here. I had to raise myself." Anger settled into his voice. "At least you had a dad, even if he wasn't your true father. You weren't alone. You had your mother, too. She cared for me and then abandoned me as she did our father. I had nothing. There's no way you can understand that. My father thinks he knows pain but he doesn't know abandonment. He doesn't know the anguish."

His father only stared at the furnace with those eager eyes. Was he blocking out all that Tommy said? What should Eric do with the hammer?

"I told you how I followed him here. How I never slept. He would tell me to stay in bed or the monsters would get me, but they were going to get me no matter what. Now, they're going to get you."

He clamped a hand on his father's shoulder; the man did not respond. Tommy punched him in the face. His father screamed in surprise and pain but did not turn to him.

Tommy stepped back, took a breath. "I saw him take Vanessa Wiles. A teenage whore. I remember seeing her name in the paper. Said she was missing. But I knew better. I saw my father grab her outside of this house. She screamed once. I stayed outside for hours, hoping for another scream, but none came.

"I made you and Ed come here because I needed to know the truth. I expected to find my father and maybe Vanessa's body, but I found something better, *much* better. This house really is special, brother, and while I may hate my father for leaving me for this place, I accept it because this place is bigger than that—it's bigger than everyone."

Eric lowered the hammer, but not all the way. This could be one of Tommy's tricks. That was a possibility, but the strength of Tommy's emotions gave his words credence. He had endured great pain and it had molded him into a psychopath.

Tommy raised his scarred hand. "The house marked me as it would have you. We are destined to do its work, and it starts right now with our father."

The anger Eric had only minutes earlier now completely vanished. He lowered the hammer even more. He couldn't kill someone, certainly not some tied up sacrifice. "The house never told me to do anything," Eric said.

"Yes, it has. You just haven't listened to it. Do this, do it with me, and all the world will be ours. There is no stronger bond than that between brothers. We are brothers forever as created right here in this house."

Eric needed to stall him and find a way out for himself. *Like you did when Ed needed you.* "Why isn't the house . . . taking Katie?"

Tommy seemed to notice her for the first time. The fingers entered her mouth, filled her throat, but came out empty. The surprised expression on Tommy's face gave way to a flash of aggression. He pounced on Katie, seized her head in both hands. Her chest was rising and falling. *Oh, shit.* The fingers slipped over Tommy's legs, explored. "It can't take her because there's no way in. It needs blood."

Tommy lifted her head. Katie's eyes opened. She screamed. Tommy paused, and in that moment Eric found something he dared call hope, and then Tommy slammed her head down against the concrete before Eric could yell, *"No!"* The back of her head caved in with a crunch. Gray liquid and blood oozed out. Tommy stepped back and the fingers eagerly leapt into Katie's fractured skull.

"Is that what you wanted to know? How this has to be done." Tommy turned to his father. "You have the hammer, Eric. The glory is yours."

"No."

404

"It's too late for cowardice. You can never leave. You must do what the house wants."

Eric let the hammer sag in his hand. "No. It ends now. I won't do anything. Too much blood has already been spilled in this place."

"I'm sorry, brother, but you don't get a choice."

"You always have a choice." The hammer dropped from his hand, clattered on the floor.

Tommy bowed his head, defeated.

"The house can't keep us here, not if we refuse to stay," Eric said. "This place isn't God or even *a* god— it's a sewer of hate and misery that traps injured souls and manipulates them with lies. You aren't its slave, Tommy. You're another one of its victims."

Several seconds passed before Tommy shook his head side to side. "You stupid, stupid, fool." He turned, fresh rage in his eyes. "I gave you the chance for eternal glory, for power you can't imagine. And you stepped back. You're my brother and you will not shame me like this."

"Untie me," Tommy's father said, "and I'll help you deal with him." He was out of his trance now, eyes frantic with bloodlust.

"No. *I* will do what the house wants."

"Tommy—"

But that was all Eric got out before Tommy charged and plowed him against the stone wall. Eric's back smacked the wall but he was quick enough to keep his head forward, preventing a skull-crushing collision. Tommy bared his teeth and growled as he pulled Eric toward him and then thrust him back against the wall. This hurt even more and managed to nick the back of his head. The world swirled for a moment.

The hammer was somewhere nearby on the floor. The radiating red converted the floor into a blood pool. Tommy's father—(*not my father*)—swayed as if he might fall over. The world started to settle back on a level surface and then Tommy drove Eric into the wall again. Pain flushed throughout his back and around his sides. His head only grazed the wall but that was enough to set the world on a tilt again. He couldn't breathe.

Tommy gripped Eric beneath his chin and brought his other hand back for the knockout punch. Three fists swirled before Eric's eyes. Tommy only wanted blood. Eric felt that if he stepped forward his legs would give out on him, but he had to try. He couldn't surrender. He owed that much to his mother.

The punch rocketed forward and Eric hit the elbow of Tommy's rigid arm. The pressure broke his hold. Eric dropped to his knees as Tommy's fist crashed into the concrete. He howled, falling away, clutching his scarred hand that throbbed now with broken bones.

Tommy raised his arms over his head, good hand covering injured one to form a battering ram, and released from a reserve of pain a scream that sprouted goose bumps on Eric's sweating arms. Tommy came at him and Eric dove forward on the floor between his legs.

Tommy's hands crashed onto Eric's back. Eric fell flat on his stomach, air rushed out of his lungs. Tommy laughed, amused and enraged. Eric's hands flailed across the concrete and found the handle of the hammer.

Somehow Eric found the strength to adjust his grip on the hammer, flip onto his side, and drive the claw end of the hammer into Tommy's calf. Tommy's shriek echoed throughout the basement, drowning out for a moment the furnace's rumble. From the corner of his eye, Eric watched the fingers ripping off one of Katie's breasts.

Tommy stumbled several feet, grabbed the hammer, and yanked it out of his leg. Blood soaked his jeans. He held the hammer before him like the injury was the tool's fault. Eric tried to scramble to his feet and couldn't; the floor was slipping beneath him. Tommy's father hopped toward his son, "Untie me. Untie me and we'll get him."

Spinning with the hammer in his hand, Tommy pointed it at his father who immediately stopped, lost balance, and collapsed. He hit the floor with a heavy thud and cried out. "I will do what must be done," Tommy said. "And that will start with you, *father*." The last word dropped as an indictment.

The hammer arced through the air toward the man's face. Something crashed onto the stairs and stumbled rapidly down the steps. The distraction lifted Tommy's head at the last moment: the head of the hammer cracked across the man's nose. Blood spurted out in a wave.

"*EHHRRRIC!*" He recognized the garbled scream right away. Why he had come here didn't matter. Timing was the important thing. For once, Eric was glad to see his brother.

His *real* brother.

CHAPTER 34

Steve dropped off of the last couple steps and stumbled into the light. His clothes stuck to him from sweat. *Not sweat, something else.* Liquid fell from Steve's clothes steadily, pattering the floor wherever he walked. He moved with the drunken gait of an experienced alcoholic, unsteady but direct. He stopped, scanned the scene. "I warned you to stay away," he said more to himself than to Eric. "Don't come here. Hudson House wants you."

Tommy stepped away from his father. "What do you want, junkie?"

Steve shuffled toward Tommy but spoke to Eric in a voice laced with tears. "I'm sorry, bro. I'm sorry for not keeping you away from this place. It's my fault. It wouldn't let me do more. It haunted me, tracked me through endless nightmares. I tried to warn you. I knew it would come to this. The house showed me this. I've stopped nothing. All those cards did nothing—Hudson House wants you and now it has you. I'm sorry, bro." His shirt was ripped, hanging open where the demon tattoo glistened.

Eric managed to stand. "Cards? You left those Halloween invitations?"

"Something sour, something sweet, loads of goodies for you to eat," Steve said in a monotone. "You're invited because HH wants you."

"Brothers Forever."

"That's right, bro. It wouldn't let me write anything else. I thought I was making a difference sneaking those cards into your locker, but I was only doing what the house wanted. I couldn't see that until today, until we spoke. I saw it in your eyes—I knew you were coming here."

"Enough of the sob story," Tommy said. "We're all here now, linked to this place in one way or another. If this is what the house wants then I am proud to do its will." He raised the hammer and stepped toward Steve, who paused, raised his own hand. The gesture surprised Tommy, halted him.

Faintly, underlying the potent candied-apple stink, another smell lingered and grew stronger. At first Eric couldn't place the smell, unable to decipher it from the overbearing candy aroma, and then a flame flashed out of Steve's hand and Eric remembered the can of lighter fluid.

"I won't let this place live," Steve said.

Tommy didn't panic. "You can't kill it. God never dies." He lunged toward Steve, bringing down the hammer. Steve raised his other arm in defense and the flame caught the underside of his soaking shirt. A wall of flame erupted from his arm, blocking his face. The hammer vanished into that fire.

Within seconds, the fire completely consumed Steve. Tommy tried to pull back, the hammer no longer in his grip, but couldn't. They tangled together and fell, Steve on top. Their screams mixed—the sound of animals in a slaughterhouse.

Flames rippled across Steve's back, melting his shirt and his flesh. The fire covered his legs and then jumped onto the floor. The fire burned steadily on the concrete and then raced up the stairs, tracing Steve's path. Steve meant to take the house with him and, surprisingly enough, the fire seemed to be catching.

Maybe the place can *be destroyed.* That optimism faded with his brother's cries as he showered flames over Tommy. *I knew it would come to this. The house showed me this.* The house knew what it was doing. It had planned this. You couldn't stop God's will; you could only fool yourself thinking otherwise while you fell right in step with His wishes.

Tommy landed a punch that knocked Steve off of him. Steve recoiled from the hit, fell back toward the stairs. The flames eating his body pushed both the darkness and the red light away. Steve's hands curled into fleshy balls and his nose was dripping onto the floor. He had stopped screaming and now stood as a burning statue.

Tommy's laughter rolled with the fluctuating peaks and falls of a psychopath. He stood, back to the furnace, red light radiating across his face, hammer in hand.

Smoke wafted off burnt patches on his clothes. The fingers that had torn apart three bodies now curled around Tommy's feet and crawled up his legs. His laugh made it clear who was going to win.

"You can't fight God," he said.

Tommy's father rolled back and forth on the ground, gargling on his own blood and saying something again and again that might have been *Help me.*

Tommy appraised him. "This is how the house wants it."

His father begged in gagging, desperate noises.

The hammer cracked him between the eyes, burying into his brain. "The sacrifice is done," Tommy said.

Some of the fingers leaped at the man's exposed brain and started spelunking for human tissue, but a few remained on Tommy's legs. Did Tommy realize what was going to happen? Was it all part of the house's will?

Steve dropped to his knees. His arms hung limply, skin oozing off like candle wax. His clothes had completely burned off and his skin had blackened in places while bubbling in others. The gruesome sight should have brought forth the bile Eric had been battling, but it didn't.

"E*hhh*ric." Steve's lips had melted off and now his teeth were blackening in his jaw.

Steve fell forward. His face splashed on the concrete and the fire ate away at his body.

"I'm your real brother," Tommy said. "He was a drug addict. We are united here in this place. Accept the burden, brother. Accept it and discover glory."

"You're wrong. Steve *is* my brother. You're the addict."

"There is so much you don't under—"

Tommy screamed. The fingers had discovered the bleeding gash in his calf as Eric knew they would. They dug deeper into his leg while other fingers braced the leg in place. He tried to move and fell over. His leg snapped. The fingers were stuck to his legs like the tentacles of those ocean sea creatures. Sometimes the tentacles were lined with sharp claws.

The first fingers pulled back from Tommy's leg with a flabby chunk of tissue that could be calf muscle. It vanished into the dark hole. More hands with hungry fingers emerged from the hole. Some went for Tommy's father, others for Tommy. He screamed and screamed until his shouts shrank to hollow gasps. The fingers worked quickly. Tommy was soon without one leg and then neutered and then his guts spilled out across the floor for the fingers to pick at.

Tommy's mouth moved but no words came out. Eric stepped toward him. In a hollow, pathetic voice, Tommy said, "The house is everything." Then his eyes rolled back in his head and he fell limp.

Eric watched for several minutes while the furnace rumbled and the fingers tore at Tommy and Tommy's father. *My father*, Eric thought. Biologically, that man might be his father, but he hadn't raised him and, no matter what he said, he hadn't really loved Eric's mother, not the way Eric's father did.

Yet, grief was a weird thing. It had driven Eric into yellowed newspaper articles of kidnappings. His father had abandoned life for the endless adoration of photographs. Tommy's father had sought comfort from a house that promised glory but delivered instead madness and misery. What was the measure of love? Or guilt?

Eric stepped to what remained of Steve's burning body. Eric had once hated Steve more than anyone, feared him, loathed him. Steve hadn't served well as an older brother—he had been a tormentor, a ridiculer, a crucifier. Love had not been in their shared vocabulary. Steve may have even enjoyed breaking Eric's nose four years ago. Vengeance for mom.

Her death *had* been Eric's fault. The engagement ring proved that. She had made a mistake with Tommy's father and had paid for it once the living proof of that mistake stepped across the threshold of this place. She had signed the contract, and Eric had been the executor. The house had placed a burden on his shoulders: a burden of pain.

In the end, however, Steve had proven himself to be the better brother. Driven unstable by nightmares and fears for Eric's fate, Steve had come here to take down Hudson House and had saved Eric's life.

The fire had diminished, but Steve was no longer recognizable, nothing more than a mass of charred flesh. Eric was not disgusted. That was not his brother on the floor of this place. What was his brother had simply vanished, transcended the darkness that almost destroyed him. Eric loved his brother, now and forever. He hoped Steve knew that. Somehow, *someway*, he hoped Steve took that love with him when he left. Brotherly love was deep—it ran in their veins, after all.

The fire marking Steve's dripping descent continued roaring on the basement steps where it spiked five feet high or more. There was no more than a foot of safe space on the individual steps and even then attempting to ascend them would certainly char his skin. That was if the gathering black smoke didn't kill him first.

He moved back from the steps. His brother's remains glowed like the embers of a dying fire. The fingers ripped apart Tommy's face, pushing through his eyelids and destroying his eyeballs while other fingers crawled out of his mouth and then yanked out his tongue. His father's torso still remained, though the fingers had already removed his head.

In this house of death, in this basement where evil took human shape, Eric would die. He knew that very clearly and was not afraid. He hadn't wanted it to come to this, but when playing against Fate, you were always dealt a losing hand. He wouldn't fight it. He would be proud to die where his brother had sacrificed himself and where their mother had conceived him. The only question was whether to set himself on fire or feed himself to the fingers.

Sudden cold raced up his spine. Eric turned around to face the woman in white. Her face shimmered a few inches from his. She smiled, touched his hand. Cold coursed up his arm and across his body, soothing, relaxing cold. Then she turned and led him to the stairs.

She didn't pull him, but he went with her in-step. She paused at the bottom of the steps before the growing peaks of fire, and smiled. The smile hung in Eric's mind while he followed her up the steps. Her face held so much beauty that were she real, Eric would kiss her, love her. She wasn't real, though, only an illusion sent to save him.

The fire popped and cracked around him, but Eric's body remained cool even when he stepped directly onto the flames. The woman did not turn to him again, her long, brown hair obscuring her face. She did not pause when they entered the pantry, but moved directly to the shut door. Flames licked at the walls while a brilliant array of colors swirled beneath, melting and reforming endlessly. Eric tried to pull back, not wanting to touch the door covered with the whirling colors. Without pulling him, she walked *through* the door and he followed. For the few seconds that he was passing through the door, roasting coals surrounded him and the stench of baking skin filled his nostrils.

The cold serenity returned when they were in the kitchen. The fire continued in here as well. Wallpaper peeled, charred, and melted. They continued through the kitchen into the coat room and into the foyer where flames slithered up between the floorboards.

Steve's Trans Am sat half in the living room. The wall had collapsed around it, covering the car in debris.

Fire raged across its hood and burned across the floor straight through the living room to the dining room. Outside, the night was still. No one had noticed. *Or they were too afraid to*, Eric thought.

The front door stood open. When the woman released his hand, the cooling sensation drained away. He stepped toward the door and turned back. The woman stood there, a faint smile tickling the corner of her lips.

"I'm sorry, mom," he said.

Still, he couldn't leave. He partly feared not being able to leave, that the door would shut on him or the walkway would open and suck him underground, but he was more afraid that the house wanted him to leave because it knew he would be back. Eventually, he'd come back. The house had its plans and there was nothing Eric could do to alter them. *HH is collecting and you're past due.* That fear—the fear of recognizing his own helplessness—kept Eric frozen in place.

His mother dropped her head back, raised her arms, and howled. The sound echoed not in the house, but inside Eric's mind. Her arms ripped open in long gashes. Blood seeped from the wounds and flowed down toward her face.

Eric ran out of the house before the blood hit the floor.

* * *

The teenagers spraying shaving cream on each other and the scattered trick-or-treaters still making the rounds didn't acknowledge him. None of them noticed the demise of Hudson House. It was easier to turn away. That was how it had always been. Kids had gone in there and never come out, but it was easier to turn away. Easier to ignore the truth and get on with life. People are afraid to face the darkness—they're afraid of what they might see.

Though he ran more quickly than he had four years ago, Eric's legs were smaller and his house farther away. Even when he made it home, he still heard the fire crunching away at the floors of Hudson House. Would the fire level the house? Would the place finally die?

Eric entered his father's study. It was time for a full confession. "Dad, I have to tell you . . ."

His father lay on the floor. In one hand he held a folder piece of paper and in the other a framed photograph, the one he had been admiring earlier. Eric didn't need to run to his father to confirm that he was dead. Suicide or something popping in his brain, the house had gotten him, too. The house had a plan, a grand scheme, and Eric was its pawn. Ed's mother had been right. God was cruel, and we are all His pawns.

Eventually, he found the nerve to go to his father and touch him; his body was already cooling. Eric waited for the tears, but they did not come. He wanted only to sleep. He was completely alone now—just him and that goddamn house.

He took the piece of paper and read it. The tears started slowly and by the time he finished, he couldn't stop crying.

The letter, written in lovely cursive read,

Dear Son,

You are only just born, but there is a heavy burden placed on you already. I have done something shameful for which I'm afraid you may suffer. There are things you deserve to know, but which I can never tell you. I love you so much. Always remember that. And whenever you read this, I want you also to remember that none of this was your fault. None of it. Love is a curse, Eric, but it is also a blessing. Love is everything. Never think otherwise.

Love forever,

Mom

He tugged the framed picture from his father's hand. He had never seen most of the pictures on his father's desk, too nervous to go close enough to view them. They were of his mother, of course, younger photographs when his parents had been dating, had been young lovers infatuated with each other.

This picture caught his mother forever in a gesture that suggested dancing, her face a glorious smile, her dress a startling white, her brown hair flowing toward her waist, the background a sparkling field of ivory. It was when she had been young and beautiful and when she had betrayed her husband and conceived a child with another man in a place of Hell.

CHAPTER 35

Eric ran back to Mangle Lane and sprinted toward the far corner where it intersected with Jackson Drive. Before he made it halfway, he knew everything was ruined. Hudson House had not burned to the ground.

There was no fire, no smell of charred wood. Steve's Trans Am was parked on the gravel driveway. The house stood as it always did: strong and formidable. The large maple in the front yard swayed its branches back and forth and somewhere deep inside the house someone was laughing.

Eric walked onto the lawn and went to the porch and climbed the steps one creak at a time. Behind him, kids were running around and laughing. They had not seen what had happened here at the corner of Mangle Lane and Jackson Drive. They had turned away from the darkness and been spared.

Eric was not as lucky.

He stood in front of the solid front door and knew Tommy was right. This was his destiny. Right here. If he turned his back on this place and walked away and somehow managed to carve out a life for himself, the house would find a way to bring him back. Maybe he'd get married, have a family. And one day, his son would walk up these steps and seal his own fate. There was no escape.

Eric opened the screen door and then grabbed the front door knob and turned. The door opened with a gentle *swoosh*. Eventually, he'd make his way back down to the basement, but first he needed to pay his respects. As he walked up the stairs toward the third floor, the front door closed behind him. Something held sway here, something that dealt in death, and it decided what happened next and how much blood fell.

Dear Reader,

Thank you for reading. As a special bonus, please enjoy a Hudson House story, "The House on Mangle Lane." There are many more stories to share about the house on the corner of Mangle Lane and Jackson Drive and I sincerely hope you enjoy this one. It was, up until this edition, available only as a separate ebook. It is my pleasure to offer it here.

Thank you,
Chris DiLeo (writing as J.T. Warren)
July 2011 (updated June 2018)
P.S. After the story, please enjoy an excerpt from *The Devil Virus*, available soon from Bloodshot Books.

1
1981

Soon it would be Halloween. On that night, the house would show him what it really wanted, and how it would satisfy his every desire. The house on the corner of Mangle Lane and Jackson Avenue had stood for thousands of years, though none of the suburban neighbors surrounding it would have ever recognized the house as a holy sanctuary, as a gift from beyond, as a blessing from forces far greater than the human brain could even comprehend. For the residents of the Stone Edge Development, the house was just an abandoned building where teenagers sometimes gathered to drink and smoke pot and wasn't it past time for the Town Council to have the place condemned and razed already?

They didn't understand. They couldn't comprehend what the house offered because they had long ago shut out their minds to things of unlimited possibilities. For most people, the house was so far in the background it didn't even exist. They were too weak to let in the mighty forces that lived and pulsed through every inch of Hudson House. They let the towering evergreens surrounding it keep it separate from their lives. They walked or drove past it quickly. They never turned to admire the mighty oak tree in the front yard or the simple, yet inviting design known as the American

Foursquare. Aging plywood that matched the gray tones of the sagging front porch covered the lower windows, but the third floor windows, dormers, were open and protruded from the house like engorged eyes. The house watched the world around it and for the one it invited to look back, the one who stared into those eyes, the house offered divine promise.

Hudson House would give him what he wanted, but only if he did its will.

Thy will be done. He smiled.

He walked down Mangle Lane slowly, though his heart pounded frantically. It was tough to control his excitement. He wanted to run there, fall to his knees beneath that oak tree and stare up at those third floor windows and declare his faith. Someone might notice and then the police would be involved and things could get difficult. If he did something so blatant, the house might still shield him, but he was in no position to test the power of Hudson House. That could come later.

First, the house demanded a sacrifice.

Wind pushed his coat open behind him like a cape. The brisk air soothed his hot flesh and filled his nostrils with the gloriously sweet aromas of apples and firewood and pumpkin pie. And beneath that pushing breeze was the undertow of the house. It pulled him closer with invisible arms that had gotten so much stronger as the hot summer melted into the cool fall.

The house was building its strength and it needed him to help.

Narrow flashlight beams crisscrossed back and forth inside the first floor.

He stood across from Hudson House on the opposite side of the street. Hands in his pocket, occasionally tipping back on his heels and gazing up at those open windows, he might have been an innocuous resident of this town just out for a stroll. He might have been like everyone else.

Except for the hot energy boiling inside him.

Except for the things he had to do.

Except for the blood that must be spilled.

Except for the almighty power he would soon wield.

Several teenagers erupted into laughter from inside the house. At least a few of the kids were girls. That gave him the chance to pick the best of the litter.

Thy will be done.

He moved across the street and toward the perimeter of the property where the evergreens stood as giant sentries.

2

Vanessa Wiles wasn't scared of Hudson House. It was just some abandoned building that elementary kids thought was haunted. Some girl had hanged herself on the third floor. She had used her father's neckties to do it. Vanessa didn't believe it. The house was too *average* for it to be scary. Haunted houses were hulking beasts with ornate architecture that spiraled to the sky and whipped back down around itself in complex webs.

Hudson House was just a three story suburban home on a block with nearly identical homes. Only the house at 51 Mangle Lane had been empty for as long as anyone could remember.

Carly had talked her into doing this and though it was stupid sneaking into an abandoned house to drink a few beers and smoke some pot, Vanessa didn't mind being inside. It was barren and smelled a little stale like the girl's locker room a day after a varsity soccer match, but it was somehow calming, welcoming.

The boys, on the other hand, were kind of stupid.

"I told you the door would be open," CJ said. "They board the windows but leave the door open. There's practically a sign inviting us in." He shoved Hector in that stupid playful, pseudo-violent way boys always do. He probably really wanted to hug Hector, maybe squeeze his ass. Non-threatening violent behavior between males could signal homoerotic tendencies. Vanessa had read that in a psychology book in the library when she did her research paper on kleptomaniacs. It was amazing how easily she got off topic.

"You think something's funny?" Hector was staring at her.

She hadn't realized she was laughing. By the time she noticed all eyes had turned on her, including that bitch Paula's and Will (who everyone called Whitey for some reason she hadn't really figured out), the play in her mind had led CJ and Hector to a porn scene where

Hector was wearing leather and CJ had on a little miniskirt.

Vanessa shook her head, looked down at the flashlight in her hands.

"That's what I thought," Hector said.

"Shut up, dick head." CJ pushed him again and then the two were mock wrestling in the large, empty space, which might have been a living room in some distant past.

There was no furniture anywhere. No signs of when anyone lived here. The walls were bare and clean without even a lighter spot or two where a picture might have hung. The place was so quiet too. Obviously the house was empty so it'd be quiet but there was something weird about noise here. Even as CJ and Hector groaned and grunted (bringing back that leather and miniskirt scenario and inducing more laughter she had to stifle), their sounds didn't seem to echo through the house, not even into the adjacent room, probably where the old family once ate dinner beneath some dim chandelier. Maybe that girl had been thinking of killing herself while eating right across from her father.

It was as though the sounds the boys made died after only a few feet.

Like the house ate them. The thought came from the darker regions of her mind and she tried to push it back into that mental abyss, but the thought persisted. They could scream and shout but the noise wouldn't go any further than a few feet. No one outside would hear a thing if something happened. Cold bumps sprouted across her arms. Still, though, she wasn't afraid. Not exactly. Not yet.

"We should have brought a chair or something," Carly said. She giggled like that was some kind of joke. She wobbled on her feet as if on the deck of a ship out on choppy seas.

"Why don't you sit on the floor," Vanessa said. "Before you fall."

"I know, right." Carly's legs tangled and she had to spring her arms out at her sides to prevent falling. She looked like a drunken tightrope walker, which she sort of was.

Whitey passed the joint to Tim, the last member of this gathering but the one most likely to vanish into the background. He took it gently and brought it to his pursed lips.

"You're not trying to kiss it," Whitey said. "You're just smoking it." He slapped Tim on the back.

When Tim finally got the joint in his mouth, his inhalation lasted a second or two before he bent over in a flurry of coughs. That brought the other three boys together in collective howls of amusement.

All the boys were on the football team but Tim was the kicker. This apparently meant that he was inferior in every way to all the other players. That seemed stupid considering the game was called FOOTball, but Tim was smaller, almost frail compared to the other guys, especially to CJ whose shoulders were wide and stretched his shirts to the breaking point. The way his chest tapered to his waist and his spindly legs reminded Vanessa of the action figures her little brother Kevin played with.

Hector and Whitey were somewhere between CJ's girth and Tim's skinniness. And that was exactly where she was—between Carly's tiny body with her perky breasts (she stuffed her bra, no doubt) and Paula's large hips and fat ass. Carly always got the boys and Paula always hung out with them. Vanessa always went for the ride and always went back to her own bed without having so much as a wandering, interested eye travel her way. She had known Carly her whole life and that had gained her access to worlds she never would have known as a loner, but that still hadn't helped her get anywhere with the boys. Carly had dated CJ on and off for the past two years—they were currently in an off phase—and Vanessa was their constant background set piece. The guys were losers anyway. At least that's what she always tried to tell herself.

Tim was looking at her now. He stood in place like a mannequin; his eyes bore down on her. CJ slapped him on the back and he blurted out a few more coughs to his teammates' delight, but he kept staring at her. She almost turned away, but maybe there was something to this. Maybe this was her night to get somewhere.

"Gimme that." Paula ripped the joint from Tim's hand and sucked on it hard. She joined the boys in their group.

"You could play checkers on that ass," Carly said. She stumbled again and grabbed Vanessa's arm for stability. "Maybe even water polo!" Her laughter pierced Vanessa's ears and the stench of beer on her breath almost made Vanessa gag. She pulled from Carly's grasp.

Carly hit the floor and bounced like a bag of sticks. Her head didn't touch the ground and she kept laughing, even harder now, so there was no harm done. She probably wouldn't even remember the fall tomorrow. She'd look at her hip and say, *Hey, where'd that bruise come from?* and that would be it.

Beams of light trailed across Carly's body like greedy hands. CJ, Hector, and Whitey laughed as they moved their flashlights from Carly's red face, across her giggling breasts, and down to the crotch of her jeans.

"That's the sweet spot right there," Whitey said. "It's calling to you, bro." He hugged CJ across the shoulders with one arm.

CJ smiled; the shadows on his face made his eyes look huge like the wolf in that fairy tale. "I already hit that," he said. "What don't you take the plunge?"

"Hector?" Whitey asked. "Care to go deep sea diving with your pole first?"

"Forget him," CJ said. "His pole isn't long enough."

"Fuck you guys," Hector said.

CJ and Whitey stared at him in silence for a moment and Hector began to step away as if he knew something bad was going to happen.

"That's your problem," Whitey said. "You're looking to fuck us when we ain't gay pervs like you."

"At least I didn't eat any stank pussy."

"Hey!" Carly yelled and then erupted into laughter.

"You even know what it tastes like?" Whitey asked.

CJ and Whitey moved in-step toward Hector like stealthy predators.

Hector pointed at Paula, who stopped, joint still in hand. "You said she stank of dead tuna fish and moldy ass."

Even Carly stopped laughing.

"Oh, shit!" Whitey stepped back and pushed CJ into the spotlight.

CJ smiled at Paula. It was that smile which got him anywhere and everywhere with girls. He was cute and strong, sure, but it was his smile, so boyish and disarming that made the girls want to jump him, that let him string them back and forth like a Yo-Yo.

"I never said that," he said. "You can trust me."

"You said the mole above her cunt looked like a piece of dried shit," Hector said.

"Asshole!" Paula launched herself at CJ. She could have been a raging hippo or a stampeding rhino.

Whitey and Hector stepped out of the way as Paula crashed into CJ and the two of them stumbled backwards into the next room. Paula screamed that CJ was a fucking shit head, an asshole who deserved to have his nuts cut off. CJ batted away her fists and spiraling arms while he laughed and said she ought to douche once in a while, give a man a reason to stay down there, it was stifling.

432

"Douche!" Carly yelled. She rolled back and forth to the rhythm of her own laughter.

Paula had managed to push CJ all the way to the far wall. Though he was still laughing, he was having a harder time fighting off her blows. Paula's fist smacked him in the side of the head and then across the face. Whitey and Hector moved closer, backs to Vanessa and Carly.

"Hi."

It was Tim. She had forgotten about him, but there he was, still staring at her like one of those nerdy kids who watched girls like scientists watched amebas. Football players didn't act like this. They weren't intimidated. But Tim was a kicker, after all. Probably inexperienced with girls, which was kind of cute.

"Hi," Vanessa said. Her body warmed. She smelled the faintest trace of a sweetness she knew but couldn't identify. His cologne, perhaps.

"You're so pretty."

"Thanks." Carly grabbed her foot and used it to keep her in place as she rocked her body back and forth.

Tim stepped closer. "I mean, like, really pretty. I'm sorry I've never noticed it before."

"That's okay." Heat radiated through her. Coming here had felt right, like something good was going to happen. Tim wasn't the cutest or best looking kid in the world but he was a boy and that was a start. She had taken the time to straighten her hair and put on some makeup. Not too much where she'd look like a whore like Paula, but more than Carly used. She could go *au naturel* and the boys would still try to grope her. She never seemed to get a zit or anything.

"Want to get out of here?" Tim asked.

What should she say? She was seventeen and this had never happened before. She had to play it cool, keep her heartbeat under control. "Where do you want to go?"

Far away it seemed, Paula was smacking CJ and spitting curses at him. It was like they had stepped outside, not simply a few feet away. Vanessa and Tim were practically alone. It was a trick of noise again. The house could be magical.

Tim stepped closer. His hot breath fluttered something inside her. "Something is not right here."

His voice had changed, lost pitch or tone or something. She brought her flashlight to his chin. Bloody veins filled his eyes and he smiled with only half his mouth like he'd forgotten how to do it the whole way. Heavy breaths fell from his mouth like exhaust from an engine trying to get started.

The heat vanished in a wash of cold, prickly skin. "Are you okay?"

"No." Tim moved even closer. His body odor itched her nose. "You're going to die here."

3

He had no idea how much time had passed. It didn't matter. Hudson House made its own time. When he eventually left here, when the sacrifice had been made, he would walk back to his house and sleep. He

434

would feel as if no time had passed at all, though several lifetimes might have bloomed into existence and been shattered to bits in that time. The house controlled those things, so he didn't have to worry about it.

He couldn't tell if he was sitting of standing. The evergreens had taken him in, absorbed him, hidden him. He was somewhere on the outer edges of what most people considered reality. He was on the cusp of penetrating the far deeper worlds where this house ruled as the almighty. Soon. Very soon.

A young man in a suit was walking a dog past the house. The man stopped to appreciate the house and jealousy raged within him. Who was this asshole in a suit with a stupid dog on a leash? He had no right to look at Hudson House. *It was mine. Mine!*

The man rubbed his eyes and yawned. He shook the leash. "Come on, already."

The dog was sniffing at the edges of the lawn which had overgrown enough for people to say, *shouldn't somebody cut that?* but not enough to any of them to want to go far enough to see the job handled. The grass would grow no longer. The house knew what it was doing. People didn't want to see the house and it didn't want them to, either. Only the chosen ones.

Only him.

The dog stepped onto the grass as if afraid the ground might give way at any second. Perhaps it would. Perhaps it would swallow both the dog and his asshole owner. Serve them right for looking at his house.

Laughter erupted inside the house. The flashlight beams shot out around the plywood-covered windows like a sunrise in a magical world.

The man stared at the house for a moment longer and then turned back to his dog. "Are you gonna go or you a tease like your damn mother?"

The dog looked up, tilted its head.

"Well?"

More laughter from inside and the sounds of a scuffle. Maybe the teenagers would beat each other into bloody near-lifeless masses. That would make things easier, though it would ruin much of the fun.

The dog whined.

"It's grass. Piss! Shit! Do what comes naturally."

The young man shoved the dog all the way onto the grass. It froze. Then its back legs started to shake and the hair on the back of its neck stood up in a large puff. The dog growled almost inaudibly.

"Hell's wrong with you? Are you gonna piss or what?"

The young man yanked on the leash and the dog yelped. The sound echoed down the block. The dog jumped off the lawn and ran into the street. It pulled the young man after it. A moment later, they were at the corner and then gone somewhere down Jackson Avenue.

Dogs might sense the power but their owners certainly didn't. The young man hadn't noticed the beams of light at the windows or heard the laughter from inside. The house kept those things contained. But not for him. The house wanted him to see and hear everything. He was the chosen one. This house was his destiny.

He took the knife out of his pocket. It felt heavy and fit his palm perfectly. Like it had been created only for him.

4

"That's not very funny," Vanessa said. In fact, it was downright scary. She had agreed to come here with Carly and a couple of the "football jocks" and now Carly was rolling around on the floor like a drunk and Tim was telling her she was going to die. He was supposed to be kissing her right now. What the hell had happened?

"It's not a joke," Tim said. *Dead.* That's what his voice sounded like. Like the voice of the dead.

"What's wrong with you?"

"I saw something. I'm trying to help."

"This isn't going to get me to make out with you." In her mind, however, she briefly imagined a sweaty session of vigorous groping.

"He's back."

"What? Who?"

"Hox Grent."

CJ had let Paula continue her barrage until she was breathing too heavily to yell anymore and her shoulders too sore to throw punches. When she stepped back from him, he smiled, and she called him an asshole.

"I'll be your backdoor man, baby."

437

"You the man, CJ. Whole hog!"

"Talk about hogs." CJ tilted his head toward Paula.

She was too tired to fight him again. Instead, she gave him the finger and turned around. "I'm leaving."

CJ was quick: he grabbed her arm and smiled that damn winning smile of his. "I'm sorry," he said. "We're just goofing. I never said any of that stuff."

"Douche!" Carly cried out amid more laughter.

"You know who he is?" Tim asked. "Hox Grent?"

"Yeah, so?"

Hox Grent had kidnapped kids back in the fifties and killed them in the basement of this house. He'd been caught and imprisoned. That was almost twenty years ago. Vanessa knew all the stories from kids at school and had heard some of the facts from her parents. The kids said Hox was possessed or something. Vanessa's parents had said Hox was mentally deranged. Perhaps the two conclusions weren't that far apart. He'd apparently chopped up the kids and fed the pieces to his dog. Only one body had ever been found, though speculations ran that Hox had killed eight, maybe ten or even more.

"He's coming for you," Tim said.

"Stop being a dick," she said. She sounded strong but her heart was racing and cold sweat broke out in the middle of her back beneath her bra strap.

"I want to help you. *Please*." Saliva dripped from the corner of his mouth in one long stream that stretched toward the floor.

If he reached to touch her, she would punch him in the face. Something was wrong with him, maybe from that joint, maybe something else (or maybe he was just being a dick) and now he was talking about Hox Grent who killed teenagers thirty years ago, and more goosebumps were forming along her legs and up her back, which felt like hundreds of spiders racing across her flesh, so if he even dared to come one step closer, she would scream and punch him and kick him in the crotch and run. Carly would have to fend for herself. This was all her fault anyway.

"At his sentencing, Hox said one thing you might want to remember. He said, 'Lock me up if you must, but it will not end anything.' What do you think he meant by that?"

Tim started to lean toward her as if for a kiss and Vanessa's hands, gripping that flashlight, were coming up, aiming right for his chin, which would knock him backwards and give her an open path to the front door, when Paula shoved CJ hard and yelled that he was a stupid little faggot with a small dick.

CJ actually hit the floor on his ass, but he was already laughing before Paula even made it past Tim and Vanessa. "Just for a few minutes?" CJ called. "The boys just want to see your strategy. You use your tongue so well. It's like getting blown by a cow."

Hector and Whitey collapsed onto each other with rolling waves of laughter.

Paula stopped, faced them. "You guys have fun blowing him. You know you want to."

A second later she was out the front door and down the steps. The door banged in the frame like the sound of a gavel smacking a judge's bench. Just like the sound Hox heard when the jury sentenced him to one hundred fifty years.

CJ regrouped with his buddies. He shrugged. "I tried." They slapped him on the back as if he had just scored a touchdown. Hector and Whitey took turns calling Paula a bitch and a fat whore.

Tim's eyes widened. "You better run."

"Get away from me!" With Paula gone and Carly in her own world, Vanessa's world shrunk to the small square of floor space beneath her. And beneath that where Hox chopped up his victims for homemade puppy chow.

The other boys sauntered over. They stood behind Tim like backup singers.

"Tim giving you a hard time?" CJ asked in a voice he'd use talking to an infant.

"Not likely," Whitey said. "Boy's limp as a noodle."

Vanessa cut through their stupid laughter. "Something's wrong with your friend."

"He needs to douche!" Carly yelled.

Whitey pinched his nose, waved his hand in front of his face. "Amen to that."

"I'm serious!" Vanessa said.

Tim hadn't moved any closer, but his mouth drooped out of the smile into a weird sort of open "O" like a zombie, and even his eyes sagged like those of a rotting corpse. Fresh drool slipped from his mouth.

"You should have listened to me," Tim said.

The boys leaned closer. CJ patted his shoulder. "Tim, you okay?"

Tim wavered back and forth as if his body had forgotten how to stand still, like he was a patient after a lobotomy. Or someone inflicted with an evil spirit.

"It's too late now," Tim said. His words slurred together. "Hox is here."

Vanessa swallowed something bitter in her throat. "What's wrong with him?"

"Nothing a little punch to the balls can't solve," Whitey said. "Care to go first, Hector?"

"Real funny."

"I thought so."

"Come on, guys," CJ said. "Tim could be really fucked up. What the hell was in that weed anyway?"

Whitey shrugged. "I don't make the shit."

"Are you ready?" Tim said.

"For what?" Vanessa said.

Tim's head snapped up straight, his mouth tightened, his eyes narrowed. *"TO DIE!"* His hands seized her throat and she fell backwards over Carly's legs. When she hit the floor, the world went black.

5

Unlike adults who couldn't see Hudson House or children who recognized the power immediately and rightly steered clear, teenagers saw the house, and sometimes the potential it held, but never fully. That made them the perfect victims.

The house could lure them in, or even bring them near, and he could strike. The house set the trap, and he delivered the kill. He was honored to kill. Others might be revolted or appalled, but he enjoyed every moment of the stalking, the fighting, the killing. The warm blood that coursed from their bodies and over his was a fresh baptismal every time he sent the knife home. And with every stab and every gush of blood, he was born anew.

Hudson House had given him a new life. He was forever indebted to it, but he would be rewarded. In time, he would get his divine blessing.

The front door opened and a chubby girl lunged out onto the wooden porch. She slammed the door shut behind her and paused. She rubbed her eyes, muttered a curse under her breath, and headed down the steps and across the walkway. The path led to the driveway. She would walk right past him.

He rested the knife on his thigh and dried his hand on his pant leg. The temperature outside may have been dropping, but the one inside him was boiling over. The only way to keep it from bursting out of his head lay in this knife and in the flesh of this girl.

She's not the one.

He knew it before she walked past him and down the sidewalk. Knew she wasn't the one. There would be someone else, someone better. Someone the house wanted. She would come. He knew that as well as he knew he would one day die to preserve the glory of this house. But in death, he would reign forever.

For now, he waited.

6

She didn't realize she was awake at first because the darkness was just as thick in this house as it had been in her mind. Her head throbbed as if it had been struck with a mallet. She tasted iron in her mouth. Blood. She had bitten her lip. Or someone had hit her. Tim had grabbed her throat with hands that were far too strong for his narrow frame. She could feel where the bruises were going to form.

She sat up. The boys were gone. So was Carly.

"Thought you were dead." A flashlight beam struck her between the eyes. She blocked the light with her hand.

"Tim?"

"Sorry. It was CJ's idea. I shouldn't have jumped on you. It was really stupid." He was sitting on the bottom step of the stairs by the front door.

She stood. Her legs felt made of gelatin. "Where's Carly?"

Tim gestured up the stairs. "Second floor."

"She was drunk."

Tim shrugged. "She didn't fight them."

Vanessa stormed straight for Tim. How could she have ever found him attractive enough to want to kiss?

He stood and placed his hands on either newel post where the railing started. The stairs went up a few steps, came to a small platform, and then turned left to a much longer flight. Carly was up there with two stupid jocks and she had no way to protect herself.

"Carly!" Vanessa's shout faded into the darkness. *Eaten.* "Let me up there."

"I can't do that."

"What? Are you a slave? What are they doing up there?"

"Nothing they haven't done before."

"What?"

"She just needed a little push this time." He held up a red and white beer can. "Hers had something special in it."

"You drugged her!"

"Not me. CJ. He loves her, you know."

"Let me up there."

"Just go home, Vanessa. Carly's going to be fine. Probably having a grand time. Maybe she'll even remember it."

She slapped him across the face before she realized that's what she was doing. He straightened his face and stared at her. Unlike before when his mouth had drooped and his eyes even sagged for his performance, Tim's face tightened into a shield and pure rage burned from his eyes. She was stepping back as he hit her.

The first hit cracked her jaw. The second knocked her back to the floor. Pain radiated through her knees and into her jaw and across her face. Tears spurted. Snot bubbled from her nose and over her lip.

"Look what you made me do, you stupid bitch."

From upstairs, CJ asked what the hell was going on.

"Just a little disagreement," Tim said.

"Fuck it," CJ said. "Bring her up here. Carly passed out."

She saw them gang-raping her. Saw two of them hold her down while a third took his time with her and then rotated with the others so each guy could say he had smelled her and boy, did she stink like rotten beef. The rape wouldn't be enough. They wanted humiliation.

Tim reached for her arm and Vanessa brought the flashlight right up into his jaw as she should have done earlier. He screamed and stumbled back to the steps and then fell into an awkward sitting position on the first step. He held his face in both hands and lowered his head between his knees. He moaned like she had pulled out his tongue.

She should tell him that's what he deserved. She should make him lead her upstairs so she could get Carly and get out of here. But that wouldn't work. CJ, Hector and Whitey wouldn't be so easily defeated. If she went up there, she'd walk right into their hands.

Her flashlight had broken. She dropped it and watched it roll to Tim's feet, next to his fallen beer can. A small puddle of beer looked like piss. Tim didn't look up. He sounded like he was crying. She almost felt sorry for him.

445

Finally, she left Hudson House and vowed never to return.

7

As promised, the house delivered her right into his arms. She was crying like the other girl but she had the mark on her—the house wanted her. Her skin glowed like she was radioactive and her eyes burned like tiny flames trapped in her skull. This was the one and he was happy. He could wait forever if he needed to, but knew the house would give him what had to be done and for that he was thankful.

He would grab her when she walked past him on the driveway. He'd pull her into the trees, cut her up a little to get her to stop fighting, and then he'd bring her inside. Not just inside, of course, but down into the basement. Down for the feeding.

She descended the steps and headed across the front lawn in a direct path for the sidewalk.

Shit. Was the house testing his dedication?

No time to wonder about the greater forces at work.

He jumped from the bushes and ran after her.

8

She was halfway across the front lawn when the rapid footfalls echoed around her like an approaching tornado. The boys were coming after her; they were, in fact, attacking from all angles. Her head swam and the world turned into a smeared watercolor.

"No!" She held up her hands and ran for the sidewalk, but it wasn't there anymore. Only grass. Grass everywhere. A goddamn field stretched before her into infinity. The house across from 51 Mangle Lane was there but so damn far away. She couldn't run that far. What the hell happened? *I've been drugged, too.*

On her desk in math class, someone had carved, *Hudson House is cursed.* Her mother told her when Vanessa was in grade school to stay away from that house, that bad things happened there. That meant Hox, didn't it? And he was in prison, wasn't he?

Something crashed into her, drove her to the ground. Blades of grass sprung up around her like giant trees. They canopied above her and someone, a giant, too, stood over her like a god. It was a huge, hulking shadow before towering black trees, like something grown in Hell. *This is the last image I'm ever going to see,* she thought.

It would have been easier for her if that were true.

9

There had been no reason to worry. There never was. When the house offered a new victim, there was never a battle or fight. He approached, attacked, and the girl fell. Every time the same. Efficient as a slaughter house.

She cowered in the grass before him. Tears coated her cheeks. She tried to curl into a ball but she couldn't. The house wouldn't let her. The grass kept her in place. Now, she was ready.

If that young man and his dog returned, would he see this spectacle? The dog would bark, perhaps, but the man would never know why. Even if he sliced the girl's throat right here and let the baptism commence beneath the night sky.

This was the power of the almighty. He tucked the knife back into the sheath he had found at a thrift store. He took it with him everywhere. No one ever noticed, of course, because of his long, black coat. Black like the night.

Like death.

Thy will be done.

10

Razors ripped at her. It was the grass. It tore her shirt to taters that slipped free from her body. Her jeans came next and her underwear. Blood sluiced across her skin as the giant pulled her through this immense forest. Freezing air bit at her like millions of tiny mouths full of serrated teeth.

This was a hallucination, brought on by a beer laced with something.

No, the pain was too intense, the visions too real.

How much blood could she lose before death finally granted her peace?

You're already dead, a voice inside her said. The voice was the sound of a cancer patient taking his final breath. *There is no peace. This is forever.*

She wanted to scream and cry and fight but the voice was right. This was it. Her final existence. Please, please, *please* just let it be all darkness. Cut me, tear me apart, but please don't let me see any more.

The giant trees parted in an amazing doorway of blinding red light. It pulsed and throbbed with life. The giant—a god (most certainly a devil)—dragged her toward that light. It wasn't light, no, it was a river. A river of blood. She was going to drown there, again and again for all eternity.

When the light took her, her body filled with an immense heat that engorged every inch of her body, every hair on her head, every cell inside her. This was Hudson House. A place of evil. But also a place of power. She was an offering to that power. The house would feed on her for all time and beyond.

The shadowed figure pulled her ever closer to her destiny.

"Are you Hox Grent?" The words floated out of her and into another plane of being.

11

The question halted him. The victims often begged and cried and pleaded, but none had ever been so direct.

The boiling heat inside him began to seep from his eyes. He leaned close to her so she could feel it.

"No," he said. "I'm not Hox Grent. I'm someone far more blessed."

12

She came out of the river into an even darker world. Something groaned down here, huge and hungry. The world filled with the pungent smell of candied apples. The aroma was so sweet that it stole Vanessa away into another life.

It was a blessing.

When the house began to tear her body to pieces, Vanessa thought about being a little girl and going to the annual Pumpkin Festival. Her mother always bought her a candied apple and her dad always tried to get her to go into the haunted house of terror, but she never did.

She was too young, far too small to withstand the horrors inside.

This book was originally published under the pseudonym J.T. Warren. Chris DiLeo is the real author.

The picture to the right is Chris' father Warren (used previously as J.T. Warren's author photos) in full costume on Halloween. Growing up with a father so enamored with the macabre, Chris unsurprisingly writes stories of dark and bloody things.

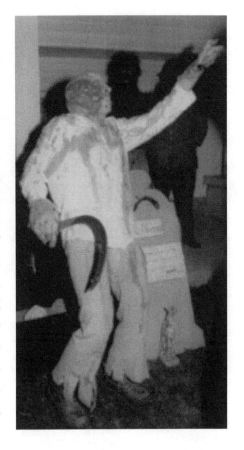

Chris is a public school teacher who has successfully lured hundreds of students into literary waters through works of horror. He hopes his writing will further encourage interest in the written word.

Chris is a member of the Horror Writers Association and author of *Blood Mountain, Hudson House, Meat Camp* (co-authored with Scott Nicholson), and *The Devil Virus*, coming soon from Bloodshot Books.

Connect with Chris on his website, Facebook, Tumblr, or on Twitter.
www.authordileo.com
@authordileo
http://authorchrisdileo.tumblr.com

Still with us? Excellent. Now, please enjoy a teaser of DiLeo's novel *The Devil Virus*, available soon from Bloodshot Books.

In *The Devil Virus*, a priest must venture into a nightmare world to save his daughter from a demon.

THE DEVIL VIRUS

The night before the accident, before I started on my personal road to Damascus, I went into the little room off the kitchen that had once been the garage to check on my father. I found him in the bathroom on the toilet, his sweatpants bundled around his ankles, his sweatshirt sagging to reveal a narrow, liver-spotted shoulder, one arm draped over the curved lift-assist bar, chin on his chest. Ben Masters appeared to be sleeping —or dead.

Dead on the toilet: an ignominious end for a once-adored father and priest.

Relief offered a selfish respite from this life of eldercare with its constant weight of responsibility, but I thought of Phoebe asking after my dad's heart attack, *Is grandpa dying?* and her immense relief when I assured her grandpa was going to be fine, though I had no reason to believe that but as a father and a priest, I knew it was the thing to say.

"Dad?"

The room smelled of disinfectant and old-man odor. The sliding-glass shower door stood open to reveal the plastic seat and the hand-held shower head, a crime scene whose victim was youth.

Naomi had painted the room a light blue and decorated with matching floor mats, towels and a soap dispenser, which was supposed to make it homier, but instead it felt like a cheap, crammed motel room. Medicine bottles were strewn across the counter, his pill case with little boxes for each day of the week open and tipped, pills scattered. The light from the bulbs around the mirror caught the silver edge of a nail file sticking out over the sink.

"Dad?"

He mumbled something, probably Latin. He'd been doing that a lot recently, revisiting his classic seminary education. His doctor said it was part of the mind's regression, reverting without connective logic, and his thinking was going to get more jumbled, an old film reel coming unspooled and entangled.

I shook him gently and he woke slowly in bumbling degrees with guttural chokes and a long trail of white phlegm slipping off his bottom lip.

One eye was bloodshot, a remnant of the stroke, and the other featured a grayish-blue cataract that made everything fuzzy for him. Fuzzy like his brain.

"You okay, Dad?"

He grabbed my arm, squeezed hard, and stared at me for several uncomfortable seconds.

"It's a goddamn waste," he said in a crackly voice. "Resisting like this."

"You're okay, Dad."

I helped him up and tugged up his pants, my head turned away in privacy, as he stood there without helping. Thankfully, what was in the toilet did not require a wipe and I flushed it away.

"You fell asleep."

"I was dreaming."

"Anything good?"

"'Thou shalt not be afraid for the terror by night; nor for the arrow that fly by day.'"

"Sounds like one of the Psalms," I said.

"Well?"

"There's a lot."

He shook his head and started the fragile trek out of the bathroom. This Bible game was a new thing. Biblical passages were the only thing he had no trouble keeping straight.

"'All things are possible to him that believe,'" I said.

My father grunted. "Gospel of Mark. Chapter nine, verse twenty-three."

He stumbled on the next step, fell to one knee, but I snagged his arm before he could go full sprawl.

"Goddamn it." He punched the carpet with surprising force. "What is the point?"

"You're okay, Dad. I got you."

I helped him onto the bed where he sat, hands on his knees, breathing in short, hollow gasps. The hand he used to punch the floor looked a bit strange, darker or something. Maybe dirty. Who knows what he might have been doing with it.

"What's with your hand?"

"What?"

I gestured and he held it up for a moment before saying it was fine and covering it in his lap. Black lines crisscrossed over it and around his knuckles like some bizarre tattoo. It might have been black pen.

"What did you do to yourself, Dad?"

"Do?" he said as if the word were nasty. "What do you mean?"

I huffed like some impatient schoolteacher—Naomi would have been so proud—and told my father he needed to be honest with me. "I won't be mad, Dad, but if there's something wrong with your hand . . ."

"There's nothing wrong with it."

"Or you did something to it."

He glared at me and I waited. I'd read posts online about eldercare some of which were very troubling, particularly those about elderly parents reverting to almost infantile behavior. Staging tantrums. Throwing food. Hurting themselves or other family members.

"You remember that Quincy Toft boy?" my father asked.

"Doesn't ring a bell. Are you going to show me your hand?"

I thought of yanking his hand free and holding it high for examination, but if he was regressing into childish antics, he probably wouldn't react very well. So, instead, I grabbed the plastic tube connected to the oxygen generator, this bulky thing by the bedside, and my father let me slip it on around his ears and angle the nostril stubs into his nose. I had to reach across the bed to turn the machine on and it came alive with a loud beep and settled into a rhythmic rumbling hum and exhaling sigh.

"Why did you turn this off?"

"I don't need it."

"Dad, you fell asleep on the toilet. Oxygen deprivation."

"You're a doctor now?"

"You're not one, either."

He took a long inhale of machine-produced air and sat a little straighter. His white hair flapped like a wing on his head and he rubbed his feet back and forth across the blue carpet that had been worn thin in a path from bathroom to bed. Crumbled tissues lay scattered around. I started picking them up.

"You can't just decide you feel better and don't need oxygen. And what about your pills? Did you get them confused again? Are you going to show me your hand?"

"He killed himself," my father said.

"What? Who?" I pushed his glass of water back from the night table's edge.

"Quincy Toft. He was a little kid. Scrawny. Kind of kid who fell over swinging a T-ball bat. Never had any friends. Followed kids, begging for them to let him be their friend. Followed them everywhere. Throughout school. On the playground. Down the streets in town. Any time you saw a group of kids, you could bet Quincy was ten steps behind, scurrying after them in a Buffalo Bills jacket that billowed around him like he was a puffed-up balloon. Always following and never included. Must have been like that from the time he was seven or eight until he was about ten or eleven."

I smelled Vicks vapor rub and one of those flower-scented Plug-Ins Naomi added all over the house. Dad said that smell reminded him of Mom. A busted blood vessel had taken her years ago. Phoebe hadn't even been a year old at the time.

"What happened when he was ten?"

He didn't say anything for a moment, just stared at his hands, the one still hidden beneath the other. They had morphed into pale maps of scraggly blue veins with tissue-paper skin. His nails had yellowed, too, like his teeth.

"He swallowed a bottle's worth of Tylenol. Sat there in his bedroom with the pile of pills next to him and swallowed one after the next. If you think about it, you can even see the way his throat must have started constricting after the first couple dozen. But he choked them down. Almost eighty of them. Then he wrapped a plastic bag around his head, one of those with the big stupid smile and Thank You for Shopping printed on it. Strapped duct-tape around his neck. To be sure, I guess."

When he sermonized, my father liked talking around things, using metaphors and anecdotes, preferring an apropos fable to a direct discussion. *A metaphor is a sermonizer's best friend* he told me when

I was preparing my first homilies. *And if a metaphor isn't apt, use an anecdote. And if you can't recall one, make it up. But don't make it too direct. People get suspicious of stories that snap together like puzzle pieces.*

Along with a *metaphor is a sermonizer's best friend,* my father also believed *the Devil is in the details.*

"This boy's family attended Saint John's?"

"You don't remember? Somewhere else, then."

He was referring to all those churches he visited as part of his pilgrimages, a self-ascribed addition to his priestly duties that sent him for a week or two on a trek of New York churches at least once a year. He took me with him a few times but they were dull affairs.

Either Quincy Toft attended one of those other churches or this story was a fabrication, an intermingling of frayed memory frames on the cutting room floor of my father's mind, maybe a lost sermon he never delivered.

A rather macabre one.

"The boy's parents were out. They came home late, didn't check on him, found him the next morning. The bag was stuck to his face. Whitish vomit had hardened around his lips and clogged his nose.

"Quincy told his parents angels were hunting him. They came for him at night. Big, bright lights, enormous things, horrifying. Like the way abductees talk about aliens. Parents thought the boy had a hyperactive imagination."

"That's very . . . unsettling, Dad."

459

"So are angels. Remember what the angel said who appeared before the shepherds? 'Fear not.' Why say that if an angel doesn't look frightening? And how does Saul respond when an angel appears to him on the road to Damascus? He is 'trembling and astonished' and those traveling with him are 'speechless'—and afraid."

"Don't the angels say they bring good news?"

"And Saul is blinded," he said. "Imagine how bright it must have been. How awful that brightness must be."

"But he's not blind for long," I said. "A symbolic blindness. Psychosomatic, perhaps."

"The liberal interpretation," he said.

"New wave Episcopalianism," I said.

He was joking—he'd been a barely disguised liberal, yet since the stroke, his moral compass seemed out of whack.

My father believed, as I did, that a priest's job, an Episcopal priest's in particular, was not to dictate interpretation: it was to offer numerous ways to examine a fragment of scripture, turning it over slowly like a prism in a blade of light to see all the possible colors.

Post-stroke Ben Masters was more of a literal-minded believer. If the pulpit were still his, he might advocate public stoning, as per Leviticus.

"You should get some sleep."

I pulled back the sheets Naomi washed twice weekly and helped him slide in. He kept his hand hidden all the while.

"You're not going to show me your hand?"

"No visit from my beautiful granddaughter this evening?" he asked.

"Not tonight, Dad."

"Is she going to wake the whole neighborhood?"

Phoebe and her nightmares.

When she was in the grip, really letting it rip, her vocals could shake the house, even make the wine goblets in the china cabinet stir. For an eight-year old and someone so small, Phoebe had impressive lung power. If someone were walking by on the street outside, he'd think she was being murdered. Her "screaming fits," as Naomi and I were calling them because that sounded better than "night terrors," though it amounted to the same, had been getting more frequent, yet all the online parent guides assured us it would get better, even if it got worse first.

"She'll grow out of it," I said.

"It's hard to fight it. 'The thief cometh not, but for to steal, and to kill, and to destroy.'"

"Gospel According to John," I said.

He waited for the chapter and verse with full recognition of his continued victory in this little game.

"Goodnight, Dad."

"That Toft boy," he said, stopping me at the door, "was an example."

"Of?"

His ailing eyes rolled up toward the ceiling. "There are worse things than nightmares."

———

461

Three nights previously, I woke after two in the morning and for a moment I thought maybe I would get up anyway; I felt pretty good, pretty rested. I could polish up my sermon for Sunday. Almost immediately, however, exhaustion weighed me back into the mattress, the feeling of being rested no more than a tease.

I started to fall back asleep and—

Heard something downstairs. A creak of floor, a faint accompanying murmur. I knew it was my father. Walking around and talking to himself. I almost got up, but my body wouldn't get moving. If he wanted to walk around at night when no one was there to help him up if he fell, I supposed that was his decision.

————

The road to Hell might be paved with such assumptions.

Made in the USA
Middletown, DE
11 September 2024